WYTCH HUNT

BOOK II OF THE TYRNING CYCLE

TIM FOX

WYTCH HUNT
BOOK II OF THE TYRNING CYCLE

COPYRIGHT

INTRODUCTION

Right, well let's get to it, shall we? I mean there are 135,000 brilliant words of narrative (the overwhelming majority of which I did not invent) waiting for you only a few lower case roman numeraled pages hence.

Wytch Hunt is Book II of the <u>Tyrning Cycle</u> trilogy. If you're not already coincidentally knowledgeable about topics such as simulacrum golems and smartass demigod Gas Station Air Hoses then it really might be better if you set Book II aside until you've consumed the nearest electronic copy of *Scavengyr*.

A couple of general non-spoilerish comments, just so you're not completely blindsided. First, in the *Tyrning* universe "y"s in words where there aren't usually "y"s denote Folk magyk. Second, you need to know now that wytches are, for the most part, genuinely unpleasant people. Who knew? Bytches is probably a good description. Third, it only seems fair to tell you before you get invested in *Wytch* that you're absolutely going to be high-pissed at me at least twice (one of those times you may elect not to forgive me, particularly if at the relevant point in time you're wearing nonwaterproof mascara and you forgot to buy more Kleenex the last two times you went to the supermarket.)

Finally, a word about the fact that there are an incredible number of chapters in my books. I believe short chapters are a kindness to both late night nodder-offers, as well as needy readers who may have had an absolutely dreadful day and are desperate to feel a sense of accomplishment about something, anything that day. That and it's hard for me to hold a train of thought long enough for it to have much more than a locomotive and a caboose.

I mentioned in the Introduction to *Scavengyr Hunt* that the Tyrning Cycle trilogy rotates around my tri-Trues: True Hero (please remember that for me "Hero" is always gender neutral), True Love, and True Choice. True Choice takes center stage, as the first among equals, in this second installment. The other two Trues are interwoven throughout the narrative but it is free will that is *Wytch Hunt's* tentpole. Unfettered. Unimpeded. The absolute right of every being to make his/her/its own decisions. There are, of course, always two sides to every coin. Positive-negative, black-white, privilege-obligation, reward-consequence, gyft-pryce.

The trilogy construct is working out nicely for character development. The principal agonists you met in Book I have pretty much taken on a life of their own. Actually, some of the secondary players have now gotten a little mouthy and are passively-aggressively asserting themselves. They uniformly seem to be of the opinion that it's necessary for you to hear all of their back stories as well. It has reached the point that I sometimes feel as if I'm merely scribing events the characters have related to me as opposed to actually creating the events myself.

In the past, whenever I've seen writers express that kind of statement, my general response has included one or more of the following words: fatuous, windbag, verbose, tedious, crackpot, and/or blahblahblahblah. Those words may actually have been appropriate in those previous cases. I can assure you they don't apply to me. Free will is practically dripping off the pages of Book II.

Enough of the [fore + (play or shadowing)]. I'll leave you with this significant Easter egg...er, thought. We're all human, well most of us. Clearly the mouthy Gas Station Air Hose isn't. We each want things to occur on a timeline that is uniquely our own, that satisfies our individual needs and desires. Sometimes we want an event to get here quickly. Like Christmas, when you've finally gotten all of your shopping done. There are other times though we pray for Time to slow down, so one special moment might last a lifetime. There are innumerable things we want from Time every single day. Which is all well and good, but have you ever stopped and asked yourself:

What does Time want?

I hope you have as much fun reading *Wytch Hunt* as I did writing it. Enjoy the ride.

Tim.

ACKNOWLEDGMENTS

To Mom. I told you in the *Scavengyr Hunt* Acknowledgments the *Tyrning Cycle* series wasn't going to be your customary book club fare. That's even more true with Book II. Remember, your favorite son loves many, many words—both great and small—from the shortest expletive to the longest onomatopoeia. And I love you.

To Dad. Even though you haven't been with us physically for several years now, I think of you frequently while I write this trilogy. Most especially the portions concerning Seeking the Center.

To My Progeny, My Brothers, and All My Relatives of Every Possible Degree of Consanguinity. Three guesses as to what you're getting for Christmas 2017. It's better than a lump of coal. Heavier anyway. Am I right or am I right?

To My Friends Who Read My Books. Thank you. You have no idea how much an encouraging text to, "please hurry up and get through, I'm tired of waiting," means to me. Regardless of whether I'm wallowing in a creative doldrum at that time, or writing like a madman, every one of your thoughtful and heartfelt comments is a huge boost. So, again, thank you.

To My Beta Readers. Karla Burnett, Holly Davis, Christie Greer, Diane Holitik, and Tyler Thompson. Reading a 135,000 word draft off of a PDF file makes for tough slogging. It takes iron discipline, a well-organized mind, and perhaps most importantly—a generous and encouraging spirit. Thank you for all of your help and your encouragement.

To KHT. If there's anything worse than proofing a 135,000 word PDF draft (see description of that terribly onerous activity in the immediately preceding paragraph) it has to be signing up for that drudgery after having already spent the last eighteen months of adult nights listening to a word-wracked author dissect, in minute detail, that week's massive plot breakthrough—knowing with absolute certainty you will receive a despondent text from him no later than 4:30 a.m. the very next morning, now characterizing said massive breakthrough as "banal rubbish." Whatever category of sincere appreciation and gratitude is the next one on the chart above the conventional category of sincere appreciation and gratitude, that's the category of sincere appreciation and gratitude I am acknowledging to you. Well, that and your continuing and much appreciated tutelage on the magykality of "y"s.

To the UnFading One. We are all your children, each of us. Thank you for the blessings you give us every day and by whatever name we choose to call you, please help us to remember to always Seek the Center in our interactions with all of your creatures, both great and small.

PANTHEON OF THE MOIETY

AMARANTOS

PRINCIPES

CHRONOS

AURORA

SOL

LUNA

RULING COUNCIL OF THE MOIETY

ARCHON

The Alberich
King of the Tuatha Dé Danaan

SENESCHAL

The Marid
Suleyman of the Djinn

PARLIAMENTARIAN

The Raja Jinn Peri
King of the Malay Faeries

The Márku
Empress of the HuldreFolk

The Proteus
Regent of The Olympians

HUNTS SCHOOL ADMINISTRATION AND FACULTY

PRINCIPAL

Chiron

HUNTSMISTRESS

Lilith Empousa

HUNTS TEACHERS

Professor Daedalus Hardcastle
Doctor Delphi SilverTongue
Professor Sprite Elphinstone

HUNTS FINALIST TEAMS

AYLLU
Incan/Mayan Realm
"clan"

YAXKIN
"Center"
Allyu Prime Direction

XAMAN
"North"

NOHOL
"South"

LIK"IN
"East"

CHIK"IN
"West"

KABILA
Swahili Realm
"tribe"

KATI
"Center"
Kabila Prime Direction

KASKAZINI
"North"

KUSINI
"South"

MASHARIKI
"East"

MAGHARIBI
"West"

OMADA
Greek Realm
"party, group, or team"

BORRAS
"North"
Acting Omada Prime Direction

NOTOS
"South"

ANATOLIA
"East"

DYSI
"West"

QUINT
"Five"

PLEME
Serbo-Croatian Realm
"tribe"

SREDINA
"Center"
Pleme Prime Direction

SEVER
"North"

ISTOK
"South"

JUG
"East"

ZAPAD
"West"

SHUZOKU
Japanese Realm
"tribe or family"

CHUUSHIN
"Center"
Shuzoku Prime Direction

KITA
"North"

MINAMI
"South"

HIGASHI
"East"

NISHI
"West"

SLÄKT
Swedish Realm
"group of people related by blood, marriage, law or custom"

MITT
"Center"
Släkt Prime Direction

NORD
"North"

SÖDER
"South"

OST
"East"

VÄST
"West"

"When mortals were infants, both the Principes and the Folk regularly trod the Earth plane. Chronos is Amarantos's Seneschal, her First Born. Even Sol, Luna, and Amarantos must bend their knees to Time. She has always held herself apart from all other living beings."

LEX IMMORTALIS

CHAPTER UNUS

"WHY IN THE FIVE HELLS ARE HER EYES STILL BANDAGED?"

It wasn't the venom suffused roar itself that ripped Väst from torpor's comforting embrace. It was the voice's familiarity. It belonged to one of her teammates. Nord. What is Nord doing in my bedroom, was her next thought. Followed in quick order by—who is he screaming at? And then—whoever they are, why are they in my bedroom?

She opened her eyes. Well, she tried to but both lids registered significant resistance. Even with her muddle-headedness her internal warning system kicked in, a claxon alerting her she needed to play possum until she figured out what was up.

Väst squinched—making the smallest flutter she could with her left eyelid. I was right, she thought. There's something taped over my eyes, holding them closed. Panic rose. She almost started screaming, but her logic center held fast. Remain perfectly still, she cautioned herself. Something is terribly wrong, feign unconsciousness until you can get a handle on what is going on.

"As I've explained several times Prime, your Fifth should have been dead in the arena. She was in fact dead under any clinical definition, until..., well, until..."

What the hell? Nord isn't the Släkt Prime Direction. Mitt is. Who is Nord talking to? I don't recognize the other voice. Wait, what? Dead? How can I have been dead? What is the matter with you Väst, she asked herself. Get a grip. It has to be significant that I can't even remember how I got here. Wherever here is. Focus. Mitt...Mitt. You know something important concerning Mitt. Don't you? Mitt did something. Right? Wrong? Good? Bad? What was it?

One thing's for sure, she decided. The bastard who taped my eyes shut and then doped me senseless is getting stone cold junk-punched as soon as I get back on my feet. She forced herself to lay there motionless, her mind straining to remember details. Any details. Something has happened to Mitt. Something terrible,...but damn it, I can't remember what.

Nord was getting progressively louder as he worked his way toward defcon crazy. "Right. I got that part, dumbass. We all saw when that Creature healed Väst. Focus your little bitty brain on this part. She's been unconscious for five days now. The start of the second term was delayed for a week because of the Combat Challenge. Second term classes start first thing Monday morning and attendance is mandatory. If our Fourth isn't in Orientation, Släkt is going to lose points."

The infirmary, Väst realized. I'm not in my room, I'm in the infirmary. Nord is talking to one of the physicks. Good start, Väst, but you need to get on top of this. Quickly. Five days? What the hell? Wait, did Nord just call me "Fourth?" I'm Släkt's Fifth Prime.

Why can't I remember? You're a smart girl, catalog the symptoms: sleep, warm-fuzzy-feel-good feeling, and amnesia. That's it. They've dosed me with a soporific of some kind. Why? Apparently I was injured. The physicks must have been keeping me knocked out for therapeutic reasons while I healed from whatever it was that happened. Now back to Mitt. What happened to him, and why is the physick talking to Nord like he's our Prime Direction?

"I've tried to explain it to you several times now, Prime. The Cooshie's intervention saved your Fourth's life." Väst heard the physick's voice take on a measure of awe, as he began to dissemble. "It was a miracle, even by magykal standards. The healing properties of the Cooshie are well-documented from many ancient texts, but there have been no incidents of elfhounds choosing to heal one of the Folk in the last several thousand years."

Nord rudely interrupted the man. Again. "Blah, blah, blah. Write some stupid egghead paper about those lowlife Creatures on your own time. I don't give a shit about that animal—or about history—or about you, for that matter. If it healed her, why has she been in a coma for almost a week? And why are her eyes still bandaged?"

"The fact that she is alive is a miracle. She was struck by Fragarach. There has never been a reported instance where someone lived after being cut by that particular sword of power. In addition to the chest wound, Väst suffered severe trauma to both of her corneas when she was sandblasted by the Mistral wind. The entire medical staff has worked in shifts around the clock, applying our strongest magyks. Even with all of our efforts, there is a fifty-fifty chance she won't ever see anything other than light and shadows.

"We have been dosing her with a potion to keep her comatose to accelerate her healing process, and because, well, because..."

"Because what, you idiot?" Nord screamed. "SPIT IT OUT!"

"There is some unknown component in her magykal aura."

"WHAT?"

Even for Nord that's a lot of decibels crammed into only one four-letter word, Väst thought.

Nord continued with his tirade. "Are you saying she's damaged goods? If so, I need to tell the HuntsMistress that the

Creature colluded with Omada to sabotage us, and we need to be assigned another new Fifth."

So much for the notion of "all for one and one for all," Väst thought. Actually, if I'm diminished, cutting me loose is the smart move for the team. Now let's rewind to that whole potentially permanently blind scenario.

"Our entire medical staff has examined Väst. Each of us has a different healmagyk specialty. Her aura seems intact, although it is difficult for us to fully encompass her aura, because, as I'm sure you know, her magyk is royal strength."

"But?" Nord asked verbally, as Väst's mind whispered the same question to itself.

"But something is evaporating, leaving a void."

"A void?" Nord asked, incredulous. "Who ever heard of a void in someone's aura. What kind of mumbo jumbo is that?" Nord demanded stridently.

"All of her primary, secondary and tertiary magykal components are in the appropriate places. It appears the Cooshie's touch is somehow gradually healing her. From what, we haven't a clue."

"That's it," Nord replied. "We're getting to the bottom of this. Wake her up!" he demanded. "Now."

There was a short pause before any response. "As Chief Physick, I am charged with the well-being of all students at Hunts School. In that role and in the appropriate exercise of my professional judgment, I have made the determination Väst needs to remain sedated for a minimum of another week. Two would be better."

"As Släkt Prime Direction, I hold the contract binding all members of my team. You can take your worthless 'professional judgment' and shove it up your ass. I have the authority to make health decisions that are in the best interests of the team. I say wake her up. Now!" Nord again demanded.

"Prime, I must warn you again that such action could be life-threatening," the voice replied.

"Do it now Physick, or I'll show you life-threatening."
Väst heard the slick snick of sliding steel. She knew that sound
well. Nord kept a stiletto in a leg sleeve pocket at all times. "Class
meets Monday morning. That's three days. The team loses points
and may be out of the competition if she's not in class on
Monday morning. However, the team is still in the running if
she's only blind or partially brain damaged."

Väst heard the physick inhale sharply. Nord has placed
the knife against his jugular, she thought.

"Get it done. On my instruction. Immediately."

"Upon your order…Prime."

"Have her ready for class Monday morning Physick, or
I'll be back to finish this conversation."

Väst heard the dagger being resheathed, followed
immediately by the heavy tread of Nord's boots as he turned and
stomped out of the room.

Where's Mitt? He should be here looking after me. He
certainly wouldn't tell the medical staff to do something that
might blind me. What happened in the arena? Damn that potion,
I need to be able to think.

A name flashed across her mind's eye—Quint!
Quint…he did something. We were fighting and he…he killed
me. Can that possibly be right? Yes, it is. He killed me, and I
wanted him to. I tried to tell him I didn't want to kill him but that
I had no choice. He doesn't know about the geas, no one knows.
How could they? The compulsion prevents me from telling
anyone.

That's it, she told herself, focus on Quint. Right. Okay, I
know he killed me, but then he must have done something that
saved me. Damn it, I need to remember, was Väst's last thought
as the warm, pleasant lassitude reasserted itself and Morpheus
carried her back into oblivion.

CHAPTER TWO

Elle sat quietly at the library conference room table as the rest of the Winter Formal Committee members filed in and took their seats. Angie Alison was Chair of the seven-member committee. Tension was already high between she and Angie, what with the grade point race for valedictorian coming down to decimal points. Because of that, Elle hadn't even tried to get the nod to be committee chair. She and Angie each had plenty on their resumes for college, and Elle didn't want to do anything that might inadvertently cause their grade competition to go nuclear.

This was the final organizational meeting of the entire committee. The dance wasn't until the first day of February, so right at twelve weeks away. Which seemed like a long time until you delved into the school calendar between now and then. There was the week off for Thanksgiving, first term finals, and then the two-week Christmas break. The high school state football playoffs weren't being held until the first couple of weeks in January. Basketball would be in full swing for most of the twelve-week period, which meant the gym was being utilized for practices and games. The combined press of school, holidays and extra-curriculars made it crunch time as far as finalization of the broad strokes for the Formal.

Their group hadn't had any problems deciding most of the foundational issues. They'd approved their top three band choices at the first meeting, and Angie had been authorized to negotiate the best contract possible with any of the three. Starting early on that detail had paid huge dividends. It was costing them a sizeable portion of their budget, but they'd been able to book their number one choice—*Plato and the Sorry Apologists*. Terrible name but they were the number one dance band in the tri-state area and booking them for a gig during the busy dance season was a major coup. Venue was covered, as the gym had been reserved for quite some time for both the night of the dance and the two preceding evenings. The committee had even unanimously decided on the caterers for the dance.

They had been at an impasse though since day one on the single biggest decision—the theme for the Formal. Decorations, props, attendee wardrobe choices—all of those decisions hinged on the theme. There was a small pool of companies providing first-rate services for large dances. They all knew from prior experience working on similar committees that all of the fabulous theme packages were booked well before Thanksgiving. After this final major decision was made, the activity would devolve to the worker bees of the numerous sub-committees.

At their last meeting Angie had tasked each of them with deciding on their number one theme choice, together with obtaining the necessary names and contact information of the lowest priced providers. She had advised them it was her intention to begin calling tomorrow to finalize a deal.

Compounding things, the varsity football team was playing this evening. Based on their lopsided victories in the first few games it looked like the Nemeton Screaming Oracles would be contenders again this year for the state title. Under her brother Barton's steady quarterbacking they had won State the last two years. The dance itself was scheduled for the Saturday night immediately following the Friday night state championship. Principal Davis had decided that it would be a nice, extra touch for the dance to be a celebration of the Oracles winning their third state championship in a row.

Most of the committee members had spirit squad obligations so they had each been allotted only three minutes for their presentation. As they had previously been unable to get a majority on any theme, Angie had texted them earlier this morning to advise the decision would be by plurality vote. Whichever idea received the most votes was the winner.

Elle wasn't as enthused about the whole Winter Formal thing as she might have been. Tal hadn't even mentioned the dance yet, so she was currently flying solo. Granted, it was still three months off but most of the seniors were already hooking up. On top of that, Tal had been acting strange the last few weeks. Even stranger than usual, she thought.

She'd already had a number of date offers—she was a Sellars after all and her family owned most of Nemeton. Several of the candidates might have interested her in the past, but not now. Not with Tal's arrival this school year. Hints had been repeatedly dropped during their evening phone calls, as well as at the movie last Saturday night. There was no question he was into her big time but for some reason he wouldn't jump in with both feet. Sure, the whole daytime nonverbal communication thing made personal conversations a little dicey but it wouldn't have taken a short minute for him to ask her in writing. Or to bring it up when they talked on the phone...every night...about everything...except going to the dance together. If she hadn't known better she would have thought he didn't even know about the dance. She discarded that possibility on the grounds of ridiculousness. He had been present several times during school when her friends discussed it with her.

When Elle finally reined in her wandering attention, Ginger Allred had finished her speech trying to convince them they should go with *Grease*, and AndersonCooper was halfway through his presentation. He was making the case for an *Urban Cowboy* theme. In furtherance of his cause he'd even worn chaps and a bolo tie. Which were definitely not furthering his cause.

AndersonCooper's last name was Rivera. Both his parents had lifelong daytime television addictions. Word was his parents had nearly gone with the "cute" play and named him Geraldo. Thankfully, they'd resisted the urge. When AndersonCooper finished, there was polite applause. The kind of hand-patting clapping that if it had been converted into words would have been, "oh, sweetie," over and over.

It was Jessica Holly Bartney's turn, which meant Elle was on deck. Jessica Holly did a nice job—complete with mockup artwork drawings—of presenting *Great Gatsby* as her choice. It wasn't a bad idea, Elle thought. The period presented lots of opportunity for interesting formal wear, coupled with some serious bling accessorizing. She toyed with the idea of voting for that idea instead of her own before deciding it was bad form. If you believed in yourself and the choices you made then you should proudly stand up for those choices.

"Elle, you're on the clock," Angie intoned.

"Thanks. I appreciate all of the hard work everyone has put into their ideas. I didn't go with a particular movie as a theme, I picked *Enchanted Forest*. I know it sounds corny at first but if you think about the concept you'll see it allows for an extremely wide variety of wardrobe choices, any supplemental backgrounds would be relatively easy to knock out…"

Jessica Holly was so excited she interrupted Elle. "Oh…oh, we could get some strands of light blue Christmas rainfall lights and place them up in tree canopies, with single blinking lights for the forest fairies, and…"

Angie quickly shut Jessica Holly down. "You've had your turn. Please allow Elle the courtesy of her remaining time."

Houston, we have a problem, Elle thought. Angie must be really invested in her idea, whatever it is, and doesn't want anybody jumping on my bandwagon. Shut it down, Elle, she told herself. "That's about it, Madam Chairperson. I have the name and contact information of a local vendor who will commit to providing the major set pieces, as well as a themed photo booth setup."

"Thank you," Angie said curtly. Mary Katherine Eanes was next with her theme, *The Timeless Art of Georgia O'Keeffe*. Mary Katherine's family vacation last summer had been to Santa Fe, and Ms. O'Keeffe's work had clearly made an indelible impression on Mary Katherine, as well as her entire family. The Eanes had recently gotten both a new puppy and a new kitten. Both of which were male. Both of which were now named Georgia O'Keeffe. Elle tried to act like she was paying attention to Mary Katherine, everyone else saved the energy.

Amber Nicole Floss was the next to last speaker. Elle had always wondered if in choosing her name, Amber's parents had been subconsciously trying to steer their daughter toward a career in the porn industry. Amber hit the ground at Mach Three, passionately pleading for her choice—*Xanadu*. She reminded everyone her daddy had a seventeen percent ownership interest in all three Nemeton area Sonics, with an option for a fourth store that was going to draw from the lucrative Marianna market. Amber was absolutely convinced she could sweet talk Big Daddy—ick, that's what she called her father—into letting them use the Sonic waitresses. The waitresses could come in wearing silver spandex and roll around on their "roller skatey thingamabobs," handing out whatever appetizers the caterer prepared. She even threw in a bribe of a few hundred free orders of Sonic tater tots to sweeten the deal. While she was in the moment, Amber went ahead and called shotgun on dressing like Olivia Newton John.

When Elle politely pointed out to Amber she was trying to call dibs not shotgun, Amber told Elle to "shut her piehole and mind her own lexicon." When it became clear no one else was going to vote for her idea, Amber crammed all of her props into her Hello Kitty backpack and stormed out of the meeting. On the way out she told all of the girls she hoped they each had a big volcano zit the night of the dance, and she told AndersonCooper she hoped his date's dress shields didn't function properly.

Angie was the last to present, and she was totally prepared. Elle had no doubts Angie had rehearsed her presentation in front of the mirror with a time clock. She wants those awards and scholarships as badly as I do and she's got the skill set to reach out and snatch them. From me? I don't think so, Elle thought. Never yield.

Angie's concept was for a Venetian-styled *Midnight Masque Ball*. It's a great idea, Elle thought. Everyone can come fancy or plain. As far as outfits, everyone could afford something. With the emphasis on the masks it gave everyone a chance to be special. Some would be store bought, others homemade.

To make the evening more mysterious, everyone would be required to wear their masks until midnight. At midnight there would be a group unmasking with the crowning of the Formal king and queen occurring at the final stroke of midnight.

The only real flaw in Angie's proposal was set design and construction. She hadn't been able to find any set rentals for the idea so there would have to be substantial set building by the committee members. Not to mention there was no way in hell Principal Davis would allow them to pour hundreds of gallons of water into plastic swimming pools to replicate Venice's canals.

When Angie was through—after two minutes and fifty-seven seconds—she called for a vote. Mary Katherine abandoned Georgia, making two votes for *Midnight Masque*. Jessica Holly went with *Enchanted Forest*, and there was one vote each for *Grease* and *Urban Cowboy*.

Damn it, damn it damn it, Elle thought to herself. I wanted to win, but I don't need this hassle with Angie. I can't change my vote though.

Out of nowhere it was AndersonCooper who saved the day. "Ladies, it's clear my proposal ain't gonna hunt. We have to make a decision today. Things will go a mite smoother if it's one we can all support. I'm thinking I could get behind a friendly merger of *Midnight Masque* and *Enchanted Forest*. Gives us all the drama and mystery presented by the masks and the wonderful backgrounds and photo opportunities of a romantically lit forest.

He looked over at Ginger who nodded her head. "That's two for my proposition. Anyone else care to change their vote?" In the end it was unanimous.

Now that that's done, Elle thought, all I have to do is get Tal to ask me to the dance.

CHAPTER TRES

When Tal had first walked into the gas station's Ladies' Restroom, at least a million years ago—well, back in the summer anyway—which in relative terms now seemed like a million years ago, the climate difference between Hunts School and Earth plane proper was minimal.

It was sizeable now. On Tal's walk to Hunts School from Nemeton, Fall had engaged in a minuet of swirling puffery for him. Kaleidoscope-patterned dervishes of recently deceased leaves skittered first here, then there, unable—or unwilling—to determine their final resting place. The leaves, together with the spitefully cold-shouldered rain, were certain harbingers of the approaching meanness of Winter.

Today at Hunts School, the weather was idyllic. Per the usual. It was the Friday of the first week following Samhain. Second term classes should have started this week. But after what happened at the Combat Challenge...

He'd last spoken to Borras on Monday morning. The previous Friday, Tal had gone straight from the infirmary to the Samhain feast. There had been zero privacy to talk details about everything that happened after he blacked out in the arena. As the first mortal to attend Hunts School, Tal knew he'd always been perceived as an oddity, most probably an extremely weak

15

link in the Omada power structure. Other students shrank from him now, almost as if even his slightest touch might infect them with some mortal disease.

Overnight he'd gone from oddity to freak. A potentially dangerous, murderous freak, at that. The other students now saw him as the winner of the first Combat Challenge in millennia, the owner of a magyk ring gifted to him by one of the Elder Children, and as the cunning trickster whose machinations had resulted in the death of the Prime Direction of one of Omada's main competitors to win the Tyrning. In only one term at the school Tal had amassed a pretty horrific curriculum vitae.

On Monday, Borras had briefly filled him in about the arena events after Tal passed out and was stretchered to the infirmary. Borras confirmed that Mitt had died. It was a Combat Challenge and the Folk were prohibited from intervening until the actual fight between Tal and Väst was finished. Which, as Tal had guessed, left Nord as the Släkt Acting Prime. Definitely a negative turn as Nord hated Tal more than anyone else at Hunts School, which pretty much meant he hated him more than anyone else in the known universe. Even though Mitt had violated the Hunts Rules, Borras told Tal the scuttlebutt was some deal had been reached between the Archon and the HuntsMistress that allowed Släkt to remain as a Hunts Finalist team and that they had also been allowed to pick up a new Fifth from one of the three losing teams.

Feelings were still mixed on his own team as to Tal using a wish of Aurora's ring to save an opponent belonging to the most significant—and potentially most deadly—opposing Finalist squad. Notos hadn't spoken to him at the Samhain feast and was apparently still high-pissed that Tal had made him look like a serious dumbass in front of the entire school. Borras and Tal agreed Tal should take a sabbatical this week, to give everyone else some space to sort things through. Not hanging with the team right now was okay with Tal because he was still angry with Notos about any number of things. Tal had pulled out all of the stops and managed to finagle the win. He was pretty sure he'd done it in a manner that was in accordance with "Seeking the Center," whatever that was. Really. There was a Hunts Rule for every other aspect of the Tyrning procedure. Why wasn't there something in writing about what was, and wasn't, "Seeking the Center."

Tal knew with certainty Väst had survived the Combat Challenge, at least while she was in the arena. There was a total news blackout about her after that. None. Not whether she subsequently died, whether she was maimed for life, whether she'd gone back to her Realm. Nothing.

After walking around the grounds on Monday, Tal had walked the length of Grass Grow, the school's expansive front yard. He had then crossed River Run and walked up to the edge of Forest Fell. Tal knew he'd been lucky last time he entered the forest and had no intention of pushing the matter. His hope had been that perhaps Arthrys had been on patrol nearby, or that Perun might step out of the woods. He owed him a major thank you for saving Väst.

She has to be alive, Tal told himself. I'm...I'm...in love with her. Even though it is her sworn obligation to put me down if I'm blocking the path to Släkt victory. His feelings seemed oddly mercurial. When he was at home, there wasn't enough time to talk with Elle on the phone, or to go to the movies with her, to email her, or simply to sit and think about her. As soon as he passed the Gas Station Crossing those feelings seemed to recede, to be replaced by his overwhelming need to see Väst, to be with her.

Even though he'd won the Challenge, and his team was still in the running to win the Tyrning, Tal felt profoundly defeated. Emet had done his best to reason with him, he really had. Emet's counsel came from his perspective of logic and reason. Tal realized his feelings had nothing to do with either of those things.

Whether because of his lack of knowledge about Väst's status, or some more general post-first term malaise, Tal hadn't been able to make himself re-engage in schoolwork during the next three days. Some of his time was spent visiting with non-Hunts students. Talking to them about their cultures and their lives. Learning. Experiencing the new and the unknown had always been therapeutic for him.

Every one of them had given up a significant portion of their life span to attend Hunts School. They'd put their lives on hold to try to win the Tyrning, leaving friends and loved ones behind. They couldn't use their psuche names at Hunts School. Initially everyone was given a student number. Those that scored high enough to make it on a competition team were given a team name. Then if they were subsequently booted out of the Hunts, that name was taken away and they were demoted back to their student number.

Almost a hundred years of building relationships, friendships, in some cases intimacy, or maybe hatred. All of it done without once being called by your real name, only by some impersonal student identification number. Harsh, Tal thought. It is really truly harsh.

Most of the last three days though had been spent with the people that made him the happiest at Hunts School—his fellow musicologists. During first term, he'd played with six or seven different groups, a revolving cast dropping in for sessions every now and then. Those diverse groups had coalesced down to his regulars, which consisted of himself, three other guys and two girls. He had been able to teach each of them how to use Earth-style six-strings. In return they taught him how to play any number of funky stringed instruments from dozens of Realms.

All of the rest of the group were proficient on keyboards, which interestingly were remarkably similar from Realm to Realm. The universality of music, Tal thought. He was a quick learner and although he'd never been much on the piano, there were a large number of fun Folk percussive instruments he mastered. Lots of amazingly different kinds of shakers and janglers and clackers. Many times Tal wished his entire Hunts School experience could have been used to learn and play Folk music.

Because he was the only human at the school, his group named him their de facto leader. Tal accepted graciously, although they all knew that as good as he was, every one of the other five were even better. He only had to play a song one time and their voices and fingers picked it up perfectly the next time through.

They'd known he was beat down this week. They did him the courtesy of not even mentioning the Hunts, the Combat Challenge, or anything about Väst. Instead, they announced to him that between the members of their little group they didn't want to be numbers anymore, they wanted to have names. Tal knew part of their plan was to help divert his attention. He appreciated it and it worked. Initially they wanted him to dole out their new monikers. Tal told them that was no good. If they were going to have new identities, they should choose the names themselves.

During the hundred-year Hunts School curriculum, the entire student body was taught about Earth plane events, including "current events." Tal laughed when he heard the phrase the first time as "current events" was everything that occurred in the three hundred years since the last Tyrning. Earth Realm was of major significance in the Folk universe. It was the only plane that operated on electricity instead of magyk, and it was the plane where Amarantos had chosen to site the Prime Omphalos.

It had taken the other five several hours to work through a plethora of choices and shouted suggestions, and they'd all had a blast. Even Tal. It was the first time in weeks he remembered smiling, let alone belly-laughing. They went through dozens of musician's names. All the way from Pan, Orpheus and Bragi from ancient mythology to Mozart and Wagner.

Okay, Tal thought, so I had a little influence in the final selections. The guys went with Jimi, Jethro and Elton. The girls were very pleased to henceforth be known as Ella and Janis.

Afterwards, as they tuned their instruments, Ella suggested the next logical step seemed to be a name for their group. Tal gently reminded them that Omada was still in the running for the Tyrning, which of course meant that he might not be alive next week…or the week after that.

Another round of fun, this time with dozens of different suggestions for their band name. The final decision was unanimous. From this point forward they would be rocking together as "Old School." After a leisurely lunch break in the cafeteria, where Tal loaded up on ambrosia and nectar, they played songs until it was time for Tal to head home. He promised his group he would study up that evening on some songs they could learn, with an eye toward compiling a few actual sets of song covers. Even though they all knew that given Tal's position as a Hunts Finalist he wouldn't ever have the time or opportunity to perform with them for the rest of the Hunts School.

He'd felt a little better on the walk home Tuesday evening. That night, and the two succeeding nights, he and Emet immersed themselves in learning lyrics and chords for some of Tal's favorite songs. Well, they were actually Emet's favorite songs too. For obvious reasons. Still, it was pure pleasure and he and Emet got to share some quality hours.

On both Wednesday and Thursday, Tal played professor for his group. Their eyes were as big as saucers the first time he played them, "Mama Told Me Not To Come," by Three Dog Night. He imagined the awe on their faces was probably the same as that of the teens of the mid-1950s the first time they heard Chuck Berry getting his guitar freak on in "Maybelline." They went crazy over all of Tal's rock tune selections, whether power ballad or hard rock. It seemed that all manner of Folk loved them some rock and roll.

The others learned so quickly that they were actually able to develop five solid set lists, with everybody getting a chance to take their turn singing lead vocals and playing guitar solos. It was one hundred percent undiluted fun—with zero percent chance of anyone being killed or maimed. Those three days of simply being a teenager rocking out with other kids his age—okay, fine, several of them were hundreds of years older than him—had been restorative. Hunts School was still about death but for the first time for Tal it was about life as well. Sure, the primary purpose of Hunts School was the Tyrning. The Hunts were intended to select the best team to rule the universe for the next three centuries. From day one Tal had willingly shouldered the burden of the heaviness of Hunts School. He was now getting to glimpse one of the secondary purposes of the school, the sharing of the talents and art of different Folk cultures for the students to take back to their home planes.

So here it is, Friday morning, Tal thought, as he briskly strode across the dew-heavy carpet of Grass Grow. He was still worried about Väst and desperate to see her and touch her but he was also ready to get back to the books. The most direct route to achieve that goal was the library, which is where he was headed. To start preparing for whatever new terribleness the truly evil HuntsMistress was going to throw at the competitors. How does somebody get that job anyway? Is there a universe-wide contest to find the biggest, meanest asshole?

As he passed the front doors, Tal nodded his greetings to the sentries. There was no response. Of course. They were the guards at Buckingham Palace multiplied to the nth degree. Well, if the Buckingham guards were identical half-naked indigo blue all-tatted up eight-percent body fat gods with trapezius muscles the size of large meteorites.

He quickly navigated his way to the main entrance of the library. His focus today was going to be Moiety background reading, learning information the Folk students had known for at least a hundred years, maybe their entire lives. After a productive morning, he was getting ready to take his lunch break when he noticed a massive tome laying on its side in one of the back racks. He was pretty sure the binding was red leather but it was so caked with grime it was hard to tell. He wiped his shirtsleeve gently across the front of the book, removing enough gunk to see the title—*From The Beginning: The Architecture of Hunts School and Its Immediate Environs*. Tal quickly flipped through a few pages. There was even a chapter devoted to installation of the murderous Keres. Tal didn't care what the grownup's official investigation had concluded, the hellhounds release had been intentional. By some extremely powerful bad actor.

This is exactly what I need, he told himself. Since there clearly wasn't much demand for the book, he asked the librarian if he might check it out for a few days. She agreed, he signed the library card, and carefully stowed the volume in his backpack.

His next stop was the cafeteria. The pleasant weather—coupled with the still tense situation with Notos—inspired Tal to fix a to-go tray from the cafeteria, remembering when he reached the end of the line to grab himself a half-full ewer of nectar. He saw the rest of the Omada across the room. He walked over and told Borras he was going to do some studying out on the front lawn. The Omada Prime nodded and let him go.

Tal nodded to the sentries as he walked out. No response. Of course. After walking down the massive front stairs, he decided the foot-wide marble lip of the fountain was a perfect place for a reading picnic. As he spread out his food and his books, he realized he was always in such a hurry coming and going from campus that he'd never simply had a chance to hang out at the fountain like everyone else.

He stood up and slowly walked the entire circumference of the fountain. The central jet shooting out the top of the structure must be seriously magyked, he thought. The culvert sized column of water rocketed intact hundreds of feet into the sky, before reluctantly conceding to gravity, at which point it erupted outward into a falling penumbra which bathed every single one of the dozen dozens of perfectly carved sculptures of men, women, and beasts. The main basin was so large not a single drop spattered outside its perimeter. Then there were the forty or fifty ancillary fountains, issuing helter-skelter from tridents, or horns, or mouths gaping wide. Tal tried to compute the hourly water volume in his head. Not enough data for specifics, he conceded. It was clear, however, that even if all of the smaller jets recycled from the reservoir there must be thousands of gallons erupting from the main jet alone every minute of every day. There was no indicia of hydraulic piping for either supply or removal. Where does it come from and where does it go, Tal wondered.

If it was sunny, as it was today, there was a nimbus of hundreds of small constantly shifting rainbows. The water sound wasn't so loud as to prevent conversation, but it was of sufficient volume to insulate private conversations against eavesdropping.

It's exquisite, Tal thought. That's the word. Every muscle, every sinew. Every eyebrow, every hooked talon, every expression on every face. Every nuance of every detail—perfectly wrought in snow-white marble. If Dante and Michelangelo had been given an entire quarry of flawless Carrera marble and asked to jointly expend every jot of their creative genius to sculpt a world made solely of marble and living water, that masterpiece would have been Fountain Flow. Exquisite. Yep, that's about right, Tal decided. Exquisite.

After stuffing himself on ouberos snake, Tal chugged about half of his nectar. He looked over at all of his books. Might as well look at my new loaner, he decided, as he hefted the book onto his lap. Damn thing must weigh ten pounds. After glancing at the table of contents, he flipped over to the chapter about Fountain Flow.

The first couple of pages were concerned with the original placement of the fountain, more than a hundred Tyrnings past. Dang, he thought as he did the math, one hundred times three hundred is thirty thousand. Fountain Flow isn't even the oldest part of Hunts School and it's thirty thousand years old. This part of Arkansas would have been inhabited by Great Plains tribes back then. In the modern era it would have been the Quapaws. Thirty thousand years went back even further than Paleo-Indian, back to the Ice Age in North America. Damn! Fountain Flow was constructed on the Hunts School campus while most of the Earth was encased in ice and snow.

Tal read a couple more pages. Seems the fountain had been designed as an ornate—and extremely heavy—cover stone to encapsulate a Plutonium. The first letter is capitalized, Tal noted. That's the first time I've ever seen plutonium used as a proper noun. There wasn't any additional information on that subject in the fountain chapter. Tal made himself a note to google it when he got home.

Later in the chapter he learned Fountain Flow was only the structure's colloquial name. Some of the words in the full name were an ancient Folk language that might as well be called "gobbledygook" but he wrote down the words he thought he might be able to translate when he got home—Phylaca, gens, and "Lernaean Spring."

There were vibrant, glossy full-page photos of each of the sculptures and smaller fountains, each of which was identified and thoroughly discussed. Tal didn't know most of the names listed in the book, but he knew enough to realize the sculpted figures represented the water-related gods, goddesses, deities, and creatures from many different Earth plane cultures. As he scanned the two-page spread of the fountain layout, he saw the northern quadrant was populated with Lir and Sinann, representing an Irish Realm, and Vedenemo of the Finnish Realm, as well as Sedna of the Inuit plane, and Njord of the Norse Realm. In the Eastern quadrant were Yam, a Canaanite plane sculpture, Mazu, from one of the Chinois Realms, as well as Anuket and Osiris from an Egyptian plane. In the west was Kanaloa, from a Hawaiian Realm. The Southern quarter section included Tangaroa of a Maori plane.

Supplementing the larger sculptures were a number of small naiad-type carvings, as well as several hippocampi scattered around. There was a pair of broad chested, long-bearded trident wielding dudes with human heads and torsos but their lower parts were both horse and scaly, long-tailed fish. They were identified in the book as Bythos and Aphros. Tal wrote the names on his ever expanding list.

There was a serpentine creature with multiple heads whose body curled downward around the central jet, ending with its tail twined around the feet of the largest sculpture in the fountain. Tal looked for its name. It was a hydra—the nine-headed version.

Far and away the largest statue was of some chick named Mokosh, from the Slavic Realm. Slavic mythology had never been part of Tal's reading itinerary. Well, before Hunts School anyway. Tal resolved he and Emet would spend some time that evening going over his list of fountain unknowns, which included figuring out what was up with Mokosh and why she was the centerpiece of Fountain Flow.

Tal guesstimated the sculpture was about forty feet tall, if you measured from the bottom of her sandal clad feet to the outstretched tip of the slender blade held in her left hand as it stabbed upward toward the heavens. In her right hand she was holding a cornucopia, with a great volume of water gushing out. The words *"fons vitae caritas"* were carved deep into the cornucopia. Looks like the Latin google translator and I will also be spending some quality time when I get home, Tal thought.

Tal finished the chapter, closed the book, and began gathering his things to head back inside. Walking back up the stairs and past the sentries, it hit him. A whole chapter in that very large book devoted to the fountain and not a single word about where the fountain's water originates. Or where it goes.

CHAPTER QUATTUOR

The last time She'd summoned him, She'd made him use his teammates' bindings to slaughter them. That's not quite accurate, he admitted, as he furtively moved from one building to the next. When he reached his target, he scurried through dank hallways to the steam room, their rendezvous point. It was the only functioning portion of an otherwise abandoned campus building. The constant hissing of the disintegrating steam pipes provided an almost impenetrable white noise against any guards on campus authorized by the Archon to use hearmagyk.

It had been his choice to kill them. Just as it had been his choice many centuries ago at the Battle of Camlann to live, whatever the cost. Disfigured and dying, he could have told Her no. But he didn't. He told Her he would trade anything to live, to rule as Archon. To that end, he'd used his authority as Prime Direction to rape his teammates of their free will. He'd twisted the unbreakable binding of their contracts to compel them, turning them into the Crestfallyn. Thin, faceless slices of their former selves. One had died in the process, the other three lived—after a fashion. It was the basest betrayal in the history of the Moiety.

She'd convinced him his team could still have all they wanted. He could be Archon for life, they could have their full lives back, and She could have…well, whatever it was She wanted. Apparently unforeseen events kept happening, causing Her plans to go awry. It all revolved around that damnable mortal. They had waited centuries for Her to tell them the time was ripe, and finally the Munedan was born and his face promised to Borras. Then somehow the human made an unprecedented passage through the Gas Station portal. That was worrisome, because it was one of Sol's avatars. Which meant one of the Principes was taking sides in the affairs of the Folk. The Dust Child joined one of the teams which was down to four members. It couldn't have been coincidence. That team had no viable options to replace their fallen Prime Direction. They were dead in the water—until the human showed up.

Each new twist lead to another obstruction. Borras was prevented from taking the Munedan's face because one of the Omada had royal level deathmagyk. The release of the Keres, the Hell Hounds, hadn't yielded the desired result. She'd fixed things so the official investigation had run into one dead end and then another. He knew Alberich hadn't given up. The combination of the Archon with his own power and that of his accursed seer wife was formidable. Even though the "official" investigation was concluded, he knew they wouldn't let it go.

As a result of Borras's failure She modified her plan yet again and made him kill all of his teammates to thrice-blood a blade. Again, that was his choice. It's what any sane person would have done, wasn't it? Any sane person who was promised all of the power of the known universe for their entire life? Out of everything he'd done, over his several thousand years of voluntary servitude, creation of the knife was easily his blackest deed.

At Her command he'd helped Her fix the Combat Challenge so the Dust Child would die. She'd even stepped in somehow to goad the leader of the Släkt. Once more a seemingly impossible event thwarted Her carefully crafted scheme. How would any Munedan meet Aurora? Why was a Principe giving a Dust Child any gyft, much less a magyk ring? What could a

Munedan have possibly done that prompted the leader of the Cooshies to heal one of the Folk? The Creatures had remained neutral for many Tyrnings. Even the Puca only participated to the extent necessary to fulfill their obligations under the Lex. There was no way any Creature was going to voluntarily save one of the Folk.

Still, She seemed to have an infinite number of contingencies. When one plan went sideways, She moved on to another version. He had no idea about the source of Her magyk, or what it was She hoped to get out of her efforts. Best not to peer too deeply into that blackness. It was clear She had substantial power. After all, he was walking around Hunts School, the single most warded place in all of the known Realms, fully disguised as someone else. Not only had She accomplished that feat but She had the magyk to prevent anyone from detecting what She'd done.

She was waiting for him when he arrived. He never saw Her and She only spoke to him telepathically. She was here though, he could see Her form through the clouds of steam. Unable to stop himself, he began tracing the now hidden scar on his face in the ritual She'd taught him.

'Have you discovered anything new about the mortal?'

The vehemence in Her voice immediately took him to his knees, blood dripping from both his nostrils. Be careful, Malabranche, you've never seen Her this angry. He slowly stood, wiping the blood on his jacket sleeve. The coat would now have to be destroyed. 'No,' he thought back to Her. 'He has been healed by the physicks, and the HuntsMistress and the Archon have reached an agreement...'

'Fool!' She screamed in his inner ear so loudly that this time it was his ears which bled. He could feel the blood slowly trickle down the outside of his cheeks. 'I know all of those things. Have you nothing for me?'

"No, Mistress,' he responded.

'The blade? Is it safely hidden?'

"Yes, Mistress.'

'Good. If all else fails, that blade will get us each what we want.' Then She changed gears on him. 'The Tyrning Year field trip. What is it?'

'As you have requested, I have made efforts for it to be some type of event with the closest Earth plane high school.'

'Excellent.' She sounded almost gleeful. 'That presents multiple opportunities which need to be weighed. I will give you further instructions. A month from now. Here. Same time.'

And just as surely as Mordred knew She'd been there when he'd first arrived, he knew now he was alone.

CHAPTER FIVE

As Emet carried him home from the gas station, Tal told him about their extra research project for the evening. Emet, being who he was, was in his own emotionless way as nerd-happy as Tal. Emet would probably have characterized it as "nerd-interested." Same difference in this case, Tal decided.

As usual, Emet dropped him off once they got to the populated areas and they proceeded to the house by separate routes. They were both convinced their subterfuge had lasted because they'd been extremely careful not to violate Rule One—they couldn't ever be seen together. Any lesser inconsistencies would be rationalized by their family and all of their acquaintances. As long as there wasn't irrefutable proof there were two Tal Smiths then no one would ever seriously consider the possibility. Not even Elle.

After dropping his backpack in his bedroom, Tal logged on to his laptop and quickly scanned the notes Emet had typed for him about today's activities at Nemeton High. He then efficiently took care of the actions necessary to maintain their deception with his family members. He played a few games of knockout basketball with the twins. Next was the family dinner during which he volleyed questions about the events of the day at Nemeton High.

Tal took a little longer on that evening's phone call with Elle than he'd allotted timewise in his and Emet's schedule. She'd wanted to tell him all about her work on the committee for the upcoming Winter Formal, and he'd wanted to listen. To every word she said. It really is curious, he thought. While I am at Hunts School I am overwhelmed by Väst. Besotted doesn't overstate the situation, but as soon as I pass through the Gas Station Crossing…

Focus, Tal, you and Emet have a lot to do tonight. It was always hard for him to refocus on pretty much anything else after having contact with Elle. Everything about her derailed him. Her thoughts, the way she expressed herself. Even the timbre of her voice, which, he decided, was like a summer afternoon thundershower. The kind of welcome and much needed event that makes you want to immediately stop what you're doing, run outside, hold your hands up, and raise your face to the heavens to be baptized. The kind of downpour that washes you clean as you spin in place, grinning like an idiot for no reason whatsoever. Or maybe for every reason whatsoever. The kind of storm that while it nourishes your life, also reminds you with the occasional rolling fusillade of thunder, that it has the power to dramatically alter your life—to even end your existence.

Elle spoke with this lilting cadence which made Tal want to agree with her about everything. How could any rational individual possibly gainsay any postulation made by that brain, expressed with that face, emanating from those lips…

The ding on his cell told Tal that Emet had texted him. Following their normal protocol, Emet was upstairs in the attic until they were both certain Thea and Pell had fallen fast asleep. Looking down Tal saw it was actually the fifth text he'd received from Emet. All of them exactly the same.

'Earth to Tal. Tal, come in.'
'Earth to Tal. Tal, come in.'
'Earth to Tal. Tal, come in.'
'Earth to Tal. Tal, come in.'
'Earth to Tal. Tal, come in.'

"Sorry, sorry. I got lost thinking about Elle," Tal whispered.

'I noticed,' came the typed reply. 'There was something I forgot to mention earlier. I'm pretty sure she wants you to ask her to the Winter Formal.'

"WHAT? WHY AM I JUST NOW HEARING ABOUT THIS?"

There was a moment's pause before Emet's response. 'Looks like I'm staying up here awhile, I hear some rustling from the adult area.'

Tal switched to typing mode himself, just in case. 'Don't you think that was kind of an important thing to remember?'

'I'm sorry, Tal. It seems to be getting more and more challenging to prioritize each day's information in the same order that you would.'

'I know. Sorry for the yelling thing. Well, I'm not calling her back now. You and I need to cogitate on this a bit. There shouldn't be any Rule One issues. I can go to the dance and you'll stay here.'

'Right. No possible "no same place at the same time" violation. Should be a no-brainer. Where do you want to start on the research?'

Tal and Emet had learned from prior projects that their thought patterns generally took them to the same online resources, so rather than duplicate efforts, Tal took Mokosh and Emet jumped on the Plutonium project.

About an hour later, Emet opened Tal's bedroom window and jumped in, closing it behind him. When he saw Tal's questioning look, he slowly lip-synced the words, "They're out. I'm sure."

"Okay," Tal whispered in reply. He went first, telling Emet what he'd learned. The two composite creature statutes in the fountain were Bythos and Aphros, representations of the two most famous ichthyocentaurs. Which was the fancy name for centaurs who had a fish tail in addition to being part human and part horse. The stories alleged them to be Chiron's half-brothers.

Emet had been assigned the Latin research. ' "Gens" in Latin can be translated as tribe or people,' he typed. 'Or folk,' he added.

"Folk makes sense," Tal replied.

' "Phylaca" is one of the several Latin words for prison.'

"Which at first thought makes no sense," Tal answered.

Emet quickly tapped his response. 'It does all seem kind of like a word jumble. Let's throw our other data into the mix.'

Tal started with the results of his Mokosh research. Slavic mythology varied widely from Eastern Europe to Central Russia. There were a couple of reasons for the disparities in the mythology. First, the Slavic culture covered substantially more geography and cultural diversity than most myth schemes. Second, the Slavic myths weren't even reduced to writing until the ninth century. Important information since it meant that most of the Greek stories were reduced to writing more than fifteen hundred years before the Slavic stories were set to paper.

In certain respects the Slavic pantheon loosely mirrored some of the Norse gods and goddesses. There wasn't as much cross-pollenization or exact counterparting between Slav-Norse as there was between Greco-Roman myths, but there were similarities.

Some sources indicated that amongst her many functions, Mokosh was the goddess of rain. That fact, together with the information that the rough English translation of Mokosh is "wet," made sense to the boys why her statue would be in the fountain with all of the other water gods and creatures. There were, however, any number of prominent water deities, such as Poseidon, not represented in the fountain. There didn't seem to be any logical nexus between the many water gods represented in the fountain and those that weren't. They couldn't find any information suggesting why Mokosh, a lesser known deity only tangentially related to water, was the centerpiece of Fountain Flow.

Although there were many variations in the Slavic stories, Mokosh was universally described as the wife of Perun, who was

Thor's Slavic counterpart, as well as the head Slavic deity. Tal noted that even though she was generally described as Perun's wife, she was almost as frequently described as being Veles's lover.

'Veles?' Emet typed.

"The Slavic god of the underworld, who also happens to be Perun's chief rival. He has counterparts in almost every culture. Some sources say Veles was patterned off of Arawn, the Welsh god of the underworld," Tal replied.

Emet quickly type-replied. 'Like Persephone with Hades, she splits her time between the living lands and those of the dead?'

"A little bit like that," Tal confirmed, "except that Mokosh's actions were voluntary. She was, apparently, very much her own woman, equal to or greater than any male deity."

'Her story then is substantially different than the mytheme paradigm used to explain the Earth's seasons,' Emet replied. 'In those stories it was always the male deity of the underworld who would capture or take an Earth goddess to his realm for part of the year. One of the consequences being Winter.'

Tal continued with his data dump. "Sometimes Mokosh was depicted as a hideous crone and other times she was a rocking pulchritudinous centerfold. The goddess of both birth and death. Best I can tell, she is a conflated version of Hecate and Aphrodite." Which, Tal realized, also made her unusual, if not singular, in all of the stories he'd ever read.

The differences between the Earth plane cultural myths involving the deities and creatures, and the real life facts involving the Folk and Creatures bearing those names made Tal realize, again, that each of us sees only our finite—and infinitesimal—piece of the many faceted jigsaw puzzle of Creation. We will never fit, he realized, until we make a genuine effort to understand those who seem different. Because they probably aren't—different. Because they probably are—us. Different shapes, different edges. Same Creation puzzle at the center of all of the countless planes of existence.

"Here's the last of it on Mokosh," he continued. "Some Slavic myths describe her as the gatekeeper of a magical spring that flows from the underworld into the land of the living. It is the pathway she uses to travel between the quick and the dead."

Emet smiled broadly at that bit of information, and typed, 'Now it makes sense.'

"What? What makes sense?" Tal asked.

Emet quickly began typing his report on the Plutonium. It started with only one word—'hellmouth.'

Tal raised his hands palms up, in a questioning motion.

'Plutonium is the Latin root word, and Ploutonian is its Greek counterpart for the same concept—a hellmouth.'

Tal momentarily forgot the need for stealth. "You mean there really is such a thing?" he asked loudly.

Emet quickly raised his finger to his lips, then leapt to the window before stopping to listen for any noise that might indicate if Tal's outburst had woken one of the adults. After about a minute they both decided they'd caught a break and Emet walked back and took his seat on the bed facing Tal.

"Really?" Tal asked, this time in a whisper.

'Yes,' Emet typed. 'A Ploutonian, named after Pluto, the Greek god of the underworld, is a hellmouth or hell gate.'

"Wow, just wow," Tal replied.

Emet continued with his typing. 'The most famous Ploutonian was called "Pluto's Gate" and is located in the ruins of Hierapolis in Turkey. However, the hellmouth concept didn't belong only to the Greeks. It appears most cultures have stories about a connecting bridge or path between Earth and Hell. The list includes several caves in Greece and Italy, Mount Etna, a location in China, a hellmouth in a desert in Turkmenistan, as well as sites in Japan, Iceland, and Ethiopia. Two of the more interesting plutonians are a certain spot in the Paris Catacombs and a place actually named the "Seven Gates of Hell" in Pennsylvania.'

"What the hell?" Tal asked.

'Exactly,' Emet typed in response. 'It's pretty weird stuff. There really is a field in Pennsylvania with seven gates in it, and the legend is that if you go through all seven in the proper order, you're…'

"Hell bound," Tal finished. "How'd you like to go to that high school?" Tal asked, muffling his mouth as he laughed.

Emet smiled in return. 'Just wait. I've saved the best for last.'

"What?" Tal asked, leaning forward.

'The Greeks also believed there was one at a place called the Lernean Spring,' Emet typed.

"You mean Fountain Flow," Tal asked, so excited about the information he almost yelled again.

'No, the Lernean Spring was a well-known site in ancient Greece. The Greeks thought the spring was one of the gates to the underworld.'

"In other words, the Greeks thought it was a magic spring," Tal whispered.

Emet's keypad clicked rapidly. 'You got it. Not just anybody could go through it though. Ordinary folks died. Only some heroes successfully made the passage. You get one guess as to what guarded the entrance to the Lernaean Springs hellmouth.'

"Ms. Empousa?" Tal asked.

'From what you've told me,' Emet typed in response, 'you are really close, but no. It was the hydra.'

"Holy crap!" Tal exclaimed, before realizing he'd again gotten way too loud. "See you in the morning," he whispered to Emet who had already leapt out the window in response to the heavy tread of Pell's footsteps on the hallway's hard wood floor.

CHAPTER SEX

When she woke this time Väst instantly knew she was in her own bed. There's just something recognizable about the feel and smell of your own mattress, your own pillow, your own comfy red blanket. Not as comfortable, of course, as the magykally woven blankets of her Realm, where only the finest fairy silk was used in the palace bedrooms. Careful, Väst told herself. You may be being watched. You may also be blind, she added. She forced herself to lay still, to listen for any indication of someone else's presence. Take a few minutes, she told herself.

A hundred years. Even for the Tuatha Dé that's a meaningful span of time. A hundred years since I last saw home, since my parents hugged me and told me they love me. They're not supposed to even know which one of the students is me, but I bet Mom has figured it out. Awaymagyk is one of the rarest gyfts and she pretty much sets the all-time standard for strength. She almost single-handedly put her team over the top against Dad's squad. Of course they hadn't been together at that time. With the whole "no fraternization" rule and all that.

Last year during the Snype Hunt was the only time in a century I've been able to use my own magyk. It felt so good to be whole once more, to feel the adrenalin rush from using the powers the UnFading Spirit has given me. As soon as that Hunt was over though, we were transported back to Hunts School, to our magkyless state.

All of us, we left not only our old lives behind but large pieces of who we are when we agreed to accept the opportunities presented by the honor of attending Hunts School. Families, relationships, children, all of those things.

Väst had noticed over the decades that the absence of their magyk had changed everyone. Some for the good. Others—like Nord—had soured and rotted in its absence. She understood the magykal ban was an intentionally designed part of the winnowing process leading up to the Tyrning. Didn't make it any easier to bear, for any of them.

Surely that's long enough, she decided. There's not been a rustle of cloth, not even the slightest inhalation of breath. She was alone. Now for the other matter. Time to find out, she decided.

She slowly opened her eyes—and saw nothing. Inky darkness. Blind, she thought, as she frantically bolted upright. I'm blind. In a few moments though her eyes adjusted, and she saw the sliver of a column of light outlining the pulled curtains. Thank Amarantos, I'm not blind.

She sat up on the edge of her bed, taking a moment to assess her status, to see if there was any remnant of the sedative she'd been given. Nope, I feel fine. Actually, I feel better than I've felt in years, she thought.

A quick glance to the magyk-powered clock/calendar sitting on her nightstand told her it was Sunday morning. Good, nowhere to be until tomorrow. She got up, went into the bathroom, and turned the shower on. As she was washing her hair she tried to pull all of the recent events into focus and assemble them in proper chronological order.

She and Quint had been their respective teams' chosen champions for the Combat Challenge. Under the Hunts Rules, it was a fight to the death. He hadn't understood she had no choice but to kill him. She'd tried to tell him but the geas on her had the same non-disclosure gag magyk as Quint told her had been placed on him for when he left Hunts School campus for Earth plane proper.

She'd done everything she could to not wound him, she even slammed her huge sword into the arena floor to give him time to find a way to kill her. Ultimately her sword of power, Heaven's Will, was too strong for her to overrule.

Luckily Quint had tricked everyone into thinking he was holding one magyk sword, Skofnung, when he was actually holding another—Fragarach. Väst paused in her scrubbing. He is so smart, and so cute, and so…so…good-hearted. And when he sings to me, well, it's unbelievable.

Her brain redirected itself back to the event chronology. Quint had remembered Fragarach's power over the winds. He'd summoned them, all of them, and they had scoured her, and burnt her, and frozen her. She remembered the agonizing pain as her skin was first scraped off, layer by dermal layer. Then her exposed sinews and muscles were burnt all the way down to the bone by the Sirocco he'd summoned. After that he'd used the Mistral's cold to freeze her. Finally, her last breath was wrenched from her by the Typhoon's water cocoon. Tal hadn't wanted to do any of it, he had been openly weeping. Not from the possibly mortal blow she'd given him when she'd sliced him with Heaven's Will, but for her. He was crying for her pain, for her loss.

After Tal had used Fragarach's power and released the winds to assault her, she'd watched his eyes as Fragarach took his strength from him and used it to trip him and drive itself through her chest. She remembered the blurred mass of her dark blue aortal blood as it first spurted, then sputtered, and finally seeped out of her chest. By then it was like she was seeing through bloody curtains but she still saw his eyes begging for her to live as she labored to take each breath, not knowing whether it might be her last. Then he'd unexpectedly grabbed his own hand and started praying to one of the Principes—Aurora. Yes, yes, that was it, excited that she could recall more details. He'd called on

Aurora to heal her, and then Quint had fallen over himself. Dying, because her sword had also mortally cut its adversary.

As Väst stepped out of the shower and began toweling off, she continued stitching the timeline together. A rainbow curtain had shimmered into being. It parted and a giant silver wolf stepped out of thin air. No, not a wolf—a Cooshie. And not just any elfhound, it was their leader himself—Perun. She knew Perun because he had saved both she and Quint's lives once before, during the Keres' attack.

Perun had first bent low so that he could run his tongue across her burnt forehead. Soothing had immediately radiated outward from where he touched her. He'd then gazed straight into her eyes, without blinking, speaking to her telepathically. 'You must hold tight to your lyfe little one. I have sufficient magyk to heal you but I cannot bring you back once your soul has begun its journey to Veles's domain.'

The echo of that conversation brought a cold shiver to her shoulders. Veles, the King of Five-Hells. Väst remembered she hadn't even had the energy to respond, so she had merely formed the words in her own mind. 'Let me go, Lord Perun. Save, Quint. Please.'

'That is not the wish that has brought me here this day,' Perun had replied. 'I have been asked if I will make you whole. I have decided that it is of the Center that I grant such request.' The great beast's lips had then retreated, baring his fangs in a jagged, lupine grin. 'Worry not about the mortal, little one. The Dust Child's wheel yet has many turns.' Then the huge maned head had leaned forward again, and gently—so very gently— licked her ruined eyes, one at a time. She knew she should have felt even more pain. To the contrary, his touch brought surcease. After that Perun used the same gentleness to touch her several more times, in the places where the damage to her body was the greatest. She'd watch him pause then—he had looked puzzled— before he leaned forward and sniffed the black, crackled remains of her torso, right above her heart. He leaned forward, until his face was over that part of her, and remained there until a single teardrop fell on her chest. 'Sleep now, little one. The wish has been honored. It will take time but you will be made whole.'

That was it, Väst thought as she sat down in front of her makeup mirror and began brushing her hair. The whole sequence. A Munedan, bereft of magyk himself, had been able to call upon the magyk of one of the Elder Children to enlist the aid of one of the kings of the Creatures. On the Hunts School campus. The place most heavily warded against unauthorized magyk in the known universe, and Quint had been able to accomplish all of that to save her.

All of Väst's pent up emotion suddenly coalesced into four words. If it wasn't for the compulsion geas laid upon her a hundred years past, she would have said the words out loud. Even though he was gone, she would have offered them publicly, for all to hear. Regardless of the consequences, she would have said them repeatedly, and without any reservation. She would have said, "I love you, Quint."

CHAPTER SEPTUM

"Well?"

"Only the vaguest of signs and those were all extremely disturbing," Alberich replied, before falling backwards into the red moire pattern of the overstuffed armchair. "I started looking immediately after the Samhain feast. I have now physically inspected this entire campus, using both my own magyk as well as the magyk lent to me as Archon by the Hunts School itself. I'm pretty much spent, Aine."

Aine walked into the kitchen, and returned several minutes later with a tray containing a pitcher of nectar and a plate full of ambrosia. When Alberich glanced sideways at her, she smiled in reply. "What? I can't sneak some much needed sustenance from the cafeteria for the exhausted ruler of all of the known Realms?"

"Thank you," Alberich replied, as he took a proffered cup of the nectar. After taking a long draw with a corresponding sigh, he added, "That is so good, Aine. Sometimes I'm not sure whether it's the restorative power of the cafeteria's food and drink itself, or merely the 'fond memories' of them from my time as a student here at Hunts School."

"By 'fond memories,' I'm sure you are referring to meeting me," Aine joked, as she came and sat down on the ottoman by the left side of her husband's chair.

"Exactly," he replied wanly, efforting to put his arm around her.

"I know you're exhausted Alberich, but I need to know whatever little you did actually learn. It might help me focus when I go spectral."

Alberich dipped a foothill-sized scoop of ambrosia up with his spoon and ate it. "I'll be fine—after a little rest. I went in reverse order chronologically, last to first, in my search."

"So you started in the arena?"

"Yes. I searched the entire arena complex and got no meaningful reading. Until I touched the sand."

"Ooh, I'm not sure I would have thought of actually laying hands on the sand," Aine said, breathing in quickly. "I know you're Archon of the Moiety, with all that entails, but sometimes you surprise me with how clever you are."

Alberich, Lord of all of the known Realms, looked at his wife and actually blushed. A little. "For both of them, it was literally their lyfeblood, his red and hers blue, that soaked into the arena floor."

"What did your reading tell you?"

"There was Principe magyk used."

His wife paused before replying. "That explains how the wards were overridden. Alberich, the Principes have never shown any interest in the Hunts or the Tyrning."

"It is yet another unprecedented event in this Tyrning year."

"Who was it?" she asked quietly.

"Their magyk is far beyond even that of the Archon. The rainbow curtain indicates Aurora was involved in some fashion."

"Or that could be a clever deception by one of the others to throw anyone off the trail," she replied.

"That was my conclusion as well," Alberich said, nodding in agreement. "I learned from the mortal that the Cooshie that appeared was Perun."

"Their Chieftain, Alberich? How? How does a mortal have access to Principe magyk? How did a human entice the leader of all of the elfhounds to heal one of the Folk? It's been thousands of years since a Cooshie helped heal one of the Folk."

"I don't know," Alberich responded. "It was well played, though. Like all of the Folk in the arena, we were prevented by the Hunts Rules from interfering."

"It wasn't everyone else's flesh and blood who was dying, Alberich."

The Archon sighed, suddenly looking weary again.

"I know, Alberich, and I agree with you," Aine continued, placing her hand on his leg. "Someone I know intimately seems overly fond of quoting this part of the Lex—'The Law must apply equally to the greatest and the least'."

"I was right at the breaking point, Aine," he replied. "All I had to do was stretch forth my hand and…"

"That's not all you would have had to do. You would have also had to violate the Oath contract. There has never been an Archon who violated the Hunts Rules."

"Luckily for us there was a clever mortal who knew the Rules only applied to the Folk—not the Principes nor the Creatures."

"I told you weeks ago after I returned from skrying in an attempt to find our adversary that I feared our daughter's fate is somehow tied to that of the Dust Child."

Alberich nodded his acknowledgment. "What little I found reinforces your thoughts. After the arena, I checked the Omphalos ziggurat. There are simply too many legitimate trails coming and going from the Omphalos to separate them out.

"Next, I laid hands on the walls of all of the hallways and also in every classroom in the Temple of All Things, trying to find any remaining magyk threads. I found nothing. I went from there to both the boys' and girls' dormitories. The good news is I found nothing amiss where the students spend either their waking or sleeping hours."

"Then neither the Finalists nor the other students are complicit in the plot," Aine announced. "That is something, Alberich. It is heartening that the individuals who may end up running the Moiety for the next three hundred years aren't part of whatever conspiracy exists."

"I agree. From the dorms I went to the front of the school and combed through Grass Green all the way up to River Run. There were some remnants of the hellhounds' magyk but their stench hid any clues as to how they were released."

"Principal Chiron said his investigation revealed naught as well," Aine said.

" 'Tis so," Alberich commented. "After that I went to the Earth plane proper."

"What? You haven't been to see the Dust Children in more than a hundred years and you didn't think to ask me to go with?" Aine asked, in mock anger.

"You know it is not something I do lightly. My Emissaries are the only Folk beside myself allowed to pass through the Gas Station Crossing wards. They risk themselves each and every time because they must travel subject to my Bane."

"You found something?" she asked.

"Several things. I noticed Luna has an avatar next to her twin brother's Gas Station."

Aine drew breath so fast it was almost as if she'd been punched in the stomach. "That is bad news. Luna has refused commerce with both Folk and mortals for eons."

"I can't figure out what's up. It is yet another sign of Principe involvement this Tyrning Year. I went from there to the Dust Child's house. It's in a town named Nemeton."

Aine smiled a little. "That name is no coincidence, dearest."

"I don't think so either. It was in his bedroom I found the most information. About quite a number of things," Alberich said, with a small grin.

"What? What?" Aine asked anxiously.

"Well, there is a simulacrum golem residing there."

"WHAT?" Aine exclaimed. "How is that even possible with the Bane?"

"It should have been impossible. I quickly reviewed the Hunts Rules. Guess what? There's a loophole, at least when a mortal is on a team. Which has never occurred before now. Each Tyrning, the Archon approves the Rules for that cycle, so they become engrafted into the contract with the Hunts School itself. There is a rule that says where one teammate goes, all of the others may join him or her."

"The mortal chaos effect once again," Aine mused.

"Yes, and evidence of some real teamwork by Omada. I wondered how the mortal was juggling making the required attendance at Hunts School as well as his Earth Realm duties and responsibilities. Now we know. We also know one of the Omada has royal level creationmagyk."

"The highest level if he or she can fabricate a functioning simulacrum golem under those circumstances," Aine added. "What else?"

Alberich cast his eyes downward a moment before responding. "There was also deathmagyk. Two separate trails."

"Are you sure it wasn't the same Folk, just from different times?"

"No," Alberich replied. "One had been there numerous times. It was only the barest trace. Aine, it was one of the Crestfallyn."

His wife placed her hand to her mouth. "We thought they were gone. It's...it's been so long."

"The other trail was royal level deathmagyk."

At those words the color ran from Aine's face. She was shaking as she slowly stood. "That's not possible. It would mean one of the Omada is a scion of the King of..."

"Exactly," Alberich said, motioning for her to come sit beside him in the large chair. When she did, he placed his arm around her waist. "His or her name must have been in The Book or Principal Chiron would not have admitted them to Hunts School."

"But the prophecy, the Lex, the Hunts Rules…"

"It has been clear all year this Tyrning is different from any other," Alberich responded softly, as he pulled her closer to him. "After I returned to campus I decided to check all of the rest of the buildings, even the ones that have been vacant for hundreds of years."

"What did you find?" Aine asked, clearly still shaken from the previous disclosure.

"In the old physical plant, the one that is abandoned except for some ancillary steam operations, I found more evidence of Principe involvement—and of death."

"You couldn't tell which one of the Elder Children?"

Alberich again shook his head in the negative. "No, their magyk is too far beyond us. It wouldn't have been reliable information anyway. I think they have sufficient magyk to trick us if they care to do so."

"But the death? There has been no reported change in either the administration or student census, has there? No one has been reported missing?"

"No one."

"That means someone was on campus who shouldn't have been here, and that they've now been murdered. How many, Alberich?"

The Archon looked down before lifting his eyes back up to meet his wife's. "Three."

"Three," Aine repeated, her shoulders falling. "Someone has thrice-cursed an object. The school wards protect the school. What kind of magyk could defy the wards?"

"I think you know the answer," her husband replied. "I am going to have to sleep for awhile to restore myself. I want your promise you will not go astral until I am here to watch over you." She hesitated. "Aine, this is a dangerous puzzle we are trying to solve. Promise me."

"I promise, beloved."

CHAPTER OCTO

Väst's satyral-shell hairbrush split in half, yielding to the adamance of the inlaid green and yellow marble floor. She stared wide-eyed at herself in the mirror, overwhelmed by her revelation. For almost a hundred years she'd been helpless against that geas. For that entire period she'd struggled to reclaim her own will in every manner she could imagine. Including spending hundreds of hours in the library reading through some of the most ancient texts from dozens of Realms.

All of my effort, for naught. I was clueless as to who had magyked me, or why. Even more puzzling was how? I was fine when I left my home plane and traveled to Hunts School using the Prime Omphalos. Whoever it was, caught me the moment I arrived at Hunts School. In that brief moment, when for the first time in my life I was deprived of my magyk. I was completely defenseless as I felt it inserting itself into my aura.

It wouldn't have mattered if I'd been at full strength. Whoever laid that compulsion on me was much more powerful. I couldn't even make a dent in the spell when we all had our magyk returned during the Snype Hunt. I couldn't tell anybody else to try to get some help either. The geas stopped me from mentioning it, directly or indirectly.

Who can be that strong? Who is so strong they can lay a magykal binding upon me on the Earth plane? Not just Earth Realm, but here at Hunts School itself? And why?

At that thought, her body involuntarily shuddered. In the early decades the compulsion was only about little things, probably designed to strengthen its hold on me. It manipulated me at every turn: my test scores, my physical aptitude results, all of them so that I would be ranked where I would be placed on the Släkt. All along it made me flirt with Kentro, accidentally run into him at lunch or by Fountain Flow. It made me weave the intricate spider web that was designed to get him to fall for me, to trap him.

She hadn't been able to stop doing it to him, and he couldn't resist her. The evil plan came to fruition last year when it made me…when I… . Stop it, she told herself. Just, stop it! You tried and it was too strong for you.

After Kentro's death she'd hoped maybe its purpose had been fulfilled, that it was done controlling her. Then Quint showed up this year, and she felt it more strongly than ever before. It was only a few days into the first Hunts term when she'd realized Kentro's death had merely been a chess move designed to allow Quint to be placed on the game board.

From the first day of class this year the geas had made her compel Quint. Of course he believed with all his heart that he loved her. What chance did a Dust Child have against such powerful magyk? When the Keres attacked the students, he'd saved her life at the risk of his own. He genuinely thought it was because he was Seeking the Center. She knew better. He had no free will with her around.

Kentro had been a truly good man, someone who studiously sought the Center. She'd felt respect for him, even though he was an opponent, and felt shame for her part in his death. Even though her actions were involuntary. Quint was an entirely different matter. Sure, he was also a good guy, someone who without even knowing it, innately sought the Center. He was also so damn hot.

As Väst bent down to pick up the pieces of her broken hairbrush, she admitted consciously what her subconscious already knew. Her ability now to speak words, to express feelings that had been forbidden her for a hundred years could only mean one thing. "No, Amarantos, please don't let me be right," her prayer barely whispered. Väst's mind raced as it rewound the events in the arena. What were Perun's exact words to her? He hadn't only been healing her, Perun had also been trying to give her a message of some sort.

"Oh no. No, no, no," she sobbed, loudly this time, her hands falling forward to grasp the cold gray stone of her vanity. "Please, no," she prayed. "Perun didn't say the wish was that I be healed, he said he was there to make me whole."

She fell forward, her head between her arms, her weeping now racking her entire body. "Oh, Quint, what have you done? You may have killed us all."

CHAPTER NINE

"Thea, you've been scrubbing that same tater for going on five minutes now. If you're trying to rub it until you start a fire, that ain't gonna happen. If you're only wanting to make sure it's clean, I'd say 'mission accomplished'."

Thea stopped, and wiped her brow with the back of her hand before placing the potato into the colander with the rest of its now pristine brethren. "It's Taliesin, Pell."

"What now?" Pell asked, walking over to the sink to hug his wife from behind. He knew she loved the kitchen because cooking was life affirming to her, but she especially loved the picture window over the kitchen sink because it afforded her a good view of the twins' outdoor activities—whether they were playing basketball in the driveway or throwing the football in the front yard. The kitchen was also the place where she found her center, dating back to before she even met Pell. Back when it was just she and her oldest child, only the two of them pitted against some pretty macabre goings on.

"Call it mother's intuition, or whatever, but something is not right."

"Seems like the situation with that jackass Barton Sellars and his two knuckleheads is under control."

"I haven't heard anything recently about them," Thea confirmed.

"So what is it, Thea? Tal's been more diligent than ever with his studies. Everything so far at Nemeton has been aces, and it appears that he's setting the curve in almost every class."

"I don't know. Ever since his eighteenth birthday it seems like he's not quite right about half the time. It might only be that his nonverbal research project is starting to wear on my last nerve."

"When we agreed to let him do it, he told us he needed it to help him with early admit scholarship offers. That means he'll have to be done with it by Christmas Break." Pell paused before continuing. "You could always ask to see a draft of his thesis."

"No, I don't want him to think I don't believe him. Pell, he used to tell me everything. We both know he's been talking to some girl every single night and he's never mentioned her to us, or brought her around to meet us, or…"

"So now we get to the bottom of it. Do you really expect your eighteen-year old son to discuss the details of his first real relationship with you? Really?"

That got a little smile from her. Well, half of a little smile anyway. "No. But he's left us in the dark on that and we never even got to see him run in an intramural track meet and now he says the season is over for the winter."

"Tell you what, sweetheart. School's almost out for the holidays. Let's all enjoy our first Christmas in our new home and then we'll have a serious sit-down with him. Deal?"

"Deal," she said, leaning back into him.

CHAPTER TEN

Even though Tal and the entire family were out eating lunch, Emet remained hidden away in his attic bolt hole. Studying. The Nemeton High School semesters and the Hunts School Hunts terms didn't sync up. Emet had finished up his mid-term exams only this week while Tal's first term had formally ended a week ago, on Samhain—the first of November. The second term of Hunts School customarily started the day following Samhain but the Finalists' classes had been delayed a week because of the Combat Challenge. Which Tal had won. Although it almost killed him.

While Emet studied, trying to get a running head start on next Monday's classes, he thought about how shaky Tal had looked when he'd picked him up at the Gas Station following the Samhain feast. The Archon's magykal healing in the infirmary had taken care of Tal physically, but he was totally wiped out mentally. When Tal hadn't even been able to hold on to his back, Emet had carried him like a baby. Much closer to town than usual, closer than caution dictated.

So much had happened in the past week. Tal hadn't spoken much for the next couple of days after the Combat Challenge. To help Tal out Emet covered Tal's customary Halloween chaperoning of the twins. They were still at the age where it was all done before dark, so Emet hadn't been expected to speak. He smiled thinking about how excited and gleeful Remy and Romy had been, knocking on doors, getting their favorite candy, staring at the other kids' costumes. Then while Tal gradually returned to his old self, Emet had done as much as possible for him over this weekend. There was no way though for Tal to bail on church today, or on the family Sunday lunch.

The boys had even discussed Tal going to Nemeton this past week, instead of Emet. The thought being it might help get his mind off of the Hunts School events. After discussing the pros and cons about academic results as well as the Elle dynamic, their decision was there was no need to rock the boat. They kept their schedule the same, with Tal heading off to the Gas Station early each morning. Sticking to their plan had worked out better than either of them could have guessed. Tal ended up spending most of the week playing music with his non-Hunts classmates, which had been huge for his mental health. And it had given them the opportunity to learn about Fountain Flow and Mokosh. The largest negative which continued to weigh on Tal was the total lack of information about Väst. The few casual inquiries he'd been able to make yielded no information. There was a total absence of information about whether she was dead or alive. Or maimed.

After Emet finished his reading he turned his attention to reviewing some of Tal's notes from several months ago, early in the first term of Hunts School. Periodically reading Tal's notes fleshed out Emet's understanding of what was going on at Hunts School. Tal went back and forth between the mortal and Folk worlds so he had the entire picture. Since Emet was created late in the evening on Tal's eighteenth birthday, he had replicate knowledge of Tal's tumultuous first day at Hunts School. But that was it.

Emet's mind wandered as he reread the earliest notes. Tal's eighteen birthday had started in an excellent fashion. Off to school, an activity he enjoyed every single day. Learning and the resulting knowledge—Tal greatly enjoyed both the process and the result. At lunch he was scheduled to have a date with Elle Sellars. She was even baking him a cake.

Then Elle's dickhead brother, Barton Sellars, and his sycophant two-pack ambushed Tal in the parking lot before class. They put a burlap bag on his head, and drove him out to an abandoned gas station in the middle of nowhere, where they threw him out of the still moving truck.

Sol's Gas Station. That was the name of the defunct service station. Right behind it was a junkyard—Luna's Timeless Treasyres. Tal hadn't known then that "y"s were important magykally. While Tal was there the Air Hose hissed at him, telling him to go to the Ladies' Room. Then he'd received a written note from the Service Bay, telling him not to be late for the first day of the Tyrning Year—and telling him that he was to go to the Ladies' Room. After that there was a message from out of order Gas Pump No. Unus that "worlds depended" on Tal—and that he needed to go to the Ladies' Room. Finally, Gas Pump No. Duo also chimed in, telling Tal he needed to "bind the contract"—and go to the Ladies' Room. Tal did what most any teenager would do under those circumstances—he yielded to the apparent adult authority of all of the individual components of the abandoned gas station. He went to the Ladies' Room.

As soon as Tal entered the Ladies' Room, the door had slammed shut behind him. He wasn't in a gas station bathroom though, he was on the outskirts of the Hunts School campus. Tal quickly realized he wasn't in Arkansas anymore. In short order, he met Borras, the largest person Tal had ever seen. Borras was Acting Prime of something called the Omada. When Borras asked him to perform some ritual called "binding the contract," Tal went with his gut feeling and agreed. Tal soon discovered he was the only human being at a school with students from every other known plane of existence. All of them ran on magyk. Humans were the only beings whose bodies ran on electrical impulses. Which was why "Children of the Divine Spark" was one of the many Folk names for mortals.

That evening, the Omada had shown up at Tal's bedroom window, barely in time to run off the faceless spook that had haunted Tal's life since infancy. A Crestfallyn, Borras had said. Because Tal decided to accept the challenge to "Seek the Center" with the Omada, the team realized Tal needed a doppelganger. Anatolia, one of Tal's Omada teammates with royal strength creationmagyk, formed a simulacrum golem out of Tal's spit, hair and blood. Tal had activated the golem by placing the lyfeword on the inside of his left thigh. The lyfeword was "Emet."

My name. I am golem.

Since that time Tal and Emet had been separate beings, both physically and cognitively. Initially, Emet's logic patterns were the same as Tal's. How could they have been any different? He was an exact replicate of Tal in every respect. Well, except he had no feelings, and as a golem he was mute under the Lex Immortalis. There was also the little matter of his lyfeforce being magykal, not electrical. Which made him faster and stronger than Tal. Other than those things, he and Tal were pretty much the exact same. At that one fixed moment in time.

They hadn't had much time recently to talk about ancillary results and unintended consequences but both he and Tal recognized an amped up type of evolution was in progress. As hours turned to days, which then became weeks, they were receiving completely different sets of daily stimuli. Emet was learning new things at Nemeton High, as well as addressing and nurturing the daylight hours portion of the growing relationship with Elle. He was even experiencing actions and events with Tal's Mom and Pell, as well as the twins, that Tal wasn't participating in firsthand. On the flip side, Tal was exposed daily to a truly other worldly education at Hunts School.

Every day now Emet was making command decisions that had once been deferred to Tal. Each day brought change in their relationship. They were becoming more and more equal partners in their lives, and Tal was becoming more and more okay with it. They were much closer than twin brothers. Well, twin brothers where one twin was a fully functioning emotional person and the other was basically an emotionless automaton.

Back to Tal's notes. The Hunts School terms for this year's Tyrning Year revolved around three of the four major pagan Earth Realm cross-quarter celebration days—Samhain, Imbolc, and Beltane. The ancient holidays were called "cross-quarter days" because they were halfway between the solstices and equinoxes. Lughnasadh, the fourth feast day, occurred during the summer. It would normally mark the end of the summer term at Hunts School but as this was a Tyrning Year, the hundred-year Hunts School cycle came to a close with the installment of the new Ruling Council on Beltane. All of the students not receiving administrative positions at Hunts School or diplomatic postings would return to their home planes to share the knowledge and experiences they had accrued during their tenure at the school. Many of the students were of royal or prominent political families and they would help guide their planes until the next Tyrning. The next crop of students wouldn't arrive at Hunts School for another two centuries of EPT—Earth Plane Time. At which time they would begin the hundred-year cycle leading up to the next Tyrning.

Second term classes would end on Imbolc, the first of February. The third term would end right before Beltane, the first day of May. Ms. Empousa, the HuntsMistress, had kept the nature of the second and third term Hunts a secret. Presumably, Tal would find out about the second term Hunt when classes resumed tomorrow.

Car doors and excited chatter from the twins interrupted Emet's musings. *Tal and our family are back.* Emet paused, before renewing his document review. *Interesting,* he thought. *Several months ago my first thought would have been "my family," before I corrected myself. Yet another change. They were gradually becoming "our family" in addition to them being Tal's family.*

It seemed to Emet his life was becoming more off-kilter intellectually. It was impossible for emotions to be the causation.

His shared experience from Tal informed him about all of the attributes of the different types of emotions but as a golem he was incapable of actually feeling them. His brain understood them intellectually. Period. In an effort to stay grounded and as a way of trying to teach himself a more complete understanding of feelings, he'd developed an, *If I Was Human Right Now I Would Be Feeling...'* game.

Listening to all of the various happy sounds of the Smith family members, he decided he'd play his game. *If I Was Human Right Now, I Would Be Feeling...'*

Wistful.

CHAPTER UNDECIM

"PLEASE SHUT IT! I'M TRYING TO SLEEP IN HERE." The alicanto's chattering outside her window continued unabated. Väst rolled over and smushed the pillow down around her ears. "Stupid bird. I don't have any gold or silver to feed you and even if I did, not at this time of the morning…"

Morning? Is it morning, already? she asked herself. Five-Hells, I must have slept like one of the dead. She vaguely remembered the combination crying jag-epiphany in her bathroom, after which—totally spent emotionally and physically—she'd nosedived headfirst into her bed. Okay, she thought, relaxing back into her bed. That was Sunday morning.

Was Sunday morning? "Shit!" she exclaimed, realizing it was now Monday morning. Class starts back today with Orientation first thing this morning. Nord will kill me if I'm late. She rummaged in and around the "needed laundering a week ago" clothing pile at the foot of her bed. After finding undergarments, sniffing a pair of jeans in the appropriate inappropriate places to determine their acceptability, and throwing on her least wrinkled blouse, she ran into the bathroom, threw a couple of handfuls of cold water on her face, and brushed her teeth.

Seeing her haggard magyk-worn visage in the mirror brought all of the recent events into sharp focus. Quint will be at Orientation. If he's still alive. That realization initiated an acrimonious exchange between her heart and her head. Heart went first, then Head. Is that the proper order, she wondered. Surely whichever is the more important voice should be the one having the last word.

Heart led with—I'm sick of the lying and the deception. Someone has used me for a hundred years for some nefarious purpose. I'm finally almost free of the geas and can talk about it. First thing is to tell Quint I used compulsionmagyk on him, to apologize, and then tell him how I feel about him. After that, I need to tell Dysi—and the rest of Omada—how sorry I am about my part in what happened to Kentro. Then I'll have a long talk with my teammates. Finally, I'll notify Principal Chiron that someone is using powerful magyk on Hunts School campus, so that he can investigate the matter.

Don't be a silly romance novel inspired twit, Head replied. You bound the contract with Släkt and your primary obligation is to do everything you can to help your team win the Tyrning. Telling anyone about your involvement in Kentro's death will probably get your squad dishonorably discharged from the competition. At a minimum, there would be an assessment of some major level punishment. Which would put Släkt at a competitive disadvantage. As far as your infatuation with the mortal, that is all it is. He is a novelty, the only Child of the Divine Spark you've ever met, so you like playing house with him.

Heart interrupted. It's not infatuation, I have genuine feelings for him.

If you don't mind, I wasn't through with my argument, Head countered. Even if we assume for purposes of this discussion that you are actually in love with a human, you know that can never come to any good end. You're Folk royalty and have an obligation to your people, regardless of whether your team wins the Tyrning. You'll still be alive hundreds of years after he has returned to the dust. Additionally, you have no idea what magnitude of consequence you might unleash upon everyone here at Hunts School if you try to expose the unknown person. And have you even stopped to ask yourself how he's going to feel about you after you tell him he didn't voluntarily put his life on the line for you? Not once, but twice. That he only did so because you were the instrument of dark magyk that robbed him of his free will? You clearly haven't thought things through. The only logical choice is to continue playing your role in this drama. What you'd better be hoping, dumbass, is that the spell is so powerful some vestige of it remains to keep Quint in line.

There's no need for name-calling, Heart rebutted. As far as my obligation to my team, you left out the part where we are, all of us are, supposed to always be Seeking the Center. With respect to your point about Quint and his feelings about me and my feelings for him…well, as far as that goes…you need to remember that…the only thing I have to say to you about that is…

Point well taken.

CHAPTER DUODECIM

Tal shambled across the verdant expanse of Grass Grow. For his entire academic life, the first day of school—and of each new term—had always been banner days. It was like Christmas, except the presents were keys that opened doors leading him from ignorance to knowledge. Every first day, until now, Tal had experienced a huge endorphin spike as he anticipated what secrets were about to be laid bare for him to learn.

He realized his shamble had slowed to a shuffle, but did nothing to hurry himself along. Instead, he turned his attention to musing about the difference between adrenaline and endorphins. Most people think an endorphin rush and an adrenaline rush are the same thing. They're not. Endorphins are a type of neurotransmitter, enzymes that allow for signals to move from one synapse to the other. Exercise is the most common activity that can create an endorphin, but it's emotions like stress or pain that are the release triggers. Even positive emotions, like joy, can create an endorphin high. Adrenaline, on the other hand, is a natural hormone that is produced and released when a person encounters some type of dramatic event. For Tal, First Day had always been a day of happiness, a day his endorphins kicked into full gear with their natural opiate effect. That is, until today.

He felt his steps slow to whatever is slower than a shuffle. A dawdle, probably. Surely dawdling is the last step before complete stoppage. I'm not sure I've ever dawdled before, he thought. It seemed like the more his brain flooded with recent events, the slower his physical gait.

Tal wasn't looking forward to the first Omada team meeting of this term. Even though everyone on his team had had a full week to settle, he knew they all were disappointed in him for violating the no-fraternization-with-the-enemy "dangerous liaisons" policy. It wasn't a Hunts Rule, but the unofficial policy had been fully explained to Tal the first week of school. It made perfect sense, actually. You really shouldn't be mugging down with someone who might end up trying to end you with a shiv. Or a magykal sword.

There was something about Väst though, something that kept him from telling her "no," every time she summoned him to their trysting place. And that last time, she'd ratcheted the heat up by taking her blouse and bra off and underneath had been the most perfect, translucent, blue-veined breasts…

Dead stop, Tal reported to himself. You've now come to a dead stop. It's okay, he responded, I haven't heard the fifteen-minute gong and I'm almost to Fountain Flow. So he stood there and continued to think.

He'd used one of his three irreplaceable wishes to save someone on a competing team. The consequence of that action was there were now six teams competing in this term's Hunt, instead of the customary five squads. Saving Väst's life had been all he could think about though. Two wishes gone. Aurora told me to use them wisely because I would need them four times and that using my three wishes would cost me someone dear.

Släkt had been given the opportunity to replace Mitt with a team member from one of the three squads that didn't make the cut. Tal's act—noble from his perspective—had backfired. Not only did they have to face an additional opponent in this term's Hunt, but Nord, the nastiest, vilest living being he'd ever met, was now Acting Prime for Släkt.

So why was he dreading the first day of class so much that he almost couldn't make himself walk up the broad front staircase? It was partly the discord with his team caused by his treasonous act. But that wasn't the real problem.

Tal had now pretty much come clean about all of his secrets. Pretty much. The team knew about his magyk ring, given to him by the Lady Aurora, one of the four Principes, the Elder Children of Amarantos. The fact that the ring only had three wishes, and that he'd used two of his three wishes to save Väst's life didn't sit well with them. It wasn't only Notos who had jumped his ass. Even Borras, who had supported Tal at every turn since they'd bound the contract, had been disappointed in his lack of judgment. Borras, the only one who didn't turn his back on Tal when it was belatedly discovered he was a Dust Child.

So here he was, the first Munedan to ever be on the Hunts School campus, much less on a Hunts Finalist team. He'd won the first Combat Challenge held in over ten millennia. Yet something was weighing him down, big time.

It wasn't because he'd had to embarrass Notos in front of the entire school as part of his winning strategy. Notos was a known factor. He'd repeatedly heaped abuse on Tal, screamed at him for all of his actions during the Challenge, and he would continue to be abusive in the future. No, Notos was a constant that Tal's brain had already factored into his daily school world.

It wasn't the lying to his Mom and Pell. He and Emet were successfully running their subterfuge while efforting to keep the deception to a minimum. Tal would tell them everything when he could. It was physically impossible for him to come clean now anyway, because of the nondisclosure binding laid on him whenever he left Hunts School campus.

It wasn't Barton Sellars and his two cretin lapdogs. Emet was doing great at avoiding them at Nemeton High. Those three were going to be in for a really rude surprise if they cornered Tal's simulacrum golem.

It wasn't even that he had a deadline to deliver Aislinn to Helblad, the head honcho draugr, by Coronation Day—or have his head chopped off. Well, that might be the cause of a reasonable amount of consternation, he conceded to himself, but that whole issue was off in the distant future at this point.

If he was Sherlock Holmes, deductive reasoning would have narrowed the possibilities to one issue—a girl. Although it was only one issue, it had two subparts. When he was home in Nemeton, he desperately wanted to be able to go to school with Elle. He wanted to date her, to talk to her, to find out everything about her that she was willing to share with him. When he was at Hunts School, trying to "Seek the Center," and save all of the known worlds, he wanted to be with Väst. To sing to her, be with her, to hear her laughter ring through the hallways. I can't be with Elle because I'm here, and I can't be with Väst because she's one of the enemy.

Väst. My feelings for her, her feelings for me. I've saved her life twice now. Well, provided that she is in fact alive. She's going to want to be all over me when I finally get to see her. Again, if she's alive and not maimed. Not that I don't want to jump her bones right in front of anybody and everybody. I can't, though. We can't. It has to stop. I'm simply going to have to find a way to let her down. Easy.

Three gongs? HOLY CRAP! That's the five-minute bell. I must have daydreamed through the first two alarms. I have to get all the way across the main building to the Hunts Orientation room on the back side of the gothic section, he thought, as he took off at a dead run up the stairs.

CHAPTER TREDECIM

Tal wasn't sure it was possible for the HuntsMistress to be in a blacker mood. If so, he didn't want to be anywhere on the same plane with her when it happened. She invariably wore her Puca during school hours but today, today she was dressed full metal jacket. If there was a piece of armament that could possibly be attached to her clothing, she was wearing it. Today she was dressed as Laura Croft meets the Terminator.

As if her attire wasn't sufficiently intimidating, during the first five minutes of Orientation she hadn't said one single word. Instead, she'd silently stalked the entire classroom, rubbing her left index finger over the top of one of the shuriken attached to her chain-link belt.

The nevereverending five minutes were spent stopping in front of a team, where she gave each of its members the laser death-eye, before moving on to repeat her actions with the next squad. All the while she fondly stroked the gleaming throwing star, her finger now a leaky faucet, leaving deep blue Rorschach blood blots on each team's books, papers, even their clothes as she passed by.

That first nevereverending five-minutes had ended approximately ten minutes ago. During the subsequent I-just-thought-the-first-five-minutes-were-nevereverending ten-minute epoch between then and now she'd been standing directly in front of the Omada table. Staring at Tal. Unblinkingly staring. Wrath of God staring. Tal knew she was hoping he'd have a heart attack—or wet his pants. One of the two. He hadn't known what to do, so he'd sat there motionless, hands folded as if in prayer, eyes cast downward in the universal posture of submission.

Tal heard every wooden chair in the room jerk when the HuntsMistress finally spoke. "Today is a tragic day for this venerable institution. This Tyrning's selection process has been tainted. This iniquitous stain is an indelible black mark on me personally and on my legacy as a HuntsMistress. I worked diligently for many centuries to earn my position. And for what?" she asked, as she made a wave that encompassed everyone in the room.

"For the first time in the history of the Tyrning we will have six teams competing in the second Hunt. Why, you might ask? Why has this ignominy been heaped upon me, and upon this Tyrning? The reason is not a Why. It's a Who. A Who that is the author of this calamitous situation. We owe this entire unprecedented slap in the face to millennia of our proud Folk tradition to the first—and hopefully the last—Munedan to ever be admitted to Hunts School."

Tal heard a snigger from behind him and to his right. The Släkt table. Of course. The HuntsMistress had heard it too because Tal saw her shift focus and begin moving back in that direction. Tal slowly lifted his head and turned his head to follow her. The Släkt had come in the back door of the classroom so it was his first chance to see Väst, to confirm for himself that she was alive. And apparently not maimed. She looked like she'd lost some weight, and was a bit disheveled but she was still the most beautiful woman in the room. He stared at her, hoping she would look up and meet his eyes. Give him some sign that she was okay, that they were okay. She didn't.

The HuntsMistress stopped right in front of Nord. "Did I say something amusing, Acting Prime?" she asked.

"No, HuntsMistress," Nord replied, although the tightness at the upper corners of his lips betrayed the echo of a smirk.

"I didn't think so. From where I stand, your team should have been stripped of their Finalist names, reassigned your student numbers, and should, at this moment, be taking regular Hunts classes with the other thousands of losers at this school. Your original Prime Direction was incompetent," she added. "His replacement apparently even more so."

In a split second it was like all of the muscles in Nord's face cramped in an uncoordinated pattern. Tal knew he had never in his life seen anyone as angry as Nord was at that moment.

The HuntsMistress wasn't anywhere done with him, either. "Släkt remains in the competition only because of a misguided act of pity by a human." She was now giving Nord her baleful laser eye of death, daring him to spar with her.

Nord couldn't help himself, he took the bait. "Perhaps the rules of the Combat Challenge were too complicated for his limited human brain," Nord replied, staring straight back at her in challenge.

Oh, you've done screwed up now, Tal thought. Rule number one in avoidance of agonistic behavior is to look down or away. Silverbacks take it as a challenge when pretenders to the throne stare at them aggressively.

Ms. Empousa took a deep breath before continuing. "Just so we're all clear, Acting Prime. The entire school is laughing at Släkt. I personally made sure that written messages were sent through the Prime Omphalos to all of the known Realms telling them what has happened. Before long…the entirety of the Folk universe…will be laughing…at your team. Most of all, they will be laughing at you Acting Prime."

Ms. Empousa leaned forward and stuck her index finger right between his eyes, the blood steadily dripping on to his nose. "From this Tyrning forward, Släkt will be the code word for any team of bumbling, incompetent losers. How does that make you and your superior Folk brain feel, Acting Prime?"

Nord was so angry he couldn't even respond. His face was scarlet, his facial muscles now gone into rigor.

The HuntsMistress removed her finger before leaning toward Nord until her face was only inches from his. "I think everyone here fully understands. Except you, Acting Prime. I'm not sure you realize just how big a joke you and your team are to everyone else. So, before we move on to today's class lesson, I need to make sure you understand."

Please no, Tal prayed silently to himself. Please stop it. Whatever you are doing, whatever you are about to…

"Stand up!" she ordered, as she stood to her full height and stepped backwards. Nord hesitated a moment before doing as commanded. "Now walk over in front of the human," she demanded.

Let it go, Tal pleaded to himself. Please let it go. This is going to be bad. Really, really bad.

Nord looked like he might refuse but he knew he couldn't, he knew it would cost his team much needed points. He walked slowly over to the Omada table.

"Now, get down on your knees."

Tal quickly looked around. None of his teammates, no one else in the rest of the room could even bear to look at what Ms. Empousa was doing to Nord. Tal had no choice but to watch, he didn't want to cost Omada any points.

The HuntsMistress was the puppeteer, and Nord her marionette. Nord jerkily lowered himself first to one knee, then to both.

"Now, Acting Prime, I want you to thank Quint of Omada for taking pity on the Släkt."

Tal knew if there was any possible way to accomplish it, that Nord would physically rip his tongue out of his mouth rather than acknowledge a debt to a mortal.

Nord's mouth worked but no sounds came out, it was if it was a gearbox rusted shut. Finally, words issued in an odd robotic cadence. "Thank you Quint of Omada, for taking pity on the Släkt." Nord started to rise, but the HuntsMistress placed her bloody finger firmly on his shoulder, pushing him back down. "Oh no, Acting Prime, you're not quite done yet. Now, thank the Dust Child for making you his bitch."

Tal heard a gasp from several team tables.

"Say it," she said icily, "and mean it when you say it. Or we will repeat the exercise over and over every class until you get it right."

Nord, Acting Prime of Släkt, his fury now an almost visible pall over the entire classroom, looked directly up at Tal and forced himself to enunciate the words, slowly, as if each word was costing him a piece of his soul. "Thank…you…Dust Child…for…making…me…your…bitch."

"See that wasn't so hard, was it?" Ms. Empousa asked, laughing. "Now that I think you fully understand your status, Acting Prime, you may cease groveling in front of the mortal and scurry back to your seat."

The only sound in the room as Nord shakily rose to his feet and staggered back to his seat was quiet sobbing from the Släkt table. Tal remembered that exact sound from the Combat Challenge. It was Väst. Weeping.

The HuntsMistress pivoted on a black, three-inch stiletto heel, and walked toward the chalkboard. When she got there, she began writing and talking simultaneously. "Because of the unfortunate events of the Combat Challenge we not only have six teams still competing, we have also lost one week of valuable time. The top three teams who will advance to the final Hunt will be announced at the feast on Imbolc.

As of today, you start with clean slates. All of the teams are equal in scoring, having zero points. Your class schedule has been reduced this term to only three classes: Orientation, Combat, and Wytches. I will be teaching Orientation and Combat, Professor Elphinstone will be teaching Wytches."

"Five-Hells, she's trying to kill all of…," Tal heard someone from the Suzoku table whisper involuntarily, before being stopped midsentence, presumably by one of his teammates. Tal had learned that lesson last term. He would wait until he and Borras were alone to ask for answers to all of his questions.

"As you may have surmised, even with your pea-sized brains, the Hunt this term is a Wytch Hunt. Wytch Hunts are rarely used and it has been a few Tyrnings since one was last utilized. Since I'm sick of all of your whining, I am going to allow you to use your Pucas for your Journeys this term.

"Now all of you get out. I get sick just looking at you. I can't believe I have been stuck with such a worthless, talentless group of Finalists."

As the teams filed out, Tal saw Nord turn and stare at him. If hate could burn sufficiently to cause a person to spontaneously combust, then Nord would be a five-alarm inferno at that moment. Väst had already left the room with the rest of her team.

It wasn't until Tal and his team had almost reached their team room that he realized why Ms. Empousa had humiliated Nord. After last term's events, she knew Principal Chiron and the Archon wouldn't allow her to personally do anything to Tal.

She humiliated Nord because she wants him to kill me.

CHAPTER QUATTUORDECIM

Väst trudged along, about four feet behind her nearest teammate. They were headed to the first Wytches class, following the team meeting hour. Mitt might not have been a contender for the best team leader in the history of the Hunts but at least he'd always tried to keep the Släkt on task—winning the Tyrning while Seeking the Center. That was the goal set by the Hunts Rules and the Lex Immortalis.

She'd known since the first month the teams were organized that Mitt had a major crush on her. The unofficial policy against inter-squad relationships was frequently discussed, the fact that intra-squad liaisons were also generally a really bad idea wasn't covered anywhere near as often. Any activity that could unnecessarily degrade the operating efficiency of a team was verboten. She'd hooked up with other non-Hunts Finalist students, they all had. After all, they were all healthy, consenting Folk in the prime of their lives. The Hunts School curriculum lasted a hundred years. No sane person was going to remain celibate for that period of time and the Hunts School wards prevented any need for an on-premises day care.

As far as all of the students knew, the wisdom of the non-fraternization warning had been validated yet again this Tyrning with Kentro's death last year. She was the only person who knew that relationship hadn't been consensual—on either end.

Kentro's death left Omada at only four members. One of the remaining four, Dysi, had become a nonfunctioning basket case and the betting money was she wouldn't recover in time to suit up for this year's Hunts. With less than four non-maimed members, Omada would have then been eliminated under the Hunts Rules. The betting money might have been right, too. If Borras wasn't legitimately a contender for the best Prime Direction ever, and if Quint hadn't miraculously appeared to rejuvenate Omada.

Within one short school term the hundred-year long game had altered dramatically. This year it was Släkt on the ropes because of an emotional attachment. Mitt's feelings for Väst caused him to lose his shit—and then his life—in the arena. If Tal hadn't saved her, Släkt would have been down to three contestants, and therefore eliminated.

Mitt had always been able to keep Nord under semi-control. What had just occurred in the secure confines of their team meeting room would never have happened if Mitt was still in charge. Nord had yelled, thrown things, all the while ranting and raving about how many different ways he was going to kill Quint. At one point he was so angry that when Ost gently reminded him they were supposed to win by Seeking the Center, he'd grabbed him by the throat and was choking him blue until Söder was finally able to pull him off. Mitt's replacement, Fem, their new Fifth Prime, compounded matters. From his actions, and inactions, thus far, Väst was afraid Fem liked and approved of Nord's leadership style and his goal to take Quint out.

Väst was limited in what she could do about team matters. They had all bound the contract. As Acting Prime, Nord now held their oaths. If he ever found out about her and Quint's relationship, Nord wouldn't hesitate to use her to kill Quint. There was no doubt in her mind that Nord would kill her if there ever came a time she wasn't needed anymore to help the team win.

There had been so much going on in Orientation that it hadn't been hard to avoid eye contact with Quint. Släkt's hasty departure insured there wasn't any accidental meeting with him. After Ms. Empousa used Quint to humiliate Nord, Väst knew she'd have to have a firm game plan before further communications with Quint. She wasn't fully healed from the geas, but she could feel the Cooshie's healing steadily working to remove the remnants of the compulsionmagyk placed on her.

There was still no clue as to who had laid the geas on her or their ultimate purpose, but as it stood right now, only she, Quint and the Cooshie knew the exact wording of Quint's wish. Until she knew more about who had conjured the magyk and what they were after, it was important the perpetrator didn't realize there had been a change in her status.

Back to the game plan vis a vis Quint. I'm not going to be able to avoid him during Hunts classes, she concluded. If I try to avoid him, he will seek me out. Which increases the possibility of a discoverable encounter. Ignoring him doesn't do any good timewise either. I'm on the clock as far as being able to count on the geas to keep him interested in me. Which is apparently what the unknown malefactor wants to continue happening.

All of which means I'm going to have to play rough to keep his attention, Väst decided. Her shoulders slumped as she slowed even more, losing ground behind her teammates. Tal would, of course, be in Professor Elphinstone's class.

What should have been a joyful, exuberant expression of genuine affection between she and Quint was going to become a subterfuge to achieve a designed result. He's never going to forgive me when it all comes out in the wash. I can't even imagine how I would feel if our positions were reversed.

There's no choice though, Quint. For your own good and for the good of the entire known universe, I'm going to have to make you have sex with me.

CHAPTER QUINDECIM

Tal really liked Professor Elphinstone. He sometimes wondered what the professor looked like in his real Folk body. The professor's magyked form, as well as his teaching style, was that of the quintessential patch-elbowed nebbish academic. In real life he might have pretty much any type of phantasmagorical appearance. He might even be squishy and twelve-tentacled— with patches on all of the elbows of his tentacles. I wonder if tentacles have elbows. Focus, Tal, focus.

"Today we will only have time to address the broad strokes of this term's Hunt. As I'm sure the HuntsMistress told you, it has been quite some Tyrnings since a Wytch Hunt was utilized. Battle Hunts had a consistent track record of causing the highest average mortality rate. The deaths in Battle Hunts, however, were principally mortals not Folk. As you all experienced first hand last year, Snype Hunts are second in total body count but first in Folk deaths. Battle Hunts are now banned." The professor sighed, before continuing, "As are Snype Hunts after last year's catastrophic losses.

"Wytch Hunts are the third deadliest Hunt statistically. Not for total number of deaths or maimings, but because the percentage of casualties among actual Hunts contestants is the highest of any Hunt category."

Well, there's some interesting info, Tal thought. Does nobody else think it suspicious that the HuntsMistress has programmed the two deadliest permissible Hunts for this Tyrning?

The professor stopped his speech and slowly looked around the room at all of the teams. Ignorance must have been writ large on all of their faces. "Ms. Empousa did go over the dangers of the Wytch Hunt with you, didn't she? It's part of the mandated Orientation presentation for that Hunt."

Crickets.

Followed by more crickets.

What's a group of crickets called, Tal wondered.

Lines appeared, going every direction on Professor Elphinstone's face. I've never noticed before, Tal thought, but worry lines are predominantly horizontal, while consternation lines travel on a diagonal axis, all of those lines cross-hatching with fear lines, forming vertices evidencing adulthood.

"Well...okay then. I feel certain the HuntsMistress advised you that as a condition precedent to allowing her to utilize a Wytch Hunt this term, the Ruling Council mandated all Finalists would be allowed to wear their Pucas."

An orchestra, Tal remembered. That's what a group of crickets is called—an orchestra. A lying, murderous bitch—that's what a Ms. Empousa is called.

Professor Elphinstone whipped his kerchief out of his front jacket pocket and started dabbing at his forehead. Poor guy, Tal thought. If he's going to be on the same faculty as Empousa they should give him headbands. Lots of them. Really wide, absorbent terrycloth ones.

"Well...er, I'm sure she ran out of time and didn't want to make you late..."

Oh yeah, that was definitely the reason, Tal thought. It had nothing to do with first humiliating me and then whipping Nord into a blood frenzy.

"I'll touch on a few general points with the remainder of our time and then we will take up a detailed discussion of individual wytches tomorrow. That will give you a chance to begin your reading." The professor cleared his throat and began with his best professorial tone, "Wytches. What are they and where do they come from? Wytches are not Folk, nor Creature…"

Holy crap! That only leaves one category, Tal realized.

"Neither are they categorized as 'mortal normal,' though all wytches began their existence as mortals." The professor looked over at Tal with the smallest hint of a smile. "For one or more reasons, they chose to leave their mortal lives. as they knew them, and become initiated into the Cult of Nyx. From that point we categorize them as 'mortal suspended'."

Nyx, Tal mused. I know that one, at least the Earth Realm version. She was the Greek goddess of night and she was one tough mother. Literally. Even Zeus had to think twice before messing with her. Don't know how she fits in with the Folk Realms though. Tal wrote "Cult of Nyx" down, to ask Borras later.

Professor Elphinstone was obviously more comfortable now that he was within the parameters of his prepared lecture. "Folk contact with wytches is almost nonexistent. There are no first hand accounts of Folk interaction with wytches in their pre-wytch phase. They were only a few hundred random humans scattered amongst hundreds of years and millions of mortals.

"We only have two sources for our limited intelligence about them. The first is the oral and written histories of the Earth Realm, their myths and legends about what the Dust Children refer to as 'witches.' This information obviously must be taken with a grain of salt. The wytches existed long before humans were aware of them and their actions have no doubt been greatly exaggerated, and in some cases glamorized.

"Second…," with that Professor Elphinstone took his already sodden handkerchief back out of his front coat pocket. The professor cleared his throat and squared his shoulders before continuing. "Second, is the information we've obtained from teams that have participated in the two previous Wytch Hunts. One of the Hunts was ten Tyrnings past, the other was two Tyrnings later. " He paused again to dab at his brow. "Actually, that's not quite accurate and you all need the most accurate information. The second source of information is what was obtained from debriefings obtained from the surviving team members. In both of the prior Wytch Hunts there were multiple Finalists who were either maimed or killed."

And there we are right back to it, Tal told himself. If I had a nickel for every time someone got killed or maimed at this school...

The professor's movement toward the blackboard pulled Tal back from his reverie. "The second Wytch Hunt was only allowed because the Ruling Council believed the results of the first one might have been an isolated situation. And, quite frankly, because the Ruling Council during that Tyrning wanted to know more about wytches and their unique power to syphon."

Tal felt a collective shiver from the room's occupants at that word. He wrote it down. Syphon.

"I'm going to write some rules on the board. They will remain here the entire term."

Like the admonition about Forest Fell on the Orientation classroom board, Tal thought. "FOREST FELL IS NOT PART OF HUNTS SCHOOL. IT IS UNWARDED. TRESPASSING MAY RESULT IN DEATH [OR WORSE.]"

Professor Elphinstone turned his back to the class and began writing on the board.

<u>MANDATORY RULES – WYTCH HUNT</u>

1. Wear your Puca at all times during each WH Journey.
2. Never take your Puca off during a WH Journey.
3. There is no conceivable situation where you should take your Puca off during a WH Journey.

4. Under no circumstance should you take your Puca off during a WH Journey.

5. No matter what happens don't take your Puca off during a Wytch Hunt Journey.

6. In case Rules 1-5 above are unclear, please refer to Rule 7.

7. <u>IF YOU TAKE YOUR PUCA OFF DURING A WH JOURNEY, THE WYTCH WILL KILL YOU [OR WORSE.]</u>

Professor Elphinstone turned back to face the class. Tal noticed there was a rivulet of sweat pouring down the left side of his neck, dousing the back of his white button-down collar. Tal made a mental note. Based on the professor's perspiration quotient, he was deadly serious about the Pucas being worn at all times.

"Okay," the Professor said, "that'll do it for today. Tomorrow we will begin on page thirty-eight discussing specific wytches."

CHAPTER SEDECIM

"Quint! Quint, love, we've got to go."

"Huh?" Present status—drowsy or somnambulant, his nervous system reported in response to Väst's repeated, urgent shaking of his left arm. The report was quickly contradicted upstairs by Central Processing. Status error—drowsy is an incorrect assessment. Ganglia get your afferent nerves in line. Stat.

"And not a word to your teammates that we're back together."

Central Processing was still having enormous difficulty effectively communicating its instructions. It's an endorphin overload, you knucklehead neurons. The correct conclusion based upon all available data, is that you feel better at this moment than you've ever felt in your entire life. Are you morons or neurons? Snap out of it, and start firing.

"Quint," Väst repeated as she wriggled into her thong before standing, then bending over him to grab her bra and shirt.

And boom! His system crashed again as the optic nerves processed the images of Väst's blue-vein marbled, gravity-defying breasts, still-excited swollen nipples surrounded by rose-hued aureoles gently swaying over his face.

"Again," he muttered, his left hand reaching for the nearest breast.

"No," Väst laughed, as she lightly slapped his hand away before standing erect. He saw her face redden a bit as she smiled at him. "I'm afraid three is all we have time for now."

"G-g-green," Tal stammered, as he watched her finish dressing.

Väst's hands immediately stopped what they were doing as her head instantly dipped and pivoted so they were eye to eye. "What, Quint? What did you just say?"

Tal could feel his blood start to return to its normal flow. He was still dopey, that was pretty much the only way to describe it. Overwhelmed, Central Processing posited. Yes, overwhelmed. "When you, well, when you came. Actually, each time you came," with that remembrance he felt a little sideways cocky grin forming. "For a split second, I could swear you were an angel— with the most beautiful green wings."

It was two short beats before Väst's reply. "I have to admit I've never had that effect on a guy before. Makes a girl feel kind of special. Weird special, I guess," she added. "But special nonetheless. I'm leaving," she announced. "Give me a couple of minutes before you go."

He nodded, his hands beginning their search among the blankets and pillows for his clothing.

"Quint, I'm not kidding. You can't tell anybody. Especially your team."

Memory chose that moment to insert a seemingly random thought. I saw an article on the internet last week about hypothermia water training in SEAL simulation training. Whether in the forty-five degree ocean water off of San Diego or a swimming pool full of ice water, same net physiological result. As it turns out, it wasn't a random thought. That was the instantaneous effect Väst's words had on him.

Clarity. Body numbing, mind numbing. Clarity. His teammates were only on the cusp of forgiving him for his previous "not-actually banging just mostly making goofy goo-goo eyes" relationship with Väst. Now that we've, now that we've...with that thought a new endorphin tsunami flooded his rational processing, leaving no capacity for motor control function execution. It took several moments before Tal could turn to respond. By then, Väst was gone, the door clicking shut behind her.

CHAPTER SEVENTEEN

It was well after midnight. Emet was in his attic nest, his Biology book open to a chapter detailing the various effects of pheromones. After the evening's debriefing with Tal, he'd thought it might contain some useful information. Anything that might help him rouse Tal out of his funk. There's nothing helpful, he concluded, closing the book and turning out the small light on his apple-crate nightstand. The light was well-shaded, of course, so that it couldn't be seen from outside his little area.

Tal had related the events of his tumultuous day at Hunts School. Including the rendezvous with Väst, without the intimate details of their physical interaction, of course. It did lead them to a prolonged discussion of Tal's extremely strong attraction—and feelings—for both Elle and Väst. After that they spent considerable time discussing the many downstream scenarios that might arise from Tal's decision to secretly continue with Väst. A decision that would dramatically affect not only Emet, but might have repercussions for the entire Smith family.

Emet understood that Tal believed he made his choice because it was the right thing to do. The whole "right" thing versus "wrong" thing still remained elusively beyond his mind's fingertips. Emet could diagram a decision tree faster, and probably better, than Tal. However, even though he understood the concept of the morality of any given choice, he couldn't feel the "rightness" of a decision.

He wasn't going to give up trying to comprehend what it felt like to feel. So, he silently mouthed the words, *'If I Was Human Right Now I Would Be Feeling...'*

Nord had called an evening strategy session for the Släkt. Väst had begged off, telling her teammates she felt nauseous and was probably going to hurl. Which was the truth—she did...and she had. Given her recent near death experience, the team didn't make a big deal of her absence.

It was Quint, however, that made her feel nauseous....and ridiculously excited. Though he was clearly inexperienced, he had wanted nothing more than to please her today. Children of the Divine Spark! I'll say, she thought. Pretty sure I passed out twice when I came. It wasn't only that his body was electrical, hers magykal. All of her previous experiences now seemed only practice, being with him was completeness, fulfillment.

He was everything she could have hoped for in a lover and a companion. Cute, witty, and just so damn smart. The simplest caress from him excited her. I've been alive for hundreds of years, and now it turns out I've only been merely existing. Take whatever romantic tale or story you like, from any of the countless Folk Realms, and Quint made her feel like all of them rolled into one simultaneous experience.

They were perfect together—except for two things. The competition, which regardless of the outcome would be over soon enough. And that damn geas that had originally bound him to her.

Which brought her full circle to her present physical status. The reason that instead of being elated at the genesis of a love that might last her lifetime she was both physically and mentally heaving. You have no choice, she told herself. His life, maybe countless other lives, depend upon you continuing to use him, doing whatever you have to do to keep him ensnared as the geas disintegrates.

She stopped thinking long enough to run to the bathroom to once again heave her guts into the toilet. With her head hovering low over the bowl, waiting for the next wave, she realized she was...

Tal was his usual considerate, fun-loving self all day at school today, Elle thought. No talking during the school day, of course. Per the usual, he'd silently walked beside her in the hallways between classes. It had been his written suggestion during lunch that they spend their study hour in the music room. Him on the guitar, and her at the piano. The entire hour flew by as they took turns playing a game of follow my melody. One would take the lead, the other move into counterpoint and then they would seamlessly shift. It was lovely. That lopsided grin of his told her he had enjoyed it every bit as much as she had. It was way past time for them to get much more physical. She'd decided that would be a discussion point when she called him tonight, and that she wasn't going to wait any longer—she was going to ask him to the dance.

From the moment he answered his phone though she'd sensed a wrongness. How could someone of such substance be so fucking mercurial? It made absolutely no sense, he was easily as into her as she was into him. Her brain reminded her there would come a point when she would remember her life had been wonderful and complete before he walked through the Nemeton High front doors only a couple of months past, that she was blessed with innumerable gifts both material and spiritual. There would be time tomorrow for her to go full bore hellfire bitch on his ass. Tonight, however, she had no choice other than to lay sobbing, curled in a tight ball underneath her favorite blankets, watching her guaranteed not to run waterproof mascara stain her pillow, while she felt...

"It was the right thing to do. It was the right thing to do." Tal had placed that exact quote, whispered in his most persuasive internal voice on a closed end loop that had been running all night long as he tossed and turned. Sleeplessly, desperately, hoping that lame message would finally end and that it would be replaced with a recording that reassured him he hadn't just turned his back on the most important woman he would ever meet, even if he lived a dozen lifetimes. The message didn't change, and as the alarm to get up went off, he felt only one thing...

hollow.

lovestruck.

empty.

wrong.

CHAPTER DUODEVIGINTI

"Our best available information—which is admittedly sketchy—tells us there are only several dozen actual wytches in the known universe."

Tal glanced quickly at his teammates and around the classroom. Almost everyone was either staring at Professor Elphinstone with steely-eyed concentration, or heads-down feverishly scribbling down his every word. It was clear the Folk students knew no more about wytches than he did. He'd made a couple of hopefully subtle attempts to catch Väst's attention but each time he'd looked over at the Släkt table, Nord was glaring death at him. He gave up, deciding the smart play was to give the professor his full attention.

"The primary reason there are so few wytches as well as so little information about wytches is the prohibition against Folk magyk on the Earth plane. As an indirect consequence of that restriction, no new wytches have been covened in the last fifteen hundred years. Your team score this term will be based predominantly upon the results of your Wytch Hunt. Your test scores in this class, as well as your Combat scores, will constitute the other portions of your final ranking for the term."

He walked over to the blackboard and began writing. "There are three possible scoring components for this term's

Hunt. First, a relatively small number of points will be awarded if your team actually makes verifiable contact with a wytch. A larger number of points will be awarded to any team that can convince a wytch to provide them with a talysman. In the unlikely event that more than one team is able to obtain a talysman, the third and most heavily weighted component will be utilized." He wrote the words as he spoke them, double-underlining them as he went. "The combined power ranking of both the wytch and the talysman received."

A talysman? Tal wondered. So, something like "eye of a newt." Or maybe they have a bobble head doll of themselves. How much for one of your broomsticks, ma'am? I guess wytches might have something like baseball trading cards. Only much, much weirder.

"Unlike other Hunts and because you will be wearing your Pucas, you will be allowed to make as many Journeys as your team can physically withstand this term."

That doesn't sound good, Tal thought.

"Even though the Prime Omphalos will deliver you within Journey range in a plane with a wytch present, the odds of you actually encountering a wytch are miniscule. The Pucas should insulate you from any permanent physical or mental injuries that would normally be caused by multiple Journeys within close proximity to each other. Remember, you must have four living non-maimed teammates attending the final presentation to remain eligible to win the Tyrning."

Tal had by now joined the faction of the class who were trying to write everything down verbatim. He could hear pens and pencils scratching all over the classroom. As he looked at what he'd written so far, it occurred to him that it didn't seem quite right that the most repeated words in his high school senior year class notes were "death" and "maim."

"There will be no blackout periods this Hunt. It is possible for all remaining Finalist teams to be Journeying at the same time. Perhaps to the same plane, as where you go on the Journeys will be determined by the Prime Omphalos." Professor

Elphinstone stopped writing on the chalkboard and turned back toward the students. "For the last ten minutes today, I will entertain questions. Please keep them about wytches generally, we will discuss individual wytches next session." Tal saw the professor scan the room, his mouth squinching a bit as he became perplexed at the absence of questions. Then his face changed to one of those kind of smiles which suggests revelation. "Let me be clear. I am welcoming questions at this time. An exceptionally good question might actually garner points for that individual's team."

Hands exploded vertically from every table.

"Yes," Professor Elphinstone said pointing at Sredina, the Pleme Prime Direction.

"Is there any Realm where we might find more than one wytch?"

"Excellent question," the teacher said, turning to write a note in his ledger book. "The answer is no. Once a wytch is initiated into the Cult of Nyx, they are required to live separate from each other, on completely different planes. There are of course none remaining on the Earth plane because of the magykal bane." Professor Elphinstone paused a moment before adding, "It is, I imagine, not only a very solitary way of life, but an immensely lonely one as well. Next question?" This time he pointed to Nohol of Ayllu.

"What magyks do the wytches typically possess?"

Again the professor scratched a quick notation in his book. "Nicely done. That's the single most important question you could ask—and one for which we do not have a good answer. We do know all wytches began their existence as Munedan. Which of course means they originally had no magyk of their own. We also know that upon completion of the initiation rites, Luna bestowed a familiar upon each new wytch."

So everybody gets a black cat to go with their pointy hat and their broomstick, Tal thought.

"I don't get it," Kati of Kabila remarked. "They give up everything in the world and they get a pet?" A small round of nervous laughter syncopated throughout the tables.

Tal noticed Professor Elphinstone wasn't smiling though. As he walked back to the chalkboard, he said, "You know better than that. For every gyft, a gyftpryce must be paid. Imagine the gyftpryce that must be paid for a mortal to become virtually immortal. Luna has made wytches unique in all of the known Realms. The familiars are...," the professor had now reached the blackboard, and he scrawled the next words as he said them, "magyk syphons."

The entire room suddenly became as silent as a graveyard. The usual whispered chatter among team members, gone. All nervous tics and motions of any shape or kind, gone. Tal glanced quickly around the room, including his teammates. Not even an eye blinking. Holy crap! These Folk have been away from their family for decades, hundreds of their classmates have died, hundreds more seriously mutilated. Yet those two words on a chalkboard have terrified them. Each man, each woman, every single one—they're rattled.

As he took his next breath, Tal sensed a new smell pervading the room, a distinct, acrid tang. I know that particular stench. From every time I've ever been bullied, or woken from a nightmare with that ghoul whispering that it was going to take my face. Fear sweat. The idea of a magyk syphon has them all scared shitless.

Professor Elphinstone seemed a little unsteady himself as he addressed the subject. "As I've mentioned, Folk contact with wytches has been sporadic. The principal reason is that, other than survivors of the prior Wytch Hunts, no Folk who had personal contact with a wytch lived to tell anyone about it. Our best information is that the familiar is a conduit that allows the wytch to draw the magykal essence from Folk and Creatures. Somehow, Wytches steal your lyfeforce and use it against you."

There was a substantial amount of uncomfortable butt shifting in seats across the classroom as Professor Elphinstone paused. "You will be wearing your Pucas. As I've made clear, there is no circumstance in which you should remove your Puca.

Our notes from the prior Wytch Hunts indicate the only reason there were any survivors at all was because of the presence of the Pucas." He turned back to the class, his face now smeared with a dusting of chalk dust as he glanced at the clock, "Okay, time for one more question."

Tal looked around. Out of the earlier forest of hands there wasn't even one remaining tree of inquiry. Without even thinking, he raised his hand. He saw a "you better not fuck this up" look from Notos. "Yes, Professor, I have one," Tal announced. "Are wytches still Children of the Divine Spark, or did they trade in their souls for their immortality?"

"Double points to Omada for a question on a philosophical issue," Professor Elphinstone replied. "The simple answer is—we don't know."

The gong sounded and everyone somberly collected their backpacks and filed out of the room.

CHAPTER UNDEVIGINTI

Tal discreetly performed a sit-rep as he and Borras walked to the cafeteria. They were using one of the smaller arterial hallways, so it was sparsely populated during the lunch period. More importantly, there were no other Hunts competitors. "I've got a couple of questions," he said.

"Shoot," came the response from several feet above his head.

"The 'Cult of Nyx.' I know who Nyx is according to Earth plane lore. Who was she according to the Folk?"

"To start with, the question is more correctly phrased as, 'Who **is** she?' not 'Who **was** she'," Borras replied.

"I don't get it," Tal said. "I realize many of the Folk are long-lived relative to us humans but Elphinstone said some of the wytches have been around for thousands of years."

"Nyx is one of many names for the female twin."

"Whoa, there," Tal said, stopping in his tracks. "You're saying Nyx is another name for Luna? As in Sol and Luna? She's in charge of wytches?"

Borras replied with a grin stretching most the width of the hallway, "For someone who is a genius in many respects, you are an absolute dullard when it comes to the most commonly known facts. Yes, Child of the Dust. Nyx is Luna, an Elder Child of Amarantos. Sol's twin sister," Borras added as he began walking again.

"So, that's what's up with the junkyard," Tal mused, as he started again as well.

"Pardon?" Borras asked.

"I keep forgetting it was dark the only time you and the team have been to Earth plane. Behind Sol's Gas Station there is a well-secured junkyard. The padlocked gate has a sign that says, 'Luna's Timeless Treasyres.' "

Now it was Borras's turn to stop their forward progress. "It says those words? It says, 'timeless treasyres'?"

"Yes."

"Spelled with a 'y' in treasyre?"

"Yes."

"Is that all it says?" Borras asked anxiously.

"There's the usual 'keep out' warning…and the unusual 'trespassyrs will be slayn.' Apparently drawing and quartering as well as disemboweling were also possibilities but they were scratched out. I thought the whole thing was a joke because of all of the misspelled words."

"There were 'y's in places that mortals would not use 'y's?"

"You got it,"

" 'Y's are magykal, never forget that."

"Got it," Tal replied.

"No really, it could be very important." The behemoth rubbed his chin, pondering something. "Quint, something's up. You've met the Lady Aurora, and she gave you a magyk ring."

"So?"

"So, all the rest of us here at Hunts School are Folk from thousands of different Realms, and none of us have ever met Aurora. You've also met several of Sol's avatars."

"If by 'several avatars' you mean two out of order gas pumps and a leaky air hose, then yeah, I have."

"Again, none of us have ever met Sol. Or any of the four Principes, for that matter. They are the Elder Children, and believe themselves to be significantly more important than the Folk."

"You mean kind of like most Folk think they're way more important than humans?"

"Sadly, that is true," Borras replied.

"The Principes may have more juice, Borras, but you're the one who's been telling me that we are all Amarantos's children."

"Fair statement. You've now met two of the Principes, and they have both provided you with assistance."

"The air hose was a little mouthy for my taste, but yeah, fair statement."

"I've been at Hunts School for right at a century. Our teachers have been here for a number of Tyrnings. Hunts School has been here, well I don't even know how long it's been here..."

"The point being..." Tal urged.

"The point being that Sol has always provided an avatar to be the gateway to the Hunts School. Obviously the gateway has changed form almost every Tyrning."

"Makes sense. A gas station wouldn't have meant to much to the area inhabitants of three hundred years ago," Tal added.

"Right. But in all of the different references to Sol serving Amarantos as the gatekeeper of the Hunts School's access point to the Earth plane, never has Luna been mentioned. Now you're telling me she has an avatar in the form of a junkyard right next to Sol's gas station."

"Lost here," Tal quipped.

"Quint, you need to be very careful," Borras replied, slowly and deliberately.

"I get it. I have absolutely no intention of ever climbing that fence. For any reason. Anyway, I'm sure there's all types of rusty timeless treasyres in there but I'm current on my tetanus booster shot, so it's all good."

Borras put his catcher's mitt sized paw on Tal's shoulder. "Serious business, buddy. Very serious business. Tyrnings come and go, every three hundred years. I understand three hundred years is a long time for mortals, it is for some of the Folk as well. To the Elder Children, three centuries is the span of a single beat of their hearts. There has never been any indication of interest by the Principes. Until now. You have somehow become an important player in a game which interests the Elder Children."

"I don't know, Borras…," Tal replied, the suddenly discovered gravity of his present circumstances threatening to crush the words from his mouth.

"You need look no further than the ring on your finger. In the history of the Moiety there has never been a gyft of Eldermagyk to a Hunts contestant."

"Back to my original question. How does this hook up with the story behind the Cult of Nyx?" Tal asked.

"To answer that question, I must first tell you the story of Munedan and Corcra," Borras replied, as he stopped at the cafeteria entrance. "It is a lengthy tale. Comestibles first. When we're through, we will find a quiet nook in the library where we won't be overheard."

"Good plan," Tal agreed as they got in line for a tray.

CHAPTER VIGINTI

After they each triple checked the area for lurkers, Borras and Tal took seats at a table all the way to the back on the fourth floor of the library. The entire student body shunned the area as it contained the library's collection of copies of every book and scroll concerning sexually transmitted diseases from all of the known Folk Realms.

"Okay, let me have it," Tal said, anxious to get the scoop on the Cult of Nyx.

"When mortals were infants, the Principes, as well as the Folk, regularly trod the Earth plane."

"Even Time?" Tal asked.

Borras smiled a little at the question. "Rarely. Chronos is Amarantos's Seneschal, her First Born. Even Sol, Luna, and Amarantos must bend their knees to Time. She has always held herself as being above even the other Principes."

"She?" Tal asked, stunned.

"Of course," Borras responded.

"So Father Time is actually a chick. Who knew?"

"Apparently everyone in the entire known universe—except humans," Borras replied seriously.

"So you're saying Sol is the only guy Principe and he has three sisters?" Tal asked. "That doesn't seem right."

"Why not," Borras asked. "Isn't there a popular Earth Realm song with the title, 'Who Runs The World?' which has as its lyrical answer, 'Girls, we run this motha'?"

"Yes, but if you're going to say it right you have to yell 'yeah' after 'motha'."

"Sorry. They didn't teach us that part," Borras replied.

"I'm not believing the Prime Direction of my merry band of aliens is quoting a Beyoncé tune to me," Tal said laughing.

"The study of Earth Realm societal institutions, including current cultures, is a large portion of the Hunts School core curriculum. We have studied contemporary Earth plane music, art, and fashions. Of course the only possible opportunity for first-hand observation is the ritual Tyrning year field trip."

"Field trip?" Tal asked. "Nobody's said anything about a field trip."

"If you'd been here for the last ninety-nine years, like the rest of us, you would know there is always a Tyrning Year field trip for the remaining Hunts Finalists. It is always the second term of the Tyrning year. In the past there has been minimal contact with mortals…"

"Makes sense," Tal said, interrupting Borras. "This neck of the woods was sparsely inhabited last time y'all were here."

"True. The field trip though has always been a huge deal. It is the only chance most Folk ever get to visit Earth Realm, which is unique among all planes of existence created by the UnFading Spirit. The details of the field trip are a closely guarded secret, known only to the HuntsMistress, Principal Chiron, and the Archon. Ms. Empousa will eventually give us the details in Orientation."

Tal interrupted him again. "The most appropriate place for a field trip for her is Death Valley."

"Let me finish the story," Borras said. "Amarantos encouraged the Principes to help the Dust Children. Sol and Aurora took much pleasure in teaching their new little brothers and sisters about Amarantos and about Seeking the Center."

"This whole concept, 'Seeking the Center,' it was taught

to humans?"

"Absolutely. Although mortals were yet immature in their methods of communication, the message was given to them."

"Which might mean many of the Earth plane religions were begun by individuals who were trying to express that message to others," Tal said, as the full importance of what Borras was telling him began to settle in his mind.

"Yes, Quint. Peace, harmony, grace, love. They are all gyfts from Amarantos to those Seeking the Center."

"Luna—she was aloof, like Chronos?" Tal asked.

"No, in fact she was the opposite. Luna helped mortals more than all of the other Principes combined. It is said she was not then as she is now."

"What do you mean?"

"Luna and Sol are twins, and were originally inseparable. Each shone as brightly as the other. During the day, Luna let Sol take the lead, teaching and leading mankind with the warm magyk of his golden light. When dusk's brush painted its dark crimson streaks across the edges of the heavens, it was Luna's turn. In the beginning, night was as bright as day, except it was lit by the cool magyk of Luna's quicksilver radiance. Humans worshipped them both equally. Borras paused in his narrative. "You know one of our words for mortals is 'Munedan?' "

Tal nodded. "Yeah, but I assumed it was only another jacked-up Folk spelling. You know, for the word 'mundane'."

"You shouldn't make assumptions," Borras remarked.

"Right. Because when I do I make an 'ass' out of 'u' and 'me,' " Tal quickly replied, smiling.

"No, it's because when you assume it means there is no objective basis for the conclusion. Who in the world ever said 'because you make an ass out of you and me,' anyway?"

"It's a thing, I swear."

"Not anywhere in the known universe."

"Forget it. If 'Munedan' isn't a Folk slur calling mortals ordinary, what does it mean?"

" 'Beloved of the Moon.' A title once spoken with

reverence by the Folk, its continued use is now a grim reminder of an epic tragedy."

"Which was?" Tal asked.

"Munedan was the name Luna gave to her mortal lover."

"No way," Tal replied. "A Principe and a human? That's like a ten dating a one—it doesn't happen." You would do well to remember that equation on a personal level, when it comes to you dating either Elle or Väst, Tal told himself. "I know this chestnut, Borras. Let me guess, their love for each other never waivered but being mortal he soon grew old and died while she remained eternally young and mourns him to this day."

"No."

"What do you mean, no? It's the old star-crossed lovers storyline. It's a classic fairytale narrative, Borras."

"That may be true, but this is not a fairy tale. When Luna first gazed upon Munedan, he was already betrothed."

"To the other person, to Corcra?" Tal asked.

"Yes. Corcra, who was Crown Princess of the Alfar."

The Alfar, Tal thought. Wait a minute, that's Arthrys's people. "Corcra was an elf princess?"

"Yes. Her name means 'purple' in the language of the Irish Realm. Princess Corcra was so fair she was like unto the brightest piece of the rain's bow brought to life."

Having met Aurora personally, I have a pretty good understanding of how gorgeous Princess Corcra must have been, Tal thought. "There's no way this was a political marriage," Tal said. "Not between human and Folk."

"It wasn't. Munedan and Corcra held True Love each for the other."

"Wow, Munedan must have been some kind of Adonis himself if he had both elvish royalty and the Moon herself all bat shit crazy over him."

"It is written of Munedan that he was as beautiful as the sunrise of the first summer morn, his mind keener than the finest dwarf-forged blade, and his laughter so pure it healed the brokenness of all who heard its sound."

"That's a pretty decent resume. Too bad he was apparently also a low down two-timer," Tal said.

"No, Quint, he wasn't."

"That leaves Luna out in the cold, then."

"If only it had ended that way. When Luna first approached Munedan, he respectfully rejected her advances. No one had ever had the temerity to tell her no, much less a human who should be worshipping her as a god."

"You know what they say about a Principe scorned…"

"Hurt and shamed, Luna flew into a jealous rage." Borras halted his story for a moment. "It is one of the few recorded instances of a full-on Connyption. Totally out of control, and being a Principe, when her magyk flared into eruption, it took…she took…she took his free will from him."

"You mean she laid some compulsionmagyk on him," Tal said quietly.

Borras nodded his assent. "All of the almost limitless power of a Principe unleashed against a Dust Child."

"Well, as soon as Munedan found out about it…"

"The Principes' magyk is so far beyond our ken she was able to disguise the geas. Munedan had no idea until much later."

"That evil bitch," Tal said.

"It is not of the Center to judge others without first trying to see the world through their eyes, Quint. Some who have experienced its force might argue that True Love itself is a form of compulsionmagyk."

"It was still a bitch move, Borras." Maybe, that's the Earth plane origin of the word "moonstruck," Tal thought.

Borras continued. "After that, Luna and Munedan were inseparable for quite some time, while Luna held Munedan in thrall."

"What finally stopped her?"

"After Sol learned of his twin sister's action, he made many attempts to bring her back to her senses, to help her understand how wrong her actions were. Sol's intervention finally proved successful. Luna realized her compulsion was tearing

111

Munedan apart, and that although she had his physical attention, that Munedan would never be able to return her love absent the return of his free will."

"It finally sunk in that her actions had not been in accordance with 'Seeking the Center'," Tal added.

"Correct. So Luna removed the compulsionmagyk."

"And?"

"Munedan continued his relationship with Luna."

"Oh, hell. Why?" Tal asked.

"No one knows for sure. It may have been because Munedan had developed feelings for her independent of the geas. More probably it was because of a pattern of behavior or a sense of obligation that was developed while he was under the compulsion."

A kind of corollary of "Stockholm Syndrome," Tal thought. "There's not going to be a happily ever after for Munedan and Luna, is there?" Tal asked.

"Even the Principes are subject to the Lex Immortalis, Quint. Luna had committed several serious violations. She took Munedan's free will from him. Just as importantly, she interfered with one of Amarantos's rarest gyfts—True Love."

"Yeah but Munedan ultimately chose to be with Luna so that fixed any of the original problems."

"It doesn't work that way. Given the beginning of their relationship, there was no way to ever separate the strands of freedom and coercion. Their relationship did not begin consensually and could never be legitimated."

Tal felt the other shoe fall. Heavily. "There's not a happily ever after for Munedan and his elf princess either, is there?"

"Most tragically there's not, Quint."

"This is a terrible, awful story, Borras. And depressing. It is a terrible, awful and depressing story. Plus, it makes no sense. How could Munedan have been truly in love with Corcra and then while that was going on fall in love with Luna, compulsion or no compulsion. True Love lasts forever."

"Perpetual is not a synonym of self-perpetuating," Borras

replied.

"Now you're starting to sound like Myrddin," Tal replied.

"Thank you," Borras replied, smiling.

His smile this time, Tal noticed. It's a little different than the normal Borras facial response. A touch of enigmatic perhaps.

"True Love is a matter where humans' short-life spans have hampered their more perfect understanding. True Love is the rarest of commodities—it is an echo of the depth of Amarantos's love for each of her children."

"I'm with you so far," Tal said.

"Between her children, it may be a once in a lifetime thing. It may also be a never in a lifetime thing."

"By listing those two choices, you're not saying it can also be a more than a once in a lifetime thing?" Tal asked.

"Yes, that's exactly what I'm telling you," Borras confirmed, nodding his head to emphasize the point.

"I'm afraid your stupid human has a more imperfect understanding of what you're saying."

"Amarantos is the Center. She chooses every moment to be of the Center. She chooses every moment to love each and every one of us."

"Now you've lost me," Tal replied. "There's no choice involved there. You say the UnFading Spirit is not only God but she's our parent, as well. We're her kids. You gotta love your kids, don't you?"

"We all have free will, Quint, including the UnFading Spirit. Just because we know she will always choose to love us no matter what we do doesn't mean such decision isn't a choice she makes every moment of her eternal existence. Without the unfettered ability to choose, True Love cannot exist. It has many imposters—infatuation, covetousness, lust—which may exist absent free will. Not so, True Love."

"Guess I hadn't really thought about it in those terms," Tal said solemnly.

"Neither had Munedan. He learned too late that True Love requires a heart's entirety. He also learned that whether you're speaking of the physical or the metaphysical, there simply isn't room in one body for two hearts."

"The True Love he felt for the elf princess, wasn't that real before Luna interfered?" Tal asked. He didn't understand why, but it mattered greatly to him that there be a logical resolution that permitted a better ending for Munedan and Corcra.

"It was."

"So, it was still real after Luna left the scene?"

"True Love is not a treasyre that may be secreted away in a strongbox for safekeeping. We do not possess or own True Love, except for each unique moment in time. Like the UnFading Spirit's love for us, it requires a constant, never-ending choice. It is a gyft which must be both freely given and accepted every minute of every day."

"But…"

"Whether you have a mortal's lyfespan or that of the longest lived of the Folk, we are all the same in one respect. There will never ever be room in one body, in one mind, for two hearts. True Love must be…it requires that it be…relentlessly cherished."

"Relentlessly cherished," Tal repeated softly. "Damn, Borras, where did all of that fancy talk come from?"

"Do not forget Quint that I am hundreds of years older than you."

"You can't tell me with all of the magyk energy of the Folk and the Principes, that someone couldn't merely wave a wand and say 'abracadabra' to fix things."

"Abracadabra is what you say when someone sneezes. How would that have helped?" Borras asked, clearly puzzled.

"Fine. Gesundheit, then."

"Good health to you as well, Quint. Why are you saying these strange, inappropriate words?"

"Never mind. Corcra still loved Munedan, didn't she?"

"As much as ever."

"Surely Chronos could snap her fingers and hit rewind

for all three of them, couldn't she?"

Borras laughed. "No, Quint. Chronos may be the most powerful of us all but Amarantos alone has the magyk to undo what has already been done."

"Are you saying there was no way the Luna—Munedan issue could have been fixed magykally?

"There was only one way Munedan could be restored to his original heart, the one that belonged with Corcra. The Kiss of Lethe."

"The what?"

"It is a magykal decoction made from a plant that only grows in one small part of the Five-Hells Realm."

"So you can't just pick it up at the neighborhood pharmacy?" Tal asked.

"No, it is one of the rarest of elixirs."

"They got some though, didn't they?" Tal asked, a splinter of hope began working its way back into his thoughts.

"Yes, a dose was procured. If properly administered, the Kiss would kill Munedan's metaphysical heart, the one which had been compromised by Luna. The medicine would cause him to forget, and he would be restored. It would be as if he had never met Luna."

"And if improperly administered?" Tal asked.

"It would kill Munedan's ability to ever feel anything again."

"Damn. But if it failed, wouldn't he still have the memories of having been in love with Corcra? Wouldn't he remember how wonderful that felt?"

"Yes, he would remember the feeling but he would no longer be able to make it his own."

Like a golem, Tal thought. I wonder if that's what it's like for Emet? To have the memories of my emotions but not be able to actually feel anything about them. Or about anyone. "Luna gave Munedan the Kiss?"

"Yes. In fact she was the only one who could do so."

"Why?"

"You know the answer, Quint, based on everything you've learned about magyk since you first walked on campus."

Tal chewed his lower lip a little as he thought. "The Kiss of Lethe magyk required that an equivalent pryce be paid. By Luna."

"That is correct."

"She had to forgo her love for Munedan totally and without reservation, didn't she?" Tal asked.

"Yes," Borras replied. "Now the rest of it."

Tal gave his lower lip another good chewing. "Oh, damn. The Kiss of Lethe affects both persons. For Munedan to forget forever, Luna had to be forced to always remember. Which meant for the entirety of her Principe existence she would remember her love for Munedan without there ever being any possibility of him returning her love. That is why she had to be the one to administer the potion." He set back in his chair. "I don't care who you are or what you've done. That's harsh."

"Someone had to pay the gyftpryce."

"The elixir? It didn't work, did it?" Tal asked sadly.

"No," Borras confirmed, shaking his head. "Although Luna said she was would do it, when the moment came there must have been some small selfish part of her that refused to let Munedan go completely."

"What happened to Princess Corcra?"

"For the remainder of her life she only ever had the heart that loved Munedan. She returned to her Realm, but as each day went by she grew more despondent."

"Why couldn't Munedan give her the Kiss of Lethe?" Tal asked.

"He was human and incapable of performing magyk. But that wasn't the only problem. He himself no longer possessed the necessary heart for the Kiss of Lethe to work for Corcra."

"Then what?" Tal asked, fearing he knew what was coming.

"Corcra mourned until her body wasted away to nothing, and she died."

Tal found himself overcome—almost about to cry, sitting in a library among the largest collection of treatises on STDs in the universe. He didn't even know the princess, whoever she was, however many millennia ago she may have lived. It didn't matter. He wiped his nose on his shirtsleeve. "Go ahead, Borras. Finish it. Can't get much worse than this."

"Luna saw what she had done. That she had ruined Munedan's life and that the elf princess had died as a direct result of her selfishness. Like all of the rest of us she didn't want things to be her fault. Munedan felt responsible for what had happened to Corcra. He couldn't stand himself nor could he stand the sight of Luna. He hid from her during the times she walked the Earth plane."

"Luna's feelings, they had to go someplace," Tal said. "It's the same principle as a magykpryce."

"Yes, and because Luna selfishly held her feelings close, they first turned shrill, then festered within her. She began refusing to help teach mortals about Amarantos. She hid her face from mortals as Munedan now hid his face from her. She dimmed her radiance so that darkness and evil could claim mankind's nights."

"What about the Folk?"

"She abandoned them as well. Her feelings that were once blessings, she came to see as curses. Humans learned to seek the safety of day and to avoid the unwholesome mysteries of the night. Except for the few who themselves felt betrayed by True Love."

"The wytches. That's where the wytches come along," Tal said, spellbound once again by the skein of the story.

"Yes," Borras replied. "Luna accepted them as her own and over time they became the Cult of Nyx—Cult of the Night. Since they were human, at least to start, they had no magyk of their own."

"Which is why she created the magyk syphon thing that Professor Elphinstone told us about." Tal saw Borras, who had been willing to face down every menace so far, shrink a little as he said the words, "magyk syphon."

"Quint, I'm not sure you can understand how hard it was for us to leave our magyk behind for a hundred years. It is part of who we are, who we've each always been. It is our lyfeforce and the source of replenishment of our lyfeforce at the same time. For someone to violate us, to kill us maybe, by taking it for their own is almost unfathomable. We don't know what other consequences it might have for us. What if it were to leave us soulless, unable to be gathered to Amarantos. It's terrifying."

The gong sounded, signaling ten minutes until the next period. Which for the Hunts Finalists was Combat. Borras threw all his stuff in his backpack, and began double-timing it out of the library. "Lecture's over."

"Wait," Tal said as he started running to catch up with Borras. "You said Luna renamed Munedan. What was his original name?"

Borras didn't slow down, merely turned his head and whispered over his shoulder so that the answer would be hanging in mid-air, waiting to knock Tal down as he walked through it.

"The Alfar call him Lailoken, 'Time's Fool'."

"Myrddin?" Tal asked, stunned.

"Yes, Quint. His psuche name was Taliesin."

CHAPTER VIGINTI UNUS

Combat had been the last class of a long day. Every time they practiced together, he and Piras improved as a team. Typically, the two of them were head and shoulders above the rest of the Finalists. Not today. They lost two sparring matches, and pulled only a draw on a third. Tal hadn't been able to focus even though Piras had done his best to get Tal in the game. As they'd seen on their first day together, Combat could be extremely dangerous.

Tal simply couldn't get Myrddin's origin story out of his head. Neither the part of the tale he now knew from Borras, nor the unfilled spaces between. Each known fact raised its own legion of unknown questions. Myrddin began as a human. Was he still human? How could that be? He must be several thousands of years old. Myrddin had magyk, Tal had seen him use it. How did a mortal exercise magyk? Even the wytches apparently had to have a syphon, whatever that was. Did Myrddin go back and forth through time? His appearance underwent radical changes but did that mean he was a time traveler? Was Myrddin behind the Conundrum that brought Tal into contact with Excalibur? Borras has said Corcra was a princess of the Alfar. What relationship, if any, did she have to Arthrys? Why were Arthrys and his clan chosen to protect Myrddin's Star in Forest Fell? Tal's head was still spinning as he took Piras off and stowed him in his gym locker. Maybe most importantly, what did it mean, if anything, that both he and Myrddin had the same psuche name.

As usual following his last class, when everyone else headed off to the sports arena for some non-potentially deadly exercise or back to the dorms for a little rest and relaxation, Tal headed the other way. To the front of the Greek temple portion of the main school building, past the impassive guardians, out the mammoth double front doors and down the four-lane-wide marble stairs. Toward the Gas Station Crossing.

Tal was always rushed going to meet Emet but this afternoon he found himself walking round and round Fountain Flow, still lost in pondering Myrddin's saga. When he finally paused, he realized he was looking at the side of the fountain that was full frontal Mokosh.

"Okay," he said quietly, hoping the rush of falling water prevented any eavesdropping, "I don't normally talk to strangers. Particularly strangers who are in fact inanimate objects, but today's already been stranger than normal even by Hunts School standards, so I guess there's no harm in chatting up some wet marble.

"Emet and I—Emet is my simulacrum golem—well, we did quite a bit of research on you recently. I don't know about the whole alleged adultery thing—not judging or nothing—because us Munedans might have gotten that part of the story wrong, and that may or may not be what actually happened in the Folk planes, and I realize I'm kind of rambling, but anyway we found that on the Earth plane the Friday that falls between October 25th and November 1st is the day you're supposed to be honored. I realize I'm almost a week late but it's been kind of a rough couple of weeks what with me almost dying and everything. Anyway, for what it's worth, I wanted to drop by and tell you Happy Mokosh Day. Or Merry Mokoshmas. Or whatever the appropriate greeting is. Have a nice day."

"Have a nice day?" he asked himself. You're losing it, Tal Smith. First you start a conversation with an inert chunk of marble and next thing you know you're wishing it top of the morning. And smooth move bringing up the whole maybe sorta adultery thing, Pretty sure that's a sore subject even if you've got a heart made of stone.

As Tal turned on his right heel to head on out across Grass Grow, a sparkle caught his eye. It was a sunbeam playing across the near side of the fountain. During the split second it danced across Mokosh's sword, he could have sworn he saw the words *'cor aut mors'* etched into the sword. That one I know from Western Civ, Tal told himself. It was one of his two favorite legendary Roman fighting phrases. The most famous being, *'Ave, Caesar, morituri te salutant.'* Which roughly translated to "Hail Caesar, those who are about to die salute you." *'Cor aut mors'* means "heart or death." Basically, "live with honor or else you've never really been alive."

In the blink of his eyes, the fountain's spray fractured the sunlight and the words were gone. If they were really there to begin with, Tal decided, as he headed homeward.

CHAPTER VIGINTI DUO

Every school term was the same, mortal or Folk. It seemed like it took forever for it to start but after the first few weeks Tal always felt like he was hurtling toward the denouement. Whether he was ready or not.

He'd spent a good amount of the couple of days immediately following his and Borras's conversation about Corcra and her Taliesin internally debating what had gone down. Everything about the sequence offended his sense of fair play and precipitated really heavy pondering. Could True Love truly be such a fragile construct?

The time required to keep up with both his schoolwork at Hunts School and with Emet's activities at Nemeton High, as well as getting prepared for the impending holidays, required that he put the Myrddin issues on the backburner. He decided the easiest way to get the answers to most of his questions was simply to ask Myrddin when he saw him again. If he saw him again. Which meant there were now two things on his backburner list—Myrddin and Elle.

For many reasons, Tal's second term at Hunts School was materially different from the first term. His classes were smaller, as the Hunts Finalists had been winnowed from nine teams down to six. He noted with interest the smaller class size appeared to have a direct inverse correlation with the level of tension. Best Tal could calculate, it was a logarithmic scale. Like the Richter scale. Reduction of even one team precipitated at least a tenfold tension increase. They'd lost three teams. Which resulted in an approximate thousandfold tension increase. First term there were times he'd felt like he was breathing tension instead of oxygen. It was now so pervasive he felt like he was chewing it. What's it going to be like when four more teams are dropped at the end of this term?

Another major difference was that he had now proven conclusively that as a human he was not a complete and total liability for Omada. Well, proven to everyone but Notos. In Combat, the other squads were reluctant to spar with him and Piras, knowing that if Tal wanted to, he could "accidentally" maim them and take them out of the competition. He wouldn't, but they didn't know that. As a result, except for his mediocre performance the other day, Tal was earning top marks for Omada every week in Combat.

Nord and the rest of the sour grapes contingent muttered about Omada's unfair advantage because they had a mortal. Which was funny when Tal thought about it because the Folk deemed humans inferior in every other category. Even Tal's own teammates, if they were being honest, would have to admit their prejudice.

A third major difference was sex. Lots and lots of sex. It was almost as if Väst was afraid to let him go more than a day or two without a ridiculous amount of stupidly pleasurable nakedness. His Old School mates had remarked several times that he never seemed to have time to practice with them anymore. Borras had gotten a little suspicious the third time Tal turned down a joint visit to the library, remarking that such refusal was "very un-Quint like." After that Tal made sure to go wherever and whenever Borras asked and that he was never late for team meetings. He'd felt bad for a week or so about his potentially treasonous actions but finally resolved that it was, well, it was…nakedness…and sex. With someone he was crazy about who gave every indication of being crazy about him.

During his first term, Tal had gotten the broad brush strokes down of being a student at Hunts School and a Finalist in the Hunts. Not that he didn't still have way more to learn than everybody else. He did, but he had a great group of teammates. Well, a great group—and Notos.

Tal also had Emet helping him back on Earth plane proper. He'd realized over the last few weeks that something unexpected, but wonderful, had happened—he'd been given an opportunity to get to know himself. Really know himself, and he found out he was somebody worth knowing and liking. He was fun to hang out with, and a loyal friend. He initially thought there would be a little more friction, like having out of town relatives come stay about two days too long. When there wasn't, he realized it's because even when we are golemless, we all have to learn how to live with ourselves everyday.

Another difference was more personal in nature. His self-image had changed radically. Not that there weren't some things about himself he really hated. Emet about drove him up the wall with that freaking ice chewing. Man, was that an annoying habit. Tal had resolved he would quit—as soon as this school year was over.

Even though Emet could type as fast as a speeding bullet, Tal still had to wait until Emet finished typing before he could respond. It had made Tal realize he didn't listen to others nearly as much as he should. Watching Emet learning how to navigate his interactions with other people without the ability to feel the emotions attached to such relationships caused Tal to think about how lucky he was to be human, to be able to feel. Whether it was his love for his Mom and Pell and the twins, or the strong emotions he felt for Väst—and if he was being honest, for Elle, the ability to feel was a daily miracle he had always taken for granted. Not any more. Tal often wondered if the learning experience was reciprocal. What was Emet learning from getting to know himself by interacting with Tal?

CHAPTER VIGINTI TRES

The bell rang, and Professor Elphinstone leapt right into the day's lecture. "Today we will begin our general discussion about wytches. As you can imagine, disenchanted humans from every part of the Earth plane petitioned Luna to be initiated into the Cult of Nyx."

Which is why almost every Earth culture has stories and legends about witches, Tal thought. Apparently the almost universal fear was—and is—well founded.

"You will notice a continuing theme in this term's classes about wytches. That theme being we have little reliable information about wytches. The first reason is that the precise nature of their relationship with Luna has been obfuscated by her Principe-level magyk."

The professor walked over to the blackboard and began writing names. "Who can tell me what the following witches have in common: Angele de la Barthe, France, thirteenth century. Mother Shipton, sixteenth century, England. Agnes Sampson of Scotland, seventeenth century. Catherine Monvoisin of France, seventeenth century. Maret Jonsdotter, Sweden, seventeenth century. Marie Catherine Laveau, Louisiana, nineteenth century, and Agnes Waterhouse, England, sixteenth century?"

Receiving no answer from the class, the professor continued, "What about if I include the Trier, Germany witch trials in the last part of the sixteenth century during which over three hundred fifty people were put to death? Or the Fulda Witch trials in Germany? During a single three-year period over two hundred people were executed as witches." Professor Elphinstone looked around the room again. "Nothing? How about if I include the Salem witch hunts?"

It's not geography, Tal thought, as he quickly scanned all of the information on the board. The names don't have anything in common. They're all females. Deductive reasoning leaves only the time periods. But they're all over the place. Well, not quite. No one is listed earlier than the thirteenth century. He raised his hand, making him the immediate recipient of the inevitable stinkeye from Notos.

"Yes, Quint of Omada?"

"They all lived subsequent to Arthrys's original magykal ban on the Earth plane."

"That's a start. You've analyzed the relevant factual information but it's of no use without the corresponding conclusion."

Think, Tal, think. Wytches were human, then they got these magykal syphons or whatever. But all of these women lived after Arthrys's ban. "They're not wytches," Tal almost yelled.

"Good. Very good," Professor Elphinstone said, as he walked to his desk to write points for Omada in his ledger. Tal saw Borras look over at him and smile. Dysi softly double-tapped his ankle under the table to evidence her approval.

The professor walked back over to the chalkboard. "Each of these individuals was labeled a wytch and most of them were executed because of it. They were, however, most certainly not wytches."

Sredina of Pleme didn't even bother raising her hand. "So what you're saying is that all of those women were innocent?"

Professor Elphinstone walked over to his book with a frown. When he got there he scratched an entry onto the page.

Pleme just lost points, Tal thought. I need to remember there is a definite downside to volunteering.

"That is a poor conclusion, unsupported by the information you've been given. Those individuals may or may not have committed murder, or treason, or wreaked mischief and terror among those poor souls unfortunate to be in their lives or in their way. La Monvoisin was a well-known poisoner. Alice Kyteler is sometimes referred to as the original black widow after having four husbands die inexplicably. Agnes Waterhouse named her cat 'Satan' which would have been enough for some people right there. To the extent they themselves claimed to be wytches, they were charlatans and liars—or perhaps merely insane." He walked back over to the board and wrote, "Witch does not equal wytch."

A hand went up from Kusini, Third Prime of Kabila. The teacher nodded his head in acknowledgment. "Are there good wytches, Professor?"

"There are no 'good' wytches, sometimes referred to in human texts as 'white witches.' The overwhelming majority of mortals were and are ignorant of the Folk. The Children of the Dust believed the Folk who walked Earth Realm to be gods or other various types of superhuman beings. Any stories involving supposed 'white witches,' what is commonly referred to as the 'Glynda Syndrome,' are most likely based on Folk who performed noble deeds while Seeking the Center."

The bell sounded ending the period. "Alright then, read ahead. Tomorrow we are going to start talking about specific wytches."

CHAPTER VIGINTI QUATTOUR

"I hope you took my admonition to heart yesterday and began your readings last night concerning those individuals who have been verified from historical data as members of the Cult of Nyx. These are confirmed wytches who will qualify for Hunts points if you meet them—and survive the meeting. Which brings up something that can't be over-emphasized or repeated too much." Professor Elphinstone pointed to the far side of the chalkboard where he'd previously written this term's Journey Rules.

Got it, got it, got it, Tal told himself. Under no circumstances am I to take Piras off on any of this term's Journeys. This place would be a lot more fun if the main entrée of knowledge wasn't inevitably served with a side order of death or dismemberment. I guess that could be death and/or dismemberment, he decided.

"Except for those wytches encountered in the two previous wytch hunts, we know nothing about wytches other than their time on Earth plane prior to Arthrys's original ban. This means each team's individual study may yield major results. There are hundreds of thousands of texts in the school library. Any one of those books may contain an undiscovered clue concerning wytches. In addition to the Folk writings and treatises there is also a sizeable collection of Earth plane books in the library.

"Wytches originated from all of the Earth plane continents." Professor Elphinstone stopped for a moment, a small puzzlement kinking his brow. "Well, probably not Antarctica but certainly the other six. Previous scholarly study provides us with some information concerning the relative strengths and weaknesses of the initiates in the Cult of Nyx. Most importantly, we are certain the top three in the Nyx hierarchy are also pyschopomps."

Psychopomp. Tal wrote it down and underlined it twice, to help remind him to ask the team.

"As you are aware, prior to any magykal ban, Folk commerce with mortals was common across all of Earth Realm. The myths and stories arising from such interaction are better preserved in some cultures than in others. For example, let's start with Greek culture. Some of the more well-known Greek wytches are Circe, Hecate, Cassandra, and the only confirmed set of Triplets—Deino, Enyo and Pemphredo."

Wow, Tal thought, three sisters apparently all done wrong by love. Definitely a country hit in there. Gotta be. Top ten if you add a dog and some repeated and excessive whiskey consumption.

"Circe reportedly turns people into animals. Hecate is the guru of poisons. The story is the triplets fell in love with the same male. Because of their unique circumstances, Luna required an additional condition for them to be accepted into the Cult of Nyx. All three were required to give up their eyes and their teeth, leaving only one of each for them to share."

Yikes! Tal exclaimed inwardly. Triple yikes, actually.

"Cassandra was a Princess of Troy, which as you know was a legendary human kingdom. She is one of the few instances where we know the name of the male portion of the love gone wrong equation. Something tragyk happened between she and the Apollo of that time."

Note to self, Tal thought. Folk and human combos seem to end in disaster. He looked over to Väst but she wasn't looking his direction. She invariably did an excellent job of ignoring him in public.

The professor continued on with his lecture. "If you go looking for Cassandra, take especial care. Most of the stories about her generally involve snakes. Snakes and perhaps a chest that if you open it and look into it, you go mad.

"Switching cultures and geographic areas, let's turn our attention to the area often referred to in Earth histories as, 'the cradle of civilization.' There are several wytches named in Jewish and proto-Jewish reference sources. Chronologically, Lilith would be the oldest."

Don't guess that's the same Lilith as our HuntsMistress. Tal scribbled on his notebook, sliding it toward Borras so he could see it. Borras shook his head no, before writing, "Stupid question, magyk syphons won't work on Earth plane, and especially not on Hunts School campus."

"There is also Herodias, who reportedly can fly, and Jezebel. By all accounts, Jezebel was one of the meanest, nastiest humans that Luna initiated into the Cult of Nyx. In Earth plane stories her own retinue defenestrated her, leaving her corpse as chow for stray dogs. We know, of course, that story is an embellishment as she survived the episode, with assistance from Luna.

"Then there is the Wytch of Endor." Professor Elphinstone stopped to walk over and write the word "necromancyr;" on the chalkboard. "Who can tell me what a 'necromancyr' is?"

Tal was pretty sure he knew but resisted the urge to raise his hand. Minami of Shuzoku decided to try his hand. "Someone with the magyk to bring another back from the dead."

"WRONG!" Professor Elphinstone exclaimed as he strode to his desk and wrote in his ledger. Kind of shook everyone in the room up a little. They'd never seen the professor angry before. "All of you. You're supposed to be Seeking the Center as an integral element of winning the Hunts. You should all know there is no magyk that can bring the dead to life. None.

The UnFading One has reserved that power to herself and she has never chosen to use it. Never. Dead is dead. Remember that. Points deducted from Shuzoku."

Tal was shocked to see Notos raise his hand. Notos was the epitome of low profile shade. "Yes, Notos of Omada?"

"Necromancyrs are individuals who have the ability to communicate with the dead."

"That is correct," the professor said with a large smile as he wrote several numbers in his ledger. "Even in the Earth plane stories, the Wytch of Endor used a familiar—her familiar—to communicate with the deceased.

"There are other confirmed wytches listed in your textbook. Louhi, a shape shifter, is a confirmed wytch of Finnish origin. Morgaine Le Fay, Arthrys's half-mortal sister is of English lineage. Morgaine is the only known wytch having both human and Folk lineage. She is also unique in that she is the only wytch who was actually involved in a love quadrangle."

Huh? was all Tal could think.

"Morgaine was in love with Gwynefar. Who spurned Morgaine twice—first for Arthrys, then later for Launcelot du Lac."

Well, that puts a whole new connotation on the term, 'cock-blocked,' Tal thought.

The professor walked back over to his desk and sat down. "That is enough to assimilate for the day. You are discharged. There's more information in the textbook about the top three wytches but each of you is going to have to do substantial independent study to discover information about the others. If you find something for your team that no one else discovers, it might make the difference between winning and losing."

Or maybe between living or dying, Tal added silently, as he gathered his class materials to place in his backpack.

CHAPTER VIGINTI QUINQUE

Per their usual protocol, the Omada team observed radio silence between the classroom and their secure team room. Once there and after the normal discussion points had been addressed, Tal went ahead and professed his ignorance. "So, psychopomp?"

Notos chimed in dismissively. "Are all humans as ignorant as you? It's derived from the Earth plane Greek. Usually translated as 'guide of souls' or 'collector of souls.' Pyschopomps are beings who transport people from the living world to the afterlife. There are Folk from almost every Realm who are psychopomps. Prior to Luna establishing the Cult of Nyx and Arthrys's ban on magyk, it was Folk who served in that role on Earth plane."

Dysi put her hand on Tal's arm to get his attention. "The most famous Folk psychopomp in the English speaking human cultures is the Grim Reaper. There were psychopomps from many Realms though, so the concept is multi-cultural."

"Like Charon the Ferryman and Thanatos, who were from Greek planes," Ana added.

"Right," Notos replied. "You can include in the list the Valkyries of Norse Realm, Azrael of the realmless Sylphs, Mercury of Roman Realm and Hermes, his Greek plane counterpart. From the Egyptian planes there are Anubis and

Osiris, and the Morrigan from the Celtic Realm. Papa Ghede from Haiti Realm was also a well-known psychopomp."

Damn, Tal thought. Notos is like an encyclopedia of shit about death. Makes sense, he looks like he walked out of a casting call for, "The Walking (While Scowling) Dead."

"You forgot one," Borras said. Notos raised his left eyebrow. "Veles of Five-Hells Realm," Borras concluded.

"Oh, um, yes…that is correct, Prime," Notos replied, fidgeting in his seat just a bit. "That one as well."

"Okay, team," Borras said, doing his job as their leader to redirect attention to the task at hand. "We might as well split up. It's going to take a lot of individual effort to ferret out information that might give us a leg up on the other teams. It's the proverbial 'straw in a stack of needles' to think we're going to luck out and find something in one of the thousands of books but we might as well try."

I'm just going to let that whole half-ass backwards aphorism thing go, Tal decided. What's important right now is for one of us to discover a piece of intel no one else knows about.

CHAPTER TWENTY-SIX

The winter holidays were important at the Smith household. Thea loved to cook, so from pretty much Thanksgiving through the first week of January, the house was redolent with the luscious smells of cinnamon, chocolate, nutmeg, and clove. Most importantly, there was the smell of fresh cookies approximately twenty minutes into the twenty-five minute oven cook cycle. The twins always had their eyes out for any large wooden spoons that needed lick-cleaning. Who was Tal kidding? Both he and Pell were also after those icing laden spatulas.

If Tal categorized Thanksgiving as "big" on the holiday index, Christmas was all the way up to "huge." Well, huge being a relative term as far as quantity of relatives. Neither his Mom nor Pell had any siblings, and both sets of their parents had died young. So not so huge, number of people wise. The constant relocations and job changes for Pell had always left them tight on money. So not so huge, money wise. His Mom had this thing about starting over when they moved, no personal belongings made the cut—certainly none of the Christmas decorations. So not so huge, fripperies wise.

Christmas was huge at the Smith household because the love and affection his Mom and Pell had for each other and for their family exploded until it embraced every waking minute of the holidays. Which, Tal thought, is particularly interesting this year as Yule was originally a pagan festival period synced up with the pagan "Wheel of the Year." Yule was one of the four major sabbats, with Imbolc being the quarter-festival between Yule and Ostara.

After Ostara came Beltane. Which was his "deliver or perish" date with Helblad, the draugr. I've got enough on my plate right now, Tal decided. If I manage to stay alive for another few months then I'll worry about my deal with Helblad.

CHAPTER TWENTY-SEVEN

Tal left Emet upstairs to begin reviewing the Wytches textbook while he spent longer than usual hanging with the fam over dinner and then playing some hoops with Rom and Rem. One of his reasons was it would soon be too cold for outdoor basketball, so he figured he might as well enjoy playtime with his little brothers while he could. If he was being honest though, the other reason was the distinct possibility Omada might get annihilated by one of the wytches. *Carpe diem* and all of that.

By the time Tal had showered and shaved, Emet was ready to give him a primer on the most powerful wytches. Emet's first point was the same one Professor Elphinstone had repeatedly made—there was a dearth of legit info about the Cult of Nyx and its members—and about their respective egos. Who knew whether the wytches were shameless self-promoters? Or compulsive liars? Maybe more importantly, they both acknowledged that based on her track history, the HuntsMistress wouldn't utilize her discretion in any manner favorable to Omada.

Their logical conclusion was Omada needed to interface with one of the top three wytches and negotiate for the most powerful talysman they could get. Because the top three were enumerated in the textbook, Ms. Empousa couldn't rule otherwise. It had been made clear that wytch power ranking counted more than talysman strength. This meant no matter how much Ms. Empousa might try to cheat them on the talysman ranking, Omada would advance to the final Hunt if they connected with one of the three most powerful wytches. Unless more than one team made contact with the same wytch and she gave one team an inferior talysman.

Hecate, Cassandra, and a wytch named Baba Yaga were all identified as psychopomps and thus deemed the three most powerful wytches. Close behind them, perhaps only half a level or tier lower, were Morgaine and some wytch named Kanka.

The only wytch of the top three they'd never heard of was Baba Yaga, so they made the decision to independently research her for about an hour and then reconvene to discuss their results. Tal hoped they might get lucky and glean something from the Earth plane resources that the rest of Omada, and the other Hunts Finalists, wouldn't know about. I mean, he thought, Google is pretty much magic itself. Right? Emet headed upstairs with the cellphone and Tal got started on the laptop.

First interesting thing—Baba Yaga, like Mokosh—was a character out of the Slavic pantheon. There wasn't any concrete translation of her name. Grandmother or "old woman" seemed to be the most prevalent conversion for "Baba." "Yaga" was even more up in the air but it might be translated as "serpent." Something fearful, in any event.

It didn't take much longer for Tal to discover Baba Yaga was one fey chick. Instead of a broom she allegedly flew around in a mortar, using a pestle to steer the contraption. Which was either a blatant phallic reference or getting a little Charles Lutwidge Dodgson *"Alice's Adventures in Wonderland"* freaky. Maybe both.

The physical descriptions of her varied from story to story and encompassed a broad spectrum of physical characteristics. In some tales she was the classic verruca-nosed crone, in others a stone cold fox. Each story seemed to have a different list of items in her treasure trove, like a warehouse full of flying carpets. I guess any of these items would make a great talysman, he thought.

Tal heard a branch creak and Emet came flying back into the room, landing catlike without appreciable noise. Boy's got some mad skills, Tal thought, as he looked at the clock. That was a quick hour.

Emet had also noticed the vast disparity in attributes credited to the wytch. In some way having no emotions allowed Emet to look at the stories holistically, to see a common thread that Tal had missed. Emet noticed that in all versions of Earth's Baba Yaga stories, the wytch was mercurial. Capricious, she was as likely to be pictured as a helpful guide as she was a villainess.

Anecdotally, she was also an equal opportunity murderer of both adults and children. On the flip side, quite a few myths mentioned she was a firm believer in proper etiquette and responded positively to well-mannered individuals. However, depending on how she felt on any given day, she was just as likely to kill and eat visitors as help them on their quest. The wytch had a retinue. Invisible servants inside her home and three horsemen outside. The horsemen were always described as being dressed in white, red and black. They didn't have real names, being referred to only as Day, Sun, and Night.

When Tal next looked at the clock it was well after midnight and he was spent. They decided they'd made a good start and called it quits for the evening.

CHAPTER VIGINTI OCTO

The next four weeks were jam-packed at both Hunts School and on Earth plane proper. Emet and Tal successfully navigated the potentially treacherous Thanksgiving and Christmas school breaks. The non-verbal alibi was wearing thin fast and they were going to have to come up with an alternative before Tal's parents called it quits for them. There was so much going on, the pair didn't ever have time to stop and think, much less collaborate, about their next move on that front.

At Hunts School the four weeks yielded a cascade of disappointment for most of the Finalist teams. Disappointment formed a co-dependent relationship with escalating tension, both intrasquad and intersquad. Dogû of Aile stupidly provoked a fight with Ha'a'aah of Hak'éí in the cafeteria. Ha'a'aah was sent to the infirmary with a nasty five-inch gash to his left forearm. Dogû wasn't as lucky. The physicks took him away screaming in agony, a three-tined fork firmly embedded in his right eye. The remaining members of Aile and Hak'éí leapt upon each other, using whatever cutlery was available. The end result was new scars for all members of both teams, a jaunty black eye patch for Dogû until a specialist physick could heal his eye, and permanent exile from the cafeteria of both warring squads by Chef Hestia.

The other result of the fracas was the HuntsMistress's issuance of a standing order that Hunts Finalists were to wear their Pucas during all school activities. Dysi told Tal the Archon also magyked the Finalists' suites in the dormitories so that no one other than the assigned occupant and his or her teammates could enter those areas.

It was clear to all the Finalists their frustration stemmed from everyone's Journey results. Each of the six teams had logged three trips. Based on the body language of the Finalists, four of the teams—including Omada—had struck out thus far. It was impossible to tell from their body language about the Allyu. Pleme made no bones about the fact the three Journeys they had taken were sufficient to gain them entry into the last Hunt. Which means they have at least met a wytch, Tal thought. Of course they could be bluffing.

At first, Tal couldn't parse the strategy behind a Pleme bluff. Emet had come up with the probable answer. It was a given that there was a very real possibility of death or substantial physical injury during the Wytch Hunt. Any team that fell below four non-maimed members was automatically disqualified. Use of the bluff strategy would be an attempt to goad one or more of the other teams—who might be ahead of your team on non-Hunts points—into additional Journeys where tragedy might occur. It makes sense, Tal decided. It's like blackjack at a casino. Most novice players don't realize the statistically smart play is to try to let the dealer bust rather than trying to beat the dealer with your hand. A smart defense being a good offense. Tal and his Omada crew subsequently discussed using a bluff strategy themselves. They ultimately unanimously voted the plan down. Well, Notos had grudgingly made it unanimous.

On each of their Journeys, the Prime Omphalos had sent them to three very different Realms. The first week they'd been transported to a water world, or at least that portion of the Realm with the receiving Omphalos was oceanic. The surface was dotted with small islands. Their team was understandably skittish—it being their first potential wytch encounter and no one

144

having a clear understanding of the mechanics of the wytches' syphons.

This was their first Journey wearing their Pucas and none of the team reported any Journey-related adverse consequences. Tal and Piras had truly become an integrated unit. Sometimes Tal didn't even have to think-talk. The Puca knew what Tal wanted, or was going to do, simply from the shifting of his muscles.

Tal had also learned that when Folk weren't on their home planes it wasn't a given their magykal abilities would be at full strength. It varied from world to world, with the exception of Earth plane. Which was yet another huge reason why the Earth plane was so popular before Arthrys's ban. No matter who you were Folkwise, you had your full juice on Earth. Tal decided it probably had to do with Earth being electrically, not magykally, powered.

As soon as they arrived on the waterworld each of his teammates did a quick magyk self-assessment. Well, three of them anyway. Whatever Notos had magykwise, he kept it under wraps at all times. The conclusion from the other three was this plane allowed them each about ten percent of their maximum level. Still, they were all delighted. Excepting only the Snype Hunt and their one brief trip to Tal's house, it was the only time in a hundred years they'd gotten to use their magyk in any fashion.

Dysi volunteered to be the proverbial canary lowered into the mineshaft. She proposed to teleport to an island within the group's line of sight. If nothing sinister happened to her within about thirty seconds, then Borras would leap to her position and watch her six while she teleported again.

The duo implemented the plan, using the protocol to work all of the islands within their visual range. After that plan came up empty, Dysi waited on the visually farthest island while Borras leapfrogged back and forth, picking up Ana, Tal, and Notos one at a time and ferrying them to Dysi's position. They then began the search pattern anew.

At no time was there any evidence of a wytch. In fact, there was no sign of animal life of any nature on that plane. By the time of the Recall, they were mentally exhausted and physically beat down.

On their second Journey they ended up in a desert furnace hell. Like the waterworld, the squad's magyk was at a fairly low level. Physically, the second Journey was a bit more problematic. Every one of them experienced the equivalent of a semi-incapacitating migraine. The Puca easily cleared that for the team but it was yet another visceral reminder of the danger of frequent Journeying.

Even the trekking was treacherous on the desert plane. It seemed like every third or fourth step one of them stepped into a sinkhole or a deep pocket of quicksand. Luckily, the first couple of times the victim wasn't Borras so he was able to grab the endangered teammate and use his abnormal strength to jerk them clear of danger. It was a closer call though when it finally happened to Borras. It took every bit of Tal and Piras's combined efforts to hold Borras's head above the sucking sand until the others could assist in the rescue.

Ana called a halt after the Borras episode and told the team they needed to be playing the game a little smarter. She took the backpack from Borras, placed it on the ground, and rummaged around for a few seconds before producing a coiled, silvery loop. As she unwound it, Tal could see it was a rope, several hundred feet in length. They tied off to each other in the basic climber's linear manner. Once secured, they continued their exploration. From then on any individual missteps were collectively addressed and managed.

Everyone who has spent time on a beach knows that any amount of sand-slogging becomes interminable once the first few grains of sand infiltrate your footwear. It only took a couple of dozen steps before Tal felt like he was carting a small bucket load in each shoe. Walking quickly became a major pain in the ass.

The first desert denizens they encountered were some ginormous and uber-slimy—as in sinus-infection-green-snot slimy—worms, who apparently thought the team was today's blue plate special. Each time a worm appeared, Borras waited

146

until it closed in on them before taking his massive right fist, stepping toward the creature, and bopping it in the forehead. Or what Tal guessed was the forehead. There was a gelatinous mass that might be an eye—or maybe three eyes——it was kind of hard to tell under the thick layer of suppurating ick. Even with only a smidgeon of Borras's full strength, the boperation appeared to be sufficient discouragement each time it was utilized. The disgusting creatures didn't abandon all hope of a meal, but followed them from then on at a respectful hundred paces back, easily grease-sliming their way through the burning hot sand.

The next animals they met were some asshat pterodactyl wannabes—who also decided the Omada group looked like an easy meal on the hoof. Some additional instances of Borras-bonking discouraged the flying varmints, each of Borras's blows knocking a beast unconscious. The snot worms apparently weren't picky eaters and each of Omada's devoted followers nabbed a couple of orders of wings to go. Never, ever was there the smallest sign of a wytch, not even a cackle, before they were Recalled.

The first two trips, however, didn't hold a candle to what happened on their third Journey.

CHAPTER VIGINTI NOVEM

Music—and Väst—were pretty much all that was keeping Tal sane this term. There were two distinct species of pressure at Hunts School—within the Omada because they were swinging and missing at wytch contact—and between all of the Finalist teams. Ordering them all to wear their Pucas during the entire school day may have been Ms. Empousa's only non-sadistic order to date.

Tal knew his individual stress was enhanced by the events happening on Earth plane proper. First, there was the entire Elle fiasco. The lying to his parents seemed to grind harder and harder each day, even though the hairball geas prevented him from telling them the truth. He'd finally convinced them he was finalizing his paper and wanted to finish strong on his project. Which was actually, pretty much, almost the truth. He and Emet decided a few weeks ago they had amassed enough data to really prepare a research paper and Emet had volunteered to knock it out. Tal had proofed the rough draft twice now and offered his comments. Emet had done a fantastic job on the project, and Tal told him so.

Which left only music and Väst as his positive daily activities. Tal made sure he had some personal time every day to embrace each. Old School had gotten tight music wise and the

149

easy going camaraderie Tal enjoyed with his group leavened his days.

His time with Väst was always brief and hurried. He sometimes wondered if stolen time felt that way for everyone. And if there is a subjective perception that stolen time is more precious, did that mean stolen time actually moved faster than normal time. Kind of like a theory of Naked Relativity?

Being with Väst was a betrayal of his teammates' trust. Tal knew it. Used to be he felt like he couldn't stop himself. Now it seemed to be more he didn't want to. Every time he was about to engage in a substantial self-debate about karma there would be a pair of the most pliable moist lips demanding his attention. The back of a hand softly caressing his jaw, diverting his thoughts from pondering "Seeking the Center." Or the most willing and unbelievably pliant nakedness banishing all philosophical conjecturing.

Something was different though between he and Väst. He couldn't put a finger on it. Piras made several sideways comments each time Tal took him off for his interludes with Väst. Piras's remarks never progressed past innuendo into any specific objections he might have to their illicit relationship. Tal hated to tell Piras but pliant nakedness trumped innuendo every day of the week.

CHAPTER TRIGINTA

Omada was due to leave on its third Journey in a couple of hours. Tal and Borras had decided to take a walk and enjoy the sun on their faces for a few minutes. In addition to calming their pre-Journey jitters, it gave them the opportunity to discuss team matters outside the environ of their team room.

"I've combed a large portion of the library trying to dig up information on wytches that no one else might have discovered. I found this," Borras said as he pulled his backpack around in front of him, reached inside and pulled out a book with a red leather binding and the roman numeral "XXIV" in gilt lettering on the spine.

"This being?" Tal asked.

Borras sat down on the closest bench and showed Tal the cover. "Volume Twenty-Four of the current 'Encyclopaedia of Current Events of Earth Realm.' Each Tyrning an Encyclopaedia is printed which contains the history of the Earth plane following the previous Tyrning. This particular volume concerns the history of North America."

"You mean the history of the United States," Tal said without thinking, as he sat down beside his friend and team captain.

Borras laughed. "Quint, at the last Tyrning, your

ancestors lived in British Colonies, and sang *'God Save the King,'* not *'My Country 'Tis of Thee.'* "

That certainly puts human life spans versus those of the Folk in perspective, Tal thought. "I don't get it. How would one of the newest books in the library have anything usable about wytches? Professor Elphinstone told us they all left Earth Realm when Arthrys imposed the first magykal bane."

"The professor also told us the Folk really know very little about wytches and we should search in places where others may have not thought to look," Borras added.

"True," Tal said as his brain kicked in to catch up with Borras, "Pretty smart move, Prime. Any of the other teams that are looking are researching ancient texts that have already been thoroughly studied."

"It's why I get paid the big bucks," Borras responded.

Something else I'd never thought about, Tal realized. "You don't actually get paid, do you?"

"No," Borras said smiling. "Well, not directly anyway. Most of the students here are some level of royalty on their home planes. Folk with the most powerful magyks are usually royal born, so they're independently wealthy. For everyone else, extremely well-paying positions await all of the students back in their home Realms. If Omada wins, our team gets to be the Ruling Council, which is a great honor, not only for us but for our home Realms."

"What about me?" Tal asked his friend somberly. "I wouldn't be able to go the distance if we win."

"You remain a puzzlement on many levels, Tal," Borras replied gently. "How you got here. Why you're here. You're a wyldcard in many respects."

"If we win, you would get to be Archon," Tal added.

Borras looked down at his massive fingers, his brow furrowed in contemplation. "It should have been Kentro. He was not only a born leader, he was a really good guy and would have known exactly what to do as Archon. Odds are he would have been one of the best ever."

Tal reached out with his left arm and tapped Borras's cable sized wrist a couple of times. "Hey, hey! None of that. Didn't know Kentro but I know the Omada Acting Prime and he seems to be a pretty good non-human himself."

"Thank you," Borras said looking back at Tal. "In addition to whatever personal magyks the new Archon may possess, he or she is imbued at the Coronation Ceremony with all of the resident magyk of Hunts School."

Tal whistled at that bit of news. "That's how Alberich can do so many things."

"Yes," Borras confirmed.

Tal pointed at the book. "Well, what pearls of wisdom did you harvest?"

"After a couple of hours scanning the table of contents and the index it was the section on the Hweeldi that caught my attention."

Well, there's a word I never heard before, Tal thought. I guess I really am a geek. There aren't too many things as fun as learning new words. Let's see—there's mugging down with Väst and staring at her glorious nakedness…there was talking on the phone with Elle about her day, with the prospect of actually going out on a date with her…there's thin crust pepperoni and black olive pizza. New knowledge is right up there, as well. Knewledge? Yes, please. "Okay, Professor, let me have it."

Borras read to Tal from the book. "During the mid-1800s there was a nation that was tortured, beaten, starved into submission, subjected to disease at epidemic levels, and marched over three hundred miles to a poorly constructed concentration camp. Depending upon the translation, the Hweeldi means either 'Fearing Time' or 'Land of Suffering'. "

"A concentration camp that was almost a hundred years before Hitler and Nazi Germany. Which one of the European countries did that?" Tal asked, trying to think his way though the possibilities of what country would commit such atrocities.

"European historical events are recounted in an entirely different volume," Borras replied. "The North American concentration camp was called Bosque Redondo. In their own tongue, the ravaged nation called themselves the Diné, which means 'the People'. "

"I've never heard of them," Tal said.

"You know them by the English translation of their name—the Navajo."

"Wow? It was the American government that did that?"

"Yes. There were some Apaches interned as well but there were over ten thousand Navajo who were forced to make the 'Long Walk' to Bosque Redondo. There is no accurate accounting of how many men, women and children perished. Hundreds for sure, maybe thousands."

"Why?" Tal asked, "Why did we do that to them?"

Borras read further before answering. "Says here the political explanation given by Earth plane historians was that the American government undertook an aggressive westward expansion under the guise of the doctrine of Manifest Destiny."

"I sort of remember that term from American History in eighth grade," Tal replied," but you're going to have to give me a quick refresher course."

Borras read another couple of paragraphs. "The fancy explanation is that Manifest Destiny is the theory that a dominant culture has the moral right, perhaps even the moral imperative, to supplant existing—and from their perspective—inferior cultures."

Tal gave a short, abrupt laugh. "I'm calling bullshit on that one. Whether on a societal or personal level, it's bullying. Plain and simple. Every sack of crap from William the Conqueror, to Genghis Khan, and Alexander the Great spouted that same mumbo-jumbo. I can tell you, from personal experience, the 'moral high ground' depends upon whether you're the 'inferior culture' getting your face violently manifest destinied against the metal school locker or whether you're the 'dominant culture' jamming an unwanted destiny down everyone else's throat."

"It's not as two-dimensional as that," Borras explained.

"The deeper philosophical argument is that the dominant culture's educational, scientific, and technical advantages ultimately provide a much higher quality of life for the inferior culture. Things like electricity, running water, and antibiotics."

"Don't forget other wonderful gifts, such as smallpox," Tal added.

"Those unfortunate situations do occur," Borras commented as he read another page. "The book says it has been a much discussed issue on Earth plane that's even been transported from philosophic discussions to pop culture. An example being the legend of Arthrys as related in the Broadway musical, 'Camelot.' At its core is the eternal question: does might make right, or right make might. Manifest Destiny argues the former."

"It still boils down to somebody kicking sand in the face of someone else because they deem them inferior in some respect. It's easy for you to read that textbook, Borras, and talk about it analytically like it occurs only on Earth Realm. It is exactly how the Folk treat humans. For that matter, it's exactly how the Folk treat the Pucas and the Cooshies, and all of the rest of the Creatures."

Tal could tell from Borras's face he'd never considered that issue before. In seconds, his face morphed from lips compressed in self-defensive anger, to eyebrows raised upward quizzical, to complexion reddened embarrassed. "Point taken," he finally replied. "Actually, point well taken and worth remembering."

"So, what does Volume XXIV have to do with wytches?" Tal asked.

"I have a theory," Borras replied. "I've been thinking about Professor Elphinstone's comments about wytch imposters."

"Both good wytches as well as bad wytches," Tal asked.

"That factoid right there was the key which unlocked my hypothesis," Borras said. "Have we discussed any stories in class, that were pre-Arthrys, where a member of the Cult of Nyx was all sugar and spice?"

Tal let his mind run through its index cards concerning all of this term's lectures. "No."

"Exactly," Borras said smiling. "It's because there were no good wytches, there were only bad wytches."

"Your proposition doesn't hold water," Tal replied. "Good and bad wytches as well as white and black magyk appear in every Earth culture. Maybe if the white magyk types appeared in only one or two societies..."

"It was Folk," Borras said.

"Can't be," Tal argued. "When Arthrys imposed his ban, the Folk stopped coming to Earth plane."

"You're right, Quint. However, the descendants of Folk and mortals remained."

Tal rolled Borras's statement around in his brain for a minute. Of course with all of the interaction between Folk and humans there would have been relationships. Väst and most of the rest of the Hunts School girls had been all over him wanting some of his "divine spark."

"That doesn't seem to work, Borras. Humans run on electricity and Folk on magyk. I don't see how there could be a zygote..."

"Your analysis is correct. There was an interspecies incompatibility with respect to normal conceptive processes. However, there were some instances where Folk, both men and women, with royal level creationmagyk mated with mortals and there were offspring."

"Magyk must have been the dominant genetic trait."

"It was," Borras confirmed. "As Folk are the UnFading One's Second Children it trumped the human component. Thus, the Nephilim."

"The etymology of 'blueblood' is actually based on a real thing then," Tal commented. "It originated as a reference to royal Folk whose blood was blue."

"Yep," Borras confirmed.

"What about when all of the Folk were ordered to leave

the Earth plane?" Tal asked.

"Arthrys gave all of the Nephilim an irrevocable choice—for both themselves and their descendants. To use the Prime Omphalos to travel to their ancestors' home Realms or to remain."

"If they remained, their magyk would be forever checked at the almost nonexistent level that wasn't prohibited by the ban," Tal said.

"Yes," Borras confirmed. "The Crestfallyn was only able to stalk you because both its magyk and corporeal existence were at the lowest level imaginable."

Tal shivered as he thought back to the terror that had stalked him his entire life, the ghoul that had laid claim to his face.

Borras continued. "Additionally, Arthrys used the power given to him as Archon to change their blood to red, and for those that were not already in human form, they became permanently anchored in the appearance of the Munedan.

"Wow. Can't even imagine making that kind of choice," Tal responded. "Creationmagyk is hereditary?" he asked.

"Yes," Borras confirmed. "It, as well as the secondary inherited magyks, would become more and more diluted every generation. But since the ban prohibited any meaningful level of magyk, that limitation never made a functional difference."

"Which means some of the people who claimed to be water dowsers, or seers, or magicians, might have…"

"Might have been children of the Nephilim, or they might have been complete frauds," Borras finished.

"Which also means any allegations of substantial magyk were grafted from stories told about the ancestors of the Nephilim," Tal mused.

"Yes," Borras replied looking up from his book. "Time to go meet the rest of the team to head over to the ziggurat."

CHAPTER TRIGINTA UNUS

'Piras?' Tal felt like there was a furnace-fired steel bar inexorably driving itself from the center of his brain out through the back of his left eye.

'I'm on it, Quint.'

'I'm hurting bad this time, buddy. Real bad,' Tal repeated, squeezing his eyes closed just to make sure none of the contents could be poked out. 'Ah, ah, DAMN! This reaction is way worse than either of the first two trips.'

'There, that should take care of it,' Piras replied.

Tal tentatively tried relaxing his face. There was still significant discomfort but it was beginning to abate. 'Much, much better,' he confirmed rubbing his forehead. 'Thanks.'

'You're welcome. I believe the contestants were warned multiple trips might yield adverse health consequences. Humans are interesting organically. You seem to be more susceptible than the Folk to adverse effects from multiple time-proximate Journeys. However, your integration quotient with the Puca is much higher than the average Folk.'

'Your words are making my head hurt,' Tal thought-replied.

'Bottom line, Quint of the Omada, if I were not with you for this Journey you would have unquestionably suffered permanent brain damage.'

'What the hell?'

'Perhaps even a fatal aneurysm,' Piras added. 'I have alleviated the constriction of your supraorbital blood vessels and redirected additional oxygen to the area surrounding the margins of your orbits. This should substantially diminish the Journey pain and allow you to function more efficiently.'

Tal felt the flaming ingot of pain soften and begin to melt away into the surrounding tissue.

"Omada, sound off," Borras commanded.

"It was a little rocky Prime, but Orseis has me fixed up," Dysi promptly replied.

"That was a real slobberknocker," Anatolia added. "I've already thanked Caliadne. I don't think I'd be standing if it wasn't for her."

"Let's get with it," Notos said with his customary dour expression.

"I'm squared away, too," Tal said, as he mentally confirmed with Piras that the pain remnants had dissipated.

"Excellent." Borras lifted the gray carrying strap off of his shoulder and unzipped their canvas duffel bag. Like the other Journeys this term, they'd been allowed to bring one team bag. Whatever they could fit in their team bag could make the trip.

The Journeys were exactly three hours in duration EPT. Depending upon the Realm visited, that three hours could mean only ten minutes or an entire week. Funny thing, Time. Tal thought. Take one precise single moment. To one person it might be less than a heart's beat, while to another that moment might be their eternity. No wonder the Folk said Chronos was second only to Amarantos.

They had loaded the bag with only the absolute necessities. Even without his magykal strength, the bag weight would never be a problem for Borras but they had to plan for the worst. If Borras was killed or incapacitated, or in case they needed to move fast, they'd decided the duffel needed to be as light as possible. Anatolia insisted on bringing her basic medkit. There was never any knowing whose magyk might work on any given plane, or at what strength level.

In case it was one of the slow-time Realms they had also brought some potable water and a few packages of RHVs—ready to heat victuals. Tal laughed to himself. That's what it said on the package from the cafeteria, "ready to heat victuals." Most importantly, they'd included two of the three scavengyr pieces Omada had acquired last term—Fragarach and the Ring of Gyges. Fragarach, one of the major swords of power, could command the winds in its immediate vicinity and any cut with its blade—no matter how minor—was fatal. Guaranteed. One hundred percent. Fatal. Tal had successfully used Fragarach to win the Combat Challenge against Väst. Successfully, as in pretty much killing her dead. At least she would have been if he hadn't burned one of his three wishes from Aurora's ring to heal her.

The second piece was the Ring of Gyges—one of the major invisibility artifacts. Since defensive weapons had been banned in the Combat Challenge, Omada hadn't had an opportunity to use the ring in a battle situation. They had each practiced with it though, taking turns in the secrecy of their team room, laughing like simpletons each time someone winked in and out of sight. Well, not Notos, of course, but the rest of them had laughed. Practice had provided them with some extremely valuable information, most importantly that the only sense the ring masked was sight. It did not affect touch, smell, or hearing. Or taste for that matter. Perhaps even more importantly, you had to be completely naked for it to be effective.

Their third scavengyr piece, Skofnung, was stored back in the team room. After seeing what happened in the arena to Nord, the now deceased former Släkt Prime Direction, no one wanted to take a chance Skofnung's hilt might be exposed to sunlight in the uncontrolled situation of a Journey.

"All of our gear made it intact," Borras announced as he zipped the bag back up and slung it over his shoulder. "Site assessment is next." Following his training, Tal began scoping out their landing site. The Omphalos they'd been sent to on this plane was an ancient tree. It looked like it belonged to a species of giant cypress. Its age wasn't expressed in height or girth but rather in the labyrinthine limb segments erupting from the ground. The stressors of age and wind had transformed the tree into a unique work of art. As Tal continued looking around, he ascertained the Omphalos Tree was the most wizened, regal cypress, presiding over a court composed of hundreds of younger lookalikes, each growing on its own small island. The islands were shiny jewels of green plants set within hundreds, maybe thousands of small rivulets. As Tal looked over his shoulder, back upstream, he saw the water originated from a scaled down version of Victoria Falls. Rainbows and mist chased each other without pause, as the sun played hide and seek behind some elephantine cirrus clouds.

Tal had no idea what plane they were on but it was a gorgeous place. Rainbow trout—or their doppelgangers—flashed as they arched their bodies skyward, looking no doubt to snag one of the large dragonfly looking insects buzzing close to the water's surface. None of the multitude of bird sounds were familiar but together with the rushing water they were laying down a beautiful backing soundtrack. It's Nirvanaesque, Tal decided. I think Väst would love this place. And Elle too, he thought, guiltily.

"I'm not connecting any dots," Anatolia said.

"Me either," Dysi added. "I don't think it's a Realm that's been catalogued."

"No indication of hostiles in the immediate vicinity," Notos said as he continued to scan, turn, and recheck.

'I can't figure it out either," Borras announced. "Moment of truth—juice check."

Dysi self-combusted, rainbow confetti exploding silently from where she'd been standing. She reappeared on an island about twenty feet away, a huge grin on her face. Again there was the quick bloom of multi-colored instantly-dissolving particles

162

and then she was gone again, appearing three islands over, waving her arms like a madwoman, before dissipating once again. This time when she reappeared she was laughing. Another mute detonation, Dysi vanished, and reappeared standing right next to Borras. Tal assumed she was doing the Folk version of the Snoopy happy dance—which was the same as the human version of the Snoopy happy dance. Face thrown upward toward the heavens, mouth stretched a smile wide, and her feet joy-tapping at close to mach speed.

Her glee was infectious. Borras whistled happily. "I'll take that as Dysi reporting in at full strength."

"Better," she confirmed. "With Orseis helping me I think I can teleport farther than I ever thought possible."

"Anatolia?" Borras asked.

There was a small cypress knee waterside by Ana's feet. She got down on one knee, cupped her hands, filled them with water and brought her hands to her lips. She then whispered something to the water before carefully using it to baptize the crest of the cypress knee. After that she took a giant step back towards the Omada. Tal watched as the cypress knee shook itself, like a wet dog after a bath, and then it began to grow. A foot, two feet, four, then seven. Ana walked back to it, laid her palm upon the trunk of the new tree and whispered to it. It stopped growing. She turned back to her team. Wow, I only thought she was beautiful before, Tal thought. She's transcendent with her face beaming like that.

"Same as Dysi," Ana, said motioning to her Puca. "Caliadne is a blessing. I have never grown anything so quickly. Excepting our one trip to Earth plane, when I created Emet, this is the only time in a hundred years I've been able to fully use my gyfts. It's indescribable. Notos, you go."

Notos gave Ana a hard stare. What's up with him, Tal wondered. It's show and tell for everyone else and they're ecstatic to have the opportunity to go full out magyk with their Pucas.

"I am at full strength, Prime," Notos said. "Although the Puca can and does augment my physical abilities, there is, of course, nothing it can do to augment my magyk itself."

Why, the hell not, Tal wondered. Since everyone else seemed to be in the know, he let it slide. I can figure it out sooner or later, Tal decided.

"And you?" Ana quickly asked Borras, to change the mood.

Borras's reply was a doublewide grin. He squatted until his ass almost touched the ground…and then he jumped. At least Tal was pretty sure the motion could be categorized as a jump. Klipspringers are the highest jumping mammals relative to body height. They can jump about ten times their own height. The jumping king of the entire animal kingdom is the flea. It can jump about one hundred fifty times its own height.

Tal decided Puca-assisted Borras may have topped that record. He kept rising until Tal could barely see the soles of his shoes against the white clouds in the light blue of the mid-day sky. Then they started growing larger as Borras free fell back to earth. Oh shit, Tal thought, he's going to break every bone in his body when he lands. Or leave a humongous impact crater. Right where I'm standing.

When Borras landed, his oversized knees were like robotic hinges. They flexed on impact, absorbing almost all of the landing's energy. Tal was less than five feet away and felt no movement in the ground.

Borras roared with joy. "I can't believe how much I've missed being completely me. Well, not completely me," he said making a circular motion encompassing his human form, "but having my magyk restored is wonderful."

"Time for us to get moving," Notos reminded them all. "We only have a limited window to get our talysman…or be murdered and have our corpses desecrated in some bizarre wytch ritual."

Warm fuzzies, Tal thought. Warm fuzzies must be Notos's major magyk.

"Which way?" Dysi asked, taking a slow three hundred sixty degree turn.

"Even with our Pucas helping us, we're obviously not going up and over the falls," Tal observed.

"I agree with Quint," Borras said, nodding in agreement. He pointed to their left and then their right. "There are substantial outflows from the falls flanking us on both sides. It appears we can step from island to island until we get to that forest about a half mile ahead." Everyone else nodded their assent.

"I just realized, we're going to see the Wicked Wytch of the West," Tal said. "Maybe we should take a bucket of water." The rest of the team was staring at Tal blankly. "Well, you know, in case…"

"In case we get thirsty?" Anatolia asked.

"Yeah, that," Tal said, resignedly.

"Quit being stupid, Quint. You know our water is contained in bottles and we didn't bring a bucket anyway," Notos said with his usual scowl.

He has the best resting bitch face ever, Tal decided.

As Borras was about to leap away, the world rippled. That's not quite right, Tal thought. Everything is still in its proper place. It wasn't an earthquake, there wasn't a thing or a person out of place. Tal's brain told him he'd seen something as well as felt it. Even the air itself had gone all squiggly before becoming regular old air again. "Umm, what was that?" he asked.

"What was what?" Anatolia asked.

"The, umm, potentially fourth dimension space-time dimensional warping," Tal replied. Looking around he saw vacuous, vacuous, vacuous, and finally…vacuous. "Fine," he added. "The ripple, what about the ripple?"

"Great, now he's seeing things," Notos said. "Not only a human but a mentally deficient human at that."

"Borras?" Tal turned to his Prime, looking for confirmation. All he got was a negative headshake.

Dysi walked over to Borras and tapped on the canvas bag. "This is such a gorgeous place. Let's have a picnic."

"That's a wonderful idea," Ana added. "We never have time to relax and enjoy each other's company."

"It would be pleasant to sit and chat for a little while," Notos said, with a half-smile on his face.

'Piras?' Tal thought-questioned his Puca.

'Yes, Quint.'

"What's happening?'

'It appears your teammates are hungry and want to sit and eat and get to know each other better.'

This is jacked up, Tal thought. Something happened and none of them, not even the Pucas, registered it. No, no, no, this isn't right. "Borras, don't you think we should, well, that we should go try to find the wytch and get the talysman thing and all of that?"

Borras laughed affably. "Dust Children. Always in such a hurry. How are you going to have the energy to engage in conflict with a wytch without the proper nutrition?" He sat down, opened the bag, and started taking the meals out. "Notos, you and Dysi grab us some kindling. Please."

"Sure thing, Prime," Notos responded as he ran off to perform his assigned chore.

What? What? Tal asked himself. Notos is whistling and humming as he and Dysi go to collect firewood? "Prime, we're on the clock here. We have to go try to find a wytch. We're on the clock," he repeated urgently.

"Ah, ambrosia," Borras said, clearly pleased someone had thought to grab some from the cafeteria. After eating a large spoonful, he turned his attention back to Tal. "Fifth, not another word about the Hunt. I am ordering you to sit and enjoy yourself. What could be more important than eating and getting to know your teammates better in this beautiful place that Amarantos has created. There's plenty of time for us to go meet a wytch." Tal did as he was told.

They were all five still sitting there—one pensive and four nibbling and nattering—when the Recall took them home.

CHAPTER THIRTY-TWO

'Can you explain to me exactly what the hell happened on that Journey?' It was midnight and Tal had asked himself and/or Emet that same question about once every ninety seconds for the last two hours. He and Emet were alone in Tal's bedroom, the rest of the house long since sensibly having gone to bed. Emet didn't need the sleep. Tal did. He was exhausted and his old pal, the migraine, was back. Trip-hammering his poor, abused skull. Piras was, of course, back at Hunts School and the demon pain presently taking continuous shots at his brain shrugged off all mortal analgesics. Tal knew he needed to sleep but he couldn't. Not until the mystery was solved.

With Emet typing and Tal verbally responding, they'd volleyed possibilities back and forth. Dozens of suggestions proffered, then almost immediately rejected. 'I feel like we're repeating suggestions we've previously discarded,' Emet typed. Tal tiredly nodded his agreement.

Emet's fingers flashed across his cellphone keyboard and Tal's laptop dinged. 'Let's start over, one final time. If we don't nail it down, we'll call it quits.'

"Agreed," Tal replied. "Three Journeys. Two inhospitable Realms, one pretty much the Garden of Eden."

'Your team consists of four Folk, presumably all from

different planes with different magyks, plus one nonmagykal human,' Emet added.

Tal nodded. "Some event occurred. I felt it and I saw it. Two separate senses. It didn't register with any of the Folk at any level." This time there was no response from Emet. Tal knew he hadn't drifted off. Emet didn't sleep, or daydream. "Emet?"

'Tal, we have completely discounted the Pucas.'

"No, we haven't. I've told you several times how they healed each of us."

'Exactly. They're magykal beings like the Folk.'

"Right," Tal agreed, puzzled.

'The repeated Journeying adversely impacts both Folk and Dust Children.'

"But not the Puca—"

'Triangulate the data, Tal. Some magyk beings and all non-magyk are affected by multiple Journeys.'

"Right. But all magyk beings and no non-magyk were affected by the unknown 'event'."

'Journeys using the Prime Omphalos are normal, ordinary magyk from Amarantos.'

Tal smiled for the first time in hours. "I get it. Using the Journeys as our test baseline, the deviation in effect means the 'event' was not a natural magykal occurrence."

Emet mused a moment longer as he reviewed all of the causation possibilities. 'Whatever happened was an intentionally created occurrence outside of the normal magyk constructs.'

"Right," Tal said a little louder before realizing his excitement could get their conversation shut down if they woke either of the parents. "The magyk was intentionally designed to affect all magykal beings in the known Folk universe. It didn't affect me because it never occurred to the precipitator that a Dust Child might be along for the ride."

'Nope,' Emet typed as he nodded his head. 'Which leaves one remaining question.'

"Why," Tal replied.

CHAPTER TRIGINTA TRES

"Have you each consulted your Pucas?" Borras asked.

All Omada noggins engaged in synchronized nodding. The HuntsMistress had canceled Combat for this afternoon. Given the extra time before Tal had to leave for home, Borras had contacted his teammates, requested they discuss the recent Journeys with their Pucas, and called an extra Omada team meeting. Their team room was the only guaranteed secure place for them to make decisions about private team matters. Given the nature of the planned discussion, Borras had requested they remove their Pucas upon entering the team room today.

Actually, Tal hadn't been wearing Piras since immediately after eating lunch. He'd spent the afternoon with Väst. Naked. He knew he should feel at least a little guilty about it. For several reasons. The time could have been spent researching in the library. But, it was Väst. Naked. Their relationship had already caused a near cataclysmic kerfuffle between he and his teammates. Hello? It was Väst. Naked. He'd been justifying his actions by repeating to himself that it was only because he and Piras's points in Combat and his scores on the weekly tests, that Omada might still make the cut at the end of the term. His mature, adult mind told him the bottom line was he was lying and that he wasn't giving his team a hundred percent. The substantially less mature portion of his brain simply kept repeating, Väst—naked. Väst—naked. Väst… Whether because of guilt or prudence, Tal had decided he'd maintain a low profile at the team meeting and not discuss his and Emet's conclusions until everyone else had a chance to say their piece.

"Okay, let's hear it," Borras said, nodding to Anatolia, who was seated to his immediate left.

"It's not good, Prime," she replied. "The adverse sequela sustained from multiple travels within a short time period are exponential. I realize what we hear in the hallways and cafeteria from other Finalists could be intentionally misleading—or mere puffery—but there is a consistency to the grumbling from the other teams. All indications are they are experiencing similar reactions. Caliadne told me it was our Pucas' collective opinion we were fortunate with respect to the sequencing of our destination planes. For our first two Journeys we were sent to Realms where our magyk was at minimal strength. Thank Amarantos we were at full strength on the third trip. Caliadne said she had to use every bit of her synergy with me to prevent some major negative physical event."

Borras put his gigantic hand over hers. It covered her hand, wrist, and almost all of her notepad. "Caliadne's point being that if one of the minimal strength planes had been our third trip, the Puca couldn't have helped us enough to keep us physically, or perhaps mentally, intact."

"Exactly," Anatolia confirmed.

"Orseis explained it to me in pretty much the same terms," Dysi added. "She also mentioned we need to consider a scenario where some of us might be at full strength and others only at a minimal level."

It was Notos's turn. "She wasn't only talking about us. She meant we might luck out and go to a plane where the Folk were at full power but our Pucas might be restricted and unable to save us." Tal saw Dysi pale a little at this previously unconsidered element of danger.

"If Ana was at full strength, though …" Tal started to say.

"If she's not, who is going to fix her so she can fix us, human?" Notos snapped.

Borras reined the conversation back in. "Quint?"

"Piras chose to give me multiple extremely graphic scenarios. Most of the possibilities included parts of my body which should always, always remain on the inside, ending up on the outside."

"I got about the same warning from Koios," Borras concluded, before folding his hands together on the table. "So, we need to realistically assess our options."

"There is no option, Prime, if we want to win the Tyrning," Notos said matter of factly.

"That's not necessarily true," Dysi replied. "I know we've previously discussed the issue but I think it's time we put the bluff strategy back on the table. I think we're pretty high on non-Hunt points. If only two other teams get wytch points we might still make the final cut to three teams."

"We've already voted against that strategy. It would leave our hands in the fate of others," Notos said shortly.

"You know as well as I do that we won't even be eligible to win if we don't have at least four non-maimed team members present at the Hunt ceremony!" Dysi snapped right back.

"Same team," Borras calmly reminded them all. "It is both a privilege and an obligation to be enrolled in Hunts School. We are tasked not merely with trying to win the Tyrning, but doing so by Seeking the Center."

Whatever that means, Tal thought.

"We need to analyze it from a risk-reward perspective," Anatolia said.

"Agreed," Borras replied. "We've now learned first-hand the prohibition against more than one Journey a week was based on a hard physical reality. Actually, once a week may be too frequent. We've only had three weekly Journeys and the repeated travel is already about to take us out."

Notos stepped in. "Only four weeks remain in this term, Prime. The smart play seems to be to balance Dysi's thoughts with Anatolia's proposed equation."

Way to be constructive, Notos, Tal thought. Didn't think you had it in you.

"Since our travel tolerance grows less each Journey, it looks like we can only reasonably expect to survive one, maybe two more Journeys this term," Borras added. Each of the others nodded their agreement.

After a few seconds of silence, Anatolia spoke up. "We have been to three different Realms. On each Journey we ended up with the exact same result—we failed to even make contact with a wytch."

"We're missing something," Dysi added.

"I agree," Notos said.

"But what?" Borras asked." There doesn't seem to be any need to keep flailing away at Journeying if we can't figure out what's wrong."

Maybe it's time to tell them what Emet and I decided, Tal thought. The best way to test the validity of our conclusion though is to see if they independently reach the same result. He took his notebook out so he could make a list. "Let's do some collective deductive reasoning. What do we know about each of the planes?"

Anatolia started. "The Prime Omphalos was only supposed to send us to Realms where there is a wytch within Journey distance."

"Right," Tal said, writing that down as bullet point number one. " A wytch was present on each of those Realms."

"There was no indication of other Folk on those planes," Borras added. Emet and I missed that point, Tal thought. Going through this process is already proving useful.

Notos spoke up. "The first two Realms were quite hostile to our presence."

"I hadn't thought about that," Anatolia mused. "The first

two Journeys, the Prime Omphalos sent us to terrible, life-threatening places. The third plane was idyllic."

Tal wrote it down. "Two planes terrible, one plane wonderful." *This is where Emet and I got to last night—the "why" question.* As he wrote the words, his subconscious went all random on him to a conversation he and Emet had last week. The class had been discussing the history of warfare in Emet's World Civ class. About how siege battles were more likely won by strong defensive positioning rather than by an offensive blitzkrieg. *Were the conditions on the destination Realms, different sides of that same, exact coin?*

"Quint?" Borras asked, interrupting his musing. "Do you have anything to add to the list?"

Everyone else has had their say and none of them remember the shimmer, or chastising me for bringing it up. "I have the same thing to add as I did during our last Journey itself. There was a ripple. Maybe, it was only an atmospheric anomaly endemic to that Realm."

"What did you say?" Borras asked, a stunned look starting in his left lower facial quadrant and moving like a slow high-pressure front up and over his mountain range of a nose, heading toward the steppes of his right temple.

Tal saw Notos starting to get up out of his seat. "You stupid, idiot cretin of a Munedan!" he screamed.

"Stop it!" Borras said to Notos, gently but inexorably pushing him back into his chair. "Tell us what you're talking about, Quint."

"Everyone had checked out their magyk and all of the Folk, as well as the Puca, reported they were at full strength. Right after you announced we were going to look for the wytch, I felt a..., well..., the air..., it shuddered. For a split-second. After that you changed your mind and said we should all sit down and eat. When I mentioned we were on a tight time schedule you told me to shut up because everyone else wanted to sit down and eat a picnic lunch and have some quality time with each other." Tal looked at his teammates who were now all staring blankly at him.

"No really, Notos even told an amusing anecdote."

Borras looked at each of the other Omada, in turn. First, at Anatolia.

"I'm sorry Quint but that's not what happened." she replied. "We all saw Dysi take point and teleport to the summit of the humongous falls while Borras ferried us up one at a time to the top. We searched and searched and came up empty handed," she replied.

Dysi, now looking bewildered, answered next. "That's not what happened, Ana. We decided the safest course was for me to try to see what was on the other side of the forest. By the time of the Recall, I was completely exhausted from dozens of hops. I heard lots of birds and saw some medium-sized arboreal animals but there weren't any wytch signs."

It was now around the table to Notos. His anger at Tal replaced with an expression evidencing curiosity. "Interesting. I would oath-swear we decided the best strategy was to split into three teams, the mortal with Borras, Dysi with Anatolia, and me solo. We didn't meet up again until after the Recall. Same net result. No evidence of any wytch."

Borras turned back to Tal. "Did you ask your Puca during real time about this 'ripple'?"

"Yes," Tal replied. "Piras told me nothing happened, and that I was imagining things. He also said I should chill out and enjoy the lunch and the camaraderie."

Borras let out a low whistle. "Jynx," he stated matter of factly. The rest of the team nodded their heads.

"What?" Tal asked.

"Here we go again spending time on remedial education," Notos snapped.

"Notos, if Quint hadn't been with us, we wouldn't even have known we'd been spelled," Anatolia replied.

"That's true," Borras agreed before answering Tal. "A jynx is an insanely powerful subject-specific geas."

"Prime, we're all from different planes," Dysi interjected. "No one has the magyk to simultaneously jynx four species of

Folk, as well as five Puca."

"No one who is of the Folk," Borras said, ominously.

Tal noticed Anatolia had turned several shades whiter. "Are you thinking a single wytch has that kind of power?" she asked.

"Seems to be the most rational explanation," Borras replied. "We don't know anything about how their syphons work. They may have magyk from many different Folk stored up." He took a deep breath. "What does this mean for us and for our completion of this term's objective?"

That's it, Tal thought. Thank you Emet for your genius and thank your subconscious for never sleeping on the job. "It means we only have to take one more Journey—back to Realm Number Three."

CHAPTER TRIGINTA QUATTUOR

Ms. Empousa was doing her normal slinking around the classroom thing. Well, Tal decided, slinking wasn't really the correct word because she invariably walked like the entire school was her bitch. But it wasn't striding either. Stomping really didn't fit as she was wearing knee high laced up the back black leather boots with three-inch stiletto heels. High up the outside of each boot was a custom-designed sheath, holstering an ivory-handled curved karambit. Well, it looked like ivory but was probably some similar banned substance from another plane.

Actually, if the movement of a four-legged lioness who had been patiently stalking her prey for hours and who intended in the next split second to leap upon her kill, rip out its jugular, and sink her entire face snout deep in the gore of the mutilated soft tissue of its neck and chest was somehow translated to a bipedal movement, then that would be exactly what the HuntsMistress's normal gait was like. Like a predator—always stalking, always prepared to deliver death.

"Today, we're going to discuss this Tyrning's field trip. Many cycles past, before magyk was prohibited on the Earth plane, magyk was utilized to transport students to various areas of the planet for the field trip. The purpose of the trips was to observe dominant cultures of that particular era. During those

Hunts cycles, this geographical area was sparsely inhabited, with the native population being primarily hunter-gatherer groups.

"With the imposition of the magykal ban, a decision was made to limit field trips geographically. Since the last Tyrning, this area of the Earth Realm has seen a significant increase in its human population. For the first time ever in the history of the Hunts School, the Hunts Finalists are going to interact socially with the Munedan as part of the study curriculum."

Tal heard the beginnings of an epidemic of excited utterance, which was quickly quelled by some epic stinkeye from the HuntsMistress. "Shut it! All of you! If I hear even a particularly nasally breath, I'm cancelling the entire trip."

Bingo. She wins the game of "Turn That Room Into A Tomb," in one sentence.

"Principal Chiron and I have already had several meetings with the Archon himself about this trip. Setting protocols and safeguards. The Hunts faculty, the Hunts Finalists—and their dates—will be attending a pagan ritual known as Winter Formal at the school geographically closest to Hunts School."

Oh shit, Tal thought. That's...

"Nemeton High School is the name of the institution," the HuntsMistress said. "Professor Elphinstone will give you the specs." With that and without even a glance around the room, she stalked out.

Jubilant. Even the normally dour members of each of the squads were cracking wise and making giggly noises. Tal's teammates were elated. Ana and Dysi were already talking hair and wardrobe choices. Notos almost slipped up and smiled. The pretty much always serious group of Folk who were engaged in life and death battles in a bid to run the entire known universe were having gleeful conniptions about attending a high school dance.

Every single soul in the room was expressing their own version of ecstatic. Every single soul except one—Tal. His sole, repeating thought as they all marched out of the room was, "I am so screwed. I am so screwed. I am so...screwed."

CHAPTER TRIGINTA QUINQUE

"You've lost your mind," Notos replied, giving Tal one of his mid-level "you're-a-dumbass-human" looks. The Omada was back in their team room checking their equipment and reloading the team bag.

In return, Borras shot Notos a high-level shut-it look. Which apparently worked. "Why, Quint?" Borras asked. "Even if we could somehow communicate to the Prime Omphalos that we want to return to that plane—why would we?"

"Yeah," Notos chimed in. "We need a talysman, not another picnic lunch."

Tal wanted to jump down Notos's throat but he remembered all of the times Borras had stepped up as a true leader. Throwing gasoline on Notos's negativity fire wouldn't accomplish any team objective. So, he didn't take Notos's bait. "We're all in agreement that each additional Journey is taking a greater and greater toll on us. Practically speaking, I think we're down to one solid shot at scoring a home run for this term."

"I think we're all willing to accept that fact," Borras said, as he glanced around the room for confirmation. The other three all nodded their heads.

Tal continued. "We know there is a wytch on the third plane."

Notos started to say something smartass but was quickly shut down by their Prime. "Again, we are all in agreement. That is one of the conditions of being sent to any plane this term."

"We know that both Folk and Puca are at full strength there."

Anatolia raised her hand and Borras nodded for her to proceed. "I agree with everything you've said so far, Quint. We know we can physically survive Journeying to that plane. How does that translate into burning our last Journey for a do-over?"

Here goes nothing, Tal thought. "I think one of the two or three most powerful wytches in the Cult of Nyx lives on Realm Three."

"I see what Quint's saying," Dysi said, not bothering to raise her hand. "The first plane might have been bad guessing by us. We may have simply gone the wrong way and used up our time. The second Realm was physically dangerous to us without the necessity of magyk being utilized. The jynx used against us on our third Journey requires someone who wields significant power."

Thank goodness for Dysi. "Yes," Tal agreed. "Ergo, an extremely powerful wytch in residence."

"I agree with the logic of his conclusion," Dysi added.

"Assuming your conclusion is valid, why would we waste our final chance to get a talysman by going back?" Borras asked. "The jynx is going to take us out again."

Interestingly, it was Notos who answered. "There are several potential ways to cure the problem, Prime. By their very nature, jynx only affect conscious minds. Although Anatolia can't perform any magyk while we're at Hunts School, she could pack all of the necessary ingredients and equipment necessary to make a sleeping potion."

"How long would it take you to whip that up in-country?" Borras asked Ana.

"Since I won't have to look for the ingredients and can have them premeasured and ready, only a couple of minutes," she answered.

"We could take our Pucas off right after they heal us, which would reduce them to their semi-conscious state," Borras added. "Assuming we can get back to that Realm and assuming we knock ourselves out before the jynx launches, what guarantee do we have that we don't sleep away our entire Journey time?"

Before anyone could answer Borras's question, Notos stood up and slapped his hands on the table. "I think we've missed part of a multi-layered defense system. Why did we hang around the Omphalos site until the jynx whacked us? Why weren't we already off exploring like we did on the other two Realms?"

"Wow!" Anatolia exclaimed. "The Omphalos site itself is enamoured." Notos nodded his head in agreement.

I don't have the faintest idea what they're talking about, Tal told himself, very quietly.

Borras ran with Notos's observation. "Your theory is the Omphalos site has a permanent enamour to encourage anyone who shows up to stay there and not wander off until the jynx has time to kick them in the head."

Anatolia was shaking her head, worry lines having appeared on her forehead. "I don't know that I could even compute the amount of magykal energy a permanent enamour would require. Plus there's the sizeable energy needed for the jynx."

"If we head out right after healing we should get clear of the jynx blast radius," Notos mused.

"And if we don't make it?" Borras asked. "Or if we can't get outside the jynx radius?"

"That's where your friendly neighborhood failsafe kicks in," Tal replied. As they all stared at him, not understanding, he added, "Me. Your lowly Dust Child," Tal said, smiling. He could tell from their faces they still weren't up to speed. "Borras is our Prime Direction. All of us are bound by the contract, so all of you would be contractually bound to respond to any command he issues."

"That's a correct factual statement, Quint," Dysi said puzzled. "But Borras would be knocked out like the rest of us."

Tal held up his notebook and his pen and placed them in front of Borras. "I won't be, and I can deliver each of you a hand-written note signed by your Prime Direction telling you that you've been jynxed and ordering your conscious mind to reject the jynx and proceed on the wytch hunt."

"What about me" Borras asked.

"Aren't you bound by the contract just like the rest of us?" Tal asked.

"Actually, I am," Borras said, laughing a little. "So, I will also order myself to ignore the jynx. Brilliant!" Borras exclaimed, pounding the table so hard the wall sconce lights flickered. "I say we give it a go, yes?" he asked raising his hand.

As soon as all five hands were raised they headed out the door for their last wytch hunt Journey.

CHAPTER TRIGINTA SEX

"Okay, Brain Trust, what's your master plan to buy us a return ticket?"

Tal didn't really feel like he could get pissy with Notos at this exact moment. Seeing as how he didn't have a master plan. Actually, not even the structural components of a mediocre plan. He had a couple of not quite random thoughts spit-pasted together. Calling them a plan would have been a sizeable overstatement.

They were in the Prime Omphalos chamber, geared up and wearing their Pucas. It was their turn in the team rotation for departure. They knew this was the last Journey possible this term. All of their gear had been carefully repacked in their travel bag. Anatolia double and triple checked her sleeping potion items, making sure there were extra amounts of each ingredient, and that each of the ingredients was secured in a separate waterproof pouch.

There were two possible outcomes today. A Journey to an unknown plane where their Pucas might not be able to heal them, or a return to Realm Three, where there was a probability one of the most powerful wytches who ever lived, resided. In either possibility there was a good chance one or more of them might be maimed or killed. Good times at Hunts School, Tal thought.

His thoughts kept returning to the events surrounding the Omada's final first term Journey. When Tal's thoughts about draugrs had overridden the Omada Prime Direction's instructions to the Prime Omphalos. They'd ended up meeting Helblad, and obtaining both their swords of power which had kept them in the Hunts. Of course Tal had also had to treasyre bargain away his life. Unless he brought Aislinn, Helblad's several thousand year old love, back to him by the Tyrning's Coronation Day.

The salient part of that experience was what happened here, in the Prime Omphalos Chamber. The Hunts Rules provided that on directed Journeys, the Prime Direction provided the request to the Prime Omphalos. He or she occupied the pivotal center spot, in the hole within the Omphalos itself. Tal had been hanging upside down, in the traditional Fifth position, and yet it was his brain that had caused them to end up with Helblad.

His "master plan" then was to try to recreate what had happened. The Journeys this term weren't directed Journeys. It was totally up to the Prime Omphalos where to send the teams. There was no question though that the Prime Omphalos had zeroed in on his human thoughts at least one time before. Why not again? So, he was hanging upside down now, thinking about Realm Three, getting ready to announce "ready" to Borras. How does the Prime Omphalos decide where we go, he wondered. Is it sentient? Does it have free will? Those questions raised a host of additional questions, like…

"Quint?"

Focus, Tal, focus. "Ready!"

There was a flash, and some spinning, and…

CHAPTER TRIGINTA SEPTEM

"Gauggh!" Tal had tried to scream a stream of his favorite epithets and that's all that would come out of his clenched jaws. The skin of his face felt like it was on a medieval rack, being stretched up and over the crown of his head. His old buddy, the superheated metal bar, had become twins, each thrusting outward through an eyeball. The pain was so great he almost couldn't focus enough to understand Piras.

'I'm trying Quint.'

"MOTHERFUCKER!" Tal screamed involuntarily, his words being joined by similar profane expressions in various languages from everyone else.

'I must be helping some,' Piras thought-replied. 'That was at least an intelligible utterance. Quint, this is bad. I'm going to have to take you off-line for a few seconds. I consent. Do you?'

"I consent..." Tal replied, before blanking out.

"Quint! Quint!" It sounded to Tal like Borras was yelling at him from about two rooms away. Borras's English didn't sound none too good either, kind of woozyish. No, wait, that's me, I'm woozyish. 'Piras?'

'I'm bringing you slowly up to consciousness. Kind of a neural form of decompression.' Tal nodded his head in response to Piras.

"Thank, Amarantos! You're alive," Dysi exclaimed as she threw herself down onto his prone form, hugging him tightly.

Tal shook his head, both physically and metaphysically, trying to clear it. 'Piras, old buddy, is there something we need to discuss?'

'We have previously spoken about humans having a greater susceptibility to time-proximate multiple Journey fatigue.'

'Um, yeah, we have. I didn't think I was maybe-kind-of-probably going to die this trip.'

'Neither did I, Quint. But you almost did.'

Tal felt Borras's gigantic arms gently move Dysi off him before lifting Tal to his feet. "Quint? Are you with us?"

"I'm good to go," Tal said, as he wobbled a step before immediately sinking back to the ground. "Well, my knees aren't quite ready yet but I have no doubt they'll come around."

Anatolia came over and hugged him. "Quint, we thought you'd perished."

Notos chimed in, "In all candor, from a technical perspective, there might have been about fifteen seconds where you were clinically dead."

'What? What?' Tal screamed inside his own head.

"Way to almost cock the whole thing up, Dust Child. You being dead was totally going to trash your 'master plan'," Notos added dryly.

"Wait," Tal said. "You mean it worked?"

They all circled round him, each of them smiling. Even Notos. Well, the corners of his mouth couldn't quite make the upward curve but he was clearly trying. As Tal turned to look at each of them he could see the magnificent falls, the immediate landscape composed of burbling streams and small islets, each crowned with its own large scale bonsai cypress. The place really was idyllic.

"Well, don't just sit there," Borras said, extending his paw to Tal to help him up again. "We have to go try to not get killed or horribly maimed by an extremely powerful wytch."

CHAPTER TRIGINTA OCTO

It turned out to be a really good thing Tal hadn't died. For a lot of very important reasons, now that he thought about it, but most importantly because his survival was necessary for the Omada to remain contenders.

Borras had ferried them all, two at a time since he was at full strength, over hundreds of the tiny islands. The land-locked archipelago ended with the rivers and streams disappearing into a forest. "Forest" didn't quite do the area justice. The trees were different than the gnarly cypresses of the river lands. They were hoary oaks, with trunks as big as double-decker buses, their canopies tightly embracing each other three hundred feet above the Omada. It was a living cathedral, as verdant in its own manner as their landing site.

The rest of the team quickly conferred, and decided they simply had to be outside the blast radius of the jynx. With Borras's assistance they had traveled five days worth of distance in only fifteen minutes. None of them had ever even heard stories or legends about a jynx that could cover that much territory. They didn't want to waste any valuable Journey time knocked out, so they voted not to have Anatolia mix the sleeping potions.

The team was wrong. Tal saw the trees shimmy-shudder in response to a nonexistent breeze and the next thing he knew Borras was announcing it was time to stop and eat their prepared meals and that he was considering a long nap after dessert. The others all thought that was a grand idea. In response, Tal reached into his left front pants pocket and took out the sealed notes Borras had written. He passed them around to their respective addressees. The change when each person got to Borras's actual signature was almost comical. It was exactly like a Three Stooges sketch where someone thunked them right between the eyes. If there had ever been any question in his mind about the power of the contract they'd all bound, there was none any longer. It was definitely some serious mojo. The Pucas hadn't bound the contract but it only took a few seconds of silent communication with their hosts, and apparently with each other, for them to also be cleared of the jynx effects.

Borras took the lead, everyone in single-file behind him. They had no idea what to expect as far as predators, other than the wytch. As they began moving deeper into the forest, they found it was full of smaller trees that were a species of dagger trees. About fifteen feet high with a circumference about the same, their leaves were razor thin thorns, which didn't stick you so much as slash you. Ana's repeated use of her healmagyk kept them all moving, but their clothes were shredded.

The headway they made was only because Borras took a small sapling and used it as a scythe. They'd thought about getting Fragarach out of the duffel bag but didn't want to take a chance it might rebound off the dense wood and accidentally strike one of them.

"The forest is another defense," Dysi said when Borras called a water break. The Omada leader had welts all over him evidencing Ana's healing of his multitude of lacerations.

"You're right," Notos said in agreement. "It means we're moving in the correct direction. We don't know how much longer we have left but the wytch has to be within three hours standard EPT. We haven't wasted any time thus far. Well, except when the human almost died."

Appreciate the concern, Notos, Tal thought.

Then, as abruptly as it had begun, the forest ended, opening into a clearing. Even without magyk, Tal instantly realized the clearing wasn't some natural formation. The forest girdled it all around but didn't dare to trespass upon the clearing itself. Tal guesstimated the glade to be about three thousand yards in diameter. It looked to be a perfect circle. Someone had taken the time and trouble to remove every vestige of leaves, branches, fallen trunks, stumps. Any and all woodlands detritus. In fact, Tal suddenly realized, the clearing was devoid of indicia of life of any shape or kind. The birds were still singing in the trees over their heads, but there were none overflying the cleared area. In the forest, the Omada's boots had scuffed up moss and clumps of lichen. The clearing floor was sere, a desert without even the normal flora or fauna of an arid region. Hell, there's not even any rocks, he realized. No boulders, no pebbles, only sterile, volcanic looking soil.

At the circle's epicenter was a ramshackle cabin. Looks like it's straight out of the Architectural Digest quarterly issue on the top ten list of 'bad shit will absolutely go down in this craphole murder shack' fairy tale cabins. The structure was made out of all manner of slapdick boards nailed catawampus, with other half-rotten boards nailed even more catawampus over those boards. It had a couple of roughly rectangular windows covered with mismatched lumberyard reject shutters. The roof was a composite, consisting of left over lumber, some nasty mildewed plywood jutting outward at irregular angles, together with some moldy thatching covering about half the roof. I guess Death Cabin Depot was all sold out of gingerbread, Tal decided.

A classic metal stovepipe chimney—with three major kinks—jutted upward about ten feet above the cabin's roof. Several tendrils of oily black smoke were clawing their way up and out of the smokestack before congealing into a greasy miasma which loitered several feet above the roof.

Right as Borras was about to step into the clearing, Notos darted forward, stopping in front of him. "Don't," Notos said extending his hand to make sure Borras didn't cross the cleared threshold.

"What's up?" Borras asked.

"We need to proceed carefully from this point forward," Notos replied.

"He's right," Ana added. "The forest was altered to grow extra-thick so it would be a barrier. Unless you were questing, or had Borras with you, you would either die or give up and go back to the waterfalls."

"Makes sense," Dysi added. "The area surrounding the waterfalls must have been enhanced to encourage travelers to stay there and never leave."

"So if the waterfalls were a 'stay here,' and the woods are a 'keep out,' why is the clearing so easy-peasy to cross?" Tal asked.

"Because it's a killing field," Dysi whispered, almost to herself.

"You are only partially correct," Notos added. "One of its purposes is to provide a visually unobstructed kill zone. However, the clearing itself is also a defensive weapon. A tremendous amount of magykal energy has been used to terraform that circle. I sense there is nothing living within its parameters, above or below."

"Surely there's some earthworms or some roaches or some type of itchy, stingy little creepers," Tal interjected.

Notos gave him some significant side-eye. "Be assured human, that I can tell you with absolute certainty the only residents of that glade are magykally scoured bones. Lots and lots of bones from which even the marrow has been sucked clean for its magyk."

Who does that, Tal wondered. Bone marrow sucking? I didn't even know that was a thing. Why did that have to be a thing?

Borras took a step back into the trees so they would all remain hidden by the dense shrubbery. "I get the clear space, Notos. Establishing a perimeter is a common military tactic, but why the sterilization? I can't even do the math in my head for how much time and magykal energy were needed to remove all living matter from that large an area. Or how it was done, and perhaps even more importantly, why?"

Notos closed his eyes and stood motionless. A few seconds went by, then a minute. Tal could see the pulsing blue of his veins against the pallor of his forehead. Notos finally took a long, deep breath and opened his eyes. "The magyk of all the Folk and Creatures whose remains lie there was used to create and perpetuate the clearing."

"Notos!" Ana, exclaimed. "That means the wytch, that she raped them of all their magyk, used up all the lyfeforce of what must have been hundreds and hundreds of…of…"

"I'm going to be sick," Dysi mumbled as she ran behind a flowering bush. They couldn't help but hear her violently retching.

"That's exactly what it means," Notos confirmed. He turned back to Borras. "The field is sterile so that no matter your magykal ability, no one, Folk or Creature alike, can call upon the power or assistance of any other living or organic matter while in the killing field. Anyone that steps out there will be totally on their own."

"Except us because we have our Pucas," Borras reminded him.

"It's why we were required to wear them," Tal added.

"I can make the cabin in one hop. Easy," Borras said.

"To what purpose?" Notos asked.

"To make contact and get a talysman before the Recall," came the quick response.

"Remember," Dysi said softly as she walked back around the bush, "our Pucas are magykal Creatures as well."

"Right," Borras sat down on a stump, and the others took seats in a close circle. "We have no idea what to expect from the wytch. Whether this ability to syphon is immediate or gradual, permanent or temporary."

"Our magyk is our lyfeforce," Anatolia added. "If she sucks all of it we're dead. My healmagyk cannot bring anyone back from the dead."

Great, Tal thought. I know what they're all thinking—the mortal is again the weakest link in Omada. The only magyk I have is Piras.

'A not insubstantial ally,' Piras interjected.

'Sorry, sorry,' Tal immediately thought-replied. 'I know the only reason I'm still alive is because of you. I just wish there was something I could do to help the Omada win this Hunt.'

'Remember, Quint—battles are more often won through defensive strategy rather than offensive prowess.'

'Thank you General Patton.' Tal then spoke aloud, addressing his teammates. "The first thing each of us needs to do is have a discussion with our Pucas," Tal said

"Why?" Notos asked. "They're Creatures and have sworn binding oaths to Hunts School to assist us."

"Quint has a point," Anatolia added. "This is not the usual Hunts situation. The wytches are abominations against Amarantos. None of us have any idea what type of pain is involved in having our magyk stolen. We don't have the right to make that decision for our Pucas."

"I agree," Borras said. "Everyone ask your Pucas their thoughts, and their permission."

'Piras?' Tal asked.

'Mortals are a most unexpected and complicated equation.' It sounded to Tal almost as if Piras was thinking to himself and that he somehow got to listen in. 'Thank you for your consideration of my subjects, Quint of Omada. I am prepared—as are all of my people—to do whatever is necessary for Omada to win the Tyrning. I consent, do you?'

'I do.'

Each of the Omada reported in turn that their Pucas, despite the unknown risk, were good to go.

The wind kicked up, blowing a mite drunkenly. Not knee-walking staggering drunkenly mind you but clearly tipsy as it fitfully teetered its way across the clearing. As the wind wandered, Tal heard a sound like wood clacking against wood. Castanets, maybe? Do wytches play small percussion instruments? Tal pulled a couple of branches aside and squinted toward the cabin. She's got wind chimes. Lots of them. Must be a hobby. Tal squinted a little more, then rubbed his eyes.

"HOLY CRAP!"

"Ssh, you idiot!" Notos yelled at him. "You're going to let her know we're here."

"Those wind chimes, they're..." Tal replied, his voice much quieter this time. "They're made of different sized skulls hanging on vertebrae fragments. She's got skeleton wind chimes."

"Amarantos, help us," Dysi said, as she turned to grab Anatolia for support.

"Time is not our friend," Notos reminded them.

"That's correct," Borras agreed, "but it's difficult to put together a strategy when we have almost no information about our target."

"Other than she sucks the magyk out of you until she's sucked you dead," Notos added.

Atta boy, Tal thought. "Okay guys, in every war movie ever made, the perimeter was cleared much farther than the offensive capabilities of the defenders."

"Good point, Quint," Borras said. He turned to Dysi. "We don't have the necessary information to safely reconnoiter, which means we need to acquire some. If we can."

Dysi nodded.

Borras turned to address the other three. "I can jump almost as quickly as Dysi can teleport. Anatolia will remain safely in the woods. In case...in case we need her healmagyk." He placed the duffel bag on the ground, unzipped it and took out the blanketed sword and the small box containing the Ring of Gyges.

Notos interrupted "Prime?"

"Yes?" Borras replied.

"Your strategy appears sound. Unless her magyk syphon acts instantaneously with deadly force when you're both within her strike range. In which case we will be down to three members and out of the competition. Additionally, if you go down with Fragarach and the ring of power we not only lose them, she gains them."

Notos is one cold bastard, Tal thought. Not just with respect to me, with everyone. Still, his frank assessment may have just saved some lives.

Dysi spoke up. "We're probably out of the competition if we don't get a talysman this trip. There's a whole lot on the line, which is why all of us have repeatedly been asked to risk our lives."

It's the same as a gyftpryce, Tal realized. The fate of the known universe was at stake every Tyrning. The possible positive outcomes have to be in proportion to the potential negative consequences.

"I'm in, Borras," Dysi concluded.

"Notos makes a valid point about the scavengyr pieces," Anatolia added. "Do we have any information about whether wytches can also syphon magyk from inanimate objects?"

"Negative on the availability of intel," Borras replied, as he placed the sword and ring box back in the team bag. "I agree. Baby steps folks, until we know more. What kind of spread pattern do you want to cover?"

Tal spoke up. "Look. I'm the one with zero magyk here, and the most expendable as far as the competition. If the wytch is smart enough to construct this type of defensive structure, she's smart enough to have a backup offensive strike mechanism to go with it."

"What are you suggesting, Munedan?" Notos asked.

"Let Piras and I be the decoys. With his help I can easily jump fifteen to twenty feet. Predictable jumps designed to get her to try to take us out. Worst case you're down one mortal and one Puca."

'You mean one Piras,' Tal heard his Puca chime inside his head.

"While I'm doing that, Borras and Dysi can do an irregular spread pattern to see if they can determine exactly how far out her defenses extend." Tal turned to them. "I'd suggest Brownian motion." He saw from all four faces they were clueless. "Brownian motion is the random movement of atoms as they carom off each other. There is no discernible pattern to their movements."

"I get it now," Borras said. "This should help us determine her defensive boundaries, and hopefully avoid any offensive counterstrike. It's a good plan. Dysi, you start toward the left and I'll jump right. No discernible pattern to your jumping. Make your direction and your distance a spur of the moment decision." With that Borras looked to Tal. "It's 'go' time."

'Okay, Piras, are you ready for some long jumping?'

'At your command, Quint of Omada.'

'Let's go five feet forward, ten diagonally to the left, fifteen to the right, straight back. If we're still alive after that sequence we will repeat, adding about five feet to each measurement.'

'Got it.'

'Let's hope she doesn't have any mortars,' Tal said, as he leapt from the cover of the forest onto the naked field of death.

CHAPTER TRIGINTA NOVEM

The only thing Tal was sure of when he regained consciousness was that he was definitely lying flat on his back. As his eyes focused, he saw he was back in the forest, a patchwork of azure sky backlighting the myriad branches crisscrossing each other over his head.

'Piras.'

'I am here,' Piras replied.

Wow, Piras's voice seems thin, Tal thought, as he sat up. Borras was seated a few feet away, his back propped against a tree. The Omada leader was rubbing his forehead with both hands. Wouldn't mind some extra-strength Tylenol myself, Tal thought.

Dysi! Tal scanned for her quickly, finding her seated by a smaller tree, about fifteen feet from Borras. A double-wide swath of Ana's medkit gauze was tied around her eyes. Anatolia was bent over her, her hands on Dysi's temples, whispering to her. Tal could hear Dysi whimpering in pain. Which was pretty damn scary because Dysi was a tough cookie. Notos was standing motionless at the clearing's edge, using a moss covered oak bough as cover. He was so still it was like someone had borrowed a department store mannequin for some artsy forest photo shoot.

"My plan," Tal mouthed to himself. "My plan must have caused this."

'No, Quint,' Piras interjected. 'The plan was well-reasoned. If there had been a better alternative, I would have suggested it.'

'What happened?'

'I am unclear as to the details. We were making the fourth jump in the pattern you set...'

'So we were making the leap back to the starting point?' Tal asked.

'Yes. As we started that jump, something touched me.'

'What?'

'I don't know how to describe it to you because it was so wrong magykally. You know the Puca are vampyric Creatures, it is why we serve the Moiety now during the Hunts. It is our nature, there is no animus in what we do, it is how Amarantos made us. This touch, however, this touch was...malicious.'

'Evil?' Tal asked.

'Perhaps, certainly a perversion of the UnFading Spirit's gyfts. It was a violation. It not only stole my magyk, it left in its place—hate. Undiluted, angry hate. It came upon me so suddenly I would have fallen helpless to the ground except for your human legs.'

'What?'

'Yes. You were not affected at all. If we had not been synced at the time I doubt you would have felt anything. It was your electrical-based mortal body that was able to leap about three feet before we collapsed together. That is all I remember. I will check with my brethren to see if they know more.'

"What happened to the rest of you?" Tal asked his teammates, his own voice sounding more like a croak than words.

Notos never took his eyes off the clearing as he responded in his emotionless, monotone voice. "As soon as you began your third jump, Borras leapt to the right, and Dysi teleported a half-beat later to the left quadrant. They were then each on their second move when you and your Puca were attacked. Seemed like she took the stolen power from your Puca and used it against Dysi and Borras."

'Tell him the Puca agree with his conclusion,' Piras advised.

"Piras confirms your theory," Tal replied.

Notos continued. "She must have attacked Dysi next. She caught her in the middle of dissipating on a teleport back to safe ground in the forest. Dysi disappeared but this time there was no explosion of particles, nothing."

"She...she took my magyk. She took a piece of me," Dysi said before breaking down into tears again. Anatolia bent back over her wounded teammate and placed her hands directly over her eyes.

"Notos was wonderful," Anatolia added, while continuing her healing. "Dysi must have had enough remaining magyk to make it to within twenty feet of where we were standing. Without even thinking about his own safety, Notos sped out there, threw her over his shoulder, and ran back here."

"There wasn't anything to it," Notos said interrupting Ana's commentary. "Because of Quint's initial jumps I was able to plot the outside circumference of the wytch's syphoning ability." At that point he looked over at Tal. "And yes, I asked my Puca if he was willing to risk his life for your plan."

"Which leaves me, Notos," Borras said, his fatigue evidenced by the tremor in his voice. "What happened to me?"

"There must not have been time for her to process Dysi's stolen teleportationmagyk into whatever raw form she uses, and Dysi's magyk only works on her anyway. It all happened almost simultaneously. She must have burned through the power she stole from Dysi trying to abduct you, by then I had Dysi across the death line, which left her unable to access any more of our magyks. You were in midjump and she got you right before you crossed into safe air. Prime, you crumpled like a wet rag. I mean you hit the ground hard. Face first."

"Notos was back out there in a flash and somehow managed to drag you back here," Anatolia said finishing the story, as she began unwrapping Dysi's eyes. "Dysi, don't open your eyes until I do a little more work on you."

That Notos is damn strong for a wiry little sarcastic bastard, Tal thought.

"I wouldn't have been able to do it without my Puca," Notos added. "Anatolia then began working nonstop on the two of you. I don't think your injuries were lyfe-threatening, but if she wasn't as strong as she is, you would have certainly been unconscious for the rest of this Journey."

"Done," Anatolia announced. "Okay, take a look," she told Dysi.

Tal watched as Dysi tentatively opened her eyes, and immediately began crying again. "Oh, Ana, thank you for helping me but they're still not quite right."

"Tell me what you see, Dysi," Ana said, calmly.

"Everything is red or green, nothing else."

"Sssh! Stop crying. Close your eyes again" Anatolia told her, gently placing her hands back on Dysi's now closed eyes. "Vision is difficult but we're trained how to fix red-green color blindness. There. Now, try."

Dysi opened them again and a broad smile lit up her face. "They're perfect. Thank you, thank you."

"You know you're welcome," Anatolia replied before turning back to Borras. "Give me a couple of minutes, Prime, and I'll see what else I can do for you. This requires different healing than anything I've ever done before. Not only did your injuries have to be healed, but I had to restore some of your stolen lyfeforce to accomplish the healing. I'm about shot but give me a few minutes to recharge…"

Borras waved her off. "I'm okay, Anatolia. Rest up and save your strength."

"I'm sorry, guys. I really am," Tal said, as he stood and started wiping moss and leaves off his backside.

"Shut it, human," Notos said, caustically. "Your plan worked beautifully. We know the extent of our adversary's range, that she is brutally fast, and that she fully intends to kill us if we continue to try to make contact with her. We learned all of that without any of us being permanently maimed—thanks to Anatolia. We also learned it is time for us to abandon this effort."

"What?" Tal exclaimed.

Borras raised himself unsteadily, leaning on the tree for support.

Man, it must be dire if he's wearing his Puca and that's the best he can do, Tal thought.

'Both Koios and Orseis were perilously close to being overtaken,' Piras whispered in his head. 'They will recover but they need some time.'

'We don't have time Piras, the Journey is only three hours EPT,' Tal thought replied.

Borras took a couple of unsteady steps. "I'm going to be okay, I just need a moment. I guess we'd better brainstorm our remaining options."

"Prime, Quint is out for another trip and I don't think I could survive one either," Dysi said.

"Our ancillary points are high, but until Empousa announces the Journey results we won't have any idea whether three of the other teams scored a wytch meeting, or worse, a talysman," Anatolia added.

Borras leaned back against the tree, while he took a couple of deep, settling breaths. "Whether it's only this wytch or all of them, Notos's point is valid. We have an enemy who takes our magykal power and uses it against us. We have fought against opponents with magyk. We have, however, never fought against one who took our lyfeforce and used it against us."

"What if we rush her all at once?" Dysi asked. "Borras can leap to the cabin. I can teleport there."

"It's no good," Notos said. "She is clearly determined to kill us, and if more than one of us dies or is maimed we are out of the competition. Besides that, I'm not sure I understand how we translate going to war with her into a constructive meeting, much less getting her to give us a talysman."

Borras was about to announce his decision, when the first trumpet sounded.

CHAPTER QUADRAGINTA

What the hell, Tal thought. A trumpet? Out here in the middle of nowhere?

The entire team walked to the edge of the forest and watched dumbfounded as three riders on horses trotted into view from the far side of the cabin. Who knew? The murder shack has stables. Wonder if there's also a guesthouse. Although for wytches, a guesthouse would probably be like having an extra meat freezer in the garage.

'Focus, Tal," Piras reminded him.

'Thanks. Normally, I tell myself that,' Tal replied.

'Talking to oneself is not normal.'

'Right, because walking around wearing animated full body spanx is perfectly normal?' When there was no further response from the Puca, he added, 'Exactly.'

As the echoes of the trumpet blast rolled through the trees the team could hear the clomp of hooves and the jangle of the horses' bridles. The riders themselves were silent as they progressed to within fifty yards from where the Omada stood at the glade's verge. Tal noticed they stopped at least twenty-five feet short of where Notos had estimated the wytch's power ended.

All three of the riders and their mounts were dressed to the nines for battle. The horses were destriers, large animals bred to carry the weight of both armor and rider. Tal knew that in medieval literature they were sometimes also called chargers. Chargers was a less specific term which also included rounceys and coursers, but technically those were smaller animals. Each of the horse types had their strengths and weaknesses but there was no question the destrier was the king boss daddy of the warhorse world. Again, way too much Renaissance Faire-ing, Tal told himself.

'If you had not been interested in medieval jousting you would not now have information which may be useful,' the Puca noted.

'Thanks, Piras. I guess nerdery may have unexpected benefits.'

Tal continued his inspection of their adversaries' regalia. The horses were wearing complete suits of armor. Bards, that's what horse armor is called, he thought, using his eidetic memory to visualize the armor components and their names. They wore chanfrons, which covered and protected their heads. The chanfron connected to a crinet. The crinet was an important, difficult to fabricate component. It was a large, reticulated piece that protected the horses' vulnerable neck areas. It had to move easily so as not to impair the horse's ability to turn its head. The easiest way to describe its movement was that it was like an airport luggage carousel where the individual metal pieces slide back and forth to retain a comprehensive surface. At the front base of the crinet were the two peytrals. They performed the function of large kneepads and were designed to protect a horse's forequarters. On top, the crinet ended at the horse's back where the saddle was located. The single largest piece of the bard was the crupper, which covered and protected all of a horse's hindquarters, while allowing the horse to run and jump.

The riders were dressed much like the medieval fighters Tal had run into during his solo Journey last term—that still unexplained, freaky Conundrum trip. Full plated armor, with their faceplates in the down position, so Tal was unable to see what they looked like. All three sets of horse and rider were perfect replicates, except for one thing—color.

The horse and rider to the team's left were garbed in white. Brilliant white, sans blemish or discernible imperfection. The sunlight's reflection off of the White's armor made it hard to look directly at him. The couplet to the team's right was the polar opposite. The armor was apocalyptic black—the color of Tal's every childhood nightmare caused by the faceless spook.

Between White and Black was Red, although red was an insufficient descriptor. Red's armor was the wet, arterial crimson that spurts from a chest wound. It was the red your entire body feels when you let your anger totally consume you. The mind-numbing red of wholesale atrocities, and of the devaluation of one person's life to satisfy the carnal ambitions of another.

"Five-Hells," Notos finally whispered.

"That about sums it up," Tal replied.

"You are trespassyrs."

"Trespassyrs will be drawn, quartered and disemboweled."

"Trespassyrs will be slayn."

With their faceplates down, Tal couldn't tell which one of the riders said what. Or whether one of them said everything. Doesn't matter, he decided. Message delivered. Exact same message as Luna's junkyard sign, he realized with a start.

Borras took a step into the sunlight. "We would like to speak to your mistress."

Red said something to his horse, which then took a step toward Borras. "State your business."

"We are the Omada and we request an audience with the wytch."

"Why don't you come a little closer," Red said. "So that we might negotiate easier." This time Tal heard ugly chuckles from the other two as the three heads swiveled to look at each other.

"We know the boundaries of your Mistress's power," Borras replied calmly. "This is a Tyrning Year. We are on a Hunt and would have your guarantee of safe passage that we might bargain with her for a talysman."

"Ha! That explains much. Know it all Hunts School students who want a wytch's talysman. Tell me, know it all Hunts School students who want a talysman, what happens to the boundaries of my Mistress's power if she arises from her chair and treads thirty feet in this direction."

Tal saw his teammates flinch as their flight instinct kicked in. Oh shit, Tal thought.

'Knowledge, Quint,' Piras thought softly in his head.

'You're right. Red just told us it doesn't matter where the Three Stooges are, her power radius is determined by her physical location.'

Red spread his arms wide to encompass the entire clearing as his voice boomed across the open field again. "It should be clear Trespassyrs that our Mistress does not bargain with vermin."

Red must be the leader of this gang of bullies, Tal decided. He's Barton. Except with this bunch no one else gets a turn talking. Well, except maybe in that first salvo. Focus, moron.

"Leave now or our Mistress will drain the magyk from your bones and we will spread your lifeless husks to rot in the field with the multitude of other impertinent fools who dared to disturb our Mistress." Red then lifted his visor and looked directly at Anatolia. "Except for you. You're too pretty to let your bones rot. We are in need of a new wind chime and I shall ask the Mistress for your teeth and your skull."

Tal saw Borras bend his knees, his leg muscles tense. He's going to jump right through that jackass, he realized.

Luckily, Anatolia saw it as well. "No, Prime," she said quickly, placing her hand on Borras's massive forearm. "He's deliberately goading you into entering the killing field."

Seeing his ploy had failed, Red clucked at his mount, who wheeled perfectly in place. White and Black echoed the motion, and the three of them took a slow canter back to and behind the wytch's cabin.

"Well, that makes one thing perfectly clear," Notos said. "Seeing as how she could make a move this way at any moment and slaughter us, I vote we head back to the safety of the Omphalos."

"Things aren't looking good for a talysman right now," Borras agreed.

"Holy shit!" Tal yelled, smacking himself in the head. "Those are the three guys—her guys. We hit the wytch mother lode."

"Whose guys?" Borras asked.

"The wytch, Borras,...the wytch on this plane is Baba Yaga."

Dysi whistled through her teeth. "You sure?"

"Yes. Absolutely," Tal replied. "Those jackasses are all over the Baba Yaga stories that Emet and I studied."

"You gleaned this information from some Earth plane books the rest of the Folk didn't have access to?" Anatolia asked hopefully.

"Yes," Tal replied. "I didn't realize that at the time, but apparently so."

"Good work, Quint," Borras said. "What'd the books say?"

"The short version is she had three riders: white, black and red. Their names are Day, Night, and Sun. Of course the legends also said she had invisible servants in her house."

"That last part's not good either," Anatolia said.

"So you think one of those three is her familiar?" Borras asked Tal.

"Yes," Tal replied. "Actually, I wonder if it could be split between all three of them?"

"We have no idea what the rules are, so that's a possibility," Borras confirmed.

"They wouldn't cross the power limit line," Notos added. "I wonder if there is also a distance limitation for the wytch-familiar connection to work."

"You mean if a familiar is outside of her range, the conversion properties won't work?" Borras asked.

"It's a logical conclusion," Notos replied. "Won't do us any good. We don't know if it's one or all three of them and there's no way we can trick them into leaving their zone."

"The only thing protecting them is the magyk she steals from everyone else," Tal stated.

"Umm, I guess human vision isn't too sharp, but what I saw was three heavily armored warriors riding three very dangerous battle stallions," Notos said, dismissively.

"I guess you've forgotten we have this," Tal said reaching over and carefully picking up their well-wrapped sword.

"You really aren't that smart, human," Notos snapped. "Even if she can't draw on an inanimate object's magyk, the second one of us crosses the battle line she will kill that person, obtain our scavengyr pieces, and have a reservoir of power to kill the rest of us."

"Unless…" Tal started.

While the rest of them were processing, Borras got it immediately, negatively motioning to Tal with the flat of his palm. "No, absolutely not. I am Omada Prime and I forbid you."

"What?" Dysi asked.

"Son of a bitch," Notos said. "You're thinking you should go because you're human and have no magyk."

"No," Anatolia said.

"Look," Tal said. "You have all been taking turns risking yourselves. It's exactly what Dysi said earlier. I'm Omada as much as the rest of you. I know you think I'm weak and need protecting. Remember—battles are more often won through defensive strategy than offensive prowess."

'I saw what you did there,' Piras thought-spoke.

'Pretty clever, huh?' Tal replied, smiling a little.

'You've forgotten my lyfeforce is magyk-based as well. She will kill me and even with Fragarach you alone cannot defeat three well-trained warriors.'

'I'm not going to give her the opportunity to kill you,' Tal replied slowly.

There was a pause on Piras's end. 'No. It is my sworn duty to protect your lyfe during the Hunts. I will not uncouple.'

'Piras,' Tal thought kindly, 'we've never had this conversation before, but you can't stay coupled with me if I revoke my consent, can you?'

There was no response. 'Piras?'

'Please don't do this, Quint,' the Puca finally replied.

'The long-ago crimes against the Folk for which your people's service is to pay penance. That was the problem, wasn't it?'

Again the Puca didn't respond.

'Our relationship has to be consensual, doesn't it?'

Again, silence. Then, 'Yes.'

'Turn the Rubik's cube, Piras. It's the only solution to the problem.'

"Quint?" Borras asked him.

"I'm sorry, Prime. I was having a conversation with my friend Piras."

'Friend?' Piras inquired.

'Absolutely,' Tal responded.

"About?" Borras demanded.

"Piras is going to stay here, while I go…"

"NOOOO," Dysi yelled, using her Puca-enhanced physical strength to leap to Tal and to curl her arms around him. "I won't allow it. With Orseis's strength I can keep you from going." Then she sagged a little as her eyes unfocused. About thirty seconds later she took her arms from around Tal and stepped back a half-step. "Piras has told Orseis and the rest of the Pucas they may not help to interfere in this matter."

"Quint," Borras said solemnly, "the number one rule Professor Elphinstone gave us was to never ever take off our

Pucas. The wytch will kill you if you don't have Piras to protect you."

'Word,' Tal heard Piras's agreement echo in his forebrain.

"I believe I may be the only exception to that rule in Hunts School history," Tal said.

"Because you're basically a magyk-eunuch," Notos volunteered.

Rude, just rude, Tal thought to himself. Clever, but mostly just rude.

"She can't steal your divine spark," Anatolia added.

"Maybe not," Notos agreed, "but she does have at least three presumably fully trained, armored and magyked-up warriors. Without your Puca, you'd never make it past them."

"Au contraire," Tal said picking up Fragarach and the Ring of Gyges.

"Absolutely not," Notos said moving to take the pieces away from Tal. "If she can steal magyk from inanimate objects, you're giving her two powerful weapons to use against us."

"No, he's not," Borras said as he intercepted Notos and gently pushed his hands away from the scavengyr pieces. "It doesn't make sense that she can syphon the object's innate magyk. Even if she can, Quint already realized the most she can do is kill him with the stolen magyk. Neither object has compulsionmagyk, nor do they have any type of teleportation or flying ability. They would remain right where she killed him."

"And one of us would dart out there, get them, get back and let Anatolia heal us before she could send her horse boys," Notos said. "I like the plan. The worst thing that can happen is the mortal dies."

Nicely put, Notos, Tal thought. "I'll walk over there behind the tree and ask Piras to decouple and then I'll put the ring on. That way I'll be fully invisible before any of those three could possibly see me. I'll head off with Fragarach, see if I can sneak past her boys, and maybe talk her into a parlay."

"That won't work," Notos said. "If you go down we will need to know the precise point where you entered the killing field. Whichever of us goes to retrieve the objects will only have a split-second to get it done."

Tal gulped, and then realized what he had just done. He always read about it in books. People were always gulping when they had to mentally swallow some unpleasant thought—or when faced with what appeared to be the prospect of their untimely demise. Which, come to think of it, did any rational person actually believe that at any point in time their demise was timely? Focus, Tal. "Fine," he said. "I agree with the Second Prime. No time like the present."

With that he picked up Fragarach, walked from under the protective canopy of the trees and into the hostile starkness of the clearing. When he got to within about five feet of where they had decided the power line was, he communicated with Piras. 'It's time, friend.'

'Friend,' Piras repeated, clearly relishing the word as he rolled it about in Tal's mind. 'The UnFading One's youngest children are so very, very different from her other offspring.' He then shifted gears back to the business at hand. 'I do not want to leave you unprotected.'

'We've had this discussion, Piras. This is the only plan that stands a chance. Now, please. I revoke my consent.'

With that, Tal felt Piras roll himself up from Tal's ankles, over his midriff, up his chest and to the top of his head. Tal gently took the now folded Puca off his head and laid him gently on the ground.

Standing there, without a stitch on, facing the highly probable certainty of imminent death at the hands of a malicious, centuries old wytch, Tal prayed the prayer of every eighteen-year old male who ends up buck naked in the presence of the opposite sex—Please, please, please Amarantos, don't let me have any pimples on my bony white ass.

CHAPTER QUADRAGINTA UNUS

Tal swiveled his hips so he could look backward and give his squad a small wave, making sure not to turn enough to accidentally wave something larger at the team. Borras gave him two-thumbs up. Turning back toward the cabin, Tal first carefully laid Fragarach on the ground. With both his hands now free he opened the ring box, took the Ring of Gyges out, and placed it on his left hand. He still wore his ring from Aurora on his right finger. We didn't even talk about whether I should worry about my gyft ring. Well, worst case scenario, I lose it but even though it has enough juice for one more wish, she can't use it. Helblad made that real clear when we were all about to get eaten back at Maes Howe. Actually, he thought, I guess the true worst case scenario is I lose it because I'm dead.

Tal knew from practicing with the Ring of Gyges in the team room that he didn't feel any different when he wore it. Just to make sure it was working he turned back around and flipped Notos off. Double-barreled, using both hands. Notos's normally dour expression didn't change a bit. Okay, the ring is working, he decided.

Tal bent down and slowly unwrapped the blanket covering Fragarach. One nick from the blade and he didn't need to worry about what Baba Yaga might do to him. He'd end up dead. Invisible dead. The team might not even be able to find his body before the Recall. Okay, Tal, he told himself, it's go time.

One small step toward the cabin, followed slowly by a second. Tal was halfway through his third step when he felt the tingle wash over him. Moments later the riders came galloping from the far side of the cabin. There was no lazy gait this time, they were spurring their horses toward him. He quickly changed course, moving in a right lateral arc that kept him within the magyk field but no closer to the cabin. He was about fifty feet away when the riders reached his original point of entry. He could see from this angle that the Omada had retreated into the woods. Stand still he told himself, and practice deep breathing. The ring only blocks sight, none of the other senses.

The horsemen were revved up, agitated. Night pointed first to the trees, and Red shook his head. Day put a finger to his nose and then patted his horse's neck. Red nodded. They each leaned over and whispered something to their horses and then turned away from each other and started slowly walking in different directions. They're going to use the horses to sniff me out, Tal realized.

A horrendous din erupted from the tree line about a hundred yards to the far side of the riders. As soon as Tal realized the noise was intentional, he saw someone leap from the trees and start running dead on toward the cabin.

Bless his little caustic negative heart, it's Notos, Tal realized at the same time the riders reacted, digging in their heels and wheeling their mounts to attack the trespassyr. Out of the corner of his eye, Tal saw Borras giving him the high sign to head for the cabin as fast as possible. Realizing they wouldn't be able to hear him running over the noise of their horses and Notos's yelling, Tal took off at a dead run, holding Fragarach tightly off to his side. Not a good idea, he told himself as he ran full out. If running with scissors is a bad idea, running with a sword of power that can end you with one scratch has to be exponentially worse. Has to be.

Notos stopped right before he reached the critical point. At which time, both Dysi and Borras appeared from two other widely-spaced flanking points. As his team had anticipated, the horsemen split up to deal with the three-pronged assault.

Tal took one last look over his shoulder before he rounded the corner of the shanty.

CHAPTER QUADRAGINTA DUO

Immediately after rounding the nearest corner of the cabin, Tal pressed himself up against the wall and paused to catch his breath and collect his thoughts. He could hear Borras, Dysi, and Notos still taunting the riders, so it was safe to assume they were at the far end of the killing field. I'm all alone, Tal realized. No Borras, Omada, or Emet to help me out of a tight spot. The wytch's syphon had turned his team's strengths into weaknesses and his weaknesses into...well, hopefully not into sure and certain death.

Get it together Tal, he told himself. Worlds are counting on you. Or so sayeth an out of order gas pump. Roll through your options, both defensively as well as offensively. To start with, I'm not killing anyone, he told himself. Although I'm still a little fuzzy on this whole "Seeking the Center" gig, I'm pretty sure Amarantos doesn't want me murdering anyone. Killing is out of the picture, no matter the circumstances.

Fragarach was a major problem in that regard. Tal understood why they couldn't bring Skofnung with them—they'd all witnessed the havoc it wreaked when its hilt was exposed to sunlight. The logic behind forging a magyk sword that unleashed twelve berserkers when its hilt was exposed to sunlight totally escaped Tal. Their only real weapon option was Fragarach, which Tal knew from the arena was easily as bloodthirsty as Skofnung.

Early on at Hunts School Tal had learned magyk was subject to the basic laws of physics. Well, in a jacked up magykal physics universe kind of way. The principle that for every action there is an equal and opposite reaction applied to the use of magyk. When any of the Folk used their magyk it drew upon their lyfeforce. As long as the draw was a reasonable amount, their body replenished it. In situations in which an extraordinary amount was used, it might reduce the user's lyfespan, or even kill them by not leaving enough magyk lyfeforce left to operate their body.

Swords of power—apparently all objects of power for that matter—augmented their magykal ability by using lyfeforce from whoever was utilizing the object. Tal still hadn't figured out some of the nuances of that equation. Unlike magykal Creatures—such as the Talaria, the winged sandals—magykal objects weren't sentient. That, however, didn't mean they didn't have a purpose. An emotionless, overriding purpose was apparently molded into every magykal object when it was created. The imbued purpose of swords of power was to kill, maim, and create as much bloodshed as possible. During the Combat Challenge, when he'd been weak from loss of blood, Fragarach had used its magyk to override Tal's intent, and had independently tried to kill Väst.

So are swords of power murderous? Actually, that's a very interesting question, Tal decided. He'd taken a couple of online college courses to rack up a few hours of credit to put in the bank, and one of the courses had been Crim Law. Murder is an intentional act. The swords had a purpose, and killing was part of that purpose. Is purpose synonymous with intent? In any event, magyk swords were amoral. Not only did they lack the capacity to know good from bad, they lacked the ability to choose. So there we have it, he decided. Philosophical issues resolved. Absent free will Fragarach is a killer but can't be a murderer.

Doesn't help me out any. I can call upon the winds to help me while I hold Fragarach but I can't even nick Baba Yaga with it or she'll die. Since I know even a scratch is a hundred

220

percent fatal it would be kind of hard to say I used the sword in self-defense. Which by the way isn't an affirmative defense to murder in most states. It's a "justification." Justification, now there's a Medusa's head full of philosophical snakes for you.

I could cut one of the horses to scare the shit out of everyone and get them to lay off. Great, Tal, just great. Kill an innocent animal who had no choice but to obey its master instead of taking it out on one of the bad guys. Yeah, pretty sure that's not "Seeking the Center" either.

Those chuckleheads don't know me from Adam, though. They don't have any idea what I'm capable of doing versus what I'll actually willing to do. I'll just have to bluff my way through, Tal decided. Now, what about Baba Yaga. He quickly rolled through all of the information he and Emet had uncovered about the wytch. She has flying carpets, many multiples of flying carpets. Some of the stories said she also has a towel that can transform into a bridge, and others that she owns a magyk ball that will show you the way to wherever it is you want to go.

In some of the legends she's a cold murderous bitch, but in some alternate versions of the story she is willing to help out her visitors. Of course there were also the versions where her house was built on stilts and able to spin in a circle. Clearly not the case here. This dump probably has a dirt floor.

Use your brain, Tal told himself. Is there some discernible pattern in all of the stories, a constant among all of the variables, or sufficient data upon which to base an estimate similar to like when stock analysts determine a ten-day moving average for a stock price. THINK, he screamed at himself. It's all on the line here. You need to make contact and convince her to give you a talysman. How the hell am I going to know what qualifies as a talysman? And how is it I'm here, attempting to avoid being cannibalized by a wytch, and there's not even a possibility for extra credit points?

Politeness! The word suddenly whirred to a stop in Tal's forebrain. In almost every story Emet and I read, that attribute made an appearance. Baba Yaga hates it when people aren't polite. Exactly like Moms everywhere who tell their children all the time—bad things happen when you don't use your manners. I'm not sure any Mom meant that being human sushi was a consequence for not saying please and thank you but same general principle.

It's a start, Tal. The first thing I have to decide is which is more polite—showing up invisible and uninvited or showing up naked and uninvited. Shit! She might as well go ahead and get the cauldron boiling, I'm dinner on the hoof. He'd decided a couple of years ago that when his time finally came, he wanted to be cremated, not buried. There's no way in hell though that I want to spend eternity as a set of wind chimes.

Honesty! Given the time, I think I could statistically support honesty as being the polite choice in most situations. Except, of course, when your girlfriend gets a haircut and asks you if you like it, and you really don't, but you say you do. Or when Mom asks Pell if he thinks an outfit makes her look fat, and he squirms noticeably before replying, "no." Hmm, so honesty isn't always the polite choice. Which deductively means if you are always polite, then you are also sometimes deceitful. Do "little white lies" really hurt no one?

Decision. Since it involves my birthday suit, I'm going balls to the wall with honesty, Tal resolved. Figuratively, not literally. The splinters on that wall could do some major damage. He sidled three steps toward the door, ducking under the jacked up windows on the way. Taking a deep breath, he rapped on the door three times in quick succession.

At first there was no response. Then he heard some scrabbling. She's probably putting away the dirty laundry, Tal decided. Either that or weaponizing her invisible minions so that they can slit my throat as soon as I walk through the door. Yeah, that's it. One of those two things.

The door finally opened. Well, in a manner. Whatever unit of measurement is smaller than a sliver, that's exactly how much the door opened. The square root of a sliver, perhaps.

What would that be anyway? A sliverite? Tal took a half-step backward in case a sliverite-sized shiv was about to be deployed.

"Who's there?" While not querulous, the voice certainly wasn't particularly welcoming. Rusty might be a better adjective.

Tal carefully took another step back and then one sideways before answering. No need being an easy target. "My name is Quint." Manners, Tal, manners. "First, I'd like to apologize for dropping in uninvited."

"Where are you?"

"I'm invisible."

"Well, I can see that can't I?" the voice answered.

Let it slide, smartass, let it slide. "I have a ring of invisibility."

"Which ring?" came the quick response.

That information won't hurt you or the team, he told himself. "The Ring of Gyges," Tal replied.

"Interesting," the wytch said, before shifting gears. "Dropping in uninvited is impolite. Dropping in invisible is unquestionably rude. Please remain where you are while I go get something to kill you with."

As the door began to slam shut, Tal blurted, "Ms. Yaga, I didn't have a mailing address nor a telephone number, so I was unable to call or write to you in advance concerning my visit. As to the invisible part, I had to use the ring to sneak past your guards, which required me to disrobe. My two choices were to either show up at your door invisible, or to appear completely naked. I chose the first option."

"Hmmph," came the reply as the door moved back open a hair. "No doubt the right choice. On top of everything else, you probably have pimples on your ass. Do you?"

"I don't know. I really, really just don't know," Tal replied, shaking his head. So this is what it feels like to be mortified.

"There are no circumstances in which ass pimples are polite," the wytch said curtly.

What the hell, Tal thought. I wonder if random stream of consciousness conversation is a wytchy thing. "Yes ma'am. I absolutely, totally agree with you. One hundred percent. In my defense, I do try to exercise excellent personal hygiene and skin maintenance. Sometimes, I even use some of my Mom's skin moisturizer. With her permission, of course." Scratch my earlier conclusion, Tal thought. This is what it feels like to be mortified.

"I have several extra pair of my knights' gambeson in here. Hold on." The door closed only to reopen about a minute later. "Here," she said as she thrust her arm through the open doorway, extending a quilted black on black jacket-robe. "Put this on before you take off the ring."

"Yes ma'am. Thank you ma'am," Tal said, taking the garment. He laid Fragarach on the ground to free both hands to put the outfit on and cinched the belt tight so it closed in the front. Bending over, he picked up the sword of power. "Done," he announced.

"Quint, is it? Five. That's an interesting use name. That's it, then? Quint?"

"Actually, I'm Quint of the Omada," Tal answered.

There was a long pause before any response. "I see. You are from the Hunts School?"

"Yes, Ms. Yaga."

"It's a Tyrning Year, is it?"

"Yes, ma'am."

"Hmm. The hunt this term, is it a Wytch Hunt?" she asked, her tone suddenly taking on a metal-like hardness.

"Yes, ma'am."

"So you're here to kill me and take some body part back with you as proof?"

"No ma'am. Absolutely not. We are only supposed to obtain the most powerful talysman we can negotiate."

"Well, Quint of the Omada, I think it's time you took off that ring so I can look at you," she demanded.

Tal tightened his grip on Fragarach, holding it carefully, pointed downward. "Before I do that, I think we should come to an understanding concerning certain ground rules of our parlay."

His words were greeted with an ugly snort. "I'm sorry," the wytch replied. "You've caught me a little off-guard showing up uninvited. And naked. Exactly what type of understanding did you think we might come to?"

Dialogue is better than death, Tal told himself. "I thought we might discuss the terms and conditions under which you would award me a talysman."

This time his words were met with an ugly laugh. "You did, did you?" Then she looked past him. "Gentlemen, please show our uninvited guest my terms and conditions."

Tal turned and looked behind him. All three riders, now on foot, were standing motionless in a spread pattern only several feet away. Damn it, Tal thought. They've got me trapped between them and the walls of the cabin so even if I can get naked again I won't be able to escape. I could try fighting my way out but it's just me with no Puca against three trained warriors. Fragarach is a hundred percent fatal but I'd have to get past their armor to cut them. Score a huge point for the wytch. How could I have been so stupid, he asked himself.

Baba Yaga continued, "I'm sorry for the vulgar show of force but I need some questions answered before I let them kill you. In my entire time on this plane no one has ever snuck past my wards without triggering them. I need for you to tell me how you did it."

Shit, Tal thought. This is where the rubber meets the road. "I didn't set off your wards because I don't have any magyk."

"Come now. Lying isn't polite. We both know without magyk lyfeforce, you'd be dead. There's no need to be embarrassed if you only possess low-level magyk. No matter how weak, I should have been able to feed on your power."

All in, Tal decided. "I'm sorry ma'am, for the misunderstanding. I don't have any magyk because I'm human."

The door flew open and the wytch appeared mid-threshold. "HUMAN!" she shrieked, "YOU'RE A MUNEDAN?"

CHAPTER QUADRAGINTA TRES

Tal had always pictured Charles Dickens's Ms. Havisham as a desiccated husk. Well, as an insanely warped and sadistic desiccated husk. If there was a casting call for Jilted Bride Zombie, the character's description would be Ms. She-Doesn't-Even-Have-A-First-Name Havisham. She was the living embodiment of the fifty-year old wedding corsage tightly pressed between stained, age-crackled laminate pages of the wedding album from your eternally-regretted-should-absolutely-never-have-happened-in-the-first-place starter marriage, which had been left to rot in the "life's mistakes" corner of your musty attic—along with your eighth-grade honorable mention band competition ribbons—and of course, all of the terrible, awful Christmas sweaters given to you by your Aunt Beatrice.

Which was not to say Baba Yaga was Miss Havishamish. Not in the least. Tal looked down at her feet to check. Yep, she was even wearing both shoes. No—the wytch and her cabin were far more terrifying. They could probably have scared the Dickens out of the English author. Tal's eyes kept shifting and reshifting, his eyes trying to provide decipherable images but not recognizing the data being shown to them. He knew his eyes were functioning correctly, they just couldn't send coherent pictures to image processing central.

His brain started trying to assemble a border out of the jumbled heap of optical jigsaw puzzle pieces. There were colors but at the same time there weren't any colors. Which is not to say Tal was seeing only grey scales. He looked at the floor, it was narrow planks of dark wood. Tal's eyes would normally have reported mahogany. The floor wasn't that color, rather it was the faintest hint of mahogany. Or perhaps the floor color had once been mahogany before something sucked all of its mahoganyness out of it.

After a quick minute, Tal's brain reset itself to new parameters and the puzzle pieces started falling into place. This place might be a hovel on the outside, but the interior was comfortably furnished. Check that. On closer inspection, it both was and it wasn't. Nothing in the entire room was as it should be. Well, except maybe for the rusted black-iron cauldron. Hung in the middle of a ginormous blazing fireplace, its contents were boiling and splatting, making noises like those mud pot geysers in Yellowstone. Yikes!

It was almost as if every object inside the cabin was slightly out of phase. The furniture and bric-a-brac weren't see-through, it wasn't like that at all. The dining table appeared rock solid, the sofa looked ready for serious sitting. Everything. All of it, was solid, and real—and wrong. The lampshade on the tabletop lamp by the sofa was your every day drawing room red silk moiré, complete with tassels. Except, it wasn't. It was a red that eons ago had given up the ghost of being red. All around Tal, the silvers, golds, greens, the blues. All of the colors were present. They weren't faded, that wasn't it at all. It was as if none of the colors remembered how to be themselves.

With one exception—a nine-stringed guitar-like instrument displayed over the fireplace mantle. It was fashioned of several different types of hardwood. Tal thought he recognized cherry and maple. It shone as if it had been polished frequently and recently. Its strings looked to be taut, ready to be played. It's a gusli, Tal realized. Like one of the ones I've learned how to play at Hunts School. And it's the only thing in this room that looks like it's here in real time.

The cabin's owner was of the same aspect as her home. Every pleat and gather of her clothing, her skin, her arms and legs, even the features of her face. Her aging must have been arrested when she was initiated into the Cult of Nyx, Tal thought. He thought back to his and Emet's research. Having met the wytch he could understand how other people could describe her as "Grandmother of Shudders." Not because she looked like an ancient crone, but because everything about her was a hair out of phase so it made you a little nauseous to look at her.

If the wytch was still human, Tal would have guessed her to be in her late twenties. She wasn't though. Human, that is. So, ageless was the correct description. Tal could tell she had been beautiful. Not some classic knock you to your knees supermodel stunner type of beauty. He couldn't pinpoint how he knew, either. Perhaps it was the slightest suggestion in the symmetrical arc of her throat as it gracefully rose to her chin. Or the vestiges of the long unused laugh lines around her mouth. It might have been the past remembrance of a sparkle in her green—yet no longer quite green—eyes. All of these things had left the building many centuries past, leaving only haunting effigies.

Looking closer, it seemed to Tal as if agitated shadows flitted around her face and arms. Actually, around the entirety of the cabin, but she was the vortex. Not shadows, he decided. They are echoes of the shadows of shadows. It was freaky, almost as if there were some perpetual motion dance of the seven veils happening all around her body, except the veils had been replaced with diaphanous wisps of oversized post-it notes.

The only ambient noise besides the hellatious concoction plopping away inside the cauldron, was the crackling of greenish wood burning in the fireplace, punctuated by the occasional popping of resin-filled knots. That's not quite correct, Tal thought, as he concentrated. Just on the edge of his auditory range, he could hear sibilant whispers. It's the echoes of the shadows of shadows, he realized. The flying post-it notes, they're speaking. Well, they're repeating single words over and over. Tal couldn't quite make out the words. They were the echoes of the whispers of whispers and they kept tripping over each other. It sounded like they were saying the words, hope,…and love…and hate…and joy.

"If you're done staring, you may sit there," the wytch said pointing toward the sofa.

Jerked from his reverie, Tal complied without question. "I'm sorry, and thank you. I don't want to seem abrupt Ms. Yaga, but my team is waiting in the woods and the Recall might be any minute now. So, I really need to talk to you about getting a talysman and then skedaddle."

"You're still nearer to being dead than getting a trip souvenir," she replied. "You only remain alive at this point because I am curious about how a Dust Child came to be on a Wytch Hunt. As far as your team goes, Quint of the Omada, all I have to do is walk toward them across my field and within minutes they'll end up as the newest permanent residents of my world-class boneyard." She stopped, cocking her head to one side as several of the flags veered around her left ear. "Except for one of the girls who Red believes would make a lovely sound swaying in the wind on my front porch. What's her name?"

"A-A-Anatolia," Tal stammered, his poker face outplayed by the wytch's gambit.

"Anatolia. Lovely name. After I suck all of the magyk out of her marrow, I promise I'll try to fashion her spine so that it endlessly repeats her name when the wind comes to visit."

Tal hadn't realized you could actually feel the blood drain from your face. He now knew from firsthand experience that you can.

Baba Yaga continued. "Whether that happens, depends on you, on what you do. Do not worry about the Recall, this plane's time ratio is eight to one Earth Plane Time."

Tal stuttered a little "T-t-that's information they need to know. They have limited water and food and no camping equipment."

The wytch totally ignored his concerns, as she bent over and stirred the cauldron's contents. "Stew?"

Tal felt his gorge rise, as he wondered what the hell kind of meat was in the kettle? "Umm, no thank you. I'm not hungry."

She ladled a bowlful and handed it to him with a spoon and a napkin. "No need to turn up your nose, it's griffin. You know what they say about griffin meat."

Tal smiled, remembering his first visit to the Hunt School cafeteria. "I sure do. Tastes like ouberos snake."

The wytch stared at him as if he were simple. "Are you tetched? The saying is that 'griffin tastes like chicken.' Ouberos snake? Whoever in the known universe ever said that?"

I told you, Borras, Tal thought to himself.

After ladling a bowl for herself she walked over and took a seat at the dining table. She said nothing further for a few minutes, first blowing on her stew to cool it, then eating several spoonfuls. "Some would consider it bad manners for a guest to not even try the food he's been given."

Might as well, Tal thought. I don't want to piss her off. We need a talysman. And to keep breathing, he reminded himself. Yeah, that too. Hey, this stuff isn't half bad, he decided after swallowing a spoonful.

After a few more minutes the wytch pushed her now empty bowl away and sat back in her chair. "Now. From the beginning. Tell me the entire story about how a mortal became enrolled at Hunts School and finally arrived here. The story should end at the point where you beg me for your miserable life. I have lived thousands of years, and heard many tall tales. I will know if you have left something important out. If I believe your story, I may let you and your teammates live."

"Will you also grant us a talysman?"

"Being greedy is impolite. I will, however, ponder upon that while you speak."

So Tal began his tale. He told her about his Mom and Pell and the twins. About the Crestfallyn which had haunted him since birth and how his family had to continually pull up stakes and move to find work for Pell. He told her what it was like to be lonely, to be the friendless geek, and about his dreams of getting an early admission full ride scholarship to someplace far away, where no one knew him. Someplace where people didn't bully each other.

After that he moved on, to when he'd arrived at Nemeton High and how he had met Elle and fallen for her totally and completely. He could tell Baba Yaga was extremely interested in that part. Next came his eighteenth birthday and his lunch date with Elle that never happened. Then, of course, it was time to tell her about Sol the Gas Station, the air hose, the two out of order gas pumps, and the Ladies' Room.

He moved on after that to arriving at Hunts School, meeting Borras, binding the contract with him and the Omada. After that came his first time meeting Väst in class and the feeling of being helplessly drawn to her. Again, the wytch seemed acutely interested, and actually stopped him to ask some questions.

She seemed fascinated by Anatolia creating Emet. So, he told her how it almost killed Anatolia to use her creationmagyk to make him, and how the rest of the team saved her life after that. After that he explained in detail about how he and Emet had become good friends and all of the arrangements they'd had to implement to make sure no one knew there were two of them.

The episode with the Keres was difficult to describe. So much had happened since then that Tal hadn't realized how much emotion he'd been repressing about that episode. About Väst almost dying, with Perun leaping in at the last moment, and saving them. They'd been so caught up in the Hunts Tal hadn't even thought about Bati of the Aile for months. She had saved the rest of them with her shouted warning, then shortly thereafter became the first of the Finalists to die.

Next came Arthrys, Myrddin, and the Pentacle in Forest Fell. Tal told her about Aurora and showed her his ring. She asked him if she might have his permission to hold it. He handed it to her and she put it on her finger, turning her hand back and forth as she gazed at its amazing colors, the ring itself being a constantly effervescing rainbow. Even though Tal was becoming acclimated to the wytch's unusual appearance it was still hard to categorize her expressions. He thought she almost looked wistfully at the ring before handing it back to him.

Tal then told the wytch about their three Journeys looking for scavengyr pieces. The first one, the Conundrum involving Arthrys and Malabranche, where Tal had taken Excalibur from the hand in the stone. The second Journey, which had been the trip to Atlantis where he'd met Fortuna and gotten ripped off, receiving only the pair of plastic Crackerjack box pilot's wings for his prize. That was the trip, however, where Borras had stepped into the death match ring and laid his life on the line to win the Ring of Gyges.

It took a little while to relate the Helblad episode to her. She kept interrupting, asking questions about the draugr creation ritual and about Hellblad's relentless quest to rescue Aislinn from Harald RedHand. Tal paused at that point, realizing his throat was dry. I must have been talking for hours, he thought. "Might I have a glass of water before finishing?" he asked.

"Certainly," the wytch replied, getting up to pour him a glass from an ewer at the far end of the table. She walked over to hand it to him and then seated herself at the far end of the sofa.

Tal turned the narration to the Combat Challenge. He went over it in great detail. From his volunteering to be champion, to his subterfuge concerning Skofnung and Fragarach, the Släkt's trickery involving both Väst as their champion and their choice of scavengyr piece categories. He related how he felt like his insides were being ripped from within as he had to try to kill someone he loved, about how Väst mortally wounded him, and subsequently his use of Fragarach to call the winds to defeat her.

Finally, it came time to tell her about Fragarach seizing control of his arm and impaling Väst, how Nord tried to kill him with Skofnung, which resulted in Nord being slaughtered by the twelve berserkers.

"So, you killed the woman you loved?" she asked.

"Well, yes, but right before I blacked out I used one of my wishes to ask Aurora to fix her, and she sent Perun."

"You're mortal and have no magyk of your own?"

"Correct," Tal replied.

"You were gyfted a ring with three Principe-magyk wishes and you spent one of them to save a Hunts adversary?"

"I did."

"Why didn't you use a wish to save yourself?"

"Too stupid to even think of that I guess," Tal replied.

The wytch paused a moment. "Quint of the Omada, does that not seem odd to you?" she asked.

"No, not really," he replied calmly.

"You felt compelled to use the wish, right?" she asked insistently.

"Yes. Well, no. Many times I feel like I'm so head over heels crazy about Väst it almost feels like I've been compelled to be with her but this was different This decision was all my own. I'm not sure what this whole 'Seeking the Center' routine is all about but that's what I think it's supposed to feel like."

"Interesting," she said placing a finger to her lips for a moment. "I realize you were in great physical discomfort at the time…"

"It was nothing, really. Just a little old bleeding out and dying on the spot," Tal quipped.

"Interrupting isn't polite," she replied, disapprovingly.

"I'm sorry."

"Can you recall the exact words you used in your wish?"

That stopped Tal in his tracks. He hadn't really thought that much about those few moments. The emotions associated with them were still raw, and the time segment was a blur, as he had been teetering on the cusp of death. His trusty subconscious finally located the memory in long-term near-dead-as-a-doorknob storage. "I asked that she be made whole," he replied.

There was a sudden flurry of post-it note activity whirring around the wytch's face. Tal was unable to categorize her expression more specifically because she wasn't human and the ripples of echoes of the expression of an expression didn't form a recognizable pattern.

"You didn't ask that she be healed?" she asked.

"Well, sure. Well, no, not exactly, I guess. I mean it's the exact same wish isn't it? Healed, made whole?" he asked her.

"I don't know, Quint of the Omada," she replied. "Is it?"

"If answering a question with a question isn't on the bad manners list, it should be," Tal shot back, instantly regretting his lip.

"I'm suddenly feeling the need to fashion some new wind chimes," she quickly replied. "Multiple sets."

Really stupid, Tal. You can't even figure out her facial expressions, why would you think you can joke with her? "Sorry. I'm sorry. I seem to have a longstanding serious addiction to smartassery."

"Your apology is accepted. You clearly do not understand the full import of your wish. I think Time will reveal it to you, most probably in a painful manner."

Baba Yaga is one weird chick, Tal decided. "That's my story, pretty much blow by blow. Is it sufficient?"

The wytch smiled. At least he was pretty sure that's what it was. The expression began with an upturn at the corners of her mouth until her canines were partially exposed and ended up with crow's feet at both temples. That expression left quickly, succeeded by one that he knew had to be some iteration of sadness. "Yes, Quint of the Omada. Thousands of years ago, minstrels would have sung of your exploits in the great halls of the important. You would have been heralded as Ulysses or Cú Chulainn, your exploits as vaunted as Rostam."

Wow, I guess the gas pump was right, worlds depend upon me. I never thought I'd be vaunted, though. Maybe that someone might say "wowzer" or "holy crap" about my mighty deeds every once in awhile, but never vaunted. "Does this mean no new wind chimes?" he asked carefully.

"Correct," she replied.

Tal wiped his hand across his brow. "Great." Now that imminent death no longer seemed a probability, he looked around the main room. No clocks. Well, duh. Why would there be? It's not like she doesn't want to be late for spin class. "I must have talked for quite awhile."

Baba Yaga nodded. "It is almost first light."

Tal jumped to his feet, and promptly fell back on the sofa. His right foot was asleep. Solidly asleep. He started rubbing it across the rug for friction. "The Recall," he said in a panic. "My teammates must be worried to death about me."

"There's the door," she said pointing the way.

"I'm free to leave," he asked.

"If that is your wish," the wytch replied.

"There's a 'but' coming isn't there?" he asked. "I always know when a 'but' is coming."

"There are no strings, Dust Child. You and your friends may return to the Omphalos tree and remain there safely until your Recall."

"But?"

"But if you seek that for which you Journeyed to this plane, then you must tarry awhile longer and listen to my story."

"Then you will give us a talysman?"

"Then we shall trade a wish for a wish."

Shit! Tal, you aren't very good at this whole bargaining thing. See, for example, your bargain with Helblad. You suck at it, Tal told himself. How much worse can it be, though? I'm already potentially a dead man and the team needs a talysman. This whole magyk equal and opposite reaction thing is a real bytch. "And if I listen to your story and can't grant your wish?" Or won't, he silently added.

"I will be through with my story before your Recall. If you can't grant my wish"—she then looked sideways at Tal—"or if you don't want to, you may still leave. Without a talysman."

I got to get me a better poker face. "What is the talysman?" Tal asked.

Again that face, that might—or might not—have been a smile a thousand years ago. "Now that you have truthfully told me your entire story, I know exactly what you need Quint."

"Sounds fair," he said. I really need to go to the bathroom he thought but I'm not bringing that up now. He stood up and extended his hand. "I consent. Do you?"

Tal could tell Baba Yaga was stunned. "A Dust Child?" she asked. "A Child of the Divine Spark offers to bind a contract with a wytch?"

"Yes," Tal replied, leaving his arm extended, his hand, which was shaking—hopefully, imperceptibly shaking.

She stood up as well, her right arm outstretched. "I do," she replied shaking his hand crisply before sitting back down and motioning for him to do likewise. As Tal took his seat, she began.

CHAPTER QUADRAGINTA QUATTUOR

Baba Yaga began, in a whisper so soft Tal had to lean forward to hear her. "The only thing that mattered to others was that I be beautiful."

I knew it, Tal thought.

The wytch paused before continuing. It was apparent she was searching for words. She's summoning rusted memories, Tal thought. A part of her long ago consigned to Time's junkyard. "Vasilisa was my given name, but my Papa always called me Lepa," she said, unconsciously raising her hand to stroke her cheek in a gesture, mimicking muscle memory from millennia past.

Her face changed for a moment, Tal thought. The distortions moved away, she lost some of her ambiguity for a second.

"Lepa—it meant 'beautiful' in our language. Papa was a tribal chieftain. Much, much later he would have been called a tsar. He was an important man with great wealth and power. As those things were measured in those days. I believe Papa loved me—at least as those things were measured in those days.

"I gave little heed to my physical appearance. Knowledge and deeds were what was important to me. Daughters, however, were merely property back then—commodities to be bartered and traded. No more, no less, than the bolts of spun silk from the Orient. Much, much less than our region's purebred goats and camels.

"Yes," she replied to the question on his face, "even the daughters of chiefs were fodder for conquest, cats-paws in the games of grasping men. I had one brother, my twin, Molniya. Even though I was older by a few minutes, Molniya was the one who was taught his letters and how to fight, both physically and strategically. Every resource was made available to him because he was male and therefore the heir. Whatever was needed to prepare Molniya to rule was given to him in abundance. Me? I was given long dresses, a maid to comb my hair for several hours each day, and regularly trotted out as a bargaining chip for potential political alliances.

"For years I harassed my brother's tutor until he agreed to secretly teach me how to read and write, not only in our language but in Latin and Greek as well. I did the same to the Swordmaster and the Head Groom. The first trained me in the arts of war, and the latter in the skills of advanced equitation. All of this was done in secret from Papa and his Ruling Council, but with the knowledge and full agreement of my mother. As much as Papa loved me, all of their lives would have been forfeit if their actions had been discovered. Even Mama, who was first among his wives, and who he had named his Consort.

"I wanted to be self-sufficient, to not have to depend upon anyone—particularly any man—to fashion my fortune. With the skills I learned I would be able to escape, to flee far from Papa's influence, to make a life for myself somewhere where my sex or physical appearance didn't matter. Where my family's wealth didn't matter. I would have traded all of the days of my present to insure such a future."

Hold on, Tal thought. Flash back to my first encounter with Myrddin, back when he was posing as Mertin Wilt. He asked me that same question.

The wytch paused in her narration, crisscrossing her hands together several times, rubbing them palms flat against each other. She's nervous, Tal thought. He couldn't tell if she was trying to summon the spirit of a memory, or to exorcise one. Maybe she didn't know herself. "Then his family walked into our village. They were...he was...nobody. From nowhere. Travellers."

"Travellers?" I asked, so drawn into the narrative that I interrupted her.

"Magyars. The predecessors of the people you now call gypsies. His given name was Luchisty Chelo. In your tongue it is translated as, 'Radiant Brow'."

Say what? Tal asked himself. That's my name translated form the original Welsh tongue. And Myrddin's. That can't possibly be a coincidence. Can it?

Baba Yaga paused again, allowing for the slack in her recollection to be reeled in. "Many nights during my youth I had taken blankets and climbed to our palace roof, so that I might sleep the night embraced by the splendor of Zorya's skillful shepherding of the Celestials in the nighttime sky. It was my momentary escape from the fate I knew awaited me.

"Suitors for my hand repeatedly brought Papa treasure chests, overflowing with sparkling gems, mined from the farthest corners of the known world. Because of my father's wealth, the finest minstrels entertained in our Great Hall, their songs so heart wrenching our palace songbirds stood still in their cages so that they themselves might memorize the melodies."

At this point the wytch stared directly into Tal's eyes. It seemed almost—not quite—but almost, as if there was a remnant of a coal that had remained banked for centuries. "I tell you about all of the beautiful things I had seen and heard because I want you to understand that from the moment my eyes first met his, I knew with certainty that whether I lived forever, or only another moment, I would never...ever...see...or hear...or feel anything as lovely as Luch. In my eyes, there was no other of Amarantos's creations which compared to him."

Tal was spellbound by the wytch's story. For several reasons. First, the raw honesty of the tale had stripped him bare

241

to his own feelings. Yet, as she told the story, it was almost as if she were recounting something that had happened to someone else. Like if Emet was telling something traumatic from my childhood, Tal thought. Second, as she worked her way through the story, the translucent veils which normally hovered close and around her seemed to become agitated, becoming miniature dervishes whirling first around her and then around the cabin.

"Luch and his family were performing in the square on a market day. It was some silly pratfall comedy with puppets but the audience enjoyed it tremendously, most especially the children. It was because of Luch. The little ones instinctively knew about him so many of the things it took me weeks to learn. That he was not only beautiful, but that he was also kind. His family's troupe were itinerants, they had little in the way of possessions yet Luch always stopped to talk to any and all of the small ones, and to give them some candy or a trinket."

"You fell in love with him," Tal interjected.

"Before Luch, that word might have as well have been four disconnected letters. Love was an emotion which was either imagined or the exclusive province of the entire world save me. To me it was a fable. Oh, my mind acknowledged it conceptually. The reality of it though had never been entered my heart. Until Luch.

"Luch. Want. Need. Love. Each of those are four-letter words. Luch showed me the difference between want and need, and that love is a miraculous merging of the two.

"It was difficult at first to find time to be alone with him but I finally learned how to play my tutors one against the other. There were sunrise rides to meet him at the edge of town so that we might sit huddled together under one of the grandfathers of the forest. Other days I would sneak a picnic lunch for us and we would walk beside the banks of the Zbruch, laughing and skipping stones before stopping to feast on fruits and cheeses and venison.

"My favorite moments with Luch though were our sunsets together. I would sit with one of his goat hair blankets wrapped around my shoulders while he serenaded me. His voice rang like the finest crystal. Luch's fellow troupers had taught him how to play all of the instruments they used in their puppet shows and mummeries. His two favorites though were the svirel—a flute—and the gusli."

"The gusli over your fireplace? It was his?" Tal interjected.

Baba Yaga cocked her head to the left a little. "I do not recall you mentioning that you are also a bard, Quint."

"Well, never really thought of it in those terms but I guess I am. Well, sort of, I guess. I can sing pretty well and play a few different instruments," he said, as he also nodded his response.

"Such an interesting human. The gusli is an ancient instrument. How came you to learn it?"

"I taught some of my friends at Hunts School how to play the guitar." Tal mimed playing a few bars on an air guitar. "They returned the favor by teaching me how to play a bunch of their stringed instruments from different planes. The gusli was one of the instruments. There were several different versions. I learned to play the smaller, wing-shaped kind, that have between nine and twelve strings. That kind," he said pointing at the mantle.

Baba Yaga nodded, and motioned with her head that he might inspect it closer. "Yes, that was Luch's."

Wow, Tal thought, as he stood up and walked over to touch the dark wood instrument. This bad boy is thousands of years old.

"After he played and sang we would each talk about our dreams. Sunsets with Luch were when I felt more complete than I ever imagined possible. Well, not 'with him'," she said turning her head aside.

Her face, Tal thought, it was like a blush began gestating and then simply went away as the ethereal veils frenzied about her head and shoulders.

"I would have, you know," she said, as she turned back to Tal, her eyes now focused squarely on his. "I would have been with him. I would have gone anywhere with him, done anything for him...or with him. He refused me. Repeatedly. He wouldn't even kiss me, Quint of the Omada. Do you know why?"

Honesty, Tal, he reminded himself. The odds favor honesty as being the polite choice. "There weren't any Knights of the Round Table that far back, Ms. Yaga, but my best bet is that Luch didn't think such actions would be chivalrous."

"I've never thought about it using that definition but you're correct. He told me repeatedly he loved me, that he'd never loved anyone before, and that he couldn't imagine he would ever love anyone again, because I was everything he'd ever wanted. He told me I was smart...funny...strong-willed. Always he told me I was those things before he told me I was beautiful. Always. Because those things were more important to him than whether my hair was properly tressed or my gown cut in the latest style."

There's a "but" coming, Tal thought. It's sad really that one of my superpowers is apparently being a "but" expert.

"But every time he told me he loved me, he also reminded me there was no possible future for us. He told me that to men like my father, he and his family were the same as a dirt floored walkway. Both were things whose sole reason for being was for the rich and mighty to step on.

"I told Luch none of that mattered to me, that I loved him, and that I would run away with him. He wouldn't let me, even though I knew it was what he wanted more than he'd ever wanted anything in his entire life. He wouldn't 'soil' me or allow me to become 'damaged goods.' He knew the risk to me. He told me he loved me and showed me by giving up any possibility there would be an 'us'.

"His clan stayed as long as they could, much longer than they normally would have remained in one location. They had to move on eventually. Their livelihood depended upon being a moveable feast of performing and fortune-telling and bartering.

"I'm not sure the heavens have ever witnessed the sorrow I felt the night he told me his troupe was leaving at first light. He was a dutiful son. His parents needed his musical gifts, as well as his strong back, to help them earn their living. Luch swore to me he'd be back for me—when he had made something of himself, when he felt worthy to ask Papa for my hand.

"I woke early the next morning to see him one last time. I was too late, they were already gone. Empty weeks passed, becoming colorless months. Then yet another suitor arrived— Prince Osel. He came with much pomp, a large retinue, and an almost impossible number of rare furs and gold. Even more important was his promise that a male child of our union would rule not only Papa's dominions but all of the Prince's considerable suzerain.

"Luch and I had always been careful, at least we thought we had been. However, some low level courtier seeking to advance himself with my father had seen us holding hands and walking one evening and had kept the information for the day he thought to use it to advance himself. He thought Prince Osel's arrival was an opportune time.

"Papa did, in fact, reward the man. Immediately. He was drug by his thumbs into the courtyard where separate ropes were tied to each of his feet and his hands. Papa then had his four favorite stallions brought from the stables. The other end of each of the ropes was tied to a saddle pommel. The four horses were simultaneously whipped, so that they would pull with all of their might in four opposite directions. The great beasts leapt, muscles straining, their hindquarters rippling with their efforts, until the man was ripped asunder. The largest piece, with his head and most of his torso, remained alive and conscious for several minutes, the screams echoing throughout the entire village. After he finally died, all four pieces were gathered and separately hung outside the front gate of the palace, as carrion for the vultures and to remind Papa's subjects that he owned each and every one of them.

"The next day a messenger delivered a summons for me to appear the following morning in the Great Hall. I was then locked in my rooms, a prisoner from that moment until the next morning, when armed guards came to escort me to what I quickly realized was a trial. Papa was wearing his robes of state and was seated in his Judgment Chair. Mama was seated to his left. The Ruling Council and other village elders stood behind Papa in a semi-circle. To his right, also seated in a chair, but lower than Papa's of course, was Prince Osel. He too was encompassed by his councilors.

"Papa demanded I publicly swear in front of Prince Osel and the nobles of the kingdom that I had remained chaste. I was mortified, I couldn't imagine anything more embarrassing that could possibly ever happen to me. I was soon to be proven wrong.

"I swore under oath I had not been violated. Papa looked to Prince Osel for his acceptance. In response, the prince glared at me, then back to my father, before flicking his eyes toward the mounds of valuables stacked against the far wall of the Great Hall. It was clear to all he was threatening to withhold his alliance and all of its benefits.

"Osel then stood and stepped onto the top step leading to Papa's throne. In so doing, he intentionally ended up being taller than my father. A hush went through the assemblage at his gross act of disrespect. To a man, Papa's honor guards' swords came halfway out of their sheaths. At a gesture from Papa, they stood down.

"Then Prince Osel spoke. In his oh-so-very-cultured, honey-tongued, aristocratic voice. 'I have come to this country because I was assured I would find a bride of both unsurpassing beauty and virtue. My people deserve only the finest breeding stock to be their queen.' With this he looked to his lackeys who all nodded and clapped once in unison. 'A woman's word is insufficient on any matter of honor. I demand a public examination. Here. Now. Or the marriage arrangement is terminated'."

Damn, Tal thought. That Osel dude was one major dickhead.

Baba Yaga gathered herself and continued. "Mama began to stand, to plead for me but Papa reached over and grasped her arm, squeezing hard until she sank back into her chair. My brother even stood there and did nothing. Papa summoned his personal physician. A few minutes later he appeared and Papa beckoned him to his throne. After whispering a brief time, the physician walked over to me, summoning several serving girls to attend him.

"They placed several large pillows on the floor and then while I stood there, frozen in a combination of rage and shame, the servants undressed me. After making me lay flat on my back the physician grabbed my ankles and forced me to spread my legs,...and then...and then he roughly inserted his fingers and his surgical tools inside me. He kept on probing me until I bled substantially all over the pillows."

The wytch paused again. There was now a maelstrom of frenzied shadows flying around her, around Tal, around the entire cabin. "When he was finished violating me, the doctor looked at Papa and nodded his head. While I lay on the floor sobbing, I saw Papa look over to Prince Osel for acknowledgment that their political and monetary transaction was still viable.

"Prince Osel, however, wasn't done yet. It wasn't until much later I realized his actions had nothing to do with me. He was simply hiking his leg to piss all over my father to make sure my father understood how far down he was in the pecking order. Osel smiled broadly as he walked down the steps to me. I cringed, making myself as small as I possibly could, but there was nothing I could do to stop that monster from grabbing my arm, forcing me to my feet, and then twisting my arm until it would have broken if I hadn't turned in a naked, bloody pirouette for all to see.

"He spoke again. 'Only one small impediment remains. I must be assured of the undying affection and loyalty of my betrothed. I require her to formally declare, in front of this entire assembly, that she never had any affection for that peasant and that he attempted to force himself on her.' With that Osel dropped my arm and walked several steps away before turning to look at me. His greasy smile, a gash splitting his face in two.

"After everything that had already happened, the request was of no consequence to Papa. 'She will so swear,' he replied resignedly. All of my humiliation suddenly burned away, now flash-forged into obstinate outrage. An outrage which continued growing hotter by the minute. 'No, she won't,' I replied.

"The entire Great Hall grew quiet once again. It had been one thing when two men were disputing about power, it was an entirely different matter for an unruly camel to spit in the face of its owner. Looking back I can see Papa was probably embarrassed by the entire sequence of events, both for himself and for me. Whatever the reason, Papa leapt up from his throne, extended his right arm while holding the staff signifying his tribal authority, and said, 'I order you to swear you have no affection for the peasant and that the animal attempted to force himself on you.'

"Arrogance had now formed a triumvirate with obstinance and anger. 'You want me to swear?' I looked first to Papa and then to Prince Osel. There was now no vestige of the smarmy smile remaining on his oily face. Turning to Papa, I said, 'Fine. I swear on my eternal soul that Luchisty Chelo is my True Love and that if I live a thousand years I shall never love another.' Then I executed a perfect naked three hundred degree turn, in deliberate mockery of Prince Osel. I turned to him and added, 'I hope you enjoyed the show, you fatuous jackanape, because I will kill myself before you ever again lay one of your no doubt disease-ridden fingers upon me'."

'Fatuous jackanape,' Tal thought. Girl had some serious linguistic smack down skills.

"I could see from Papa's face he'd finally realized his pride and his ire had led him into making a grievous error. He had underestimated the obstinacy of his only daughter. As the chieftain he couldn't back down. He was counting on me to realize that, and to recant. In doing so, he again underestimated my strength of will.

248

"In accordance with our laws, each week for three consecutive weeks, at sunrise on Utorok, I was summoned before the throne in front of the same assembly, while Papa made demand upon me to renounce Luch. Arrogant as ever and heedless of the consequences, I thrice refused to do as requested. Papa had no choice. As I said, I believe he loved me, as love was measured back then. Refusing the thrice-ordered royal command was treason and the punishment was death."

"What?" Tal asked, incredulous. "Your own father ordered you put to death? He was the chieftain or the tsar or whatever. All he had to do was pardon you, or..."

"Even leaders must obey the law. Perhaps," she mused, "more than any other, the leaders must obey the law."

"The only option was death?" Tal asked.

"Not just death, a specific ritual death—the traitor was walled up alive in the town square."

"That's beyond cruel and unusual punishment," Tal added.

"The public nature of the punishment had a purpose. The entire community had to go about their daily lives in the market, hearing the traitor slowly dying. Pleading for mercy. Begging for food and water. They had to listen to the traitor screaming from lips so cracked from dehydration that the cries ceased to be understandable words. They were supposed to listen as the whimpering was finally replaced by the silence of death. After witnessing such suffering, no one in their right mind would consider disobeying their sovereign."

Tal felt like he might be sick. Even though it had now been hours since he'd eaten, he could feel it roiling inside him. "That didn't happen, though. You're here now."

"Mama fled the city the morning they began mixing the mortar and building the low walls of the structure. She couldn't stand it, she blamed herself for 'indulging' me for years. Prince Osel had stayed on as my father's guest so he could make sure the sentence was carried out and his honor upheld.

249

"The structure was only to be built about four feet high and five feet wide. Why waste materials and labor building a comfortable coffin for a traitor? When the walls were done, I was escorted from my room, allowed only a simple white shift to wear. The only thing that remained was to lift me over the wall, after which eight stout guards would fasten an inch thick metal roof on top of the brickwork.

"During the entire ceremony the crowd stood silent, all eyes focused inward on my impending confinement. Suddenly, almost as if one mind controlled all of their bodies, they turned toward the south end of the square and began pointing and murmuring.

"It was Luch. Whistling one of my favorite tunes. He came striding slowly up the main road, head held high, without an apparent care in the world. His hair was burnished by the light of the sun, his eyes unwaveringly fixed on mine."

"He was John Wayne, come to save you, so you could both ride off into the sunset together," Tal said, suddenly hopeful there might be happiness at the end of this story.

"No. Luch knew when he came back that we would not both leave the square alive. He wasn't a warrior, he was a trouper and a musician. He came back to our town from whatever safe refuge he and his family had found. He came alone and unarmed, knowing in advance the town would be bristling with armed guardsmen.

"I knew immediately why he had come and started screaming, 'No!' at the top of my voice. 'No! No! No!' When Luch didn't stop, I yelled at the workmen to hurry up, put me in the prison and nail the roof closed. To do whatever was necessary to complete Papa's sentence. To do whatever was necessary to make it too late for Luch to do what he intended."

Tal's gut turned sour again as he finally realized where the story was taking him—that there was only one resolution to her narrative that allowed Baba Yaga to be here today. "No," Tal whispered involuntarily under his breath.

"Papa ordered me gagged. When that didn't stop me from thrashing around, he ripped his own shirt off, and tore it into narrow strips, handing the pieces to his men to bind my arms behind my back.

"After I was restrained, Luch approached Papa and was granted permission to speak. He told Papa his entire relationship with me had been a charade he'd undertaken in an effort solely to steal jewelry and other valuables from the castle, and that he had tried repeatedly to bed me but despite his best efforts I had rejected all of his advances. Luch finished by telling Papa that…," the wytch faltered in her telling before regrouping, "he told Papa he 'cared less for me than any one of the last five cheap whores he'd fucked'.

"Osel stood there simpering but Papa flew into a rage. He would have killed Luch himself on the spot but he couldn't under the law. By making his confession, Luch had absolved me of my treason, and replaced it with his much more heinous offenses. He would now have to die the ritual death. Papa realized he couldn't kill him, Quint of the Omada, but he could beat him. And so he did. Himself. Personally. He savaged him again and again with the royal scepter until Luch was nothing more than a bruised bag of flesh filled with splintered bones. One of his eyes had been torn away from a direct blow, the other was swollen shut. His once impossibly beautiful face was completely deconstructed by Papa's violence. Throughout the ordeal Luch never whimpered or moaned. Nothing. He just took it. When he finally passed out, Papa signaled for the guards to throw him in the prison and secure the roof.

"The living tomb was heavily guarded to prevent anyone from attempting to thwart Luch's sentence. For three days and three nights I kept vigil as well, my head laid against the masonry, talking to Luch, entreating him to recant his testimony, to save himself. I apologized to him for my stupidity and my arrogance, which had created the entire situation. For three days and three nights I heard no reply. Nothing.

At dawn on the fourth day the sentries were recalled to other duties. Seeing them leave I gave up too, assuming Luch had died from his untreated injuries. I stood up slowly, my muscles cramping from dehydration and lack of use. As I was leaning against the crypt, I heard the faintest whisper of air moving across the bricks. It was Luch! Do you know, Quint of the Omada, what the last words were said to me by the only man I ever loved?"

His shoulders sagging from the overwhelming sadness of her story, Tal couldn't even respond audibly. Totally overcome, the best he could do was simply slowly shake his head side to side.

He said, "Choose Love, Vasilisa. Always."

"Later that morning—after I was sure Luch was gone—I withdrew to my rooms, intent on never leaving again. There was an emptiness in me. It's hard to describe because even though it was a void, I could feel it chewing on me, growing larger and more painful. Looking back now I guess the best way to describe the festering was that it was an abscess of guilt."

"It wasn't your fault Luch died. That's on your father and Prince Osel," Tal argued.

"No, his death was totally on me. My arrogance and my pride were the reasons Luch died. If I had bent my neck to my father's will, Luch would have lived a long and happy life. He would have married, had children, been a grandfather."

Tal almost interrupted Baba Yaga again, to reason with her but quickly decided that dialogue needed to wait until she was through.

"Food and drink were brought to me each day. I touched nothing, figuring it was only right I should suffer and die as Luch had. My plans were changed when Papa appeared at my door a few days later. He informed me that in light of Luch's confession, Prince Osel had agreed to overlook my unfortunate comments and that we were to be married the next morning.

"The rest of the day was taken up with maidservants constantly in attendance—pinning up a gown, bathing me.

washing my hair or choosing jewelry for me. I checked my door that night after they'd all left and as I surmised, Papa had ordered sentries to stand guard.

"I snuck onto the roof one last time from my balcony to make good on my promise to Osel…and to myself. Luna ruled the skies that night, the heavens were in the grasp of her unfeeling, icy magyk. I sat down for a few minutes to order my thoughts. As I tried to stand to walk toward the parapet, I realized I was so debilitated from lack of water and food and by my overwhelming sense of loss that I didn't even have the energy to throw myself off the roof. I prayed to Luna to take away my pain. To make me so I would never feel anything again. I prayed that I might have the strength to give up my life.

"The Elder Children still walked Earth Realm in those days. Luna heard my heart's petition, and appeared before me dressed only in her cold, silver brilliance. She asked me if I understood what I was asking of her, if I was truly asking her for a life devoid of feeling or emotion. I answered yes, and she reached out her hand and pulled me to her bosom.

"When next I woke, Luna had transported me to Arianhrod, her Earth Realm home. It exists not in any fixed location, but simply appears wherever her moon avatar is closest to Earth Realm. The moon itself is always full there, the moonbeams wider than the boulevards of the greatest of our cities. The house and grounds are immaculate, perfect in their silvered beauty. A cold, sterile beauty. On the trellises outside the glass-encased lunarium, the moonflowers were exquisite works of art, each having the appearance of finely glazed porcelain. The wall art, the flooring, and even the furniture, were shot through with every imaginable hue of magykal silver and white. It was not however, a kind or welcoming place for trespassyrs. The estate perimeter was guarded by the Rougaru."

"I've never heard of them," Tal said.

"That is only one of their many names throughout Earth history. Monsters, without either conscience or the ability to feel pain, they call themselves the 'Loup-Garou.' Men and women who shape shift into wolves."

"Werewolves," Tal whistled under his breath. "The moon was always full, so they were always in full beast mode."

"Yes," the wytch confirmed. "Arianhrod is where Luna eventually conducted all of her initiation rites into the Cult of Nyx. Each supplicant had to do as I did, they had to first irrevocably renounce their humanity."

"I don't understand. How does someone 'renounce their humanity'?" Tal asked.

"It is a ritual that takes hours, maybe it was even days. Time seems to pass differently at Arianhrod, so it's difficult to gauge its passing. The initiate is first required to exhaustively list their every emotion, every feeling, and then to state they irrevocably reject each of them. Sadness, pain, happiness, joy, elation, and all the myriad tints and hues in between. After that portion of the ritual is complete, they drink a magykal draught, which Luna has herself prepared specifically for the presumptive wytch. After those steps are concluded, the initiate is blessed with the Cult's symbol. It is at that moment the transfiguration occurs."

Baba Yaga stopped talking for a moment as she pushed up her left sleeve, all the way to her shoulder. High on her left arm there was a perfect imprint of a crescent moon.

"So all wytches receive that exact same ink?" Tal asked.

"We do all wear the Cult's symbol. However, it is not a tattoo, it is a brand."

Wowzers, Tal thought. Can't even imagine how tough it must be to stand still while someone scorches you with a hot iron until it sears your flesh.

"The branding is the final act of the making ceremony, it activates Luna's magyk. None of the wytches understand the mechanics, as it involves Principe-level magyk. As you know, humans are Children of the Divine Spark. Out of the entire universe only Dust Children have electricity-based lifeforce. The lyfeforce of all Folk—and all Creatures—whether created by

Amarantos or by her children, is fueled by magyk. At the time of transformation, Luna's magyk spell creates a familiar for each of the wytches."

"You seem to have three," Tal observed.

"Yes, as I was the first initiate, Luna made me Keeper of the Seal of Nyx and gyfted me with three familiars, which allows me to syphon more magyk than any other wytch."

"Which makes you the most powerful of all of them," Tal confirmed.

"That is correct. It also provided me with sufficient magyk to serve her as one of her guides for the deceased."

"That's right, you're one of the three psychopomp wytches," Tal said.

"One of innumerable names given by humans to myself and the two others like me. To some we were Azrael, to others Valkyrie, and to still others, Barnumbir."

"You're no longer human, then?" Tal asked quietly.

If the wytch had still been human, the noise she made would have been a laugh. "No, Quint of the Omada. I am about as inhuman as someone can be. The penultimate step of the initiation, immediately before the branding, was when Luna removed each of our emotions, one by one."

"You mean figuratively, right?" Tal asked.

"No, physically. She used her magyk to excise them from within us."

"She destroyed them?" Tal asked.

"No," the wytch replied. "I've given it much thought over the centuries and I've decided that uncreation of that kind must be beyond even the Principes' magyk. She does not have the power to terminate our emotions. She is able magykally, with our permission, to separate us from our emotions, giving them an external existence. They remain tethered to our physical forms but they are ours no longer."

"I don't get it, I don't understand the whole magyk syphon thing."

"My body still uses electricity for lifeforce but it's a unique hybrid of electricity. I am sustained by the magyk syphoned from other beings. Luna created the familiars to serve as converters. They somehow translate the stolen magyk for my body to use. I will never grow old, I will never die. From now until the end of Time, others will die so that I will live. Forever."

Okay, Tal thought, this setup is different than what we thought it might be. "You could stop stealing from them."

Again, the nonhuman upward tug of the lips. "Doesn't work that way. Luna laid a geas on us in case anyone regretted their decision enough to....well, enough. The magyk syphon is automatic. Any magykal being within my sphere of influence has their magyk drained from them to replenish me."

"Until they die?" Tal asked aghast, as he realized the parameters of the syphon.

"Yes," the wytch confirmed.

"Well," Tal interjected, "the magyk syphon didn't carve all those wind chimes on your front porch."

"No, it didn't. Those are bones of Folk who travelled to this plane to murder me."

"What?" Tal asked, surprised.

"In a number of Realms there are those who believe that immortality can be obtained by killing a wytch."

"Can it?" Tal asked wide-eyed.

Baba Yaga hesitated before answering. "We don't know. No one has ever been successful in killing one of us."

"That means the other bones, the thousands in your killing field, they are all from innocent victims?" Tal asked.

Quickly and coldly she responded. "Relatively innocent."

Tal rolled all of the new data through his central processor. "That is why in all of the Earth stories, wytches lived far apart from each other," Tal said.

"Yes, else the stronger of us might have syphoned the weaker."

"The fairy tales, some of those were based on actual human interaction with wytches?" Tal asked.

"Most of the tales are fabrication or embellishments. The only contact any wytch had for centuries before the bane on magyk was when humans lost their way and crossed into our domains."

"When magyk was abolished on the Earth plane, you couldn't get any more magyk to sustain you?" Tal asked.

"That is correct," Baba Yaga confirmed. "Arthrys's ban couldn't effect Principe-level magyk. However, once all of the Folk and Creatures left the Earth plane there was no longer any magyk we could steal to sustain us."

"Which means there was a wytch diaspora."

"Yes," Baba Yaga replied. "We each used the Prime Omphalos repeatedly until we found suitable separate planes. I chose this Realm because there was plenty of clean water, wild game, and a wide variety of edible fruits and grains."

"And Folk to syphon," Tal added.

"It is the nature of what I am and the geas Luna laid upon me. With my voluntary consent," the wytch replied. "Most of the stolen magyk is retained as a reservoir to provide me with lyfe. I used the remainder of the stolen magyk to create warnings, discouraging anyone from accidentally finding me."

"We noticed that," Tal replied. "The waterfalls, the forest, all of it, were designed to steer people away from your cabin. So why are there so many bones in the killing field?"

"Several reasons, I guess. Stupidity, curiosity. Fascination of the abomination," she added. "I think that's what it's called. They wouldn't, or couldn't, leave me alone. For others it was greed, requesting the use of magyk for a dark purpose. They came to petition the wytch for a love potion, or to seek the wytch's blessing to bring destruction on an enemy. Once they stepped over my threshold they were snared and couldn't escape."

I guess we might all only be "relatively innocent" after all, Tal thought.

Baba Yaga stood, and walked to the fireplace. Reaching for the poker, she moved the wood, causing the fire to burn hotter. As Tal watched, the poker seemed to alter the fire, morphing it from its normal colors of red and orange to shades of silver. She stuck the iron directly into the fire's heart and left it there, before turning back to address Tal. "We have bound a contract. What you wish from me to fulfill our bargain is a talysman for your Hunts competition?"

"Yes," Tal answered, unable to pull his eyes from the thin, glowing rod shoved deep into the silver flames.

"Regardless of the strength of any individual wytch, talysmen may be weak or strong," Baba Yaga stated, again turning the poker, the fire spiraling upward in response to her ministrations. "I am willing to bestow upon you a talysman worthy of a champion. Is that what you seek of our contract?"

Eyes still transfixed by the flames as they greedily lapped over and around the metal rod, Tal stated, "It is."

"We have made a contract, we two. Even though you're human you do understand when magyk is used there is a cost? That lyfeforce is used?"

"Yes, Tal replied. "The same is true with gyfts, a gyftpryce must be paid." Without conscious thought, he turned Aurora's ring.

"It is so," the wytch confirmed. "This iron," she said, turning and taking hold of the poker, "is the only magykal object I possess."

She's going to give me a used fireplace iron, Tal thought. Seems kind of a lame talysman to me. He cut his eyes form Baba Yaga and the strange fire, to look out the cabin window.

The wytch saw him looking outward. "The familiars are Creatures, made by Luna. Their existence is powered by my abandoned humanity, they are not mine to command to further our contract. As a mortal you have no lyfeforce magyk to expend to power the fashioning of a talysman, so the power to create it will have to come from an ancient human method. Is that acceptable, to you?"

"Absolutely," Tal replied without thinking. Their time until the Recall had to be growing short.

"Do not agree so rashly, Dust Child. The old ways require much pain." She turned back to the fireplace, rousing the silver fire until it roared, flames leaping three feet up the chimney. Finally, Baba Yaga withdrew the metal rod, showing him the superheated end. It had some sort of design on it.

Holy crap, Tal thought, as he finally realized what the iron was. It's not a poker—it's a branding iron. Shit, she's the Keeper of the Seal of Nyx. Tal's excitement excused itself and promptly fled the scene, being replaced by its understudy, cold sweat. "Umm, how much pain are we talking about?" he asked.

"Significant pain, Quint of the Omada," she replied. "Significant pain."

CHAPTER QUADRAGINTA QUINQUE

Baba Yaga shoved the brand back into the embers, silver fire hungrily enveloping it once more. "I will complete my part of the contract first. At the moment I press the brand to your flesh and invoke Luna's power, you will experience all the pain of your entire lifetime in that one moment."

Okay, this is jacked up, Tal thought. My lifetime's pain in one split-second is a little more than "significant pain." Hell, it might possibly kill me.

"If you live through it…"

And there it is, Tal thought, nodding in confirmation to himself.

"Then you can fulfill your part of the bargain. Once the talysman is affixed, the only way you will leave this cabin alive is if you successfully complete your part of the contract."

Which means if I don't do as she asks, I will not only be dead but I will have suffered the grossly understated "significant pain" unnecessarily, Tal thought. "Umm, how about if I throw this out there as a possibility, Ms. Yaga? You know, it would be perfectly okay with me, for a token involving a little less unbelievable pain. Like, maybe if you have a pair of ruby slippers you could let me have as a talys…"

"Ruby slippers?" Baba Yaga asked, aghast. "You're crazy if you think any self-respecting wytch would be caught dead wearing anything but silver pumps." She leaned over and pulled the glowing brand out of the fire before turning back to Tal. "The talysman will not be activated until the contract is fulfilled. Until then it is worthless. Do you understand?"

"Y-Y-Yes," Tal replied. Then taking a deep breath with a corresponding gulp, "So, this isn't some elaborate charade to scare the shit out of the mortal? You really are going to brand me?"

Baba Yaga merely nodded in reply, before advancing toward him, the poker held high. "You will need to be naked before we begin. The mark is traditionally placed on the left shoulder. Is that where you want it?"

This is really happening, Tal told himself. I'm about to get seared. Where? I'm going to have to try to hide it from Mom and Pell. I guess I could have her put it on my left inner thigh, where Emet's tat is. No, he quickly told himself. That is entirely too close to my boys. Well, damn. That pretty much leaves only one place.

Tal stood, a little shakily, turned his back to Baba Yaga, before unbelting and then shrugging out of the gambeson. Oh well, he thought, as he leaned over and braced himself against the arm of the sofa, this is going to solve any possibility of pimples at that location.

"Really? That's where you want the mark of Nyx?" she asked him.

Tal nodded, before gritting his teeth and clutching the sofa even harder. In the next moment he heard screaming—his—and there was the smell of burnt flesh and hair—again, his. The pain invaded his body, then his mind, and finally it assaulted his heart. All of the pain in my entire life in one moment, he thought. How can I possibly bear to live through the old again, much less the future pain? As his upper body collapsed over the arm of the sofa and onto the cushions, the torment tsunami continued to engulf him. Finally the pain drowned all sentient

262

thought, save one. Burning hair? Do I have both pimples and a hairy ass?

Tal wasn't sure how long he was out before his conscious mind believed it safe to rouse him to wakefulness. It couldn't have been too gosh awful long, the wytch was still standing behind him holding the silver-hot brand.

Shit! Shit! SHIITTTT!!!!! HOLY CRAAAAAP! My ass is on fire. If this is what hemorrhoids feel like I need somebody to just go ahead and do an assholerotomy on me right now. His central processor let Tal know all available neurons were overwhelmed trying to transport the plethora of pain messages, and that a sizeable amount of anguish was being placed in layaway to be rolled out for delivery over the next few minutes, possibly hours. SHIITTTTT!!!!

The wytch calmly walked back to the hearth and replaced the rapidly cooling iron in its place beside the fireplace. She stood there for several minutes, silent. Waiting on him.

"Why? Why was that necessary?" Tal finally asked, still near tears because of the supernova now located on his upper left buttock.

"I am Keeper of the Seal of Nyx, and therefore the most powerful wytch in the Cult of Nyx. Once your mark is activated, it will be the most powerful talysman—without exception—that could ever be obtained from a wytch."

"Okay, fine. I guess that explains the 'why' part," Tal replied. As the pain ebbed a smidgeon, his brain reminded him he was still butt-smoking naked. "May I put my clothes back on?" he asked, reaching for the gambeson.

"Not yet, Dust Child. You must be as Amarantos made you until we are done."

You mean, if Amarantos had made me with fire shooting out of the skin of my ass, Tal thought to himself.

"Are you recovered sufficiently to fulfill your obligation?" Baba Yaga asked him.

"I think I can handle it," Tal replied, his breath still coming in large gulps. "As long as it doesn't involve sitting, or running, or breathing."

"Good. Now stand up and turn around." As Tal hesitated, she continued. "Male vanity knows no bounds. I have felt no emotions for over several thousand years, Quint of the Omada. I rather doubt your equipment is sufficiently impressive to cause me to have any feelings this day."

As Tal turned he looked down at his genitals. *If I need a Viagra prescription before I'm twenty, it is absolutely not going to be your fault,* he told his Johnson. *It's just not. It's all on her.*

"The time for the Recall approaches and we must conclude the contract."

You're on the clock, Tal told himself. He stood, placing his weight all on his right leg, and turned around full front to the wytch. "I agree. Let's knock this little old thing out," he replied. "What is it you want me to do?"

In one smooth motion Baba Yaga shrugged off her clothing and calmly knelt naked on the rug in front of him. Crossing her hands in front of her chest she bowed her head. "It is a simple thing. I require that you end me."

CHAPTER QUADRAGINTA SEX

"Beg your pardon?" Tal asked, nonplussed but somehow remembering to be polite. Which included not unduly ogling the extremely shapely nude wytch.

"Our conversation today has made me acknowledge there is an impassable gulf dividing living and existing. It is what Luch was trying to tell me with his last words. I was so full of anger and self-loathing I refused to listen.

"I cannot kill myself because of Luna's geas. No magykal Folk or Creature will ever make it alive past the automatic syphon. There is little possibility another Dust Child will ever visit this plane. I've been here millennia and you are the first. I will continue in my present state until the end of Time.

"I have decided that is no longer acceptable. I want to feel again—even if the only option I have left myself is feeling the pain of dying." The wytch made a vague gesture surrounding her face and then toward the air immediately surrounding her, enlarging the gesture until it encompassed the entire room. "I need your help to accomplish that goal. For your talysman to have value it must be activated. To activate it, you must end me."

That's interesting, Tal thought. Her arm gestures, the way she tilted her head. She acted like her emotions are here, real time.

265

"I am ready," she announced, still kneeling, head bowed.

"I'm not going to do it," Tal stated firmly.

"You seem to think this is a matter in which you have a choice, Quint of the Omada. The Recall looms before you. If you don't do as I ask, I will kill you, and the Omada will return without a talysman. Even if they somehow remain Finalists at the end of this semester, we both know it is extremely rare for a team with only four remaining members to win the Tyrning. Do as I ask and there will be no other team with a more powerful talysman than the one I offer. To insure the Omada win the Wytch Hunt you must fulfill our bargain."

"You played me," Tal declared. "You kept me here until the last minute so I couldn't think this through or explore other options."

She looked up from the floor and smiled wanly. "Your team is counting on you. You have Fragarach. There couldn't be a more perfect weapon to accomplish your present task," the wytch finished calmly, coldly.

"I'm still not sure exactly what 'Seeking the Center' is about but I'm learning what it's not, and I know with absolute certainty that murdering you this morning is not of the Center," Tal replied firmly. "So, no. No, thank you."

Tal could almost feel a breeze as cloudlets of gossamer frenzied around the wytch in response.

Baba Yaga remained in her kneeling position. This time she didn't even bother to make eye contact with him. In a voice devoid of any inflection, she said, "You will fulfill your part of our contract, Quint. Or, I won't only kill you. I will walk out that door toward your teammates. As soon as they are within my range, their lives will be snuffed out and no one will ever know what happened to the Omada."

That must be what happened to some of the teams on the first two wytch hunts. Think, Tal, think. Why did she keep gesturing to herself and around the cabin just now? Why had she almost appeared in focus as a human being several times during her story? I'm not even sure that what she's asking me to do counts as murder. She wants to kill herself but can't, so I'm only helping her do it. Which makes it assisted suicide. Doesn't it? And if so, isn't there a legit argument in certain very rare situations involving debilitating, terminal diseases that assisting is the moral choice? In the abstract that may or may not be true, Tal decided. Regardless, this time isn't one of those situations.

Okay then, new tack. She's threatened me and my friends. If I kill her it would be self-defense. I either use Fragarach to stop her now, or I let her kill my friends. Of course, it's not a given she could accomplish that. I might could yell a warning loud enough for Borras and the others to hear. They're all magyked up on this plane, and all they would have to do is play keep away until the Recall.

Baba Yaga chose to give up her humanity because she couldn't stand the pain of loving Luch, and losing him. The weight of causing his death was too burdensome. So, she decided to give up all of her todays for a tomorrow where she would no longer hurt. Which also meant she gave up all of her joys, her laughters, her opportunities to love again.

This is what Myrddin was talking about, wasn't it? When I first met him as knickers-wearing Mertin Wilt. I was totally ready to relinquish all of my todays for a tomorrow that may—or may not—ever come. And it wouldn't matter if that tomorrow did or didn't come, I would still have forfeited all of my todays. This heartbeat, and the next one. I almost made the same choice Baba Yaga made, to trade in all of my emotions, all of my feelings to achieve a goal.

There is no one who can stop me—any of us—from throwing away our wants and desires. From saying life is too hard. That having dreams and goals and hopes is simply too much of a burden to bear. To give up on constantly striving to be more, to be better, because when I finally do succeed and I am more and I am better, I still won't let that be good enough.

No one can. No one but ourselves. A cold chill washed over Tal. What's that saying, "someone is walking over my grave?" Tal realized he was more terrified at that moment than he'd been when he'd first entered the cabin. I was so close to the precipice, to making the same decision that all of the wytches made. So close to giving up my humanity for a pre-determined result I desperately thought I wanted. Each of us, all of us, we can do this to ourselves, he thought, his entire body shaking in acknowledgement.

Amarantos has given each and every one of us free will. We are each flawed and arrogant and stubborn, but we each deserve to love and to be loved. Each of us. All of us. Me. Väst. Elle. Emet. Baba Yaga. Luch.

Turn the Rubik's cube, Tal, use your mind. Think harder, time is not your friend. Wait a minute, she wants me to use Fragarach, a magykal object, to end her. It's only one hundred percent fatal because it's a magyk sword. There are only two magykal objects in this cabin, the Nyx brand and Fragarach. No, Tal, that's not true. There are four—including the Ring of Gyges and Aurora's ring. I've used it twice. The Lady Aurora warned me to use it wisely because I would need it four times, and that my choice would cost someone dear. Maybe, just maybe, I already made it past that bump in the road and I'm in the clear.

Luch! Tal felt an answer begin to coalesce around Luch. Some fact about Luch solves this problem. What is it? He was handsome. She was crazy about him. His last words were to tell her to choose love. He was a minstrel. His name was the same as mine—Taliesin.

Bingo. Luch was a singer. His gusli is here. It is the only object in this entire cabin that looks like it is supposed to look. Why?

I've learned how to play the gusli at Hunts School. Coincidence? What about his name meaning the same thing as mine, despite the millennia between us? More coincidence? I don't think so. Decision made. With Aurora's ring, I will try to help her do what Luch told her he wanted her to do. She just said she wished she had taken the path he suggested. If I can, I will help her to feel again—to choose love. "Ms. Yaga, my psuche name, it's Taliesin."

His statement jolted the wytch, she rocked back on her haunches, her white-but-not white face became even whiter-but-not whiter. She wobbled a little even though she was still in a sitting position. As her tremors subsided, she slowly stood and stumbled over to the sofa—where she collapsed onto the faded cushion. "You...you are telling me you are this generation's avatar of the Shining Brow?"

Truth, Tal reminded himself again. Truth is usually the polite choice. "I do not know the answer to that question. It may be that that is still to be determined. I do know that my psuche name is Taliesin."

"And you too are a bard?" she asked.

"I do sing fairly well," Tal replied, trying to be modest.

If her features had been human, Tal would have described her as looking like she was going into shock. It's decision time, he told himself. "Worlds depend upon you." That was the prophesy of a scratched all-to-hell out-of-order gas pump. Helblad, the draugr, told me I had a clever mind and a giving heart and that I should use those gifts. Myrddin told me, well, he told me so many damn things, I can't identify anything particularly useful right now. Of course, Notos will go nuclear on my ass if I show up without a viable talysman. Speaking of my ass, damn it still hurts. Wowzer, it really, really hurts. Focus, Tal, focus.

You've already decided you aren't going to use the Answerer to murder her. She told you she's tired of merely existing and wants to feel pain again. As long as she isn't human, the magyk syphon will keep her fueled up for all of eternity. What happens if she feels something, anything? Would that mean she would become human again?

If her humanity is restored, maybe that means she will die like all the rest of us. Please, please not in a *Raiders of the Lost Ark* stupid Nazis staring at the Ark of the Covenant with their flesh melting off and their eyeballs bulging out and exploding and then their screaming skeletons being consumed by fire type of death.

Just a regular run of the mill live your life out and then finally draw one's last breath expiration of life death.

It discombobulated her that I'm a singer. Maybe music is the answer. When she was human, her strongest emotions involved the evenings when Luch sang to her. That was their most precious time together. His gusli is here. I don't look like Luch, and me standing here with my junk on full display isn't particularly conducive to engendering a heart-wrenching response. Sorry, Mr. Johnson, but it just isn't. Great, Tal thought, now I'm apologizing to my package.

He turned Aurora's ring, his thoughts racing. I only have one wish left and I don't think I get to make it a multi-part request. Aurora's gift should be used to "Seek the Center." Again, whatever that is. Even if I get that squared away, it still leaves me standing here strumming a banjo, naked.

Unless I use both magyk rings. I'll put the Ring of Gyges on and disappear. I'll still be naked so that won't interfere with activation of the talysman. What wish do I make that solves the bigger problem?

The wytch gave up her feelings, made them unimportant, and cast them aside. Why did Luna require the renunciation ritual? Why? he asked himself. Because you're no longer human if you harden your heart so that you no longer have the capacity to love. That's it, Tal realized. Baba Yaga has to be restored to her ability to love. It's as simple, and without Aurora's magyk, as impossible as that.

Tal bowed his head and turned the ring on his finger several times. The ring flashed, throwing a vivid rainbow palette into the air of the cabin. The colors hung together in the air of the cabin, like there was an indoor aurora borealis.

'Aurora, please grant my wish,' Tal whispered in his mind. 'If it is of the Center to restore Baba Yaga's humanity, let me not just be named Taliesin, but allow me to become the Taliesin of this time and place. Grant me the magyk of Taliesin. Please. And thank you for my ring and my wishes.' Tal watched as the ring flashed again, summoning the colors back into itself before it became a dull, lifeless silver.

Well? he wondered. Where's my surge of magyk? It's pretty obvious my last wish done left the cabin. My beautiful ring of many colors is now a plain silver band. Come on, Amarantos. Please. What words, what song? What song do I possibly know that is so beautiful that after thousands of years of Spockness it might totally crater Baba Yaga into feeling something again? Who has ever sung such a song to me with such unreserved love in their voice? In their heart? Well?

Then he heard a voice in his head. Not Aurora's. Most definitely not Aurora's. He would never forget what it felt like to have an Elder Child inside your brain. Fortuna? Is it the blindfolded casino employee he met in the Atlantis casino? No, it's neither of those. Whose voice is it?

Shush, little one and be still. You can't hear with your mind all scared and racing to and fro. Shush, my little son. Calm, calm, calm. Listen to me closely. I have a song I will sing to you. It has the power to make all bad things leave you alone. It has the power to heal you.

That voice! It's my Mom, Tal realized.

Still yourself, my precious child. My song will only work if you will let go of your fear. Trust me, Taliesin. Let go and listen to me.

All those early years when it was only the two of them. When Mom was barely making ends meet and having to move repeatedly, doing everything she could to try to keep me safe from that faceless ghoul. Those nights when I was terrified out of my mind. There was a song of unselfish, giving love. She used to sing me to sleep with it sometimes, back when I was so little I couldn't even say the words. It reduced her to tears nearly every time, Tal thought, especially the first time I got big enough to sing the duet lines with her. From then on we sang it together.

Be quiet, my heart's desire. I will sing you a song of love and healing.

Half of it is in Italian, Tal thought, but that's no problem. The wytch speaks Latin. Italian wasn't around when she was human but it's a descendant of Latin so she'll understand the gist of the words.

Music can heal every pain, beloved. If it is the song of your heart's desire. Let's begin.

Thank you Aurora for the ring, Tal thought. Thank you Amarantos for my Mom and everything she has ever done for me my entire life. Thank you for her example of True Love.

"Fine," Tal announced to the wytch. "I'll end you."

CHAPTER QUADRAGINTA SEPTEM

"I'll do it," Tal continued, "but I will do it my way. I'll do it 'Seeking the Center'." At the wytch's questioning look, he added, "You will remain seated on the sofa, with your eyes closed. No matter what I do or what I say, you will keep your eyes closed."

"If you leave without completing the contract, the talysman will be worthless. After I kill you, I will hunt your friends down and finish them."

"You've made that perfectly clear. I'm not leaving and you are going to die. Do you agree to do everything exactly as I said?" She nodded her head. "Good, now close your eyes."

As soon as she complied, Tal walked over to the gambeson, took the Ring of Gyges out of the pocket and placed it on his finger. Just in case she didn't keep her eyes closed. That done he swiftly strode over to the gusli. Baba Yaga had obviously kept the instrument well dusted. But the strings were thousands of years old, who knew how long they would hold up? If at all? So, none of the usual normal tuning or warm-up of either his voice or the gusli.

Here goes nothing, he thought. If the Omada win the Tyrning someone definitely needs to write a thank you letter to David Foster, Carol Bayer Sager, *et al.* Okay, Amarantos, if you're listening—this is me "Seeking the Center" and I can use whatever mojo you can give me. Luch, this one's partly for you and partly for all of the rest of us incurable romantics who believe in True Love.

As Tal played the introductory chords, he saw Baba Yaga open her eyes. He stopped. "My rules, Baba Yaga. I will fulfill the contract but you agreed to abide my rules." She nodded her head, leaned back and squeezed her eyes tightly closed. Tal began again.

I pray you'll be our eyes, and watch us where we go

As he sang the next few lines he kept a close watch on the strings. There was no apparent fraying and they seemed to still have the necessary elasticity.

Let this be our prayer, when we lose our way
Lead us to the place, guide us with your grace

The next verse was a combination of the English and Italian lines. As Tal sang the lines, the beauty of the lyrics and the music washing over him, he remembered his Mom holding him tight, showing him both by word and deed that he was safe, that he was loved unconditionally. He felt the surge in his own emotions infuse his singing, taking his voice to an eloquence he'd never felt before. When he reached the Italian lines, he saw the wytch start. It speaks to her as well, Tal thought, I know it does.

A ricordarci che
Eterna stella sei

He saw Baba Yaga mouth the English translation: "To remember that you're my eternal star." It was at this point he noticed some of the translucent dryer sheet sized whatever the hell they were things had begun flying around him and in and out between the strings of the gusli. The majority of the tiny flags were circling Baba Yaga clockwise in a column, spinning slowly at first and then picking up speed.

Lead us to a place, guide us with your grace
Give us faith so we'll be safe

As he felt himself merge seamlessly with the gusli, Tal continued the song. Immediately before playing the last verse he improvised a bridge, and as he was close to finishing the last round of the bridge, he whispered into the wytch's left ear, "Now Vasilisa, I need for you to translate and sing the words, after I sing them to you." The see-through mini-clouds were in tumult now. The wytch nodded, the first progenitor of a tear welling in each of her eyes.

> *È la fede che*
> *It is faith that*
> *Hai acceso in noi,*
> *Lit up inside us*
> *Sento che ci salver*
> *I feel it will save us.*

As the strings echoed the final chord, Tal realized he was totally spent, and drenched in sweat. To his surprise, he discovered his eyes were swollen almost completely shut from crying while he had been singing. He took the gusli back over and reverently replaced it in its place above the mantle. After making it secure he strode back across the room before taking the Ring of Gyges off his finger.

A loud gasp pulled his focus back to the wytch. She had fallen off of the sofa, face down on the floor, her arms and legs flailing as she convulsed. Then she began shrieking. Not words, sharp guttural syllables. All of the diaphanous flags were attacking her, burrowing into her skin.

Tal leapt over the back of the sofa, and knelt on the floor beside her. He gently but firmly held her arms, restraining her for a few moments until the most violent of her abrupt movements subsided. Tal then gently cradled her before turning her over.

Baba Yaga's appearance had completely changed. Well, it hadn't changed so much as been revealed. She hadn't lied. Even in her present, severely distressed state it was clear to Tal she was beautiful. Not an attention-grabbing, vampish kind of beautiful. A perfectly proportioned, everything-fit-together-just-so, young

Audrey Hepburn kind of beautiful. Where'd all that camoflaugey stuff go, anyway? With all of the impediments evaporated, she was now as much in focus as one human can possibly be to another.

In-focus and currently now limp as a wet noodle. A not-breathing wet noodle. Oh hell, no! I wasn't trying to "kill her" kill her. I mean I was trying to kill her but I figured it was only going to be a kind of "hey now you're human again so welcome to death at some point in the not too immediate future live long and prosper" kill her. Please, please don't let her face start melting.

"HELP ME!" Tal yelled. "HELP ME!"

Only seconds later the cabin door burst open, shattering into a thousand pieces of infinitesimally tiny kindling. A shadow loomed, filling the entire doorframe. There's only one person I know with that big a shadow, Tal thought. "Borras!"

"Quint, you're alive!" the giant exclaimed as he warily stepped into the room. Only after he'd scanned the entire room for threat evaluation did he step forward, allowing the rest of the Omada to enter. "Everything okay?" he asked as he tossed a folded Puca to Tal. "I'm not sure what you two have been doing in here naked but it's probably time for you to suit up."

Tal smiled grimly and nodded, as he grabbed Piras and placed him on top of his head. 'I consent, do you?' he thought to the Puca.

'I consent,' Piras replied, before flowing down Tal's body, covering him except for his hands and feet. 'I have scanned your body, Quint of the Omada. You appear unscathed excepting a pattern burn on your left gluteus maximus. Would you like for me to try to repair it?'

'NO!' Tal thought-screamed at Piras. 'Sorry, details later. Piras.' Tal felt a slight hint of a tremor. 'Recall?' he asked.

'Yes,' the Puca replied. 'The rest of the Omada felt it starting a few minutes ago. Right before the three horsemen and their horses evaporated. I'll start rearranging your blood flow.'

"Everyone get prepared to head home," Dysi confirmed.

"Did we score?" Notos demanded.

Tal ignored him. "Anatolia, can you heal Baba Yaga before we go?"

"I'll do what I can, Quint," Ana replied stepping to the wytch and placing her hands on her forehead. After a few moments, she looked up at Tal. "She's experiencing some type of total body failure. It doesn't appear to be anything physical that my healmagyk can correct. My knowledge of the human electrical system is limited."

"Human? " Tal asked, incredulous. "She's reading to you as human?"

"Just as much as you do," Ana replied.

Before Tal could answer, Notos shouldered in between she and Tal. "I'm your Second Prime and I asked you a question, Fifth."

"Shut the fuck up, Notos," Tal said sharply. "I got this covered. Now step away." Notos was so stunned by the hardness of Tal's voice that he actually did as Tal directed.

Baba Yaga opened her eyes. They were now a vibrant emerald—gemstone quality emerald. "I saw what you did there, Munedan. Our bargain was for you to "end me." Instead of using Fragarach, you used parts of me to accomplish the task."

"I don't understand," Tal said softly.

"Don't you see," she said feebly waving around the cabin before motioning for him to lean close so she could whisper to him. "You have restored my emotions to me," she said.

"What?"

"I told you, human, but you weren't listening. They were here all along. Tethered to me but not part of me. Because of you I am now whole again."

'Quint,' Piras interrupted quietly. 'You've got a couple of minutes. Tops.'

"How is this possible?" she asked, clasping Tal's hand tighter. "The Cult of Nyx oath. It was Principe-level magyk, Quint of the Omada."

Tal smiled at the wytch and nodded slightly acknowledging her courtesy in keeping his psuche name a secret.

"I'm not really sure myself exactly what went down here. I used my last wish to save you."

"What?" It would have been an exclamation but there wasn't that much breath left in the wytch. "But your story—you told me Aurora said you'd need your ring four times with only three wishes. You could have used Fragarach and saved the wish."

"Yeah," Tal replied. "That decision may come back to bite me in the ass. Hopefully the other cheek," he added wincing as he moved. "Killing you was not of the Center. I don't think my plan would have worked though, if you hadn't decided in your heart that you wanted to make the choice to follow Luch's last words to you. They contained magyk more powerful than even that of the Principes."

"Luch," the wytch breathed, all the emotion of thousands of years now unfettered. "With my eyes closed, you might have been Luchisky. I think maybe you are the Taliesin."

"What Luch told you, his last words?"

"Yes."

" 'Choose love always.' That can have two meanings Vasilisa."

Now it was the wytch's turn to smile. "Thank you for saving me while fulfilling our bargain," she stated. Seeing sadness immediately fill Tal's face, she added, "No, you don't, Quint of the Omada. This is the greatest blessing you could have given me. To be alive again, even for a few moments. To know Amarantos can now hold me in her arms and I will see Luch again. Our contract is fulfilled. Your talysman is activated."

As Tal felt Piras further adjust his body rhythms to counter the effects of the Recall, he heard Vasilisa say one final thing to him.

"Beware of Luna. She will be most angry when she learns you have freed her most powerful wytch." With that warning she was gone.

No big thing, Tal thought. How on earth would she find out what happened here, and how often will I actually have occasion to run into Luna anyway? Once, every blue moon? Damn, I'm funny, Tal thought, as Baba Yaga and her cabin faded into the blackness of the Recall.

CHAPTER QUADRAGINTA OCTO

Tal knew from his first breath—before he even opened his eyes—exactly where he was…the freaking infirmary. Again. *I should buy stock in this place*, he thought. *Of course it's not a publicly traded corporation, so buying stock wouldn't be…focus, you dumbass.* He looked to his left. Dysi was asleep in the bed next to him. His other three teammates were in the aisle about ten feet away, huddled in conversation. Everyone was still wearing their Pucas. He craned his neck back to the right. All the way down at the other end of the infirmary, on the other side of the aisle, and as far from the Omada as possible, he could see three members of Ayllu surrounding one of their number on a cot. *Who's missing? Lik"in. Oh, shit*, Tal thought. *Something bad must have happened.*

The talysman! Ms. Empousa mandated secrecy. She'll seize any opportunity she gets to boot us for a rules violation. He raised the covers and saw that from his midriff down it looked like he had a Puca body cast. 'Piras?'

'Yes, Quint, I am here,' Piras thought-replied. 'Knowing the HuntsMistress's instructions, I had Koios ask Borras to tell the physicks you would heal better if I remained in contact with your skin from the waist down. From the small amount of information I gleaned before you passed out, I thought there

281

might be additional reasons you would want the nature of your talysman to remain secret until you had time to make some decisions about its disclosure.'

'Thanks, Piras. It was a really smart play.'

'You're welcome. If the HuntsMistress hadn't ordered the Pucas to be worn during the school day for the rest of this term I wouldn't have known the talysman needed to be secret.'

When Borras noticed Tal was awake, he moved to his side, leaned over and whispered, "Thank Amarantos, you pulled through. It's a damn good thing none of us have to make another Journey this term. The physicks had to do some major repair work on two of your heart chambers. They just got through running diagnostics on the rest of us. Dysi has a small brain bleed her Puca couldn't fix, so the physicks will repair that magykally as well."

Wait, what? I've just had closed chest heart surgery. I'm only eighteen damn years old.

The double-doors at the near end flew open and Ms. Empousa came stomping in, followed closely by Tal's old buddy, the Chief Physick. Tal sat up, slowly.

"Good, you're awake," Ms. Empousa snapped. "Although I'm not sure why you're still lollygagging in the infirmary."

Lollygagging? Hello? Major repair work on two of my heart chambers, Tal thought.

"I am here to reiterate to both teams in this room the same information I have already repeated to the other four teams. If you made contact with a wytch or obtained a talysman of any nature, your Prime will inform me privately. There is to be no other communication about the talysman, even among team members. Let me make sure I am clear on this point. The only information your teammates may have is whether or not you secured a talysman for the team. Any and all other information will have to wait until Orientation next Friday morning. At that time each team will be called on to reveal its results. I will announce the presumptive team rankings at Orientation. Given the rarity of Wytch Hunts and any contact with wytches, the Ruling Council has decreed the results will not be finalized until each team formally presents its talysman or contact information at the Imbolc Feast.

Tal rolled his memory back to the information on pagan holidays section. *Imbolc is on the second day of February. Which makes next weekend a busy one. Final Orientation class for this term on Friday morning, field trip on Saturday evening, and Imbolc Feast on Sunday at noon. I don't know how I'm going to swing being gone from home all weekend.* He made a mental note to get Emet started cogitating about a solution to that particular problem.

"Now all of you, get your worthless teammates out of these sick beds and back to work." With that pronouncement the HuntsMistress was gone in a flash, needlessly scattering tray tables full of formerly sterile instruments in her wake.

Tal took a quick look out of the window. *Past time for me to get home, anyway. The team knows I scored a talysman because I told Notos. Any other disclosable information can wait until tomorrow.* As he struggled to get up, his body let him know just how badly it felt ill-treated. *Damn, even with Piras helping out, my ass still feels like someone put a blowtorch to it. No telling how bad it's going to be when I leave him here.*

'It's going to be pretty bad,' Piras thought-chimed in. 'Probably worth a steady repetition of a combination of "Holy Shit!" and "Yowzer!" to quote your usual vernacular.'

Man, I sure hope Emet isn't late getting to the gas station. I really don't know if I can walk all those miles home with this supernova on my gluteus. Today shouldn't be a problem for him. When we talked this morning it looked like it was going to be a run of the mill, ordinary school day at Nemeton High.

CHAPTER FORTY-NINE

I'll leave the Advanced Biology and Calculus books, Emet mused, as he thumbed through the contents of his locker. I need the Physics and Medieval Lit books to study this weekend. If the pattern holds, I'll have pop quizzes in those subjects before lunch on Monday. He pulled one more book out of the locker—Statistics. Tal and I need to go over that one this weekend as well. It's been awhile and I should make sure he's up to speed on that subject.

Emet closed the locker, spun the lock, and pulled on it to double-check that it closed. He'd been feeling odd since shortly after lunch. Not having any direct experience with illness, that was the best he could do as far as a descriptor. Nothing he and Tal had read thus far gave him any information about whether Creatures, specifically golems, could even be sick. During Study Hall he'd given his status some thought, trying to quantify it. Maybe he was "queasy," or perhaps it was more like "feeling faint." Something wasn't right, he knew that. Emet glanced up at the clock on the hallway wall. Perfect, he thought. I'll be right on time to pick up Tal.

As he turned left to head toward the front door, he

almost collided with Barton Sellars, Gunnar Haslip, and Fail McDermott as they came cruising around the corner. Fail had little Scooter Stanley gripped by the nape of his collar and was dragging him across the linoleum floor with Scooter's toes making contact only about every third step. This situation is unacceptable, Emet thought. No one deserves to be bullied. As he rolled through those thoughts, he felt his heart rate increase dramatically. That's odd, he thought. I don't have fluctuations in my pulse rate, sitting or exercising.

When Barton saw Emet, he brought his group to an abrupt halt, disrupting the flow of students in the crowded hallway. "Lookahere, boys," he said in his reedy voice. "It's Brainiac. We haven't seen you in a while." He motioned for Fail to pass custody of Scooter over to him.

Emet noticed Scooter was shivering and that he was totally nonverbal. Could be symptomatic of pre-shock, Emet thought. This is unjust. Hold on, my first thought was a fact-based quantitative assessment, but my second was a qualitative impression. What's up with that, he wondered as he began to feel a little shaky himself.

"Shame we're already booked for today, isn't it," Barton said to his crew, as he pulled Scooter's head back before slamming him head first into Emet's locker. "Look familiar?" Barton asked in a jeer, before slamming Scooter's face twice more. Gunnar and Fail laughed when they saw the sharp metal vent in the locker had opened a jagged gash running the breadth of their victim's forehead.

"Looks like our boy Scooter is accident prone," Gunnar said. "Any more accidents and he'll probably have to go get a band aid from the school nurse."

"Yeah, 'accidents'," Fail guffawed.

Emet looked around. The usual crowd had gathered but no one made a move to stop the harassment. This has to stop, Emet told himself. Someone has to stand against this aggression, against these three constantly picking on weaker individuals. Their victims feel pain and hurt and sadness. They have done nothing to deserve the senseless brutality being inflicted on them, he thought as a wave of nausea swept over him. Emet began his game, *'If I Was Human Right Now I Would Be Feeling...'*

As Barton pulled Scooter's head back a fourth time, Emet felt his body answer the question. In the space of one heartbeat he shrugged his backpack off his right shoulder and violently head-butted Barton—his forehead to Barton's nose. Emet felt Barton's septal hyaline cartilage bend sideways, then bend some more, before snapping like last year's kindling. Emet was careful to make sure he didn't apply enough force to shove the pieces deep into Barton's brain.

'If I Was Human Right Now I Would Be Feeling...'

Two heartbeats, three, four...

Emet's best guess at the noise coming from Barton's mouth was that it was a four-letter yowl. It was kind of difficult to make out the precise word, what with the rain of blood and mucus spray-painting the immediate vicinity.

'If I Was Human Right Now I Would Be Feeling...'

Five, six, seven...

No longer supported, Scooter collapsed to the slippery floor, leaving Emet an open path to both Gunnar and Fail.

'If I Was Human Right Now I Would Be Feeling...'

Eight, nine, ten...

Emet stepped forward, throwing his now extended arms as wide as humanly possible before slamming them closed, concussively slapping both of Gunnar's ears.

'If I Was Human Right Now I Would Be Feeling...'

Eleven, twelve, thirteen,...

Gunnar dropped to his knees in the praying position, screaming through tears as he held his head in his hands. Fail swiftly stepped forward into Emet before trying to move behind him to secure a stranglehold. There was no doubt in Emet's mind that Fail intended to kill him. Emet's only thought was that he needed this fight to be over as soon as possible. He reached slightly behind his body to get purchase on Fail's right forearm. Then he wrenched. Once. Really hard. There was a large pop as

Fail's right arm first twisted sideways at the elbow joint before also separating from the shoulder socket.

'*If I Was Human Right Now I Would Be Feeling...*'

Fourteen, fifteen, sixteen...

With his right arm now dangling uselessly, Fail released Emet, before also dropping to the floor in pain.

'*If I Was Human Right Now I Would Be Feeling...*'

Seventeen...

Conflict over.

'*If I Was Human Right Now I Would Be Feeling...*'

Eighteen...

Begin aftermath.

Scooter was, at best, semi-conscious. He was moaning and rolling around in the sticky goo on the hallway floor. Barton was gasping like a fish out of water, trying to collect sufficient breath to scream epithets at Emet. Gunnar was feverishly shaking his head and wailing that he was deaf. His bell had clearly been rung...and was apparently still ringing. Fail was holding his right arm close to his side and mindlessly keening a one-word mantra—"MOTHERFUCKER! MOTHERFUCKER!"—in the highest pitch imaginable.

Momentarily stunned, the crowd of students collectively came to their senses—realizing they didn't want any part of the present drama. Nor of any subsequent official administrative inquiry. Nor of Barton's wrath against anyone who might have seen him beaten. Nor of any accusations that by their mere continued physical presence they were Tal-sympathizers. So, the entire crowd evaporated.

Not even thirty seconds, Emet thought, as he leaned backward against the wall. I've turned Tal's world upside down in less than half a minute. What has happened to me? Why am I feeling like this? His logic center overwhelmed, Emet bent over and picked up his backpack before turning his back on the carnage and shakily walking out the front door.

'You should report this incident to someone with authority,' he thought.

'Sure thing, genius,' he told himself. 'You're only a golem, you can't speak. Remember?'

'You need time to process,' he replied.

'Clearly, you're not thinking clearly,' he told himself. 'The Sellars own this town and there is some serious shit getting ready to go down.'

'Leave me alone, I don't feel good,' he replied.

'That was Elle's brother, you know,' he told himself.

'I know that, dammit! Stop being so fucking analytical. I said I feel sick to my stomach,' he yelled at his rational voice.

'Why? Why did I feel like I had to intervene? And why am I shaking all over?'

If I Was Human Right Now I would Be Feeling...'

Everything.

CHAPTER FIFTY

Without a shadow of a doubt, Angie was going to make an excellent Fortune 500 CEO someday, Elle thought, as she wrote herself a reminder for her decorations sub-committee. Angie had even brought a printed itinerary to their committee meeting that used military time so there could be no possible misunderstanding between the a.m. and p.m. bullet points. The most important detail for Elle was when they would have access to the gym. She'd hoped it would be moved up but it remained the same—immediately after the basketball game next Thursday evening. Next weekend was packed. Basketball on Thursday evening. The football state championship on Friday—the night before the Winter Formal. With Barton at the helm, Nemeton was heavily favored to win again. School was letting out early on Friday so everyone could attend the game. Elle had to go because it was Barton's last game, and the rest of her sub-committee really wanted to attend the game. She'd already cleared it with Principal Davis for her and the rest of the decorators to take possession of the gym after the Thursday basketball game. The main set pieces would be delivered by the vendor at that time and the gym would be open for Elle twenty-four seven, from that point until noon on Saturday. After that it was time for hair and nails and getting all dolled up. It was, after all, her final major social event at Nemeton High.

As Angie continued working her way through every minute detail of the dance schedule, Elle couldn't stop her mind from wandering. Barring some unforeseen meltdown, she had the lock on the valedictorian spot. Unforeseen meltdown or crazy freak accident resulting in death, she thought, smiling to herself. For the last two weeks she'd been inundated by schools throwing crazy amounts of scholarship money at her. She had a great date to the formal. Most every other girl at Nemeton would give their eye teeth to get next to Holiman Richards. He was the school's number one wide receiver, and her brother Barton's favorite target. Although not at the rocket science intelligence level, he was pretty damn smart, extremely comely, and the word was he was as good with his hands for other fun activities as he was at using them to catch footballs. Everything was going great, her life was wonderful, things were super peachy keen, and then inevitably her thoughts drifted to Tal…

"ELLE!" AndersonCooper yelled at her.

"What? My group will be ready and we'll have the decorations timely placed…"

"Obviously, you haven't been listening," Angie snapped back. "Your beat-all-to-shit brother is bleeding all over the damn door."

Elle looked over toward the windowed door. Barton was leaning heavily against the door glass, his deeply tanned face now pasty. Is his nose crooked, Elle wondered. It is, oh lord, what's happened? Barton had a rust colored goatee made of congealed blood, with rivulets of fresh blood flowing from his nose down over the dried material and from there slowly meandering its way down the door glass.

Amber Nicole hadn't been paying attention either. She'd been doodling monograms composed of her initials together with those of her prom date. Even though it was their first date, she'd been daydreaming about their possible future together. Amber looked up smirkily when she heard Angie bark at Elle. "OH MY

GOD!! OH MY GOD!! OH MY...," before promptly fainting and falling flat out, limbs splayed snow angel wide.

Elle quickly stood up, having to step over Amber as she headed for the door. Oh sweetie, she thought as she looked down to make sure she didn't step on her. Please, please, don't ever wear "days of the week" underwear, but if you do, for the love of all that's holy don't ever wear Thursday on Friday. When she opened the door Elle was a little surprised that she had to catch her brother and steady him so that he could even remain upright. "What the hell happened to you?"

"That fucking boyfriend of yours," Barton spat, froth-foam bubbling at both corners of his mouth.

"Holiman, did this?" Elle asked in disbelief.

"Not him, you idiot. Fucking Tal Smith."

Oh no, Elle thought. NO. NO. NO. Is Tal okay, she wondered. Where are Barton's two bodyguards? Please, let Tal be okay. Please.

"The idiot school nurse wouldn't let me drive home. Gunnar and Fail had to go to the hospital. Stupid nurse tried to make me stay in her office, said I might have a concussion. I need you to take me home. Now."

"Sure, let me get my stuff," Elle replied. After leaning him up against the wall, she ran back into the room, stepping back over Thursday on Friday, and retrieved her books. She looked apologetically to Angie, who gave her a shooing motion to let her know she had it covered. After throwing her backpack and purse over one shoulder, she helped support Barton with the other, as they headed down the hallway toward the parking lot.

"HE'S A FUCKING DEAD MAN, ELLE," Barton yelled at the top of his lungs to the empty hallway. As the echoes from that roar tapered, he yelled once more. To no one, and to the entire world. "You're a fucking dead man, Tal Smith. A. Fucking. Dead. Man."

CHAPTER FIFTY-ONE

Tal had slowly and excruciatingly limped halfway home before he found Emet. He was sitting doubled-over at the base of a large live oak, about fifteen feet from the edge of the two-lane highway. "I got to tell you, Em, you picked a hell of a day to desert me."

In response, Emet barely lifted his head enough to make eye contact with Tal.

"Em, what the hell happened? What's the matter with you?" Tal asked, as he speed-limped across the remaining distance between them. Damn, Piras hadn't been kidding. He couldn't even sit down, not with the friction provided by his jeans. Wowzer! My ass is seriously distraught. "Emet?" he asked again, softer this time.

Emet didn't even get his cellphone out. 'I screwed up big time, Tal,' he slowly mouthed, over-enunciating each syllable so Tal could read his lips. 'Big time!'

"Listen, buddy, I don't know what kind of bad day you think you're having, but it doesn't hold a candle to my crappy day. And I can't really sit down right now, so if I'm going to be lip-reading a bunch, you're gonna need to stand."

In response, Emet wobbly stood to his feet, got his cellphone out of his shirt pocket and started typing, slowly at first as he searched for an efficient narrative, but in a few seconds his fingers were moving at about mach five. When he finished about three minutes later, he pushed send.

Tal's phone beep-beeped twice, letting him know he had a message from Emet. He opened the text and started reading the epistle Emet had written.

CHAPTER FIFTY-TWO

Per their usual protocol, the boys split up a few blocks from home. Tal was way late getting home, it was almost eight o'clock before he got to his block. He and Emet had discussed things on the way. They were already late and decided that whatever "worse" factor was created by being even later paled in comparison to Tal not knowing every syllable of every word and every movement, blow by blow, in today's showdown. Even given the extra time, he didn't have a chance to discuss today's Journey with Emet, or to delve into what prompted Emet to act like he did today.

Still, Tal would have almost rather had a hot poker stuck on his ass—again—than have to face Mom and Pell's anger. And disappointment. As he rounded the last corner before his house he saw them before they saw him. They were sitting on the front porch steps, backlit by the porch light beside the front door. His Mom was turned into Pell, and he was hugging her tightly. As Tal got a little closer he could see her shoulders heaving. She's crying. Because of me, well because of Emet, but it's all on me.

The adults stood in unison when Tal walked out of the darkness and into the oblong pool of light cast on the pavement by the streetlight. Tal walked silently up the sidewalk, then up the steps. Waiting, waiting, for the explosion.

There was none. Thea grabbed him, hugged him so hard it took his breath, and sobbed, "Oh, thank God, you're okay. Thank God, you're home safely. Let's get inside. Quickly." Bear-hugging Tal she turned toward the house, and the three of them walked inside.

CHAPTER FIFTY-THREE

Without letting him go, Thea walked Tal the length of the living room, to the sofa farthest away from the front door. Tal watched as Pell double-bolted the door, turned off the front porch light, made sure the curtains were securely drawn, and then turned out the overhead light, leaving the room dimly lit by only the two coffee table lamps. Okay, I expected Mom to be crying. I figured both of them would be furious. Actually, my money would have been on anger more than crying. I guess that will come later. But what's up with this whole cloak and dagger, hide in the shadows action from Pell?

"Are you okay?" Pell asked tersely, as he walked behind them, and into the kitchen.

Tal craned his neck to watch Pell as he checked the locks on the kitchen windows and doors. "Um, yeah, until you get around to the part where I've disappointed you before but never to this magnitude and I'm grounded for life. Even beyond eighteen, when I'm an adult and technically you have no further right to ground me."

"We were worried you had done something stupid to yourself," his Mom replied. "Or that someone else had done something stupid to you."

"Look, Mom…"

"We know what happened, Tal," Thea interjected.

"I'm so sorry," Tal replied.

Pell walked up behind him and put his left hand on Tal's shoulder. "There's no need to apologize, Tal."

Tal turned to look over his shoulder. "But your job?"

"Money is important, son, but there are many things more important in life than a paycheck," Pell replied

Thea leaned her head against her oldest son's other shoulder. "We've heard from half a dozen parents, Tal. They've told us exactly what happened. You know how I feel about violence but it sounds like you were sticking up for someone that was truly in danger."

"Still not sure how you single-handedly took out three varsity football players, Tal. But that's a conversation for another day," Pell added.

Thea stood and extended her hand to Tal to help him up. "Go on upstairs and get cleaned up and go to bed. There's a meeting set for tomorrow morning at the school. We will talk more first thing in the morning."

Tal saw that Pell had gone back to standing by the side of the front window and was staring out into the night. "What's going on, Mom?"

"We've already had some threatening calls," she replied.

"This is a football crazy town, Tal," Pell added. "Doesn't sound like anything permanent, but you injured three of the team's best players and the state championship is next weekend. I'm going to stand watch tonight."

"You can't stay up every night from now on to protect us," Tal responded.

"No, he can't," Thea confirmed. "We're going to wait and see what happens at the meeting tomorrow. After that we will make a decision about where we go from there. Now go to bed."

Shoulders slumped, Tal did as he was told. He made sure the bathroom door was locked before he showered. Last thing he needed right now was for one of the twins to wander in and see his brand. It would be hard to pull the switcheroo with Emet again.

After showering he got in the bed with his laptop open. "Did you hear?" he asked quietly.

A few seconds later he received Emet's typed reply. 'Yes.'

"I need to fill you in on everything that happened today."

'I have some extremely important developments we need to discuss as well.'

"Let's wait until after the meeting tomorrow. That way we will be able to bring each other totally current."

'Agreed.'

"Goodnight, Emet."

'Goodnight, Tal.'

Emet lay in his small niche in the attic. Alone. A few minutes passed and he heard Tal's breathing become steady. Emet didn't need sleep although he normally shut his brain down for a few hours of downtime. He couldn't hit the "off" switch tonight as hundreds of thoughts competed for priority. What was going to happen to Tal? What about their family? Had he put the twins in danger? Would Tal face criminal charges?

One thought though kept repeating itself, refusing to be silenced without an answer. An answer that Emet couldn't supply. 'What is wrong with me?'

CHAPTER FIFTY-FOUR

Tal and his family arrived fifteen minutes early for the Saturday morning meeting. Ms. Helen Kuciejski, the school secretary, had been called in to work. Tal assumed she would normally be irritated about the weekend work. If so, her irritation was far outweighed by the opportunity to be privy to the salacious details of the largest imbroglio in the history of Nemeton High. The Smiths were left sitting in the waiting area outside the conference room even though they could hear snippets of conversation already in progress. Heated snippets of conversation. Primarily that of a male voice. So, not Principal Davis. Had to be Mr. Sellars. The regional Croesus. Barton's father. And Elle's, Tal reminded himself, as he sighed. Wonder what she thinks about this disaster?

The intercom buzzer did its buzzing thing. Ms. Kuciejski did her punching the button thing. Principal Davis's voice crackled over the speaker, saying to send Tal and his parents in. Which Ms. Kuciejski did, lingering at the door until Principal Davis asked her to close the door—behind her. As the door clicked closed behind her, Tal was pretty sure she was finally wearing an irritated-at-having-to-be-at-school-on-a-Saturday bitch face.

Tal was closely flanked by Pell and his Mom. He felt both their bodies tense up as soon as the three of them were in the room. The reason was pretty obvious. Mr. and Mrs. Sellars were present with Barton. Mr. and Mrs. Haslip were present with Gunnar. Mr. and Mrs. McDermott were present with Fail. And Sheriff Dempsey was standing, arms folded behind him in the far rear corner.

Principal Davis had conducted a separate meeting with the three bullies and their parents prior to the group meeting. With the senior law enforcement officer of Lee County. Mr. Sellars had the whole thing already cooked. Of course he did, Tal thought.

Barton was wearing one of those clear plastic Jason masks that athletes wear to protect things like detached retinas—or broken noses. Though the mask Tal could see Barton was sporting a set of almost completely swollen shut raccoon eyes. Gunnar wasn't wearing any medical accessories but his left eye kind of sort of seemed to be drifting around doing its own thing. Fail's right arm was encased in something that looked like a two-stage sling. Part of the contraption was clearly holding his right shoulder in its respective socket, and the other portion was holding his elbow snug to his side. Gunnar and Fail were wearing extra large snarls. Not Barton though. His expression was full on smirkitudinal.

Tal felt Thea reach around his back to squeeze Pell's left arm at the elbow. Tal knew that squeeze—relax. It was a hold your position and take a deep breath arm squeeze. His Mom didn't want Pell blowing up on anybody until she had obtained as much information as possible.

"Thank you for coming…," Principal Davis began before she was interrupted by Mr. Sellars.

"Thank you, my ass!" he shouted. Mrs. Sellars looked sideways at him. "Language, Third. There are ladies present."

She's the dangerous one, Tal thought. Just like Elle is smarter than Barton, Mrs. Sellars is the queen of the Sellars royal family. Mr. Sellars thinks he's in charge but he's only the prince consort.

"Fine," Mr. Sellars began again, much calmer this time. "Sheriff, do your duty. Arrest that felon," he said pointing at Tal. "Tell Judge Pearce I strongly recommend the little shit be held without bond," he concluded, as he folded his arms.

Tal felt Pell's muscles load for action and Thea's arm tense as she tightened her hold on her husband. As Sheriff Dempsey started toward Tal, he reached back with his right hand and unhooked a pair of handcuffs from his belt. "Taliesin Smith, you are under…"

WHAM!

Tal was so shocked he asked Central Processing to replay the noise. Yes, "WHAM!" is actually the noise the conference room door made as it exploded inward, its frosted glass panes rattling in strident protest as the door bounced off a rubber backstop.

In walked a nebbish who would have been nowhere tall enough to ride this ride at any of the really fun rides at the Magic Kingdom. He was followed by a covey of endomorphs. Scooter Stanley, with two adults who could only be his parents. In accordance with their group's theme, they were all fairly short of stature, Mrs. Stanley being the tallest of the four.

"Who the hell are you?" Mr. Sellars demanded.

"Third!" Mrs. Sellars admonished.

Chastised, Mr. Sellars began anew. "Fine, who are you?"

"I am Daggett J. Noble. Of Noble, Noble, and Noble. Osceola. Here's my card." Lawyer Noble paused long enough to pull a short stack of business cards from his vest pocket. He then proceeded to pass them around the table. "What the card doesn't say," he added with a small grin, "is that I also have the incredible good fortune to be this young man's favorite uncle—and godparent. "These good folks," he added, pointing to Scooter's parents, "are Jackie, my sister, and her husband Bear."

Bear, Tal asked himself. Really? Must be a family name.

"Fine, but why are you here?" Mr. Sellars demanded. Rudely, Tal noticed, but apparently the rudeness was within what Mrs. Sellars would tolerate as acceptable societal protocol.

Lawyer Noble ignored the question. He turned first to the Principal. "You would be Principal Davis?" he asked.

"Yes," she replied, clearly as puzzled as the rest of the persons of average stature in the room.

"This is for you," the attorney said handing her a thick manila envelope. "I see the alpha male in this room is actually a female," the Lilliputian attorney said as he slid another large package across the table to Mrs. Sellars. He then turned to the Haslips and the McDermotts. "I can see from the total lack of understanding on your faces that you are the parents of the other two loutish individuals." He casually passed over a package to each of them.

"Now see here," Mr. Haslip began.

Wow, Tal thought. Mr. Haslip gets to go second to Mr. Sellars just like Gunnar goes second to Barton.

"Shut it, Haslip!" Mr. Sellars growled.

"Probably really good advice for all of you," Lawyer Noble said agreeably.

"Well, this is all well and good," Sheriff Dempsey interjected. "I'm here to make an arrest and you're impeding the administration of justice."

"You are Sheriff Dempsey?" Attorney Noble asked.

"Yes," the Sheriff replied curtly.

"Good. Just the man I have been looking for all morning. I have this separate package for you," he said as he walked around the table and handed a small box full of paperwork to the Sheriff.

"And what is this?" the Sheriff asked, having to jam his handcuffs into his front pocket so he could grab hold of the box with both hands.

"That, my dear constable, is a box with copies of fifty-three affidavits. They were prepared after my paralegal and myself worked all night long meeting with fifty-three sets of parents of mostly minor children."

"So?" Mr. McDermott interrupted.

Hey, Fail's side of the table got to say something, Tal thought. I guess there may be such a thing as a multi-generational bully group hierarchical structure.

Lawyer Noble responded politely and professionally. "So—as you have so eloquently framed the question—after meeting with the young men and women and their parents and obtaining their affidavits, I had coffee first thing this morning with one of my old law school classmates. Lowry Jargley. You may have heard of him."

"He's the Lee County Prosecutor," the Sheriff stated.

"Yes, he is," the attorney confirmed. "In addition to the underlying affidavits, in the Sheriff's box there are also drafts of fifty-three separate Informations and corresponding arrest warrants alleging commission by this troika of miscreants," Lawyer Noble performed a jury closing argument type hand flourish at Barton, Gunnar, and Fail. "The Informations allege a total of four hundred and sixty-five criminal offenses over the last three years." Lawyer Noble turned to the Sellars. "There is a three year limitations period for the subject felonies of assault and battery." He then looked over at Principal Davis. "Almost all of the felony criminal offenses were allowed to be perpetrated on school property during regular school hours."

Tal watched as the color literally blanched from Principal Davis's face.

"Because your reprehensible offspring committed many of the acts while they were of the age of majority and the victims were minors, most of the offenses will carry a statutory enhancement to their prison sentences. Given the ongoing, substantial pattern of criminal activity, I can tell you based on my decades of experience trying cases against Prosecutor Jargley, there will be no possibility of probation for any of the three defendants named in those draft Indictments."

"And what's in the other packages?" Principal Davis asked, her voice trembling.

"Those, madam, are copies of the draft of the one hundred thirty-four count *Class Action Complaint* I have prepared for filing against these ruffians, their parents, you personally, and the Nemeton High School Board. The *Complaint* alleges a number of RICO violations, which may ultimately subject you personally to federal prison time. Oh, and it requests both compensatory and punitive damages. Your family would be the proverbial deep pocket, Mrs. Sellars," he finished as he cocked his head toward Barton's mother.

The Sheriff had had enough. He threw the box on the floor, walked over and grabbed Tal by the wrist. "That's it. I've got more important things to do. I'm arresting this troublemaker and taking him to the..."

"Demp." Mrs. Sellars said quietly to the Sheriff.

One word, spoken in a whisper. That was it, Tal thought as the Sheriff's arm went limp. It's almost like she put marionette strings on Sheriff Dempsey.

Mrs. Sellars turned back to Lawyer Noble. "Counselor, I believe you used the word 'draft' when referring to the Informations, the warrants and the *Complaint?*"

"Yes, ma'am," the attorney confirmed.

"And by 'draft' you mean Prosecutor Jargley hasn't actually signed the warrants and they are not yet a matter of public record?"

"That is correct, ma'am."

"And the same is true with the *Complaint?*"

"Again, you are correct, Mrs. Sellars. I have not yet signed it on behalf of my clients."

Barton's mother turned her cold gaze back to Sheriff Dempsey. "Thank you, Demp. Your services are no longer required here. You have my permission to leave. Please leave the paperwork where it is and close the door behind you." The Sheriff didn't miss a step as he placed his box on the table and beat feet out the open conference room door.

"WHAT?" Barton said, exploding upward from his seat.

Barton's mother pivoted quickly in his direction. "Fourth?"

Again, a single, hushed syllable with the uncanny ability to control, Tal thought, as he watched Barton cow before his mother and sink back into his chair.

Mrs. Sellars turned to the Haslips and the McDermotts. "Leigh Ann, Hazel—I will call you both this evening to let you know what we decided." The other two mothers silently nodded their heads in obeisance, each firmly grasped their respective husband by the arm, and head-nodded to their kids to follow as they also left the conference room.

"Mr. Noble?"

"Yes, Mrs. Sellars?"

"As their legal representative, you have full authority to negotiate in all respects for the Stanleys and all of the other individuals and their parents?"

"Yes, Mrs. Sellars."

"Then perhaps it is unnecessary for the Stanleys to remain?"

Lawyer Noble looked to his clients to see if that was acceptable to them. They nodded their acceptance and promptly rose to leave. Scooter gave Tal a quick wink, followed by a fist to the chest to show solidarity within the geekverse.

There was a moment of silence after all of the departures. The momentary stillness was interrupted by Principal Davis who raised her hand to ask a question. Mrs. Sellars nodded her assent to the request.

"What about me?" Principal Davis asked hopefully. "I guess I'm free to go as well?"

"Oh no, Floy Jean. I'll need you to stay to make sure you understand what it is you're going to say and do. And we may need you to make copies for us. First though, why don't you be a dear and ask Helen to bring us some coffee. I take both cream and sugar with mine. Shouldn't take you a quick minute. Thank you."

CHAPTER FIFTY-FIVE

It all seems so very civilized, Tal thought. We're here for what is for all intents and purposes my educational execution and we've now each ended up with a non-alcoholic beverage of choice together with our choice of assorted cookies left over from yesterday's faculty potluck luncheon. As I have both a liquid and a solid I guess this might technically count as a last meal.

"Let's start with the nonnegotiable items," Mr. Sellars stated.

"Fine," Lawyer Noble replied, as he reached into his briefcase to secure a notepad before taking a real fountain pen out of his front shirt pocket. "Go."

"That little shit will be expelled immediately," he demanded, pointing at Tal.

Tal saw red immediately bloom across Pell's face. It wasn't just the derogatory nature of the remark. Pell knew if Tal didn't have a high school diploma he couldn't attend college this fall. An expulsion on his record also meant Tal would never receive any meaningful amount in scholarship money. Which again meant he wouldn't be able to attend college. A quick hand squeeze from Thea and Pell's color rapidly returned to some semblance of normal.

"Got it," the lawyer confirmed as he began writing. "All four of the 'little shits' will be expelled immediately."

"WHAT?" Barton screamed.

His mother turned to him. "Fourth, if you rudely interrupt the adults again, the thrashing you received from Mr. Smith yesterday will pale in comparison to the one I will bring down upon you."

Barton murmured something intelligible under his breath. Tal thought it was one syllable and had all the required letters for the word "bitch."

"I'm sorry, Barton, did you say something?" his mother asked, her words might as well have been made of cold-forged steel.

"No," Barton replied sullenly.

"No, ma'am," she prompted.

"No, ma'am."

"That's better." Mrs. Sellars turned her attention to Mr. Noble. "My husband mistakenly used the word 'nonnegotiable.' Barton will be walking across the stage to receive his Nemeton High School diploma with high honors, just like the five generations of Sellars' men before him."

Principal Davis took the opportunity to add her two cents. "Besides that, the state championship is next Friday night. All three of the boys have been cleared to play. Even all banged up. Coach Ross has told me Nemeton doesn't stand a chance without them. If they're expelled, then state law provides that they can't play."

In response, Lawyer Noble slowly scratched out the one item he'd written so far.

Principal Davis wasn't finished. "There are legitimate security concerns that need to be addressed. People around these parts take football pretty serious. There's a sizeable segment of the student body who don't approve of Tal assaulting the star quarterback the week before the biggest game of the school year."

It was Thea who responded to Principal Davis. "I'm glad you're concerned about everyone but our son. We have already received a number of anonymous threatening phone calls. It's clear from the Sheriff's participation in your little charade that Tal and the rest of our family are totally on our own as far as our personal security."

"Not totally on your own," Lawyer Noble replied with a wry smile. "Let me offer this. Masters Sellars, Haslip, and McDermott will remain in school for the rest of this school year. They will graduate with the rest of their classmates in May, participate in the graduation ceremony, and there will be no adverse scholastic activity against any of them."

"Sounds good," Mr. Sellars said.

"I wasn't through, thank you," Mr. Noble replied. "Master Smith will be allowed to conduct independent study on each of this term's subjects and receive his diploma in May as well. He will not attend the graduation ceremony. There will also be no adverse scholastic activity taken against him."

I could care less about the ceremony, Tal thought. Besides that, Helblad, Jarl of all draugrs and wights, will probably have already made several meals out of my carcass by then.

"Sounds good," Principal Davis said.

"I wasn't through, thank you," Mr. Noble replied yet again. "To insure no inappropriate leverage is exerted upon any of Tal's teachers, his final grades in this semester's subjects shall be exactly what they are as of the present date." With that, Lawyer Noble looked first to Thea and Pell for agreement.

Tal saw his Mom looking sideways at him. He gave a tiny nod. Why not, Emet had more than held up his end of their academic partnership. They had top marks right now in all of his subjects. He hadn't been at Nemeton long enough to be in the race for the Valedictorian and Salutatorian honors so those weren't in play. Tal watched as Thea squeezed Pell's hand, deferring the response to him.

"Agreed," Pell said.

"Agreed," Mrs. Sellars confirmed.

"Whatever," Principal Davis stated.

Mr. Noble wrote the graduation terms in black ink on his notepad. "Next item?" he inquired. "Doesn't even have to be a nonnegotiable matter."

Wow, Tal thought. Score one for the clever endomorph with a wicked sense of humor.

"We want a restraining order against that animal," Mr. Sellars said, again pointing at Tal.

He really doesn't need to waste time pointing, Tal thought. I think everyone here is aware that he believes me a perfidious brute.

Lawyer Noble's pen began scratching its way across the pad again. He spoke the words as he wrote them, "Mutual restraining order among and against all four of the 'animals'..."

"Stop," Mrs. Sellars commanded.

The pen stopped.

"Rather than going back and forth with these one-off statements," she quickly frown-glanced at Barton Sellars, III, "let's negotiate all of the terms. Barton can't be subject to a restraining order. First of all, he's a Sellars. Second, entry of a restraining order would be grounds for suspension from football. Third, it's duck hunting season and everyone knows you can't have possession of a firearm while a restraining order is in place against you."

As Tal scanned the room it seemed fairly obvious that only Mrs. Sellars and Lawyer Noble were aware of that particular legal technicality.

"Mrs. Smith, does Tal hunt?" she asked Thea directly.

Thea's response was polite but clearly not warm. "No."

Mrs. Sellars continued. "Do you believe at this time that he is safe on the Nemeton High School campus?"

"Absolutely not," Thea replied, looking scornfully at Principal Davis.

"Besides the sporting events and the graduation ceremony what other school events remain this term?" Mr. Noble asked the principal.

"The Winter Formal is next Saturday," she replied.

"Tal, are you presently planning on going to the Winter Formal next weekend?" Mrs. Sellars asked.

She's asking because of Elle, Tal realized. "No, ma'am. I don't have any plans at this time to attend."

"The solution to the problem seems fairly simple to me," Mrs. Sellars stated. "Tal will agree to a restraining order not to be within five hundred feet of any member of the three families. That's any member," she added pointedly. "Nor will he be within five hundred feet of school property or any school athletic function."

"I don't think so," Pell said, slapping his hands on the table. "Why is our son going to be the only one with a criminal record that will affect his college and work career?"

"Master Smith?" Lawyer Noble asked, turning to look at Tal.

"Yes, sir?"

"Is there any reason for you to have contact with any member of the Sellars, Haslip, and/or McDermott families?"

Only that Elle may be the most important person I've ever met, he thought. But I guess I've screwed that situation all to hell. At least for this lifetime. "No, sir, there's not."

"Is foregoing attending the game next Friday evening a problem for you?"

That one was easy. "No, sir."

Lawyer Noble looked down at his second legal pad. "Finally, there's staying clear of the dance. Is that a deal breaker for you?"

Well, now there's a potential problem, Tal thought. The field trip is mandatory attendance or Omada will lose major points. But we're going to have masks on and all of the Nemeton High students will think anyone they don't recognize is from Little Rock. Emet will, or course, have to stay away. No, scratch that. I might need his brains and strength on site if something unexpected happens. He can wear the exact same clothes and the same mask as me. I'm probably being paranoid. Like there's any chance of something catastrophic happening at some boring, stupid high school dance.

"Tal?" his Mom's voice jerked him back to the conference room.

"No, Lawyer Noble, it's not a problem."

"Good," the attorney replied before making a few additional notes on his notepad. "Am I to understand then that it is acceptable to all of the parties if an agreed Restraining Order is signed but that I hold it in escrow at my office? If Tal complies with its conditions for the rest of the school year, it will be shredded. If he violates any of the conditions, it will be tendered to the Prosecutor for filing with the court?"

"Agreed," from Mrs. Sellars.

"Sure," from Principal Davis.

"Tal," Lawyer Noble interjected, "I need to make sure you understand what you're agreeing to. You're eighteen and have to make your own legal decisions. If you violate any of the terms and conditions of the Protective Order I will be required to turn it over to Prosecutor Jargley for filing. You will be subject to being fined, to arrest and to imprisonment for violation of the order, and multiple criminal charges will undoubtedly be filed against you."

"I understand," Tal advised.

"Fine, fine." Lawyer Noble began writing a lengthy paragraph on the notepad. When he was finished, he wiped the nib of his pen against the top left corner of the pad to clean it.

"Now, what else do we have to discuss?" Mrs. Sellars asked.

Lawyer Noble reached over into his briefcase and took out a second legal pad. Tal could see this one already had a numbered list written on it. The attorney went down the list scratching off several of the enumerated items. He paused at number six and looked at Mr. Sellars. "It is my understanding from some of the parents that you have terminated Mr. Smith?"

"Hell, yes. He's fired and that's non-negoti…YOW! SONOFAFUCKINGBITCH! HOLY DAMN, JOSEPH AND MARY!"

Tal could tell from her body position and the tightness of her lips that Mrs. Sellars had just kicked Mr. Sellars' shin three ways from Sunday.

"There is no need for blasphemy, dear," she purred in response.

Mr. Noble flipped a couple of pages back on his second notepad, to a page filled with writing and numbers and dates. "As I've previously mentioned, several of my clients are presently minors. The three-year limitations period for any civil litigation doesn't begin tolling for the youngest of my clients until about another two years down the road. We've already discussed the time limitations for the criminal charges." He nodded in turn at each of the packages he'd previously tendered.

"Third," Mrs. Sellars began, saccharine-sweet, "I believe you may have been hasty in your termination of Mr. Smith. He should probably be reinstated, with a five-year employment contract and a twenty-percent raise."

Mr. Barton looked like was he about to experience a phreatomagmatic event roughly equivalent to the two hundred kiloton eruption of Krakatoa. Either that or simply blow an aneurism—or three. He bit his lip several times, each time that action was followed by several episodes of what looked like a severe onset of acid reflux, but he finally nodded his head in agreement.

"Thank you, Mrs. Sellars for the kind offer," Pell replied. "However, I have no desire to be employed any longer by Sellars Chemicals. In any capacity. At any price. I want only the money that I earned through yesterday."

Tal saw Mr. Sellars smile at having apparently won a round over the rabble Philistines.

"Ahem." The obvious fake throat clearing was from Lawyer Noble. "In that case I can have a separate memorandum of understanding drawn up, to be signed by both Mr. and Mrs.

Sellars, acknowledging that if there is any comment of any kind, written or oral, by them, any of their family members, known acquaintances, or by any member of any of the Sellars many companies, that negatively impacts Mr. Smith's future employment or employment prospects, that the limitations period will be deemed to have been contractually tolled on all civil causes of action against any and all members of their family." He looked over at Barton. "As well as the filing of the Informations against you for all of the criminal charges, which would undoubtedly conclude with you receiving prison sentences totaling in the hundreds of years."

It was clear from the sheen that appeared on Barton's face that the possibility of hundreds of years of hard time got his attention. Mr. Sellars spoke up, "That's ridiculous. We can't possibly be responsible for everything that our acquaintances might say. We don't control everything they say or do."

"Don't be silly, sweetie, of course we do," his wife responded, softly patting his clenched fists a couple of times. A motion she repeated until he finally relaxed them. Both of them.

"Which also brings up the issue of any type of retaliation or harassment against Tal or any of the Smiths. I presume Mr. Smith that given your job status you intend on leaving the Nemeton area as soon as the school year is over?"

"That's correct. The day after Tal gets his diploma," he said fixing a glare on Mr. Sellars that any sensible person would find extremely alarming. Tal noted that at least in this instance, Mr. Sellars fell into the any sensible person category.

"That should work out nicely as the consideration for Tal's voluntary agreement to be exiled from school," the lawyer said with a quick smile. He wrote four or five sentences on his first notepad. "If the Smiths report to me that they are harassed in any shape, fashion, or form—including but not limited to verbal, physical. telephonic, mail, internet, social media of any type or kind, instant messaging, instagram, and/or snapchat— then the agreement not to prosecute Barton, Gunnar, and Fail for criminal charges and to forego suing everyone civilly, shall be null and void."

"WHA…" Mr. Sellars started to say as he erupted out of his chair.

"We agree," Mrs. Sellars replied. Then with a terse headshake she resumed her telepathic remote control of Mr. Sellars' leg muscles and he fell back hard into his seat.

Damn! And I thought Ms. Empousa was scary, Tal thought.

"Good," Lawyer Noble stated. "I'll have the agreement drawn up by noon tomorrow and couriered to your house for your signatures. I will hold it in escrow together with the Restraining Order. I will also have couriered over my statement for fees rendered and those reasonably expected to be rendered, and you will be sending a certified check for those amounts by the close of business on Monday."

Mr. Sellars looked like he was revisiting the whole possible aneurism bursting type thing. It was Mrs. Sellars who finally spoke. "That won't be a problem, Mr. Noble. We own the bank."

Lawyer Noble took his time and calmly and deliberately went up and down the itemized list on his second notepad. Then he repeated the action before putting both notepads back in his brief case, capping his fountain pen, and replacing it in his front shirt pocket. "It was a pleasure to meet you all. Principal Davis, thank you for the coffee and cookies." He turned to look at Tal, and stuck out his hand for a handshake, which Tal stood and returned. "Just so we're clear, all of the terms and conditions are effective when you leave the school property today. Let me be the first to congratulate you on finishing your high school experience. I know you will do wonderfully as you matriculate into whatever college you choose." With that, Lawyer Noble of the firm of Noble, Noble, and Noble, Osceola, Arkansas, exited the stage.

Principal Davis followed the lawyer out of the conference room. Pell helped Thea to her feet and they headed out with Tal following close behind.

Suddenly Tal heard footsteps, followed by Barton's high-pitched whine of a voice. Softly, really softly. "You think you're clever. You and your punkass attorney. Just so we're straight, Loser, you're not leaving this town alive. You're dead, you motherfucker. You, your mommy, your step-daddy, even those two little mongrel brothers of yours."

CHAPTER FIFTY-SIX

On the way home they turned into the nearest fast food drive-through to pick up lunch. Pell's thought was that keeping a low profile, especially until after the school-related events of next weekend, was the prudent thing to do. There would be no church this weekend, no trips to the park with the little ones, in fact the plan was for them all to hunker down indoors and give the Sellars a chance to bully the entire rest of the community into compliance with the morning's agreed terms.

Tal wasn't hungry, which was just as well. He knew Emet would be starving. For both calories and information. He could tell his Mom and Pell were exhausted from the events of the last twenty-four hours. They didn't even want to debrief with Tal before letting him go to his room. Pell reminded him he didn't need to plan on leaving the house the rest of the weekend and that telephone and social media communications needed to be kept to the bare minimum. His Mom reminded him the nonverbal experiment was terminated. Immediately. Which was another one of the issues he needed to discuss with Emet.

The first thing Tal did was close his bedroom door hard enough to let Emet know the coast was clear. Next, Tal walked over and opened his bedroom window. Finally, he collapsed on his bed to wait for the golem. His mind started turning. There was so much to go over. Baba Yaga, the meeting results, the dance, and maybe most importantly—their new dynamic, now that it was no longer acceptable for Tal to be mute.

Next thing Tal knew, he was laying on his side, looking out the window at the setting sun. What? He'd been out cold all afternoon? Which, he guessed, wasn't entirely unexpected but why didn't Emet wake him? He scanned the room. No Emet. The bag of now congealed greasy chicken was still sitting on his work desk. Emet hadn't been here at all. Tal got his phone out and texted Emet. No response. No dots indicating Emet was typing a response. Nothing. He texted him three more times. Dammit. Still no response.

What if Emet left the house while we were at Nemeton High and something happened to him? He could be out there hurt...or worse. Okay Tal, you need data. Do something constructive to obtain quantifiable information. First thing is to check Emet's bed in the attic. Which would be relatively easy if I could use the attic stairs. They're in the hallway though and the entire family is awake. I'm sure the twins are going stir crazy by now. There's no way they're going to let me go up there without following me.

So it's either wait until they're all asleep or only another half hour until its full on dark. Emet always made the round trip transit from attic to bedroom and back look easy. But he's got hyperstrength from being magyk powered. I can't wait any longer than I absolutely have to, so it's the oak tree express.

Might as well spend the time productively, try to work through some of the latest kinks in our covert dual existence. We don't have to worry about Nemeton High anymore, so that's a plus. The negative to that plus is the folks are no longer going to accept Silent Tal, and I still have to attend Hunts School every day for the rest of this term. Maybe for even longer if Omada makes the final cut. Emet can't be seen around the house during the days because he can't speak. I have to be home during the daytime hours because I'm basically under scholastic house arrest for the rest of this term. Turn the Rubik's cube on that one, Tal

Smith. Emet can't be here, I have to be at Hunts School, and I have to be home because I've been exiled from Nemeton High.

Of course, I could always try to tell Mom and Pell the truth, he thought, as he rubbed the bonfire still fiercely burning on his left ass cheek. The geas prevents me from telling them anything about Hunts School, but maybe I could show them the Nyx brand. Right, Tal you need to think that through. They're going to think that while you were in the grip of whatever madness caused you to assault those three goons that you also went out and got yourself branded. Not even tattooed, branded. Like a cow. Well, a steer in my case, he reminded himself. Actually, a steer is a gelding. Bull, then he told himself. Focus, you moron. Okay, okay, if he tried to verbally explain the brand, the hairball geas would shut him down and things would be a hundred times worse than before. Nope, buddy, you're going to have to finish this charade you started and be prepared to take some hard licks when you can finally come clean.

Exiled. There's the answer. If I can be involuntarily exiled from Nemeton High, why can't I be voluntarily exiled from home? I could attend Hunts School and I won't be expected here, which means Emet wouldn't need to hang around here to get busted by not being able to speak.

What's the deus ex machina that can make that happen? Well, duh, Tal thought, realizing he'd almost actually smacked himself in the forehead. The reason for the nonverbal experiment will be the reason for my excused prolonged absence. But you're only eighteen, Tal, and things are dicey right now. Your Mom and Pell aren't going to let you travel halfway across the state in one of the only two family vehicles.

The counterpoint is that the reason they will actually let me go is that it's the safest course of action for me and for all of the rest of my family. A trip to Hendrix College in Conway will provide me with the cover I need. A trip to personally present my thesis on the generational change in the percentage increase of nonverbal communication created by the advent of the internet and social media.

So my plan is to create yet another series of lies? When is it going to stop? I know, I know, but I would tell the folks the truth if I could, and me being out of town is arguably much safer for everyone. Out of sight, out of mind. I wouldn't have to take one of the cars, a bus can provide the transportation.

I can live at Hunts School. There are special suites for all of the Hunts Finalists. What about Emet, though? He won't be able to stay here without being seen and he can't come to Hunts School. Tal decided to put that one away for the two of them to discuss. Tal glanced out the window. Okay, dark enough to go find out what's up with Emet.

CHAPTER FIFTY-SEVEN

"If you don't tell me what happened, I'm just going to get the information from Daddy."

"Ellyse Holly Sellars,..." her mother began.

Wow, Elle thought. It wasn't that long ago that I almost wet my pants when the Queen called me out by all of my given names. What am I saying, she asked herself. I'm eighteen now and it's still scary as hell. Steel resolve, she told herself. Show no fear.

"Your father has had a hard enough day without you pestering him. He had to miss his regular golf game talking to our lawyers. It's given him such a headache he's not even going to the club for drinks at the Men's Grill this afternoon. You let him be."

"Here's the deal, Mom. I'm a member of this family and I deserve to know what other people know about my family members. Tell me right now or I'll go ask Barton first."

"No, you'll set him off. We barely have him under control as it is."

"Details, Mom, or I'll get them on my own."

Her mother gave her about a level nine baleful stare.

"I'm not kidding, Mom. You know I'm not."

Mrs. Sellars stopped carving the beef tenderloin and wagged the large carving knife in Elle's general direction. "You're only interested because of that Smith boy. He's bad news, Elle. I don't know what you see in him, anyway."

"Yes, you do, Mom. You most certainly do."

Her mother paused. *She knows it, too,* Elle told herself. *She knows there's something special about Tal. Even though he's an asshole. Which makes him a special asshole, I guess.*

"Fine," her mother conceded, motioning for Elle to sit at the kitchen table. "I'll make a deal with you."

"What?"

"I'll tell you everything you want to know. In return you agree that you won't try to have any further communication of any kind with him until after the end of the school year. They're moving away immediately after that anyway so it will no longer be a problem."

Elle didn't know why she had a sudden ache in her chest. Tal had broken up with her and hadn't said a word to her since that night. They would each have been leaving in the Fall to go to their different colleges anyway, and probably would never have seen other again. Still, there was something so definite about promising that she would never see or speak to him again. *Why does my chest hurt, though? You know the answer, Elle. You thought for a brief moment in time he might be everything you ever dreamed of in a life partner. Maybe if you're being honest, you still think it.*

Well?" her Mom asked.

I can get the information from Barton but it'll be badly editorialized from his perspective. And Daddy did look pretty bad when they got back from the meeting at school. "Deal."

"Fine," her mother said, returning to cutting up tonight's entrée. "But if I'm going to go back through that whole nightmare, you need to go fix me a gin and tonic first. Go on," she said wagging the knife at Elle. "Don't be frugal with the gin."

CHAPTER FIFTY-EIGHT

What took Emet all of about ten seconds took Tal almost ten minutes. Plus a ripped shirt and a couple of substantial scratches. Actually, Tal thought, one of them almost qualifies as a laceration. I wonder if the line of demarcation between scratches and lacerations is based on length or depth. Or maybe a combination of both. He finally made it up the tree and through the small double windows in the attic. It was pitch black and he hadn't thought to bring a flashlight. He'd forgotten Emet could see at lower light levels than humans. Cellphone! Cellphone light. He wriggled his phone out of his front left pocket and turned the light on.

Emet had done a great job of arranging the boxes and stored bric a brac so it all effectively hid his nest without appearing to have been moved or arranged. Tal snaked between two pillars made of stacked plastic containers and there he was. Facedown. On a pile of blankets and quilts he'd found stored in the attic. They even reeked heavily of mothballs. I really haven't done right by the boy, Tal thought. He's had to completely make his own way, been stuck up here all by himself, and never once complained. Although I guess for him to know that he should complain would require him to have an underlying feeling of some nature. Which he doesn't have.

Tal saw Emet's phone gripped in his left hand. Like Tal, he was left-handed. Of course. Emet wasn't moving, not even with a small, rhythmic breathing motion. Tal took a couple of steps and hit his knees as he flipped Emet over and put his head to his chest. Heart was beating. Very slowly but they'd never had any discussions as to whether Emet's magyk-powered heart beat at the same rate as Tal's.

"Em," he whispered. Urgently but quietly. The absolute last thing they needed added to the mix right now was his folks. "Emet," this time a little louder with some not quite so gentle shaking. Tal wasn't worried about Emet screaming, he couldn't speak but he didn't need him thrashing and maybe knocking something over.

Five minutes later, after alternating speaking in Emet's ear and even violently shaking him, Tal was still unable to rouse Emet. It can't only be a really sound sleep, he'd have woken up. Emet is in some type of coma. Tal stopped to regroup. He was exhausted too, and the brand on his ass was sending excruciating pain pulses to all parts of his body. I'll just wait a few minutes, he decided, then I'll try again. Might as well lay down here beside him while I'm waiting.

CHAPTER FIFTY-NINE

Threep! (Sound.)

Threep! (Animal sound.)

Threep! (Bird sound.)

I looked that noise up last semester, Tal thought. On the morning after Emet was created.

It's a hisselly phrase! (Bingo, got it.) That sequence is one version of our friendly neighborhood robin's morning song.

"Oh, shit!" Tal voiced the words before he remembered where he was. In the attic with Emet. Who was still out cold. Tal checked Emet's breathing. Slow, very slow, but steady. He shook him. No response. No time to keep trying to wake him, Tal told himself. Even though Sunday morning everyone normally sleeps in until about 9:00 a.m., I can't count on business as usual this morning. I need to get back to my room, stat.

Out the window and down to his room. Down was substantially easier than up, but the oak exacted toll consisting of several more annoying abrasions, and apparently his burnt to hell ass was going to throb for the rest of his mortal existence. Let's amend that to the "rest of my hopefully long and prosperous mortal existence in which the medical profession quickly finds a cure for torched buttocks." Much better, he decided.

Tal cracked his door and listened. The folks' white noise machine was still going strong down the hall. Good, that means they're still asleep. Well, there is one other possibility, he reminded himself. No need to call up any virtual simulations, he told image processing. Same net result for me—I have a few minutes.

Tal grabbed his backpack and started shoving clothes into it until it was about to pop the seams. He couldn't take them to Hunts School with him, but he had to sell the lie to Thea and Pell. After that, he grabbed his wallet, emptied the cash and his debit card and shoved them under his mattress for Emet to pick up later. To hopefully pick up later. Tal literally shuddered at the many possibilities of what could happen if Emet didn't wake up. First of all, whatever had happened to Emet might be fatal. Second, if he didn't wake up soon there was always the possibility he could be discovered in the attic. They would all assume he was Tal and freak out and take him to a hospital and all kinds of terrible fallout would occur from there. The doctors would go bananas if they found out Emet's blood was blue.

But I can't stay, Tal thought. If I'm not back for class tomorrow morning, Omada starts getting points deducted. And I'm the one with the talysman. If given the chance, Mom and Pell are absolutely not going to let me out of their sight until after next weekend. Which would mean a guaranteed loss for Omada. Which also would probably mean that shithead Nord and the Släkt will rule the universe for three hundred years.

Write Mom and Pell an explanatory note, grab your stuff and get the hell out. After you make your bed, he reminded himself. I can leave all of my belongings at my normal drop off place and type Emet a text once I'm safely there. Our phones are password protected so he's the only one that will ever receive it. Provided he wakes up. I hate to leave him but if he were awake he would tell me leaving immediately is the smart play.

CHAPTER SIXTY

Thea and Pell, yelling. Not at each other. At Remy and Romy. Not mad yelling. Anxious. Worried. Yelling. They're both telling the boys to hurry. Multiple car doors opening and closing. Four distinct sounds. Tires squealing as Pell floored the SUV as they left the driveway.

Emet rolled over and sat up. It's full on daylight. What's going on? I don't even really sleep and I must have been out for ten hours or more. He tried to rewind yesterday's events. I went to sleep because I felt sleepy. Felt?

Why didn't Tal text me and wake me up? Phone. He rummaged around under his old blanket and found his cellphone. Four messages from Tal, all of them only "?"s. They're from last evening. What is going on with me? He looked at the time on his cell. It's only 9:30 a.m. They couldn't have been late for church, it doesn't start until 11:00 a.m.

He texted Tal, then waited. Give it a couple of minutes, he told himself. He's probably in the car with his parents and needs to make sure he doesn't get busted for texting with me. After waiting five minutes Emet decided something was definitely wrong. Maybe Tal is asleep downstairs. I heard four car doors but I also only heard Pell, Thea and the twins.

Careful, he told himself. Can't violate Rule One, Tal and I can't be in the same place at the same time. He took another couple of minutes to listen. Even with his exceptional hearing there was no sound other than the heater fan kicking on. Time to go find out what's up, he decided.

He scanned the driveway to double-check. Yep, gone. Out the window and down the tree and into Tal's room. What the hell? Looks like a bomb went off in here.

CHAPTER SIXTY-ONE

That's probably the fastest I've ever made it to the gas station, Tal thought, as he finally reached the pockmarked gravel driveway. *I hurried because I couldn't take any chances. Mom and Pell are pretty smart and may have figured out my note was a subterfuge. Once I cross through the Ladies' Room I'll be where they can't find me. My ass literally feels like there is a campfire on it big enough to cook s'mores on. If that happened I guess they'd be "ass s'mores." I'm not even going to think about looking that up in Urban Dictionary.*

Per his usual routine, Tal began removing all of the objects from his pockets. He had some change in his left front pocket and his cell was in his right rear pocket. *I can try texting Emet again.* He started punching the digits.

SHIT! SHIT!! SHIT!!! I was upstairs with Emet all night and the phone wasn't on its charger. It's dead. I can't believe I was so stupid. Review your options, Tal. It's too much of a risk to try to head back into town. There's no telling what roads the folks are cruising looking for me. Plus they've probably put out an all-points bulletin with the few people they can trust. Not to mention what might happen to me if any Barton-sympathizers catch me out and about.

No, I'll have to do this with snail mail. He got a pen and piece of paper out and wrote a note to Emet. It ended up taking two sheets, front and back. Tal first wrote down the info that would bring Emet up to speed on the last Journey and what little details he had about the field trip. Then he explained the terms of the bargain with the Sellars so that Emet would be in the know. He also asked him to try to hook up with him at the school dance on Saturday night. After Tal was done he read through it a couple of times. Feels like I left something out. He looked it over again. Yes, that. I need to tell him I'm very worried about him, that I'm sorry to leave him in the lurch like this, and that when I see him Saturday night we can draft a more permanent plan. Like where he's going to live and what he's going to eat and how we're possibly going to make it through the last half of senior year at Nemeton High. Oh, and that I love him. As things are pretty dicey in the Hunts competition right now, seems like I should tell the people I love that I love them as often as I can.

Tal placed the note in his backpack, and then shoved the backpack into its usual hiding place under the bushy azalea right in front of Luna's junkyard. Hopefully the note will stay dry even if the weather goes south. After that he turned and walked into the Ladies' Room.

CHAPTER SIXTY-TWO

Emet quickly surveyed Tal's bedroom. Much of the room's contents were helter-skelter but Tal's bed was made. Like he or Tal would make it. Teenage boy "close enough for horseshoes or hand grenades" as opposed to Thea's hospital-cornered meticulousness. What's the significance of the observable data, Emet asked himself. One—Tal took time to make his bed before he left. Two—he's gone for the day. It was a firm Smith house rule that beds were made before going about the day's business. Final conclusion—Tal conducted an orderly evacuation.

But it's Sunday morning. There's no school and it's not near time for church. And why are some of his clothes and belongings strewn around the room? More information needed, Emet told himself. He crossed to the bedside table. The auxiliary cellphone battery charger, and charging cables were still on Tal's bedside table. Next, he went to the desk. Both drawers were still partially open and their contents jumbled. The desktop contents were all out of their ordinary positions. Tal knew where everything in the room was so he hadn't been the one searching for whatever was being searched for. Had to be Thea and Pell. But, why?

As Emet moved toward the closet his foot kicked a piece of notebook paper laying on the floor. Emet bent down and picked it up.

Dear Mom and Pell:

First things first. I love you. You both know that.

Second, I am not a stupid or rash individual. You both know that as well.

Third, I've decided the safest place for me to be for at least the next week is out of sight, out of mind.

Fourth, I didn't ask first because I know your initial response was to tell me "no" even though you would subsequently realize it's a great short term solution to the present problem.

I'm taking my thesis on nonverbal communication and heading to Hendrix College to see if I can get somebody to take a look at it. There is no need for you to call the school. I haven't called ahead or made an appointment with any of the professors so they don't have any idea I'm coming. At this point they don't even know I exist. You'll completely destroy my credibility as an adult, and as a scholar, if you call them to ask about me. So, please don't.

Mom—please don't worry. Pell—please tell Mom she doesn't need to worry. Because of the deal you brokered we know I'm going to have great grades for this last term. Please give me this chance to try to prove myself and get a sizeable scholarship.

I'll call you in a few days after I've gotten there and I'm settled in. I saved enough money for the trip and you both know I'm frugal. Rather than fretting, just trust me and wish me luck.

Love,

Tal

Looking at the note Emet felt his breath catch in his throat. This is why Thea and Pell flew out of here. They think they can catch Tal, to at least try to talk him out of going. Emet reread the note several times to make sure he caught any subtext Tal might have left for him.

I get it, Emet thought. Don't know the exact details but some deal was cut with the Sellars clan about Tal graduating with good grades but not going to school anymore. Which means two of us here at the house. Not good. Plus if he couldn't get away it would have screwed up his Hunts School attendance requirement.

Where does that leave me and why didn't he give me a heads up on his plans? Well, if Tal is "out of town," I can't stay here at the house. And he didn't give me any information because he couldn't. I was in that fugue state.

Time to get moving, Emet decided. Pell and Thea know that Barton dumped him out at Sol's. Tal will have done the smart thing and gotten off Earth plane proper as soon as he could, so I can't catch him at the Gas Station. I need to book out of here before the family comes back to regroup. If I'm moving out I'll need all of our available capital. Tal would have known that. Emet stepped over to the bed and lifted the near corner of the mattress. Yep, cash and his debit card. Although debit card transactions would be traceable so using it would have to be an emergency. While he was by the bed he collected the auxiliary phone battery, charger and connecting cords. I'll zip upstairs and clear out all of my stuff so there's no sign I was ever there and book it to the Gas Station. Tal will have had to leave all of his possessions in his hiding spot. I'll turn his phone off and hook it up to the extra battery. Hopefully it will still have juice in case he ever gets to check in at the Gas Station. Emet walked over to the desk and grabbed a pen and some paper to put in his backpack. Backup communication material is the prudent play, he decided.

He leapt out the window and back to the attic, grabbed his Nemeton High textbooks and took them back downstairs to Tal's desk. He picked up the camouflaged Hunts School books and took them up to the attic, where he placed them in his backpack. Although it was a tight fit he was able to cram all of the textbooks, his spare sets of clothing, the extra battery, cords, and battery charger into his school backpack. It didn't quite zip closed but that was okay. He moved his stacks of crates so that they were disorganized and threw his quilt in a corner. It looked like it had been laying there undisturbed for months. After all of that he gave the attic a careful once over to make sure there was no sign of human—well almost human—habitation. None. As he moved toward the attic window some substation in his subconscious brain kept telling him he was forgetting something. Something that might be incriminating, if found. What, though? What? I've picked up all of my stuff.

Oh, right. The one thing of Tal's that was up here. That silly little plastic bubble with the airplane wings Tal got on Atlantis plane. He reached inside the rolled up area rug where Tal had hidden it and put it in a side pocket of the backpack.

I can ditch it in a trash bin on the way out of town, Emet thought as he jumped out the window. He carefully closed the attic window behind him, then made sure Tal's window was closed, before shinnying quickly down the oak tree. He stopped and looked back at the only home he'd ever known. Melancholy, he thought. I know I can't feel it, but that's the emotional response which Tal would have received when confronted with the same factual stimuli. Taking a deep breath, which if he'd been paying attention he would have realized was also a large sigh, Emet loped across the front yard. He then headed south, sticking

to the least used surface streets. Out of town, and toward the Gas
Station.

CHAPTER SEXAGINTA TRES

The backpack was right where Tal always placed it. Emet checked Tal's phone first. Dead. There's the reason I didn't get any further communication or instructions from him. He hooked the phone up to the battery and then turned it back off. Better safe than sorry. There's no telling when Tal might get a chance to come check for messages. As Emet looked through the backpack he found Tal's notes. He took the notes, zipped the backpack up and carefully secured it back under the azalea, covering it with a thin layer of leaves and dirt where it couldn't be seen from the sidewalk. I don't really need to remain out in the open any longer than necessary, he reminded himself. Tal said the Ladies' Room was pretty nice. Seems like as good a short term place to hide as any other while I read his notes and figure out my next move.

Emet opened the bathroom door, closed it securely behind him, flipped the light switch, and then almost fell over in surprise. The first thing he saw was a crisply made single bed in the space in which Tal had said the seating area was located. As Emet looked closer he noticed there was even a wrapped chocolate mint on one of the pillows. Beside the bed was a small table with a single chair. The table was dressed with a pressed white linen tablecloth, a pitcher of cold water, a delightful looking antipasto platter, a cloth napkin and a complete table setting for one. There was even a small vase sitting in the middle of the table filled with freshly cut royal blue delphiniums which were accompanied by sprigs of dusty miller. As Emet walked into the room he noticed there was a glass-doored marble shower which sported a rain forest shower head. Completing his circuit of the bathroom he saw there was a note taped to the inside of the door.

>Emet:

>Good morning. It is my understanding you are currently homeless. You are welcome to stay here until 5:00 p.m. this upcoming Saturday. Reservations have been booked beginning at 7:00 pm for the Hunts Finalists to utilize the Gas Station Crossing for their field trip. There are any number of Creatures and Folk who would detect your unique magyk signature if you remain on the premises after 5:00 p.m. Your existence is presently unknown to anyone other than the Omada, the Archon, and his wife.

>You will be safe while you are within this space. Any time you spend on Earth plane proper will be at your own peril.

>There are no nuts on the antipasto platter in the event you have a nut allergy.

>Tal is always very good about remembering to wash his hands and about turning the light off when he leaves. Please do the same.

>Sincerely yours,

>The Ladies' Room

Emet realized he suddenly felt unsteady on his feet. Again? What's the matter with me? First there was that whole out of control situation with Barton Sellars, then my unexplained illness, which was followed by a more than twelve-hour coma.

Something is not right, he thought as he sat in the chair by the table with his food. As long as you're sitting here, read Tal's notes, he told himself.

About ten minutes later, he reached over and grabbed some grapes while he sat back to ponder the large amount of new information Tal's notes provided. Tal hadn't had much information to give him about the field trip so that portion was only a vague outline. The Hunts Finalists were going to the Winter Formal at Nemeton High this Saturday night. Emet already knew that much from the Ladies' Bathroom. Actually, he had learned most of the details about the dance itself from Elle, he just hadn't had a chance to bring Tal up to speed on any of those details.

The blow by blow of Tal's encounter with Baba Yaga was an entirely different matter. It was easy to visualize the entire episode from the details in Tal's notes. Wait a minute, he thought as he looked back through the last few minutes of interaction before Borras made his appearance. Tal and I never got a chance to discuss that either, but my sickness must have started right about the time he used Aurora's last wish.

It can't be, Emet thought as he sat there stunned. That can't possibly have happened. I need to lay down. Never have I needed to talk to Tal more than I do right now. I can't get in contact with him until the dance on Saturday. I'm just going to lay down here and take a nap. But you don't need sleep, Emet, you're a golem, he reminded himself. 'I need a nap' was his only responsive thought before he nodded off.

CHAPTER SEXAGINTA QUATTUOR

Tal looked around the classroom. It's Monday of the last week of class for second term. Today is the day we're scheduled to get the final details from Professor Elphinstone about the field trip. "I know you're all excited about the field trip. Since Arthrys instituted the first prohibition against the use of magyk on Earth Realm, the only Folk authorized to visit Earth plane proper have been the Hunts Finalists each Tyrning year, the Archon, and the few emissaries periodically sent by the Archon to the Earth plane for cultural updating."

You can add the Crestfallyn to that list, Tal thought to himself. Of course, Professor Elphinstone knew nothing about the incursion of one of the Crestfallyn on the Earth plane. The faceless freak who had haunted Tal ever since he was an infant and who'd tried to take his face on his eighteenth birthday.

"Much planning has gone into making this excursion possible and there are a large number of rules and conditions attendant with the trip. We will go over the restrictions today, and I will repeat them during class the day after tomorrow." He stopped and looked all the way around the room. "Just so that we're all very clear about the rules of engagement.

"Because of the novelty and the many intricacies involved in this activity, Ms. Empousa has changed the scoring for this term. She has elected to make your team score on this field trip twenty-five percent of your score for this term. The Wytch Hunt will count as sixty percent. Everything else you do this term, such as combat results and test scores will only cumulatively count as fifteen percent of your team ranking."

What's up with that, Tal wondered. If Baba Yaga was telling me the truth then we were a lock for the final three. That may not be the case though with the field trip being so heavily weighted.

"All of the Faculty chaperoning the field trip will participate in your scoring. Every team starts equally with a score of one hundred. Because we expect you to listen closely to the rules and to follow them without the least bit of deviation, you will not accrue points for the field trip, you can only lose them."

Everyone but me has been here almost a hundred years, Tal thought. They've taken tests, passed physical challenges, studied and read up on the hundreds of Hunts in previous Tyrnings. They all believed they were prepared for pretty much anything. This twist is unexpected. Both the trip, and the scoring mechanics for the trip are wild cards, and the uncertainty is worrisome.

Professor Elphinstone walked over to the blackboard. "I know most of you generally take copious notes. Every member of every team needs to write down each of the rules I am about to write on this board. During your team study times, you need to drill each other on the rules. During your independent study times, you need to practice memorizing the rules. While you're asleep in your dorms, you need to dream about reciting the rules…"

Okay, I'm going to have to ask Borras about that, Tal decided. If Folk get to have self-directed dream activities that would be pretty cool. Just think of all of the people you could imagine getting busy with…

"Focus, Quint," Borras whispered, jamming an elbow the size of a pot roast into Tal's side.

Professor Elphinstone ceased talking and began writing. The only noise in the classroom for the next few minutes was the scratching of chalk on blackboard and pens on paper.

Rule One – Alberich's Bane will remain in full force. None of the students, nor the chaperones, will be able to utilize their magyk.

Rule Two – Everyone will embark on the same transport vehicles at the Gas Station Crossing.

Rule Three – The event site is the Nemeton High School gymnasium. Once we arrive at the gym, you are not to leave the gym for any reason. No wandering the halls, no exploring the grounds. The gym has bathrooms you may use. All of the food and drinks will be situated in the gym.

Rule Four – The event is a masque ball. The individuals in charge of the event have decreed that wearing of the masks is mandatory until midnight at which time there shall be a formal unmasking. You will strictly comply with that requirement. We will be leaving the event in time to be back on the transport vehicles immediately prior to the midnight unmasking.

Professor Elphinstone turned to face the class. "Obviously you don't attend school at Nemeton High School. The Ruling Council, with the permission of the Archon, has utilized its magyk to take care of all of the necessary cover details. All of the Nemeton faculty and students believe they are being joined at the dance by a busload of seniors from a high school in a place called Little Rock. It is apparently not only the Earth plane term for a pebble but is also the capitol of a geographically delineated political subdivision. The masks are what made the field trip possible, as they will make it difficult for individuals to know who is or who isn't actually from Nemeton High School. You will be able to participate in various group discussions, listen in on other conversations, and obtain a substantial amount of data about the current status of Earth Realm cultures and philosophy.

"Removal of a mask for any purpose will constitute a major penalty of fifty points." With that he turned back around, grabbed a fresh piece of chalk, and continued writing.

Rule Five – You may partake of any of the refreshments on premises but please do not try to smuggle any contraband from Hunts School. It will be detected and your team will be docked points for the attempt.

Rule Six – Please do not attempt to bring any "souvenirs" back to Hunts School. The ward boundaries will reject any items. Pay attention and learn what you can from the expedition so that you may remember it later.

Rule Seven – Customarily, only the remaining Hunts Finalists are permitted on the field trip to Earth Realm. Because this event is a dance you will be allowed to designate another student to accompany you as your date or your escort. You may choose anyone who is currently enrolled as a student.

A wave swelled clockwise signaling major approval. Of course it would, Tal thought. Everything had been so new and so different for him last term that it had taken him a long time to see the clues for all of the hookups and mating rituals. And why shouldn't all of that be going on? These students were the best and the brightest from all of the known planes, and while they were at Hunts School, they all had human form. They'd been away from home and segregated at this school for almost a hundred years. Of course people were getting down.

Tal flicked his eyes toward the Släkt table. Väst was looking at him but glanced away when she saw him looking. What the hell is up with her, Tal wondered. This last couple of days, I can't even get her to speak with me. It's not like I could take her to the dance anyway, her entire team is trying to kill me. Except for her. Well, maybe except for her. Plus Elle and her dickhead brother and his gang and all of the teachers and students at Nemeton will be there. I caught a huge break when they decided on masks as part of the theme.

The sudden screech of chalk skittering across the blackboard reeled Tal back from daydreaming. Professor Elphinstone was still writing rules.

Rule Eight – The Ruling Council has agreed to bring master costumers, cosmetologists, and some of the finest mask artisans from the Venetian Realm to assist all of the Finalists and their dates with wardrobe, hair and makeup. You may choose a plain mask or an ornate one, there is no penalty assessed for duplication of masks. However, you will not be permitted to copy anyone else's event costume.

At that point the class bell rang. Tal heard papers being shuffled behind him.

"Ignore, it," the professor said. "We're having an extended session today. Lunch will be delayed."

"Damn it," Tal heard someone in the back whisper to his squad. "It's fried Sphinx knuckles day. They always go fast."

"Shut it," his Prime Direction said harshly. "It's not like you ever solve the riddle to actually get any."

"Attention please," the professor reminded everyone, as he began scrawling the next rule.

Rule Nine – No copulating with any of the mortals. Even though they are all seniors and should have passed the age of majority. Any Finalist found copulating with a human will cost their team all one hundred points available for the exercise.

Tal actually heard some grumbling from both males and females at this point. Apparently, quite a few students had been planning on getting a little strange.

"Additionally,…"

Wait, there's more?

"Any student violating Rule Nine will be lyfetyme magyked upon their return to campus. The magyk will evidence itself anytime in the future that such student becomes SSA." Professor Elphinstone started writing Rule Ten on the board. He must have heard the whispered questions because without even turning around he said, "SSA? 'Subsequently sexually aroused,' of course. In such instances the magyked individual will become violently ill, hyper-flatulent, and cursive writing in red ink will appear on their forehead stating, *I have huge, suppurating genital warts*.'"

That'll either have to be a really small font, or a really broad forehead to get all of that on there, Tal thought. But I now have yet another example of death—or worse.

"Always…as in, mmm, like…always?" someone choked out.

"Always," Professor Elphinstone replied. "As in…mmm, like…FOREVER."

The teacher's statement provoked a new round of almost universal low-level muttering. Best Tal could tell, none of the Hunts Finalists had ever heard of someone having that type of magyk, but none of them wanted to test whether it was a bluff.

"Corsages," someone asked from the far left corner. "Is this the type of social event where corsages and boutonnieres are worn?"

"Excellent question, and yes." the professor replied. "I will ask the HuntsMistress and Principal Chiron to make sure we have an assortment of all types of arrangements for those wishing to wear them. We're almost done with the rules," Professor Elphinstone said, turning and retrieving his chalk shard.

> **Rule Ten** – This is a field trip, not a Journey. There will be zero tolerance for injuring, maiming, or killing of the Dust Children. This field trip presents the danger of a bloodpryce Rules violation.

As Tal tapped his pen on his notebook to get Borras's attention, he heard Nord mutter, "Not much of a dance then is it?" to the general mirth of his team. When Borras finally looked down, Tal scribbled a question mark. Borras wrote, "later" on his pad.

> **Rule Eleven** – This is a field trip, not a Journey. There will be zero tolerance for injuring, maiming, or killing of

another contestant. Violation of this rule will not only result in zero points for this exercise, the offending team will forfeit the competition.

Tal noticed that this time there was a wave that went clockwise and a second wave that went counterclockwise, crashing together halfway across the room. Damn, he thought. There's a goodly portion of Finalists who are upset about the whole no-maiming restriction.

Professor Elphinstone put his now substantially expended piece of chalk down in the tray at the bottom of the chalkboard before turning and walking to his desk where he opened the top left hand drawer, took out a small dark washcloth, walked back over to the chalkboard, and erased every one of the rules. "I hope you were paying attention. Now, go get some lunch. Oh, and since I've made you late, the answer to today's riddle is 'man'."

CHAPTER SEXAGINTA QUINQUE

Sometimes it was hard to distinguish the sound of Her voice in his head from the loud hissing of the steam pipes. *'Have the arrangements for the field trip been made as I instructed?'*

'Yes, Mistress.'

'The Archon will be in attendance.'

'Alberich? No, he won't. The Archon has never gone on one of the field trips in the entire history of Hunts School.'

These are unusual times, Malabranche. He is a formidable opponent. He arrogantly believes that with his Hunts School magyk and that awaymagyk scrying bytch wife of his that he can prevent anything from happening. Their attendance means you will not be able to take your weapon with you, she will sense it.'

'Then your plan won't work," he replied, as he began in frustration to stroke the hidden scars on his face. 'I don't have the power to magyk the blade on to the Earth plane. Not with the Bane in place.'

'FOOL! You doubt me? After everything I have shown you over the last millennia? If you want to quit now, I can arrange for you to join your former teammates in the grave.'

Too far, Malabranche, he told himself. You've gone too far with Her. 'I'm sorry, Mistress. I'm sorry. I don't doubt you. I desperately want to finish what I started.'

'Of course you do, Malabranche. It's why you have foresworn every vow you've ever made. When I am through, not only will you be Archon but you will have your chance to avenge yourself against that interfering Munedan. You remember him, don't you? The one who gave Excalibur to Arthrys?'

Saliva began dripping through the curled gap in his lips, one of the many horrendous mementos left on his face from his battle with Arthrys. 'After all these centuries it is finally my turn for vengeance? You have my word, Quint of the Omada shall die.'

'NO, you dolt! He must not die on Earth plane proper, his death there will not serve my purpose, and it will not make you Archon. You are to use the thrice-cursed blade to kill some other mortal. It has magyk sufficient for three deaths, three mortal wounds which Folk magyk is powerless to heal. Follow my instructions exactly. You are to select a mortal at random, someone who has no obvious connection to the Dust Child. The Archon has great magyk but if you do exactly what I say he will not be able to thwart my plan. I will be there to help you complete your task when the moment is ripe. Leave the thrice-blooded blade here. It will be placed in the bathroom at the mortal school and glamoured so that only you can see it. Remember—when darkness rules, I will glamour you invisible, and it is then you will strike.'

Who am I dealing with that has this kind of power, Malabranche asked himself. I've already answered that question a hundred times—the answer is it doesn't matter. I've murdered my own teammates to get what I want. There is no longer any possibility for redemption for me, only victory or the Five-Hells await.

After several minutes of silence he realized She had departed. He carefully unwrapped the thrice-blooded blade and knelt to gently lay it on the floor. He knew all too well what swords of power could do to anyone, no matter how powerful they might be.

CHAPTER SEXAGINTA SEX

The big reveal day had finally arrived. Tal looked around the Orientation classroom. It had been some time since he'd seen the whole group in street clothes. For the last couple of months they had been wearing their Pucas at all times during the school day as well as for their Journeys. I used to feel naked when I was wearing Piras, now it's the opposite. Funny how quickly perspective shifts when you choose to unravel your knotted up ignorance.

Same thing but different with Baba Yaga, Tal thought, his brand throbbing in response underneath his jeans. Hero or villain? Was she a victim or was that entire train of thought a conceptual non sequitur because lyfe didn't come with a warranty booklet. I wonder if lyfe operates by the same rules as magyk and gyfts—for every positive there is an equal and opposite negative.

It wasn't only the strength the Puca gave him that Tal missed. Piras had become one of his best friends and, for obvious reasons, a close confidant. He knew everything about Tal, including most of the details of his ongoing illicit relationship with Väst. Tal could tell from comments made by his teammates and from Combat class results that none of the Folk had the same intimacy or familiarity with their Pucas. The habits and prejudices of hundreds of generations of Folk weighed too heavily upon them to change in such a short period of time. Even the genuinely good individuals, like Borras, had subconscious bias. To the Folk, the Puca were merely Creatures, lesser beings to be used as tools to help Folk teams try to win the Hunts. After that they would be packed away until they were needed to provide service during the next Tyrning cycle.

Now that the Finalists weren't being augmented by the Pucas, Tal could see how uniformly haggard they all looked. Two of the six teams only had four members present, which could mean any number of things—none of which were good for the missing individuals or their teams. Despite the fact the physicks were allowed to use healmagyk while the Finalists were between Journeys, at least a half-dozen of the Folk had visible bandaging, and about the same number looked like they had only been recently released from the infirmary. No question that even with the Pucas' healing, the multiple Journeys this term had exacted their toll.

The HuntsMistress had passed the word yesterday to all of the Prime Directions that the Pucas were to be stored for the rest of this semester. No big deal, Tal thought. This morning's double session of Orientation is our last class. We have the rest of today and tomorrow to get costumes and masks ready for the dance tomorrow evening. Sunday is Imbolc. We'll have the celebration feast and the remaining three Finalist teams will be formally announced before the entire school. Those three teams will move on to the last Hunt. The members of the other three teams will, no doubt, first be humiliated by Ms. Empousa before forfeiting their names and being demoted from the spacious Finalists' suites back to the barracks areas where the general student population sleeps.

The downgrade back to the general barracks had to be a major blow. As soon as Tal had showed up on campus on Sunday, Borras had taken him to see Principal Chiron and he had personally unlocked Tal's suite for him. It has been waiting for him since Tal was initially confirmed as an Omada team member. Swanky didn't do the rooms justice. Each Finalist's suite had been designed by an interior designer who had earned the right to design the suite by winning a contest involving tens of thousands of submissions from all of the known planes. Apparently designers' reputations were made for life if one of their designs was selected for use in a Finalist suite at Hunts School.

Tal's suite contained a humongous drawing room that soared several stories upward, an oversized bathroom with about a dozen marble columns that contained a shower as big as an elevator, a magyk-jetted tub, a sauna and a steam room, and a bedroom of Brobdingnagian proportions. Whatever size mattress was bigger than "king" was standard issue for the Hunts Finalists' rooms. Whoever had won the right to design and furnish the suite given to Tal was from one of the Moroccan planes, and Tal loved everything about the Moorish-influenced furniture and wildly colored fabrics. In contrast, all of the non-Finalist students were apparently required to sleep ten students to a barracks unit with a community bathroom and shower at the end of each floor. Emet would have loved this place, Tal thought. I wish he could see it.

Borras nudged him to get his attention. Tal could see the other three Omada members craning their necks to hear. "You got the talysman? I don't want to violate Empousa's directive with any details, but most of the other teams have a bag or a box or something. You know you have to have it? That we have to make the preliminary presentation in class this morning?"

Tal nodded in response. "I got it covered, Prime." Big whoop, how long is it going to take me to tell everybody that instead of receiving a swag bag, I got the worst tramp stamp ever?

The door blew open the exact moment the bell rang, and Ms. Empousa came flying into the room. She was, of course, still wearing her Puca. Always with the dramatic entrance, Tal thought. She surveyed the room, noting who was present—and who wasn't. That's probably what an osprey looks like the split second before it dives at over thirty miles per hour to rip the life out of its unsuspecting earthbound prey.

"We will have an extended session this morning. The talysman holder for each of the teams will summarize his or her team's Journeys and provide details concerning any contacts with wytches and whether a talysman was obtained. If a team did not receive a talysman, the Prime Direction shall be the default team member providing the pertinent information. First to report will be Pleme," Ms. Empousa said, motioning toward the Pleme table for a representative.

Sredina, the Pleme Prime Direction, stood and slowly walked to the front of the classroom. "Pleme really got our asses handed to us on our first two Journeys. None of us, including our Pucas, were at more than about ten percent on the first Realm. Istok was immediately attacked by what can only best be described as a rabid, three-foot long, iridescent yellow dragonfly. Before we could pull the thing off of him, he'd been bitten in the leg half a dozen times. It became quickly apparent the creature's saliva contained some type of neurotoxin. Istok's Puca was able to redirect the blood flow away from the wound area until the Recall." Sredina looked back toward her teammates at their table. "After the Recall, we rushed him to the infirmary. It was too late for the physicks to save his left foot."

Holy shit! Tal thought. Istok lost his foot to a freakin' dragonfly?

"When the Hunts are over, he will be able to utilize a magykal prosthetic that will remove any physical limitations resulting from the amputation. It's a lengthy, painful procedure and there's no need to rush to fit him now as the magykal prosthetic wouldn't operate at either Hunts School or on Earth Realm.

"We were lucky on the second Journey in that we were all at full strength. Our luck ended there. None of us had ever heard of or seen anything like that Realm. It rained rocks and boulders there. All shapes and sizes, pointed and ovoid. The entire time we were there we were madly jumping about to save our lives. Even with our Pucas' help we all received serious bruises from being hit with some of the smaller stones. If any of the boulders had made contact it would have been game over. Sever got three busted ribs and Zapad got his arm broken. No sign of any wytch, although once we got back we realized the rock rain must have been one of her defensive mechanisms.

"It was on our third trip that we finally met a wytch. We landed in a beautiful woodland glen, a clear stream lazily looped its way through the clearing. At the far end there was a row of seven Ionic columns. Each was about twenty feet tall, chiseled from pitch-black obsidian. The columns were the backdrop to a matching set of stairs that led up to a low dais. It looked at first as if the dais floor was painted in a trompe-l'oeil design that was patterned to make it appear the floor was in constant motion. As we walked closer we saw that the floor itself wasn't moving. The entire platform was more than a foot deep in thousands of snakes, all of them writhing nonstop. Coiling around each other and around the legs of a low, backless obsidian divan—where the single occupant of the structure sat.

"The wytch gave us each a hard stare before crooking her finger at me to approach. As we all started toward her, she whispered something. I couldn't make out the words, but in response four enormous pythons slithered from somewhere outside our peripheral vision. The four snakes proceeded to coil around the legs of my teammates, up to about their waists. Smaller snakes quickly writhed up their brethren and wrapped themselves loosely around my teammates eyes and ears. The wytch wagged her finger at my squad before crooking her finger at me once more. She'd made herself clear. I was to approach her alone and our discussion was to be for my ears only.

"As I walked toward her the snakes cleared a narrow path for me. All the way to the foot of the raised platform. From close up I could see the barely there shift she was wearing was made out of cast off snakeskins. Her face was classically beautiful, her hair the smoldering red of a fire looking for any excuse to turn into a full-fledged inferno. It was her eyes though that caught and held your attention though. The vertical slit pupils were emerald viper green, with the largest sclera I'd ever seen. If the whites of your eyes can be unhinged, hers were.

" 'Find me beautiful, do you not?' she asked me, her soft voice husky, with just the trace of an overbite sibilance.

" 'Yes,' I answered her. Not because Pleme wanted a talysman but because it was the truth.

" 'Say you that I have a face that would launch many more than a mere thousand ships?' Her voice was so soft I almost couldn't make out the words.

" 'Yes,' I replied. Again, it was the truth.

"If possible it seemed the whites of her eyes grew even larger. 'Of course I do,' she replied. A huge frown appeared. 'Helen. All anyone can talk about is that fucking slut Helen,' she mumbled to herself. A small red and black snake wound up her neck, its head pausing a moment at her left ear while its forked tongue flicked in and out. 'You are Sredina, Prime Direction of the Pleme'.

"I was stunned. It was a statement, not a question. How could this wytch have any idea who I was, who we were?

" 'I have foreseen your coming. But you don't believe me do you?' she asked.

"It was the strangest thing. I wanted to believe her but I didn't. Then I tried to fake like I believed her, to suck up to her, but I couldn't. So, I forged ahead. 'We are here as part of this year's Tyrning Hunts to meet you and to ask you for a talysman.'

"The wytch threw her head backwards and laughed uproariously. A yellow and orange snake began coiling itself counterclockwise up her throat, resting its mouth against her right ear.

"It wasn't until right then I realized who the wytch was— Cassandra. The Earth Realm myths about her said she was given the gift of prophecy by Apollo and that when she spurned him he cursed her so that no one would ever believe any of the things she prophesied. In a flash it all made sense to me. It wasn't a human Apollo who cursed her, it was THE Apollo. That Tyrning's Apollo avatar. The real deal, royal-level magyk Apollo.

After falling stupid in love with the one-time captivating young Dust Child, he must have magyked her in all kinds of ways to entice her affection. When she didn't return his adulation, he then used his considerable magyk to negatively glamour her so that no matter what Cassandra said—truth or falsehood—no one ever again believed any of her foretellings. I realized I was the first person to learn the ultimate conclusion to her sad story. The part where no one ever believed her for decades on end drove her absolutely bat shit crazy.

"Living proof of that conclusion was sitting in front of me, slowly rocking back and forth, and insanely cackling. 'I see you have figured out who I am,' she laughed. Even her laugh evidenced she was a few clowns short of a circus. 'Yes, I joined the Cult of Nyx. When Luna remade me she told me she had the power to remove that bastard's curse. I told her no, I'd become used to it. Since then I've used my syphoned magyk to exact vengeance against all Folk who make the mistake of coming my way. Not only do they not believe me, they are unable to act unless they do.'

"I realized then that's why I couldn't act like I believed her a few minutes before. The wytch was utilizing her magyk to insure that without belief there could be no action. Which meant every poor slob who ever had the misfortune of landing on her plane ended up dying there because she eventually syphoned all of their magyk. One of the snakes must be her syphon. I knew we weren't going to die on the plane because the Recall would save us. So, as long as she didn't syphon all of our magyk before then, I didn't believe her crazy was a problem for us." Sredina looked sorrowfully to her teammates. "I soon realized I couldn't have been more wrong."

She paused and looked around the rest of the classroom before resuming her story. "Cassandra pointed a long, bony finger at a large vase sitting on the near right corner of the dais. It was only five short steps away from where I was standing. 'Knowing what you require for the Hunts I have hidden a powerful talysman underneath that vase. Although I am not named among the most powerful of my kind, I assure you the talysman I offer will insure you a place in the final Hunt.'

" 'Awesome,' I replied. 'What can we trade you for it?'

"She laughed loudly again, gleefully rubbing her hands up and down her legs. 'There is no cost. It can be yours, Prime. Everything. All of it. Everything you've ever dreamed of. All yours. Secure the talysman from under the vase and you will have a chance to become Archon of all the Folk Realms for three hundred years. All you have to do is tell me you believe me.'

"I tried to open my mouth to say the words. Only three short words. My mouth wouldn't open.

" 'Go on. Say it for me. As you can see, everything you ever wanted is only...five...short...steps...away.' She then let loose another foul burst of laughter. I tried to move my feet toward the vase. They wouldn't respond. I put both hands on my left calf and tried to raise my foot. Again, nothing. Then I remembered. Crazy had made it so that I had to believe what she told me before I could act on it. I focused until my eyes crossed themselves. Then I tried holding my breath until I almost passed out, thinking that might knock some jot of belief loose. No luck."

Sredina held up both arms above her head, so that her shirt sleeves fell above her elbows. There were newly healed angry red welts running up and down both her forearms. "I tried pain next." She looked again to her team, apologetically this time. "As much pain as I could stand. I swear it to you, my Pleme comrades."

Sredina then refocused on the whole class once more. "Nothing. None of the things I did or said could overcome the negative compulsion. When the Recall came, the wytch was so crazy joyful her body was convulsing with paroxysms of laughter." She looked to the HuntsMistress. "Pleme reports we met a wytch but failed to acquire a talysman." With that she dropped her head and walked back to her teammates.

"Doesn't seem quite fair," Tal wrote on his notepad before sliding it in front of Borras.

Borras quickly scribbled his reply. "What's 'fair' is a very subjective concept."

Tal pulled the notepad back to read it. "But Pleme seems to be genuinely 'Seeking the Center.' Like us."

Borras wrote on his own pad this time. "Merkez of the Aile might beg to differ. If he were still alive."

Damn, I completely forgot about the Aile. Sredina had more than likely killed Merkez last term on one of the scavengyr Journeys. Maybe karma is actually a thing, after all.

CHAPTER SEXAGINTA SEPTUM

"Next up will be Ayllu."

Yaksin stood up from his seat in the center of the Ayllu table. Instead of walking to the front he chose to remain surrounded by his teammates. All of the other teams quickly adjusted their chairs so they could see him. "We were unsuccessful in making contact with a wytch on our first three Journeys. On each of those trips we were sent to Realms where we were all at full strength. It was apparent we were affected by the multiple Journeys. Because all of our team as well as our Puca were at full strength, we believed, wrongfully as we were to subsequently learn, that the damage was minimal. Our best intel after our third trip indicated at least two of the other teams had either made contact with a wytch or made contact and secured a talysman. We took a vote about making another trip. I cast the deciding vote to risk it. It was my only chance to be Archon, for our team to be the Ruling Council. None of us wanted to be sent home as losers having come this far but I..., I convinced myself that voting in favor of another try was Seeking the Center.

"I was wrong. On our fourth Journey we landed in a Realm where our magyk was almost nonexistent. All of us, including our Pucas. Which meant they couldn't help much when Xaman suffered blinding headaches or when Nohol began experiencing repeated seizures. It was Lik"in who suffered the most though. His brain bleeds began almost immediately. I have some secondary, low-level healmagyk but there was nothing I could do on that plane. We had the basic med-kit supplies but they were of little use, he needed magykal intervention.

"If we had been sent to an accelerated time plane we would have had Lik"in back in time to be healed, at worst to be put on the disabled list. The three-hours of Earth Plane Time ended up being a month of that Realm's time. Every day we watched him slip in and out of consciousness. The first couple of days we were able to use the narcotics from the medical supplies to ease his pain but after that was all used up, he screamed constantly. It didn't matter whether he was awake or unconscious, the pain made him scream."

Yaxkin paused a moment in his story to look at his three teammates. They were all crying now, Xohol and Chik"in had turned inward to embrace each other, their shoulders heaving. "We watched Lik"in. For weeks we watched. Unable to do anything to help him, to ease his pain. I even thought about..." Yaxkin's words stumbled over each other. "I even thought about strangling him while he was unconscious. It would have been the merciful thing to do but I kept praying that in the next minute the Recall would begin and we could get him back here for healing. And so we waited. And he screamed. Unable to even keep any water down, Lik"in finally lapsed into a coma at the start of the fourth week." Yaxkin paused and squared his shoulders so he could finish the story. "Lik"in passed away less than six hours before the Recall."

With that Yaxkin looked up at the HuntsMistress. "It took Lik"in's unnecessary death for us to realize winning at any cost is not Seeking the Center. We took another vote when we got back. This time the vote was unanimous. The Ayllu are done."

Yaxkin motioned to his teammates to stand up and come around the table to where they were beside him. "I hereby release each of your from your contract." Yaxkin turned to Xaman. "I consent. Do you?"" Xaman, in his last official function as Allyu Second Prime, responded first. "I consent." Next was Nohol, "As Third Prime, I consent." And finally, Chik"in. "Fifth Prime consents."

Yaxkin bent over and picked up his backpack. "We came this morning as a matter of honor and respect to all of the other teams. We wish you all safe Hunting. The Ayllu are officially disbanded." Without waiting for comment or permission from Ms. Empousa, Yaxkin nodded to his now former teammates, his now simply good friends for life. They all picked up their personal belongings and without a single glance backward, followed their former Prime out of the classroom.

Damn, Tal thought as the Allyu filed out. Those guys had class. The universe could do much worse than to have been ruled by the Allyu for the next three hundred years.

CHAPTER SEXAGINTA OCTO

"Shuzoku, report!" the HuntsMistress barked.

Kita, the Shuzoku Second Prime, walked slowly, heavily to the front and turned to face her classmates. She carried with her a large tapestried carpet bag. The bag had hundreds of small green sequins sewn into the pattern. No, they aren't sequins, Tal realized, as they sparkled in the light. They're tiny emeralds.

"On our first Journey we were sent to a Realm which looked like it had been spawned by a blast furnace. No vegetation, no water. If we walked too quickly the air itself seared the hair off of our arms. If we breathed too deeply, it burned the insides of our nostrils and our lungs. Although our magyk was strong on that plane, even with our Pucas' assistance I do not think we would have survived—except for the fact it was an accelerated time Realm. The three-hours of EPT passed in a little less than fifteen minutes of that Realm's time.

"The second Realm was altogether different. In fact, it gave the appearance of being one of the Welsh planes. The Omphalos was a menhir, standing along a four horse cart wide roadway, only a short distance from a magnificent stone castle. There was even a moat with a drawbridge.

"We initially assumed the Prime Omphalos had made a mistake, as every indicator pointed to us being on a well-populated Realm. However, as we stood there and assessed our situation, it became clear the castle and its environs had all of the trappings of a small medieval castle and accompanying village except for the total absence of living things. No people. No livestock. As we scouted for a few additional minutes we noticed there weren't even any bird sounds.

"We followed Chuusin toward the main entrance. As we neared the moat, the drawbridge began its creaky descent, ultimately thudding onto a wooden support that was level with the cart path. We entered into a small courtyard. Again, it was beautifully wrought with stones masterfully set with mortar and joined together in intricate patterns. Filigreed bronze sconces cupped torches burning with what was clearly magyk fire. But just like the castle exterior, the courtyard was devoid of life.

"The main entrance of the castle proper contained two massive wooden doors, each bound with bronze straps several feet wide. They weren't as tall or wide as the Hunts School front doors but they were close. As he approached the doors, Chuusin gave us the signal to spread our formation a little so that we were more to his flanks than behind him. There was a huge bronze skull doorknocker on each of the doors. The detail of each skull was such that it was immediately apparent they used to belong to the living.

"When Chuusin was within ten feet of the doors they swung outward to meet him. Still no sign of life but the wytch obviously knew we were there. Past the doors we could see the great hall of the castle. Dappled with shadow, it also seemed vacant. Initially.

" 'Come,' a female voice commanded. Chuusin looked back at us and shrugged his shoulders. After all, we were wearing our Pucas and meeting a wytch was the purpose of the Journey.

"As soon as our Fifth Prime stepped through the threshold, the doors slowly closed. Immediately following the dull thud of them coming together we heard the metal on metal scratch of a drop bar falling into place.

"The torches extinguished themselves and we were enveloped by darkness completed. Suddenly the room was lit with green light that grew steadily brighter until the hall was fairly well lit. My first thought was that the torches had reignited, but I was wrong. At the far end of the immense room, steps led up to a throne. It was the throne that was providing the room's illumination.

"I'm not sure how to describe the throne. Regal? Clearly. Imposing? Certainly. Ostentatious? Hell, yes. But it certainly got the point across. The construct was about four times as tall as Chuusin. On both peripheries there were dozens of steadily decreasing gothic spires, made of either solid gold or a heavily gilded lesser metal. The spires were inset with emeralds. Dozens, cumulatively there were hundreds, maybe thousands. Most were imbedded in their raw uncut form, their colors ranging all the way from the lightest absinthe, through all the variations of Kelly green, to the darkest of hunter greens. Near the top of each of the spires, however, was a perfectly faceted cut stone. Each of these stones shone brightly and most of the room's ambient lighting was coming from them.

"Three golden steps led up to the throne's seat. It was there the wytch sat, royalty awaiting the commoners who came begging audience. I looked at the rest of the team to confirm my initial thought. The boys' mouths were wide open. So, yes, the wytch was beyond beautiful, she was a raven-haired goddess. My teammates were firmly ensnared, but because of my,...well, anyway, I could tell that she was glamoured. Actually, that word doesn't quite do justice to the magyk being used. Whatever a supersized glamour would be called, that'd be the right descriptor. The wytch was clearly using substantial amounts of her stolen magyk to fuel her vanity.

"In her left hand she held a green bejeweled orb and in her right she lightly grasped a scepter, one end of which laid across her lap. The wytch wore no jewelry except for a finely wrought golden braid that was pinned in small loops around her head. It's centerpiece was the mother of all emeralds and sat perfectly in the middle of her forehead. 'We are Morgaine,' she announced.

"I glanced around to see who else she was talking about before I realized she was using the royal prerogative. I rolled quickly through the limited information which the texts and Professor Elphinstone had given us about her. She was the only known wytch born of both human and Folk parents. She got stuck in a love quadrangle. She was hot for Gwynefar, who although initially receptive, threw her over the first time for Arthrys and later for Launcelot.

"Chuusin recovered sufficiently to remember our reason for being in that dangerous place and got directly to the point. He told the wytch there were six Finalist teams and only the top three scoring teams would advance to the next Hunt. He then advised her that based on our research, she wasn't even in the top three most powerful wytches so we were going to need a powerful talysman from her.

"All of the gems in the throne grew noticeably brighter as the wytch's resting condescending face became an active furious face. I squeezed my eyes closed. If I was going to get blasted I didn't want to have to also watch the destruction rained down on my teammates.

" 'You,' she said, pointing at Chuusin. 'Typical arrogant male. Boring.' Her eyes lasered in on me. 'We'll hear from you,' she said before looking back at Chuusin and the other guys on my team. 'Away,' she commanded. A broad green beam flashed from her forehead jewel. It first encapsulated the rest of the Shuzoku, then it lifted them off their feet and hurled them backwards. The iron bar leapt into the air and the doors flew open a split-second before they would have been smashed against them. Right before the doors slammed shut again, I saw my teammates laying in an unconscious pile.

" 'Come,' the wytch demanded, motioning me to approach and to sit on the lowest stair. Immediately at her feet. 'We grant you leave to speak with us.'

" 'I'm not having any conversation with you until I find out about my teammates,' I replied. Morgaine smiled. Well, kind of. Maybe her lips curved up slightly but her eyes held no smile in them. 'They are unconscious and relatively uninjured. Whether they remain that way until the Recall depends entirely upon you.' She motioned to me again. This time I did as directed and sat immediately below her feet. It was then she told me what my options were to secure the talysman."

Tal heard Kita's voice catch. She'd been rolling through the story without any problem—until now. Now there was some substantial impediment. Everyone in this room has lived through some really brutal events in the last hundred years, he thought. What is it that could bring her up short, now?

"Morgaine got up from her seat and slowly walked down the steps. As she walked by she rested her hand not so causally on my left shoulder."

Tal felt the self-same shudder roll through him that Kita must have felt at that moment.

"When she reached the bottom she turned to face me. 'You are charged with Seeking the Center while trying to win the Tyrning, are you not?' I nodded my response.

" 'Some things never change,' she sneered. Again there was the laugh that didn't have enough life to even reach her eyes. 'Seeking the Center. True Love. Ridiculous platitudes about nonexistent things. We shall give you two options, it is for you to decide which is of the Center.' All I could do was nod.

" 'Your first choice is thus. We will trade you a suitable talysman in exchange for ten percent of the lyfeforce of every one of the Shuzoku. Except for you. If you take this option you will keep all of yours and I will steal only from your teammates."

Lost, I looked at Borras. He wrote a sentence on his note pad. 'They would each lose ten percent of total lyfespan so it would be a much higher piece of what they have left.'

Damn, that's harsh, Tal thought. He watched as Kita got ready to continue. Not only was she obviously reluctant to tell the rest of the story, her movements had changed. She seemed sluggish, almost wooden. Tal was certain in that moment that if Kita had even tried to smile, it would have been stillborn.

"I told the wytch her first option held no interest for me. 'We assumed as much,' she replied. 'Then it shall be the other. We shall spend the time until the Recall together, you and I. You shall recount to us, in intimate deal, every physical encounter you have ever had with yourself or another. You will make such recitation while you pleasure us. You will agree to perform any act which we request, and you will do it willingly'."

Please let that be all, Tal thought, as he watched Kita's shoulders sag as she took several deep breaths and prepared to continue.

" 'Is that the entirety of the bargain,' I asked her. 'Almost.' This time her laugh was frightful because it consumed her entire face. 'You will consent to a geas that shall prevent you from ever forgetting one second of our time together. A geas of such power that you will never successfully know True Love—no matter how long you shall live.' "

I would have broken down by now, Tal thought. Then he realized that Kita's deadness was part of what the wytch did to her. He looked to the Shuzoku table. They had, of course, known nothing of this until right now. All four of Kita's teammates looked like they wanted to somehow go back in time and stop her.

" 'If I do this,' I asked Morgaine. 'If I allow all of this to happen to me then the Shuzoku shall all leave here alive and unharmed with a talysman that you guarantee will secure us a place in the top three teams for this Hunt?'

" 'We give our word,' the wytch replied.

" 'I'm sorry,' I replied, 'but your word is insufficient for me. You will have to magykswear on whatever it is you hold sacred.'

"Her anger was palpable. Energy crackled around her, finally coalescing around her forehead emerald. The energy grew and grew, in a cloud spinning around her face until it seemed as if the entire hall would explode. 'You demand an oath of us?' she screamed. 'Of us? You shall have your oath, impudent girl and then We shall exact our payment.' With that, Morgaine ripped the left sleeve off of the bodice of her dress, baring a glowing brand of a stylized crescent moon, positioned on her left upper arm.

That sounds familiar, Tal thought, as sudden heat erupted from his brand.

" 'We, Morgaine Le Fay, swear on the mark of Nyx, the most sacred and powerful wytch sigil that ever was or ever will be, that the talysman We bargain to you will see you qualified for the last Hunt.' A prong of green flame exploded from her forehead emerald to the brand on her arm, then speared outward until it pierced me through my heart, before it returned to the emerald.

"She clapped her hands over her head and suddenly we were both naked in her bedroom, on a massive poster bed as ornate as her throne." Kita stopped again. Chuusin stood quickly to go to her aid, but she waved him off. "No, Prime. I am of the Shuzoku. We will be in the final three..." She stopped. Her body rigid, her eyes squeezed tightly closed as if she could somehow physically banish what the wytch made her do. When she finally opened them, there was no light in them. They were the eyes of the deceased. "I...will...finish...my...obligation."

Having passed that juncture Kita proceeded, still haltingly. "From that moment she made me do unspeakable things to her. She required that I allow her to violate me in every way imaginable. While she abused my body, she reached into my mind and extracted every pleasant memory I had ever experienced. Of...of love. Of consensual pleasure. She took them and she made all of them repulsive to me."

Her duty to her team completed Kita sagged in place. As Tal watched he wasn't even sure what was keeping her upright. The entire room was respectfully silent.

Ms. Empousa finally broke the silence. "What talysman did you receive in exchange for your sacrifice, Kita of the Shuzoku?"

In response, Kita reached into the large, brocaded carpetbag and pulled out an object.

Wow, was Tal's only thought. Absolutely, wow! Whatever it is, that thing is gorgeous, it must be worth an absolute fortune.

Kita was holding a jewel-encrusted scabbard, the kind meant to sheathe a broadsword. Even in the relatively low light of the classroom there were hundreds of colored sparkles, each sparkle created by an inset faceted gemstone. It looked like the entire gem universe was well represented. Scattered all over one side were diamonds, aquamarines, emeralds, and citrines. On the other were tourmalines, garnets, and pretty much every other precious stone. On both sides, running the full length of the scabbard, was an unbroken line of rubies. I know that design, Tal thought. Where have I seen that before? Some art history book, maybe.

Kita answered the HuntsMistress's question. "The Shuzoku's talysman…is the Scabbard of Many Names."

The entire class exploded with whooping and hollering. Despite the fact the Shuzoku had just clearly nailed one of only three spots for the last Hunt, they were all impressed. The rubies! Tal thought, mentally slapping himself in the forehead. It's the same design as Excalibur, which before Arthrys got it from me was the Sword of Many Names. He quickly flipped the virtual pages in his King Arthur mythology storage section. All of the various Arthurian legends said the scabbard was more powerful even than Excalibur. Whoever held the scabbard wouldn't bleed from a wound. They couldn't be killed. The stories said that Arthrys didn't have it when he fought Mordred…because his half-sister Morgaine stole it so that he would die. Tal knew that wasn't entirely accurate, except, apparently, for the part that Morgaine had stolen it. Well done, Shuzoku, there's one spot that's taken.

"Thank you," Ms. Empousa said, motioning for Kita to place the scabbard back in the bag and return to her seat. "It would appear Morgaine has made good on her promise. Let me remind you the Ruling Council decreed before we started this term that given the extremely rare nature of the Hunt that the talysmen would need to be presented at the Imbolc Feast day after tomorrow or else that team will not receive its points. So, secure your talysmen well after we leave class today."

CHAPTER SEXAGINTA NOVEM

"It is Kabila's turn."

Mashariki, the Kabila Fourth Prime, took his place at the front of the class. He gave every appearance of being uncomfortable with public speaking, fidgeting from one foot to the other, then nervously clearing his throat several times before beginning his tale. "On our first Journey we landed on a Realm covered by a forest of trees that must have been a half-mile high. The Omphalos was the tallest tree in the entire forest, and we all landed on separate limbs several hundred feet apart from each other. When I looked down, I couldn't even see the ground. There were limbs running crisscross every few feet, like giant round highways. Plus, there was some type of white Spanish moss growing everywhere. Except it was sticky.

"Kati yelled at us to assemble. As I started carefully working my way toward everyone else I heard a scream. The first scream, actually. It was Kaskazini. He was on a branch below me and off to my right side. Three giant spiders had him pinned down with their pinchers. The things were, well, they had to be about eight feet long. They all had shiny jet black shells. A fourth one was taking what I had thought was Spanish moss and was using it to imprison his feet and hands, securing him to the branch.

"Then Magharibi screamed. He was above to the left of me. The same thing was happening to him. I realized if it was happening to two of us that we were all in danger. I turned and sure enough there were three coming from under my branch for me. I used my..." Mashariki looked quickly to his Prime as he caught himself before disclosing top-secret team information. "I broke free and high-tailed it toward Kati, yelling for her to look back over her shoulder.

"The largest of the bunch, she must have been the queen—if spiders have queens—was dropping on a silk cable as thick as my arm. This one was a dirty white, with enormous fangs. There was greenish ick dripping from them. She was apparently coming to finish the job her underlings had begun. We would have all died on that Realm if it hadn't been for Kusini. He used his..." He again looked at his Prime. She must have felt the information different this time because she nodded for him to proceed. "Kusini used his firemagyk like some hero out of Folk legend. He toasted the queen first, the others immediately became disorganized and he picked them off one by one. I could tell he was using his entire magyk reservoir to burn the creatures, but he didn't stop. He didn't give any thought to his own welfare, only to Kabila. He knew...he knew he'd passed the point where his own body could renew its magyk. And he still kept going.

"The spiders didn't leave for long, apparently they had reinforcements close by. Which included a new and bigger queen. All five of us were huddled on Kati's original branch of the Omphalos tree, waiting as the new Queen marshaled her troops for the next attack.

"We were at approximately half-strength on that plane. It was only because of Kusini's Puca-enhanced firemagyk that any of us lasted until Recall. Finally, he could do no more. Magharibi had to hold Kusini to make sure he didn't roll off our perch. His effort cost him too much of his lyfeforce and as we do not have anyone with healmagyk..." Mashariki stopped abruptly, looked toward Kati, his Prime, and dropped his eyes in the universally recognized submissive pose.

Tal turned halfway around to look at the Kabila table. Kati was wearing a full-scale frown. Oh shit, he accidentally disclosed confidential team information. Knowledge is power. Everyone now knows that even in a situation where the teams can use magyk that Kabila doesn't have the ability to heal its team members. Tal looked back and forth between the two until he saw Mashariki lift his eyes. Kati gave him the smallest head nod to continue, her frown easing a little. Well, well, well, Tal thought. Kati, you just committed the same offense of disclosure. You and Mashariki are a couple. Tal turned back to his notepad and wrote himself a note as Mashariki continued his narrative.

"Luckily, the Recall happened right then and we were able to get Kusini to the infirmary. He remained dangerously close to death for days, it took several weeks for the physicks to fully restore him. When Kati deemed it safe for Kusini to Journey again, we took our second Journey. This time we were deposited on a wind-swept mesa on a Realm where the Kabila and our Pucas were at full-strength.

"We landed in a large patterned circle, four or five hundred meters in diameter. Kati was in the middle and the rest of us were spaced ninety degrees apart. From her center vantage, Kati was the first to notice we were each standing in a circle, and that it was circumscribed by a thin line of powdered turquoise, or turquoise-colored sand. Lines radiated outward from Kati's circle to the rest of us. But where the inside of Kati's circle was smooth, light-caramel colored high desert sand, the floor of our four circles was intricately etched turquoise stone. The designs were stylized animal motifs, but these figures were outlined in gold.

" 'They're animal totems,' Kaskazini said. Magharibi noticed the structure, viewed as a whole, looked like a time wheel. It was Kusini though who finally added all the pieces together. 'It's a very culture specific form of time wheel. I think it's a Medicine Wheel, in some Realms it's called a Sacred Hoop.'

" 'Very good,' a new voice added. We all about jumped out of our skins. Particularly since we couldn't see the source of the disembodied voice. Kati had trained us well, so despite our surprise, we each quickly flowed into defensive positions. Well, as good as we could with the entire team being so far apart. We all glanced around the circle, and started using some hand communication gestures we'd practiced. After everyone confirmed with a head nod, we started to walk toward Kati.

" 'STOP!' the formless voice commanded. 'Whoever steps outside their circle dies.' Then the air 'popped.' Like a really hard snap of someone's fingers. If the really hard snapper was made of steel. It was that hard of a snapping 'pop.'

"Kati was no longer alone in her circle. With her now was a lanky, sun-dried youth. Narrow-featured, his grin had a hint of the lupine, such suggestion being furthered by his apparel. He wore only a mottled brown fur loincloth and a pelt wrapped across his shoulders from the same animal. That was it, except for a tiny bag hung from a plain leather thong around his neck. The bag, however, was anything but plain. It was completely covered with embroidered animal motifs, in what from a distance looked like tiny pieces of turquoise and gold. The symbols were smaller versions of the ones underneath our feet.

" 'I am Mica,' the stranger said. 'Herald for Kanka.'

"Kati answered the man. 'You are the wytch's familiar.'

" 'I am that, as well,' the man replied, dipping his head slightly in confirmation. 'Kanka has sent me to thank you for your lyfeforce and to welcome you to your death.' "

Damn, Tal thought. No wonder the Wytch Hunts were banished. Multiple Journeys that some students wouldn't survive, absent the Pucas. Add to that, all of the wytches' syphons apparently operate a little differently but they all have the same bottom line—sucking the lyfeforce out of any Folk within range.

Mashariki continued with his story. "Kati didn't flinch. She informed Mica we were the Kabila and we wished to meet Kanka and ask for a talysman. Mica's response was a laugh wrapped within a snarl.

"It was at that moment I realized somewhere in our decades of studies at Hunts School we had studied their names.

Which meant Kanka had used her stolen magyk to recreate a culture on this plane from one of the known, inhabited Realms. My subconscious seized that still amorphous bit of information and then retreated to work on extrapolating specificity.

"Kati didn't give up. She advised Mica we were individuals of substance, that we were the Kabila and had made the first Finalist cut of the Hunts, and we were now one of only six teams that remained eligible to rule the known universe for the next three hundred years.

"Mica stood motionless, thinking or scheming, I know not which. After several minutes he said, very matter of factly, 'If you move from your circles you will die.' There was another small 'pop,' and except for a few stray floating tufts of fur, Mica disappeared. Kusini started to speak but Kati quickly gave him the hand-signal for silence while putting her hand to her ear and turning three hundred sixty degrees. We all understood. We were to assume Mica and Kanka were eavesdropping.

"A few minutes later, the air popped yet again, and Mica reappeared. 'My Mistress has been wanting me to provide her with some new entertainment for many years. She is willing to negotiate with you.'

" 'Anything,' Kati quickly replied.

"Mica made what passed for his laughing sound once more. Having heard it again, I realized it was more of a yip-laugh than a snarl-laugh. 'Do not be so quick, Kabila Prime. There are times when 'anything' can mean 'everything.' Your first Hunt—what was it?'

" 'It was a Scavengyr Hunt,' Kati replied." With that Mica was gone again. This time, however, he was back in about ten heartbeats. I know because I counted each time mine thumped in his absence.

" 'Great Kanka has taken pity upon you and has offered you a bargain. You have your pick of two options. You may voluntarily forego your opportunity to meet my Mistress. If that is your choice you will be allowed to remain in this plane, unscathed, until your Recall. As soon as you return, you will have the Hunts School Principal use the Prime Omphalos to send your scavengyr pieces to this Realm.' "

Two things interesting about that statement, Tal thought. First, if they lose their scavengyr pieces, the odds are they won't win the Tyrning even if they make the cut this term. Second, Mica apparently didn't know the name of the Principal, which means that whoever is Principal of Hunts School has the magyk to utilize the Prime Omphalos for directed travel.

" 'And the other option?' Kati asked.

"The feral smile appeared once again. 'Ah, the other option is that you commit to the bargain, and in return my Mistress will meet you and provide you with a suitable talysman.'

" 'What's the bargain?' Kati demanded tensely.

" 'Oh no, Kabila Prime. The bargain will be whatever I say it is, whenever I say it is. What does it matter? You have already said "anything".' "

There's something not straight up about that answer, Tal thought, but Kabila hadn't had any leverage. Even if they could make another trip safely, they would have then been deprived of their scavengyr pieces.

Mashariki continued. "Even though Kati had the power to make the decision on her own, she looked slowly around the circle, waiting for us each to mouth the words, 'I consent.' Which we did. Kati turned to Mica, 'Kabila consents.'

" 'Excellent.' Mica replied, skipping back and forth with a little added huff-huff noise. 'What scavengyr pieces did you secure in the first Hunt?' "

Mashariki paused his narrative. It's something else he needs authority to disclose, Tal realized. He didn't even turn around to look at Kati. There is no way that Kabila wants their scavengyr artifacts disclosed. None of us have any idea what type of bizarro Hunt the blood-crazed HuntsMistress has planned for the final three teams.

When Mashariki began again he glossed over those details. "Kati itemized our scavengyr pieces for Mica. 'One moment, please,' he responded as he cocked his head to the left.

'Yes, yes, yes,' he exclaimed, hopping around in his excitement. 'Your four teammates stand upon animal totems. Each animal is the representative of a cardinal direction. Three of the four totems are not in their correct directional position. One of your teammates has to guess whether their totem is in the correct position. If the guess is correct, my Mistress will deliver the talysman to you. If the guess is incorrect, the totem beast will materialize and rend that person limb from limb.'

"Kati interrupted Mica, flatly telling him no." Mashariki stopped and looked around the room. It's for dramatic effect, Tal thought. He can tell we're all totally caught up in his story. He was giving us the business when he started, acting like he was uncomfortable speaking. He used our sympathy to lure us further into his story.

Satisfied he had their attention, Mashariki continued. "It was at this point that Mica's face became not quite so human. His nose elongated, now more a narrow snout than a nose. Any pretense of frivolity in his laugh was gone, subsumed by an ominous snarl. 'The bargain has been made. It will be fulfilled or none of you will leave this Realm alive.'

"Realizing there was nothing she could do, Kati bowed her head for a moment before looking him straight in the eyes. 'One blood sacrifice erases all debts and all the rest of Kabila will depart this Realm safely with a substantial talysman?' Kati asked the syphon.

"Mica smiled, then nodded before tilting his head to the side. He was listening again. After several moments he straightened and addressed Kati. 'Whoever occupies the Center is safe, Prime Direction. What would you do if great Kanka were to allow you to exchange places with one of your teammates?' The briefest of flutters of Kati's eyelids betrayed her as she looked at me before looking down.

" 'Aaahh, just as my Mistress thought,' Mica exclaimed. "This game just keeps getting better and better. You!' he howled pointing at me. "You'll be responsible for the lives of your teammates. Pick one that you believe is standing over the correct symbol. Guess wrong and Kabila will be down to four.'

"Howled..., I thought. Mica literally howled. MICA IS THE COYOTE! my subconscious screamed. A deity in many Amerind Realm mythologies. Often in tandem with Iktomi the Spider. Coyote is almost always mischievous, a trickster. But which Amerind plane is this facsimile patterned on? You have no other data to help you, I told myself. That's not true. You have the witch's name—Kanka. And you have the four animal symbols that we are standing on—Mountain Lion, Bobcat, Bear, and Wolf.

"I smiled with relief as my mind supplied the answer. The Lakota. Kanka has used her stolen magyk to recreate one of the Lakota planes, and Mica Coyote is a trickster in the Lakota stories. Try as I might I couldn't remember the Lakota animal spirits assigned to each direction.

"Then it came to me what I had to do. The correct order was irrelevant. These were my teammates, Folk who I genuinely believe should rule the known universe for the next three hundred years. That result needed to happen even if I wasn't there to help rule. The deal was for one blood sacrifice and Mica had already told us what would happen if we stepped out of our circles, so..."

"Oh shit," Tal mumbled under his breath.

"I stepped out of my circle. Cylinders of swirling grey smoke and red vapor rose from each of the totems, intertwining as they grew. With my teammates frozen in fear, the cylinders surrounding them reached a height of ten feet before they became to melt inward, first forming large blobs, then gaining more definition. The one now immediately to my left did the same. Then animal noises started coming from the totem cylinders. Vapor became solid, amorphous became defined, and there were now four great beasts from hell, roaring and howling, reaching out with claws to rend and tear all four of us.

"As shocked as Kati was that I had chosen to step out of my circle, she rallied, trying to save the rest of Kabila—and our chance to win the Tyrning. 'But you said…' Mica was himself in full beast mode, growling with blood lust.

" 'CEASE!' a deep female voice commanded, the word somehow reverberating clockwise to each direction. 'Cease,' to the North, and the mountain lion raking Kaskazini's flesh dissipated. 'Cease,' to the Wolf of the East and it growled one last time before disappearing. 'Cease,' to the Bobcat, and the southern totem became two-dimensional once more. The final 'Cease,' echoed across the bear, which was squeezing the last bit of air from my lungs, and it was gone into thin air.

"Mica's fury scream was bone-chilling. It was equal parts the sound of a hungry animal robbed of its prey by an alpha predator and the squall of a petulant toddler abruptly deprived of its favorite pacifier.

"Kanka materialized between Kati and Mica. The wytch's hair was made of living raven's feathers. They were blue-black with an oily sheen. Instead of fingers she had eagle's claws. Her teeth were those of a snarling great cat. Kanka was dressed in an earthy ochre stained long-sleeved full-length tanned leather dress. Two to three inches of fringe ran down the sleeves and across the hem, the fringe colors mirroring the turquoise and gold of the Medicine Wheel.

"The wytch gave her syphon a hard stare before extending the claws of her right hand. Mica shook his head no. She motioned again and this time he whined. She motioned again, more abruptly this time. Mica stomped his left foot before reluctantly untying the bag from around his neck and handing it to her. 'Withdraw,' she commanded quietly. I could have sworn that the 'popping' sound this time was made of curse words.

"The wytch then turned her attention to me. She was angry, terribly angry. 'If I had the power I would make you watch helplessly as I sucked the lyfe out of each of your teammates.' Pointing to Kati, she added, 'Her last.'

"I was dumbfounded. The wytch clearly had the power to kill all of us. My bewilderment must have been writ large across my face because the wytch paused a moment. 'You didn't even know about that provision of the Lex, did you?' she asked. 'I thought you out-smarted Coyote—and you didn't even know.' "

Know what, Tal wondered.

"But the contract Mica made with Kati was for one blood sacrifice," I replied.

" "Foolish man. Mica Coyote is a trickster. Your team should have paid closer attention to his words. There was no outcome where any of the Kabila were leaving this plane alive,' she replied."

I knew it, Tal thought. Mica said the bargain was whatever he said it was, whenever he said it was. He left open his ability to amend the contract. What a dick. A clever dick, but a dick nonetheless. If that was a valid contract though, then why did Kanka stop him mid-murder?

" 'The best of intentions are of small moment absent action. However, even the wytches of the Cult of Nyx must obey the Lex Immortalis. Your free and willing choice of self-sacrifice, as stupid as it was, prevents me from taking any of your lives until Luna's avatar passes once more over this Realm. Your Recall will happen before such time.

"With a wave of her left hand, opaque columns rose from all four of the circles encompassing my teammates. 'Here,' she said as she walked over and pressed something into my palm. 'You might want to be careful with the contents. The totem columns will remain until the Recall. I can't take any of your lives but if you choose to, you can stupidly throw them away. If any of the others step outside their circles, they die.' Kanka clapped her hands once—and disappeared.

"I secured the totem and made sure it was well hidden under my shirt. Then I quickly walked to each of the others and yelled for them to remain where they were. After that we all hunkered down and waited until the Recall.

"The talysman the wytch gave me was this," with that Mashariki reached under his shirt and pulled out the small embroidered bag, its top tightly cinched by a small strip of rawhide. He began pointing out the various designs. "This is *igmutanka,* the mountain lion, symbol of the North. Here is *igmuhota,* the bobcat, representing South. M*ato,* the bear, for the West. And this is *sunkmanitu,* the wolf—East."

Tal realized that meant the animal totems were all situated on the correct direction on Kanka's Spirit Hoop. That Mica Coyote was definitely the trickster version.

Mashariki lowered the bag to waist level. "These are often mistakenly referred to as 'medicine bags.' That's only technically correct when the bag actually contains medicine. This bag contains something that is *waken.* Depending upon the context that could mean a sacred object, an object that has been given a mystical power. Or, as in this particular case, something magykal appropriated by Kanka from another Amerind plane."

Mashariki turned to face Ms. Empousa. "HuntsMistress, Kabila's talysman from Kanka is corpse dust."

CHAPTER SEPTUAGINTA

The stillness that gripped the room described for Tal the significance of Kabila's talysman. Borras was furiously scribbling on his notepad. When he finished, he slid it over to Tal. It read, "The wytch herself is only average to above average strength. Kabila hit a home run though with their talysman. Corpse dust is used by skinwalkers to effect their transformations. It's magyk, of course, so it won't work at Hunts School or on Earth Realm, but it's unbelievably rare and valuable. On other Realms it is extremely powerful."

Skinwalkers, Tal mused, as he reread Borras's information. Holy shit. Anybody could be anybody or anything anytime.

"Släkt, it is your turn."

Tal watched as Nord picked up his backpack and swaggered to the front of the room. He did, Tal decided, he actually swaggered. As Nord passed Tal, he looked down, giving him one of his patented oily smiles. It's so greasy it's a miracle his muscles don't slide right off of his face, Tal thought.

"We'll skip all the blah-blah-blah and cut straight to the part that puts us in first place at the end of this Hunt. Släkt had a productive meeting with Hecate..." Nord paused to let the news do the wave around the entire room. "That's right. We met a psychopomp who also happens to be the second most powerful wytch in the known universe. For our talysman, she presented me with this small trinket of her affection and regard."

Nord reached into his backpack and pulled out a necklace of some kind. No, Tal quickly corrected himself. It's too big to be a necklace. It's a hollowed out round ball, covered with cuneiform-type characters, hanging from four golden chains. A thurible, maybe, like for incense? No, that's not right. It's hollow like a thurible but instead of an open space in the middle, there's a sparrow's egg sized sapphire. A damn impressive gem, easily worth a gadzooks-level exclamation, maybe even a criminy.

The first response came from Sever of Pleme. "Unbelievable. They did it. They actually did it. Släkt obtained the Hecatic Stropholos."

"What?" Tal looked to the Pleme table. Sever had been so shocked he'd forgotten the first rule of Empousa survival—remain as invisible as possible. Which had just caused Tal to screw up as well. Head down, idiot.

Sredina responded. "A strophalos is a magykal wheel used for rituals. Among scholars who study such things it is generally conceded, given Hecate's place in the wytch hierarchy, that her strophalos is the most powerful one ever."

"Consolation prize to the know it all loser from Pleme," Nord replied.

"How, though?" Sever asked. "What price could any of us possibly afford that would warrant a talysman having such significant magyk?"

"Good question," Nord replied, his smarm factor now dialed to the maximum. "Actually, we got off cheap. Seems Hecate is bored after all of these millennia and wants a Dust Child to torture. So, I traded the Munedan's life for the talysman."

CHAPTER SEPTUAGINTA UNUS

Tal's vision lasered to a pinpoint that encompassed only Nord. This must have been what it was like to look into a kinetoscope, he thought idly. There was a scream of dismay from somewhere in the back of the classroom. That's the Släkt table. Well, at least Väst didn't know about the deal, Tal thought. That's something. He heard only general background clucking from the other five team tables. It wasn't their fight.

Stay still, Tal told himself. Don't tense up, don't react. It's what the psychopath wants—he gets nothing from me. There is no way he can bargain my life away. Tal felt Borras's oversized muscles gather into coiled ropes, ready to explode into action. He'd kill Nord, Tal thought. He has the physical ability to literally tear him apart, magyk or no magyk. Or beat him so badly he will be disabled. Which is exactly why the sorry ass lunatic is standing right in front of me, taunting our team. He doesn't know if we have a talysman or not, but he's trying to get us to do something that will cost us points. Tal quickly reached over and tap-tapped two fingers on Borras's exposed wrist. It wasn't actual semaphore but it got his message across.

Surprisingly, it was Notos who calmly stepped into the fray. "HuntsMistress, as Omada's Second Prime and Parliamentarian I request a point of clarification. I am not aware of any Hunts Rule that gives the Prime Direction of one team any binding authority over a member of any other squad. He certainly doesn't have the authority to reduce our team roster during the Hunts."

In response, the HuntsMistress looked at Nord and merely raised her left eyebrow.

"I guess that's what comes of the Omada having a two-bit Second Prime Direction," Nord sneered in response at Notos. "There is no Hunts Rule that prohibits my bargain because it will not be completed and payment will not be exacted until after Släkt wins the Tyrning and I am the Archon. I will then use my authority as Archon to direct the Prime Omphalos to deliver the mortal to Hecate's Realm."

Tal's heart began pounding. *No way, there's simply no way. He can't sell me into slavery. Can he? This is the second time that sonofabitch has tried to make me a slave. The Archon does have almost unlimited magyk, I've seen that firsthand.*

Wait a minute. There is absolutely no way Hecate is giving up one of her most valuable possessions for a contingency. I'm not really believing wytches bet on the come. They seem much more the kind who always play with a house advantage. He scribbled furiously on his notepad and slid it across the table—past Borras—to Notos.

Notos quickly scanned the note and nodded. "HeadMistress, the Omada Parliamentarian requests further clarification."

Ms. Empousa tilted her head in Notos's direction.

"Would the Släkt Prime Direction kindly provide the entirety of his bargain with the wytch?" Notos asked.

Tal noticed a small tic suddenly begin behind Nord's right eye.

"More specifically," Notos continued, "would you please advise what payment is due Hecate if the Släkt do not win the Tyrning."

The tic now began to cantor, before accelerating to a full gallop. Tal watched, in horror, as Nord's nasty, squishy smile reappeared, driving the eye tic into remission. That means it's something bad, something really bad, he thought.

"Well, there is that," Nord replied. "I feel quite certain that Släkt is going to win. However, in the small chance we don't prevail, I wasn't able to leverage quite as good a bargain. Because then I wouldn't have the authority of the Archon…" He turned toward his own team table.

Maybe it was because Tal was human and the rest were all Folk, but for whatever reason he knew with absolute certainty what Nord was about to say. Oh no, Väst…

"I would only have my authority as Släkt Prime Direction to secure suitable payment. So, yes, I traded all of you," he said motioning to his teammates. "Which shouldn't be a problem if we all work together and you try as hard as you possibly can to help me win this thing. It's actually kind of brilliant, don't you think? This way I get the absolute best effort from my entire team to help me become Archon."

The roars of indignation from the Släkt table were ringing so loudly in Tal's ears that he could barely hear Ms. Empousa screaming at the top of her lungs that there would be a thirty-minute recess.

CHAPTER SEVENTY-TWO

Where am I? Emet wondered. He shook his head, trying to bounce the grogginess. What's the deal? I don't need sleep and yet that's the second time in a couple of days I've experienced total system shutdown.

Emet sat up and looked around. The Ladies' Room, that's right. I've been sleeping on a bed. In a girl's bathroom. I'm not sure my status could possibly get weirder. Then he looked at the table. Now there was a fresh pot of coffee, a small creamer full of half and half, and a plate with what looked like about four hard scrambled eggs. Oh, and a platter heaped with chocolate chip, blueberry and cranberry-apple scones. Emet knew that's what they were because he could smell them. They smelled warm, as if they'd been very recently emancipated from the baker's oven.

It was at that moment Emet realized he was ravenous. I don't feel hunger, he reminded himself. His stomach was sending a contrary message as he found himself unable to focus on anything but caloric intake. Weirder and weirder. First I'm sleepy and now I'm hungry. Something else to add to the list to discuss with Tal—I've apparently now lived with humans long enough that I'm experiencing sympathetic emotions. Kind of like that whole "ghost pain" phenomena when some people lose a limb.

Well, except you never had emotions to begin with, he reminded himself. Food, Emet. Food. Right.

As he got up out of the bed he noticed there was a new note taped to the door. He nabbed a cranberry-apple scone on his way to get the note. What time of day is it? He wondered as he walked the four steps and took the note off the door. For that matter, what day is it?

> Good morning, Emet:
>
> I knew you would take a cranberry-orange scone first but you simply must try the blueberry as well. Actually, they're all simply divine.
>
> You've already answered your first question, you're in the Ladies' Bathroom. The answer to your second question is a little more complex. Your transition is consuming substantial energy and resources.
>
> Your next two queries were chronological in nature. It is now almost noon on Saturday. You'll need to pack your items and be clear of the entire Gas Station Crossing well before 5:00 p.m.
>
> Yes, Emet, I said Saturday. You've been asleep the better part of five days. Unusual but apparently it was necessary.
>
> Eat and drink a sufficiency. Your body is depleted from your hibernation and you have a busy day— and evening—ahead.
>
> Shower and shave, toiletries are in the shower.
>
> Remember, two things. First, you are safe while you are in this room. Second, it is important while you run your errands today that you not be recognized. You have no way to communicate with Taliesin except face to face tonight at the dance.
>
> Best of luck to you Golem in the Journey you are about to take. Remember, no matter how dire

your situation, always choose love. It is the path to the Center and therefore to the UnFading Spirit.

There's no need trying to talk to the Air Hose. He's been in a pissy mood the last couple of weeks. Don't forget to wash your hands and turn the light off when you leave.

Thank you,

The Ladies' Room

What the hell? So much information to assimilate I don't know here to start. Well, that's not accurate, Emet told himself as his stomach rumbled.

Emet had just began to turn back toward his breakfast when the door to the bathroom flew inward. Emet leaped backward, landing close to the shower.

"What do you see?"

I know that voice, Emet thought. The sudden backlighting blinded him momentarily. Whoever it belongs to is extremely intoxicated.

"Nothin', it's dark." Deeper voice, words slurred. I also know that voice.

"Flip the light switch you idiot." Third voice, maybe even drunker than the other two.

Emet's eyes began adjusting to the glare at the same moment he realized the drunk individuals were Barton Sellars and his pair of idiots.

"It don't work."

"Of course, it doesn't work, you moron." That was Barton, taking control. The note said it was noon. How can they possibly be so drunk at noon on Saturday? "Hello? It's an abandoned gas station. It's why I brought the flashlight. Get out of the way."

Emet watched, afraid to move as Barton shoved past the other two, a beam of light issuing from the flashlight in his hands. If I take Barton out maybe the other two will run.

"Come out, come out, Brainiac. We have some business to discuss with you." The beam aimed right at Emet, passed over him and explored every corner of the bathroom. The shower, the bed, the chocolate scones. "Dammit to hell! No Brainiac. I just knew that pussy would come hide out here. But nobody's been in here in a long time, looks like not since we smashed everything up our freshman year. And the place smells worse than one of Fail's shits. Gauggh, let's get out of here."

"What are we going to do now, Barton." That's Gunnar, Emet thought.

"First thing is we're going to the liquor store and get another half-gallon of vodka and some Red Bulls. My sister's going to be at the dance tonight and I know that piece of shit won't be able to resist coming to see her. There are plenty of places to hide a body out back of the gym."

Emet watched as Fail jerked the door closed. He walked over to the door and listened until he heard their tires on the gravel as they left. Breakfast first, he told himself. Then errands to get ready. I have to get to the dance before Tal tonight, they're so drunk they might actually kill him if they get the chance.

CHAPTER SEPTUAGINTA TRES

Thirty minutes didn't give them sufficient time to make it to their secure team room and back, so Borras corralled the Omada down a small side hallway. He pretty much filled the hallway, which prevented anyone from sneaking up on them to listen in. Borras had asked Tal to wait a few feet farther along the hallway while he discussed a couple of things with the other three.

On his own for the moment, Tal's thoughts wandered. Probably sensory overload, he decided. In a way I guess you could say the present situation is all my fault. There must be some type of karmic intersection where best intentions collide with equal and opposite reaction. Trying to "Seek the Center," I used my first wish to save Väst's life in the Combat Challenge. I wrongly assumed using one of my three wishes was the sum total of the price to be paid for my action. Maybe it's more complicated than that, maybe there are indirect consequences which ripple out to create collateral damage. As a result of my action, Mitt died and Nord became Acting Prime. If I hadn't saved Väst's life, Nord wouldn't have the power to bargain with Hecate and the Släkt would be out of the Hunts. Väst would be dead though, his heart ached in response.

His brain next moved to Emet and to the events on Earth plane proper. Where is Emet? What's he eating? Emet's a resourceful young man, his brain replied. He'll be fine. With any luck you can get all the details when you see him tonight. That solved, his brain moved on to his Mom and Pell…

"Quint!" Although the volume of Borras's voice was dialed way down so as not to carry, the urgent tenor commanded Tal's attention. "Okay, I told the others I needed to use the remaining time to settle you down."

"I'm actually pretty…"

"Quiet," Borras whispered forcibly as a hand the size of a boule of sourdough bread clamped down on Tal's shoulder. "You have our talysman, whatever it is. You're the only one who knows the details on how we got it. That means only you can present for Omada."

"I,…"

"Quint, just listen to me. The stakes have never been higher. There are already three strong contenders to make the final cut."

"I know, Borras, but…

"Time's ticking. Empousa has forbidden us from wearing our Pucas for the rest of this term…"

"Right, but tomorrow's the last…"

"That's the point," Borras urged as he gently shook Tal. "Don't you see? The top three or four teams are going to be really close on points. With the Ruling Council's decree about talysmen presentation at the Imbolc Feast…"

"Oh shit," Tal said, finally catching up with Borras. "A talysman gets stolen or destroyed before then, that team is going home."

"Exactly," Borras confirmed as he looked around to make sure the rest of Omada still had the hallway secured. "There's something else. Because of the Combat Challenge all of the other squads know about two of our three scavengyr pieces."

"You're thinking if we get challenged a second time they'll pick no Pucas again, neutralize our artifacts, and our champion will be easy pickings for their weapon," Tal said slowly.

"Right. You have two goals for your presentation. The story of meeting the wytch and gaining our talysman is the first. The second is that whatever it is that went down with you and the wytch, you need to go up there and sell yourself as a badass."

"Well, I guess, I could…"

"No, Quint, there's no maybe to it. You can't lie, that wouldn't be Seeking the Center. Besides, I feel like Empousa has asked the Archon to magyk the classroom to disclose material lies about the wytch encounters. So, no lying but you're going to have to embellish the hell out of your saga. By the time you get through this morning, all of the other teams need to be scared to death of you. Really scared. Folk don't have much interaction with mortals, so if you sell it, you can convince them that you're a blood crazed monster."

Tal took a moment to register Borras's comments. "When you were talking to the rest of the team, you told them that's the game plan, right?"

"No, I'm afraid I was employing a little misdirection," Borras said, slowly shaking his great shaggy head. "For the ruse to work the rest of the Finalists need to see their unvarnished initial reactions to your story."

"You want me to pull the same trick I used on Notos in the Combat Challenge?" Tal asked.

"Yes."

"The rest of Omada will despise me."

"Yes, they will," Borras confirmed. "At least until we can meet in our room and I can explain our strategy to them. Can you do it?"

"If that's what you want me to do," Tal replied.

"It's not a matter of want, it's what you need to do. I'll give you some space to get your thoughts together." He patted Tal on the shoulder and walked to the far end of the hallway to join the other three.

CHAPTER SEPTUAGINTA QUATTUOR

Ms. Empousa had called the class back to order. There was a distinct chill flowing from the Släkt table at the rear right corner of the classroom. "So far we have three teams with talysmen, one team that will receive points for meeting a wytch. And one group of losers—who are also quitters," she snarked, looking toward the empty Ayllu seats.

"Remember, points for the talysmen will not be awarded until you formally present them to the Ruling Council at the Imbolc Feast. Then there's always the possibility of another Combat Challenge…"

She'd like that, too, Tal thought. Last term was the first one in many Tyrnings and the bloodthirsty bitch is trying to encourage the possibility of another student death in the arena.

"Pleme, you technically remain a Finalist team and may attend the field trip tonight. Although, how you'll look at your lame loser asses in the mirror, I'll never know."

Man, you can always count on HuntsMistress Em to make you feel good about yourself, Tal thought. Well, we should be in with our talysman. If Baba Yaga was good to her word, we should win. But that will make four teams with a talysman, including the Släkt. No one else knows it but my three wishes are gone. Everyone else knows what scavengyr pieces we have. I have to find a way to spin events without lying. To keep us from being in another fight to the death.

"Last team—Omada," Ms. Empousa said.

Tal looked to Borras, who smiled grimly and nodded for him to start the show. Tal's brain raced as he slowly stood and slow-walked to the front of the class. Borras doesn't know it but we have an additional problem the other teams don't have. They can secure their talysmen between now and the Feast. I'm wearing ours. Anybody wanting to eliminate Omada only has to take me out. It's almost as if the HuntsMistress knew it and is trying to get me killed. For about the umpteenth time.

"No time like the present, human!" the HuntsMistress snapped.

"Right, sure," Tal stumbled, having a little difficulty switching gears from thinking mode to verbal. Fine line between embellishment and lying, but as an out of order gas pump once told me, "worlds depend on me."

Tal took a deep abdominal breath, settled himself, and began. "There was no wytch contact on our first two Journeys. On the third trip our team encountered strong magyk that wiped the memories of all four of my teammates. If it hadn't been for me, they would have been clueless about the fact we had visited a Realm with an extremely powerful wytch."

Tal checked out his table. His teammates were all nodding along at this point. Back at the Släkt table, Nord had his arms folded, acting like he could give a shit. Tal knew he was hanging on his every word, just as much as Väst, who was staring straight at him.

"At that point I effectively took over as Omada Acting Prime. Solely because of my unique abilities, I was able to achieve a directed Journey back to that Realm." Tal paused because that statement got some murmurs from the class. That's right, a human accomplished a directed Journey. He gave it another couple of beats to soak in before continuing.

"I single-handedly came up with the strategy to help my teammates make it past the most powerful Jynx in recorded history." There was louder murmuring this time. They're waiting for something to happen to me for lying. When it didn't and Tal heard the scratching of pencils on paper, he knew he'd scored substantial "you die if you mess with Omada" points.

"The wytch on that plane was so powerful she had three familiars, not one. They were fully armored and mounted warriors, kitted out with a shitton of weaponry. The wytch's magyk was off the charts—she had enough juice to create a large circle of automatic death. If any of my teammates entered it, they would have perished." The Omada wore pretty much the same facial responses. The rest of the class was now extremely interested in where this was leading.

"My Folk teammates were all useless at that point so I told them to stay where it was safe, that I would go take care of the wytch and all three of her familiars." He stole another quick peek at the Omada table. Borras's face betrayed nothing. Both Ana and Dysi's mouths were large "O"s. Ever-grim Notos was more like angry-grim Notos at this point in time.

"Not only did I step willingly into the death circle, I decided I didn't need any help from some lame Puca, and so I took him off and went after the wytch stark naked." When they saw Tal wasn't going to be struck down for lying, the class's interest quotient increased dramatically.

"The wytch lived in a beat up old cabin that was surrounded by wind chimes made of the skulls and spines of hundreds of Folk and Creatures. I made contact with her, explained who I was, and told her I wasn't leaving without a talysman. A really good talysman. She told me the only way my team and I were leaving her Realm alive—and with a talysman— was if I killed her for it." He paused. "So I did," Tal stated with a small vocal flourish containing an under tone of smugness and an overtone of braggadocio.

"What?" Ana's involuntary comment was more breath than spoken word. Can't stop, Tal told himself. Use Anatolia's outrage to sell it hard. Just don't cross the line into total fabrication. He looked straight at Ana. "That's right, teamie.

When you found me at the end and I asked you to try to save her…" Careful, Tal, you can't lie. You did want her to save her. Shoulder shrug it off he told himself. So he did. Anatolia gasped again. "Me, the no-magyk weakass Dust Child. I killed the wytch. And because I'm the biggest, baddest motherfucker in the entire shithole of Hunts School, before I did it, I tortured her by making her tell me about her entire sorry ass worthless life. I had her begging me to kill her." Close to the line, Tal thought, but still true. The return of her feelings after so many thousands of years was torture, and she died as a result of having her humanity restored.

This time it was Dysi who whimpered. "Quint, how could you? We are charged to Seek the Center."

More, Tal thought, you have to press harder. "What's the matter, Dysi? You want to win the Tyrning, don't you?"

She nodded first in the affirmative, before she started wagging her head no, and softly crying. "Not like this, Quint. Never like this."

Tal looked around the rest of the room. He definitely had their attention. I'm sorry Dysi, but I have to seal the deal. "Well, you may not have the stomach to do what it takes to be a winner, but I do. I had the wytch on her hands and knees begging me to use Fragarach to put an end to her. But I didn't. That kind of death didn't interest me in the least." Right because I had no intention of murdering her.

"I made the wytch give me the most powerful wytch talysman in the universe, and then I made her help me end her lyfe. By killing her I also took out her three familiars. And their horses." All true, every bit of it, Tal thought. The warriors and their horses were constructs of Baba Yaga. They ceased to exist when she did.

Tal looked again to his teammates. Even Notos was looking a little green. Dysi and Ana's expressions had morphed from surprise into revulsion. He glanced at the Släkt table. For some reason, Väst's eyes were brimming over in tears. She looked away quickly when she saw him look her way, visibly trembling as she placed her head down on her team table.

Surely that's enough, he told himself. No, Taliesin it isn't, he thought back. There must be no stone unturned, they must all fear you no matter the cost. "Want to know which wytch it was I put down? It was Baba Yaga herself. That's right, I ended the most powerful wytch who ever lived, the leader of the Cult of Nyx." Everyone in the room was transfixed. Either that or petrified that a lowly mortal could accomplish such action.

Tal didn't stop there. He looked straight at Nord. "I didn't have to sell my teammates out to get some mediocre geegaw from only the second most powerful wytch, either."

Tal was on the receiving end of a mix of horror-adulation emanating from every rapt student in the room. Even Ms. Empousa was stunned into silence, her always taut, rippling muscles still taut but perfectly still. Which is kind of hot in and of itself…Tal, you dumbass, focus.

Nord couldn't stand it any longer. He leapt to his feet. "I don't have to sit here and listen to this low-life lying Munedan waste our time with his ridiculous stories. Show us, Mr. Big Shot. Let's see it, Dust Child. Show us your fucking super talysman to beat all other talysmen that you supposedly got from Baba Yaga."

Well, shit, Tal thought quickly. Guess I thought that show and tell was actually going to be pretty much only tell in my case. But if there was ever an instance where I had to drop trou… "You want proof?" Tal yelled back at Nord. "Here ya go, you green-teethed bastard. Kiss my ass!" With that, Tal turned around with his back to the entire class room, bent over, and mooned the shit out of Nord.

CHAPTER SEVENTY-FIVE

Elle and AndersonCooper were the last two committee members at the gym. They made one final lap around the enchanted forest, marking off each item on their checklists. All of the extension cords were firmly taped down, each of the individual spotlights were ratcheted in place to provide the optimum backlighting. The Winter Formal Committee had succeeded in transforming the gym into a place where one could almost imagine magic might exist.

Angie Alison had already left. She'd stayed long enough to make sure there weren't any problems with the band's sound check and then she split. Of course the people on the ticket subcommittee hadn't been in yet today. They'd been in charge of pre-sales and would be the first ones on-site tonight to make sure only students and their guests were allowed in. Except, of course, for the Little Rock crew. Angie had received a text from Principal Davis that the bus from Little Rock would be leaving on time. After a quick stop for dinner they would be at the Nemeton gym by nine o'clock. Apparently they had some big event tomorrow morning so they were leaving right before midnight. Kind of funny for a school to have school events on Sunday morning. Oh, well, big city folks were strange.

Elle glanced at her phone. One o'clock. Holy hell, I have

to get moving. My hair appointment is at three and I have to get showered and legs and pits shaved before then. That'll give me time to get back home and get my make-up on. Holiman is picking me up at seven-thirty for dinner.

Fingers crossed for a fun, uneventful evening. After the fiasco at the game last night, Nemeton High could use a large dose of happy. Barton hadn't come in until three this morning and Elle was pretty sure he'd started drinking again for breakfast. If Momma catches him at home house drunk during daylight hours, Barton may not live long enough to make it to the dance.

One last quick scan of her checklist. Satisfied that all details had been addressed and there were no loose ends, she nodded at AndersonCooper and started toward the door.

All details except Tal, she thought. Please let him have left town. Or gone to ground. After last night's loss, Barton and his crew were at a boiling point. It's a good thing Tal's been banned from the dance. I'd bet good money that if he showed up here tonight somebody would end up dead. Literally.

"Ready?" she asked AndersonCooper as she put her finger on the master light switch.

CHAPTER SEPTUAGINTA SEX

One thousand and one...one thousand and two...for once, even the HuntsMistress was speechless.

One thousand and three...all of the Omada remained frozen, their mouths gaping wide.

One thousand and four...Tal saw Notos close his mouth as surprise was supplanted by another emotion blooming on his wan face. What is it, Tal thought, recognition?

One thousand and five...Väst was staring intently at him, tears streaming down her face.

One thousand and six...Nord's cocky smile returned. "That's it? A burn mark on your ass is the most powerful talysman in the history of the universe? Idiot Munedan. Your talysman is shit. We're finally done with you and your pitiful teammates." With that Nord sat back in his chair, smiling bigger than ever.

The HuntsMistress leapt forward, grabbed Tal's arm and spun him around until his face was merely inches from hers. She squeezed him so hard with her Puca-enhanced strength it involuntarily brought tears to his eyes. "You killed Baba Yaga?" Tal grimaced as he nodded in the affirmative. Ms. Empousa eased her grip a little. "That brand is the mark of the Cult of Nyx, isn't it?" Tal nodded again and once more her grip was less intense. "Are you saying the wytch used the original seal itself to brand you with the mark?" Tal nodded a third time.

Ms. Empousa let him go, shoving him so hard he almost tripped over his pants and underwear, which were still gathered around his ankles. "You," she said pointing to Tal. "Pull your pants up. It's not like you've got anything to be especially proud of down there."

Well, that should be good for a few tens of thousands of dollars of psychotherapy, Tal thought, as he quickly scrunched over and pulled his pants up to his waist.

"And you," she said pointing across the room to Nord. "You just cost your team a hundred much needed points in a tight competition. For being so incredibly stupid." The HuntsMistress stepped backward so that she had a good view of the entire group of Finalists. "Quint of Omada killed Baba Yaga. She was not only the original initiate into the Cult of Nyx, she was its leader. The wytch affixed the seal of Nyx to his body. Listen up all of you dullards, I'm only going to say this one time. Baba Yaga's talysman isn't merely the brand itself—it's Quint of Omada. For the first time in our recorded history a nonwytch mortal has become a psychopomp."

What the hell, Tal thought, as he finished buckling his belt before falling back into his chair.

Ms. Empousa wasn't through. "There is no question that if Omada presents Quint to the Ruling Council at the Imbolc Feast, the Omada talysman will be ranked as the most powerful. Class is dismissed. Be out front at Fountain Flow at 7:00 p.m. sharp or you'll be left. Any team without full representation tonight will be docked significant points." Per her usual, the HuntsMistress was out the door before the echoes of her voice had stilled.

Tal sat stunned as the import of the HuntsMistress's pronouncements congealed into conclusions. One, I'm a pyschopomp and two, the person in charge of running the Hunts this Tyrning just intentionally put a target on my back.

CHAPTER SEVENTY-SEVEN

Emet had thought the twenty-mile jog to Memphis would only take him about forty minutes but it had taken him almost an hour and a half to get there and to cross the interstate bridge over the Mississippi. He'd even had to stop several times to catch his breath. I must have eaten way too many of those scones, he concluded, and they bogged me down.

Even with the added time he was in good shape timewise to get his shopping done and get back to the Ladies' Room to shower and shave and get dressed for the dance. The Ladies' Room had been absolutely correct about the Air Hose. Emet had made the mistake of giving it salutations and got spurt-misted in response. Emet knew where the air came from but didn't even want to know about the moisture component.

He'd decided the trip to Memphis was a necessity. With the outlying towns included, its population was nearing the million mark and Tal didn't know anybody there. Which meant Emet didn't either. Both factors reduced the possibility of him running into someone from Nemeton down to a miniscule level. Just as importantly, Memphis had a large number of costume shops where he could buy a suitable mask. Everyone at Nemeton High had either ordered theirs from Amazon weeks ago or gotten some cheap version from the Wal-Mart up toward West

Memphis. He couldn't take a chance of trying that store. And at this late date they were probably sold out anyway.

He'd google-mapped his options and the shop closest to him was Mr. Lincoln's on South Florence. It ended up being perfect. He and Tal hadn't had a chance to discuss outfits but they each had only one white long sleeve dress shirt and one pair of navy blue dress slacks. Odds were that's what Tal would wear. Even if I'm wrong, I'll blend in with most of the rest of the guys. Now, since we are basically the same brain, which mask would I choose? Well, he would choose, but he equals me. The traditional black Bauta mask. It covers the entire bottom half of the face and black fades away in low light much better than the white version.

Purchase made, he stopped at the corner burger joint. I'm hungry again, he realized. And worried. About Tal and Thea, Pell, Remy, and Romy. And quite frankly, about what's going on with me. He looked at the clock on the wall. Half past two. Time to book it back to Nemeton.

CHAPTER SEPTUAGINTA OCTO

Still semi-dazed, Tal watched as Borras sprang into action. He flashed a sharp split-fingered signal to Ana and Dysi. They instinctively reacted in accordance with their training, leaping to their feet and assuming defensive postures in front of Tal. Borras rocked his head backward toward Notos, who was somehow instantaneously right behind Tal. Borras then reached down and grabbed Tal, throwing him up to his feet. With a firmly ordered "Go!" from their Prime, the Omada phalanx marched double time out of the classroom. The operation had been executed so efficiently that Omada was well clear of the classroom before any of the other teams even realized Omada was booking it elsewhere.

Save only the syncopated cadence of their shoes slapping on the marble floor, there was complete silence all the way to the Omada secure room. As soon as they were all safely in, Borras placed his palm against the door, ensuring it was now locked at the highest security level.

Tal barely had time to shake off the last effects of shock before he started getting whiplashed by the emotional crosscurrents roiling through the room. Ana was livid that Tal was a murderer. Dysi was a little more restrained but still clearly disheartened by Tal's apparent absence of character. Notos was…well, he was typically Notosian.

Borras didn't give the competing emotions time to reach critical mass, even though he too was looking a little iffy after Tal's sanguinary recitation of his dealings with Baba Yaga. He's always looking out for the team, Tal thought. There are times to allow venting and times to seize control. "Stop," Borras commanded. A moment's pause. "Listen." And they did. "I told Quint he had to pump up the volume on his story. That he needed to do his best to intimidate the others so they wouldn't even think about issuing another Combat Challenge." He turned to Tal, "I had no idea though that you…that you were capable of…"

"I'm not," Tal replied quickly. "And I didn't."

"Human, we were told if we lied about the wytch interactions we would be discovered and disqualified," Notos interjected, starting to heat back up.

"There was no lying," Tal replied. "I remade the story using whatever embellishments I could to try to fulfill our Prime's request."

"So, once again you played…"

Borras interrupted the nascent eruption. "Notos! Stop!" His tone made it clear it wasn't a request. "That part was totally at my direction. Now, Quint, let's hear the unembellished story. Without interruption," he added, looking at the other three.

Tal started from the point where he used the Ring of Gyges to disappear and concluded when the Recall brought them all back to Hunts School. As he reached for the water pitcher he realized he must have been talking for the better part of an hour.

The team room was now awash with completely different emotions. "You saved her," Dysi whispered, wiping the remains of a tear from her left eye.

"Thanks," Tal replied, "but she was the one who had to make the tough decision to turn her back on hate."

Ana reached over to put her hand on his arm. "I am sorry I doubted you, Quint. Your actions were of the Center. I have some nonmagykal salves but I don't think those will help with the brand. From what you've told us, I'm guessing constant and continuous pain from the brand is probably an intrinsic part of the Nyx magyk."

"There is no one in this school who could have handled that any better, Quint," Borras stated.

Notos had to add his two cents. "You realize, of course, that you used your last wish when all you had to do was take Fragarach and…"

"Notos!" Ana and Dysi exclaimed in tandem.

"Fine," Notos conceded. "Good work on getting us the number one ranked talysman. Of course it does us no good if you're dead by Feast time."

I can always count on Notos to keep it real, Tal thought.

Borras responded to Notos's comment. "Although phrased indelicately, our Second Prime has correctly identified our most immediate concern."

"Quint stays in our secure room until the Feast," Dysi quipped. "Problem solved."

"That's a no-go, Dysi," Anatolia replied. "Field trip attendance is mandatory. Empousa repeated that again right before she dismissed us. With her revised scoring, the field trip is twenty-five percent of our term score."

"Doesn't seem quite fair," Dysi interjected. "The other successful teams are going to hide their talysmen in their secure team rooms."

"I really don't want to stay here all afternoon if I don't have to," Tal added quietly.

"Perfectly understandable," Borras replied. "If anybody is looking to take you out they will focus their efforts around trying to crack the security of your suite. One of us will go there and you will go to one of our rooms. They all have the same level of security as our team room."

"That's true," Notos added, "however, we have windows in our rooms that are vulnerable to possible attack. The windows are warded against magykal attack but I'm not sure how they'd be against a significant physical assault."

"Tal has to get ready for the dance, too," Dysi observed. "Sounds like you're thinking of a shell game?" she said to Borras.

"Absolutely," Anatolia said, already up to speed with Dysi. "I'll gather all of my makeup, my dress and mask for tonight and I'll get ready in Dysi's room. Let's smuggle Tal into the girls' dorm right now and Borras and Notos can get Quint's stuff and meet Dysi someplace to give it to her and I'll get it to Quint."

Borras nodded. "Good plan, ladies. Best we can do for pre-dance security, anyway. Let's turn to the more difficult part of the equation. The field trip itself."

"I'll be a little ruder than normal and get the back bench on the bus," Notos said. "Borras can get Quint on the bus and then the four of us will form a physical shield during transport. First on, last off. Coming and going."

"So much for our dates," Anatolia added, with the smallest whisper of wistfulness. "Please don't misunderstand me, I just feel badly for them. Since they aren't Hunts contestants we were the only way they were ever going to get to step onto Earth plane proper."

"I feel badly for them as well," Borras added. "As soon as we leave here we're all going to have to make our excuses. Tal, did you have someone you were escorting?"

"Yes," Tal replied. "Janis. Her real name, well her real name, um, number is 072457. She's from my band, Old School."

"We can't risk you out and about any more than necessary," Borras said.

"I'll be the heavy and makes sure she gets the word," Dysi stated.

"What about during the dance itself?" Anatolia asked. "We're going to be there until midnight. Which means three to four hours of exposure."

"Right now, no one knows we're at full magykal strength on Earth plane proper," Borras stated. "We need to maintain that element of surprise as long as possible. If we make the cut for this term, we still have an unknown third Hunt ahead of us next term. Ana, since you'll have your full healmagyk, you're going to need to stick to Quint like a glove. The rest of us will back off a few feet and maintain a defensive perimeter. If somebody tries something we should have plenty of juice to stop it before they get to Quint.

"Our travel cloaks are over there in the closet. People generally see what they expect to see. Even though I won't fool anyone with my size I'll still wear mine. Notos and Anatolia are only a little shorter than Quint. We will all hood up before I unlock the door, The three of us will head off toward the boys' dorm and everyone will assume it's the three guys. Quint and Dysi will go to the girls' dorm.

"Okay team," he said, now grinning broadly. "Since we won't all be together again until we meet at Fountain Flow, I think we can indulge ourselves and be happy that we are apparently going to remain in the Hunts for another term."

CHAPTER SEPTUAGINTA NOVEM

Alberich was sitting on the floor of his study, his arms wrapped firmly around his spouse. Aine had been spectral a long time. Too long in his opinion, even for the strongest wielder of awaymagyk in centuries. Even with all of his own magyk and the considerable variety of magyks granted to him as Archon by Hunts School itself, there was nothing he could do to help her. She would either find her way home to her body or she would drift. Forever.

Aine began convulsing. Alberich sent tendrils of his telepathmagyk out and through her. If I can just still her, get her heart back to its normal rhythm, maybe it will help her find her way back to her body. He began sweating as he expended more lyfeforce into her. Her convulsions subsided into tremors, the tremors became smaller twitches, and finally she was still. No, not still, thank Amarantos, her chest is rising and falling in a normal breathing pattern. She has returned. He sent more of his power over and through her again. And again. Aine finally gasped and opened her eyes.

"Welcome, home," he smiled, hugging her closer.

She laid her head back into his shoulder. Exhausted. And scared. "Alberich, something is tremendously wrong. There is an evil seeking to unravel the fabric of the universe. It discovered me searching and chased me. Me! No one has ever been able to keep up with me and this, this thing is so much faster, so much stronger..." Aine shuddered and fell silent a moment before continuing. "I could not initially come back to myself, it somehow had the ability to follow me. It might have had the strength to take me, and use me for its unnatural purposes."

Alberich leaned forward and whispered in his queen's ear, "You are safe now, dearest. We are at Hunts School and I am Archon of all of the known Realms. I think perhaps you should not go astral again until we know more about our adversary."

Her voice still shaking, Aine agreed with him. "Alberich, something is going to happen at the dance tonight."

"You have no idea what?"

"No," she said, shaking her head sadly. "I was only able to scry that it has been well-planned and there is nothing you will be able to do to prevent it, nor to mitigate its effects." When Alberich began to protest she turned and put her finger on his lips. "No, dearest. I don't know if it's because it's more powerful than you or because it would be a violation of the rules, but you have been effectively negated."

"And our daughter?"

Aine started crying. "She remains materially involved."

"Sshh, dearest. We have faced and overcome many allegedly unbeatable enemies in our time together. There are wyldcard factors that perhaps this evil doesn't know about." When he saw Aine wasn't following him, he continued. "Remember, there is a simulacrum golem of the mortal, and the Omada are not barred by my Bane while he is with them on the Earth plane."

"I had forgotten," she whispered.

"Amarantos will provide a way for those who truly Seek the Center," he added. "Now, c'mon," he said, standing to his feet and extending his hand to his wife. "We have to get dressed and masked. We are chaperones for a formal dance this evening."

CHAPTER OCTOGINTA

Dysi's suite had been decorated in the style of a grand Tuscan villa. It suits her, Tal thought. The warmth of the bright, natural colors, the crisp freshness imbued in the wall frescoes. Even the tinkling of the small water feature in her front foyer. They weren't just rooms, either. It was clearly her home. There were no pictures of her family, of course. But there were dozens of pictures and plaques and trophies from her hundred years here at Hunts School. Dysi is full of hope and promise for the future, Tal thought, and her dwelling reflects those attributes.

He turned his attention to his wardrobe choices for this evening. As he did he realized he'd been rubbing the brand on his ass. It hurt, as in like a son of a bitch, all the time. When his mind was focused on something, the pain receded to a substantial dullness, but it quickly became acute when his mind wasn't otherwise occupied.

Let's see. T-shirt, t-shirt, vee-neck t-shirt, and white dress shirt. There's a no-brainer. Blue jeans, khaki shorts, dirty blue jeans, and navy blue dress pants. And, again we have an easy winner. Anatolia had brought him a large box full of masks to consider. Fancy without feathers, fancy with feathers, attention-garnering garish, really, really tall but otherwise unremarkable, and about half a dozen basic masks. All the way from the simple

Batman-Lone Ranger style to more substantial options. He finally narrowed his selection to two: a white Bauta mask and a black one. Black it is. Fade into the woodwork as much as possible, Tal, he told himself.

I have a lot to do tonight, he thought as he walked into the bathroom to shave and shower. I have to hook up with Emet and make plans for our future. It'd become clear to Tal the last few days without Emet's counsel and friendship just how much Emet meant to him. Even though simultaneous sightings would always be a problem, Tal was resolved that he and Emet needed to plan their future together. In a bigger town, where no one knew them they could be identical twins.

I also have to do whatever is necessary to stay clear of Elle. As much as I'd like to talk to her, it isn't in her best interests. As if she'd even give me the time of day, anyway.

Then there was Väst and his feelings for her. Maybe by some miracle, Släkt wouldn't make the cut and he and Väst would get the chance to publicly explore their relationship. After all, Alberich and Aine had been on competing teams.

Seemed like there was one other thing on his list for tonight. Emet, Elle, Väst. What else? Oh yeah, You have to make it through the night without being murdered, you idiot.

CHAPTER OCTOGINTA UNUS

The Omada had gotten in the front of the line for the second of the two yellow school buses waiting at Sol's Gas to transport them to Nemeton High School. Sticking to their plan about bus seating, Notos was in front, Dysi and Anatolia were tucked in tight on his left and right and Borras intentionally made sure there was about a three foot gap between Tal and the first non-Omada person in their line.

Tal assumed the two drivers were going to be magykally "washed" of any memory of out of the ordinary details concerning tonight. Like the fact that almost seventy men and women came tromping out of a gas station Ladies' Room, some dressed traditional formal, others like they were going to a masked version of disco night at the local dance hall. The Air Hose said nothing to him as he walked by, but he was pretty sure it actually wolf-whistled at Anatolia.

It was easy for Tal to revert to his human stereotypical concepts concerning magic and to assume that Folk magyk might be similarly generic and all encompassing. That wasn't the reality of magyk—it was extremely specific. Both as to species of Folk and to individuals as well. The only thing every member of the Folk had in common was that their existence was powered by magyk, as opposed to electrical impulse. Apparently, Folk royalty were the most powerful wielders at their specific types of magykal abilities, but the species of magyk were as numerous as the grains of sand on a beach. As Tal absentmindedly turned the now dull silver ring on his finger he qualified his thoughts. His observations applied to the Folk. Amarantos's Elder Children, the Principes, were an entirely different matter.

All of the Hunts School students and faculty had been magyked before their arrival for the present school term so that they each outwardly appeared as your every day garden-variety human being. The wards protecting the school prevented the use of magyk on school property by anyone, excepting only the Archon. Even the faculty were restricted, except in specifically authorized situations. The wards couldn't, of course, stop Principe magyk. Tal had learned that lesson during the Combat Challenge when he'd used Aurora's ring to save Väst.

The Hunts School hallways were now so familiar that even in an architecturally unique building such as the main building, Tal had to consciously think about it to remember that all of the lighting, the climate control, the cafeteria food preparation, hell, even the toilets, were powered by magyk, not electricity.

He'd gotten limited glimpses of the different species of magyk possessed by his teammates on the Omada's Journeys, and at his house when Anatolia created Emet. Alberich's Bane prevented the use of any unauthorized magyk on Earth Realm. Because of Hunts Rule 5.2 that prohibition didn't apply to Tal's Omada team members. Since there had never been a mortal at Hunts School before Tal, the loophole in that particular rule had never been discovered. They had all decided that information should remain a closely guarded Omada secret.

An elbow jostle ended his reverie, bringing Tal back to the present with—Holy Crap! When the entourage had first assembled back at Fountain Flow, he'd originally thought the expedition would merit only a "Wow!" But every time he turned around there was some additional nuance or detail of the multi-layered magyk utilized by the Archon, Principal Chiron, and the

HuntsMistress, to prepare for their field trip to the Nemeton High Winter Formal.

The Ruling Council had authorized Folk with specialized magykal skills to be transported though the Prime Omphalos. Dozens of people—seamstresses, cosmetologists, haberdashers, cordwainers, and mask-makers. At first it had seemed to Tal, a little, well a little past grossly excessive. When he'd discussed the activity with Borras, he'd reminded Tal that the Tyrning field trip occurred only once every three hundred years and that in the entire history of the Hunts School there had never been a field trip where the students had been permitted to interact with Dust Children. Tal now realized that the annual Winter Formal in a tiny hamlet in the rural delta region of Arkansas was about to become a singular event in the storied history of the Folk universe, and that it deserved to be treated as such.

The girls had all been measured and shown gown designs. Several had apparently opted for ancient Roman styles with exposed breasts. Those had been quickly rejected by Principal Chiron. Almost all of the ladies had chosen to go with the most fantastically designed ball gowns you could possibly imagine. Most of the guys were more conservative, although there were a fair number of outlandish tuxedos and a few individuals who on their home planes were clearly used to wearing uniforms with epaulets and dozens and dozens of medals of super-meritorious merit.

The entire group, including the escorts, were excited. If one didn't know better, they would seem to be a diverse collection of high school students amped up about their final high school Formal, their last hurrah before diving into the deep end of adult reality. Of course, Tal knew better. Even more, he knew the future of the Folk might turn on him not dying this evening.

CHAPTER EIGHTY-TWO

Elle had to admit that the evening had been lovely so far. Holiman knew how she felt about being late and he was precisely on time picking her up. He'd chatted her folks up for the mandatory couple of minutes of small talk and even given her Mom the obligatory Eddie Haskell, "Hello, Mrs. Cleaver, you look lovely this evening." Modified to Mrs. Sellars, of course.

The only blemish on the day thus far was Barton. Best Elle could tell, when he'd woken up from last night's bender, his head hurt so badly he'd launched into multiple Red Bull and vodkas. Consuming "all the hairs of the dog that bit me," was his only meaningful statement to her before he'd lapsed into another few hours of unconsciousness.

He'd apparently gone out for a bit while she was at the gym but had come back home and passed out again. Mom had finally kicked him out of his bed about the time that Elle had gotten back from her final precheck at the gymnasium, so he'd called Gunnar and Fail, as well as a few of their other football buddies, to come over for a pool party. Their afternoon had been spent playing beer pong and doing Jäger bombs. The net result of that activity was that he had passed out again by the time Holiman arrived. Elle knew Barton was comatose when they left, because she'd heard him snoring loudly as she'd walked down the hallway a few minutes before she went downstairs to meet Holiman. I feel badly for whoever he was supposed to take to the Formal tonight, Elle thought, but the best thing for all of us is that he sleep until time for church tomorrow. That much alcohol and that much anger about last night's loss were not a good combination.

The small wrist corsage of three light green mini-cymbidium orchids Holiman brought for her complemented her dress. She'd suggested it, of course. Just as she'd suggested the limo and the dinner reservations at Authors, the finest steakhouse in at least three counties. Absolutely nothing wrong with being organized, she told herself.

At Angie's suggestion, the Committee members and their dates were now waiting outside the gym to greet the Little Rock visitors as their buses rolled up the school driveway. Elle watched as the occupants of the first of the two buses disembarked.

"Dayumm, some of those chicks are smokin'!" Holiman exclaimed.

"Down, Tiger, you've already got a date for the evening," Elle replied, as she gently patted his arm. It's not like she and Holiman were invested in each other, she thought. And as more and more of the students exited the bus she had to agree. The girls' gowns were each dramatically different in color and style. If Elle hadn't known that average high school students couldn't afford couture, she'd have sworn that's what they were wearing. Every dress looked like it had been individually tailored for its wearer. And their masks. Wow! Horns and feathers and lace erupted in unusual configurations. They were like a procession of trooping fairies straight out of a William Butler Yeats' poem.

She politely greeted a few of the visitors from the first bus. As the second bus began unloading, she turned Holiman back toward the entrance. There were a couple of extension cords she wanted to make sure were well-secured. Never hurts to be prepared.

CHAPTER EIGHTY-THREE

Elle spent the first twenty minutes back in the gym waiting for something to go horribly wrong with the decorations. She'd had nightmares about it for weeks. Some unexpected thing went haywire, the incident was blamed on Elle, and Angie was able to connive her way into the valedictorianship. Her nightmares were creative, diverse, and fairly disturbing. One had involved the electrocution of some dimbulb who wanted to get a "cute" angle for a selfie high up in an enchanted tree. Another was a double-strangulation when one of the lianas came unglued, fell to neck level of a couple, and somehow wrapped around both their necks while they were making out. Oblivious to the hazard, they both slipped and fell to the floor when the guy tried to round second in public. Elle could still see their blue-choked faces, eyes bulging three inches outward through their masks. All kinds of catastrophic possibilities had cycled through Elle's sleeping mind.

Plato and the Sorry Apologists were, however, now on their third song and everything seemed to be all systems go. Angie was on duty at the front desk, together with several of the off-duty officers providing security. They were checking identification and making sure everyone was masked. The attendees were really starting to roll in. A few of the dateless ladies were already dancing. The guests from Little Rock remained clumped together, talking in small groups, but Elle was sure they'd start mingling soon.

So, when Holiman put his arm around her shoulders and suggested heading over to the photo booth that was set up at the far corner of the gym, Elle relaxed into his well-muscled upper arm and they headed over. Unlike Barton, Holiman had acquitted himself well on the field of combat last night and had already moved on from the loss.

They were actually in the booth when she heard a guitar lick cut off mid-chord, resulting in high-pitched feedback that became even more unbearable when Angie's jet-decibel level screeching began. "Stop! What are you doing? Security! Security!"

Elle dropped her yellow feather boa and the hand sign that said "Drop Dead Gorgeous!!!" and bolted out of the booth. The conflict was on the stage where a scrum of three attackers was laying into Plato and two of his Sorry Apologists. Amps and speakers were being shoved off stage, punches were in progress, masks were being ripped off faces, and there was lots and lots of shoving. Then she heard a really loud, really familiar—if extremely slurred—high-pitched voice. "Which one of you is that sorry mother fucker?"

Oh shit, it's Barton! He must have woken up still so outrageously polluted that he thinks Tal is in the band. Elle bent down and took off her four inch stilettos, before taking off at a dead run for the stage. By the time she ran around some guests, and then through the Enchanted Forest, the melee was over. Security personnel had cuffed Barton, Gunnar, and Fail and were in the process of hauling them outside. Elle started to follow them when someone grabbed her arm and jerked her around.

"Where the hell do you think you're going?" Angie demanded, the rest of her face now even redder than her Crimson Harlot lip gloss.

"I'm going to check on Barton…"

"Oh, I don't think so. Your parents will no doubt be here any moment to save his ass once again. I'm holding you personally responsible for this." Angie started laughing hysterically. "You probably did this to sabotage me. You knew I was going to beat you for valedictorian. Didn't you? Didn't you?" Angie grabbed Elle and began shaking her. Vigorously.

Elle decided she had no choice but to slap Angie to snap her out of her crazed shock status. Right when she had her arm cranked back, Angie's demeanor flipped. It was like somebody had flipped an Angie-switch. She started blubbering that she couldn't handle the pressure and took off through a little copse in the Forest they'd nicknamed Lover's Grove, making a beeline to the hallway. No doubt she's headed to the ladies' bathroom to hide, Elle thought.

You could have heard a pin drop. There were several hundred Nemeton students in the gym, plus the Little Rock guests, and they were now all looking directly at Elle. Get a grip, she told herself. Worse things have happened at high school dances. Like what, Elle? Well…there was that one scene in *Carrie*. That was fiction, Elle. Well, if it had of been real, then that would be a worse thing.

Focus, Elle. How do we get this dance back on track? Duh, the band. If I can get them organized and back in business everyone will forget the unpleasantness and crank back up into party mode. Go help the band get set back up, she told herself as she strode quickly back toward the stage area.

CHAPTER EIGHTY-FOUR

Väst listened to the music as she looked around the gymnasium, her amazement growing by the minute. The band, with all of its electrical augmentation was simply amazing. Apparently on Earth Realm, philosophers could also wail their asses off. What Dust Children could accomplish with electricity was pretty unbelievable. She'd always felt pity for humans because of their short life spans and because they were the only children of the UnFading Spirit who were bereft of magyk. Like maybe Amarantos had given them short shrift on blessings. Now that she could observe their ingenuity and creativity first hand, she found herself beginning to reassess. Lives should be measured by how they're lived, not how long they last.

She'd noticed when the entire group gathered at Fountain Flow that none of the Omada had dates. Their Prime must have instructed them to cancel their dates and placed them all on security detail. Smart move. Borras had turned out to be an excellent leader. Talk had been when Kentro died that Omada was going to shrivel up and blow away. They hadn't. Omada had prospered and Borras appeared to have succeeded in qualifying them for the final Hunt.

Of course a large part of their success was attributable to Quint. Even with his mask on he looked handsome. There was absolutely no mistaking that lopsided grin. It was infectious, and hot. Really hot. Anybody who knew him would know that look from a mile off.

Väst would have called off her date too, except she and Ost had decided the afternoon the field trip was announced that they would come together. Ost had the rep of being somewhat of a rake when it came to the non-Finalist female students. Despite that, any number of them would have been delighted to come with him for the experience of traveling to Earth plane proper. She suspicioned that, despite the rules, he still planned to hit on some of the Earth girls.

After Nord's vile revelation this morning, she wouldn't have subjected any non-Hunts date to having to put up with him. All students, as part of the Hunts School required curriculum, had studied in great detail the individual members of every Ruling Council from the first recorded Tyrning forward. There were examples of truly great Ruling Councils, others who were basically caretaker governments. History contained every permutation of disagreements, arguments, love affairs with spouses, and love affairs with other than spouses. There were even numerous recorded instances where Prime Directions had to be heavy-handed with their team's binding to accomplish goals. There was, however, no precedent for what Nord had done. He'd bartered the life of another sentient being for the opportunity to be Archon. He'd also used the sacred contractual binding to contingently sell his teammates out so he could have the opportunity to be Archon. There is no way that Amarantos wants someone who would do such things to win the Tyrning.

No, what Nord had done was unforgiveable. It was too much like the horrific rumors surrounding Malebranche's possible actions during his Tyrning, the year in which Arthrys defeated him. She couldn't defy Nord on team matters, the contract bound her tight on those issues. She could despise him though and although she and the others hadn't been able to discuss it, she thought they felt the same. Even Fem, their replacement Fifth, who wasn't going to win any sportsmanship awards himself.

She'd just motioned to Ost that she was ready to take him up on his offer to take a spin around the dance floor when the fight erupted. Folk and human had similar responses to the unexpected fracas. Clearly beating the shit out of the band was not standard operating procedure at Earth Realm high school dances.

When things looked like they were in total disarray, Väst saw a statuesque goddess come flying from the Enchanted Forest area. Five-Hells, she could be a ruby-haired teenage Bastet, Väst thought. Just looking at the way she carries herself, I know she's beyond gorgeous behind that exquisite Egyptian lion-cat mask. And since we live on completely different planes, I'm not going to let it bother me one bit that she's rocking that green ball gown even better than I could. Well, I'm not going to let it bother me an excessive amount.

CHAPTER EIGHTY-FIVE

Not wanting to risk being recognized at the front entrance, Emet circled the outside of the gymnasium building, drifting from shadow to shadow, as he tried every auxiliary door and all of the first floor windows. He decided to be patient, to wait a few more minutes before he broke out a window or forced a door, hoping that opportunity would present itself. Tal's notes said he was required to attend this dance as part of his Hunts School obligations. Otherwise there'd be no way either he or Tal would risk violating the terms of the non-prosecution agreement. Depending on this term's Hunt results, tonight might be Emet's last chance to communicate with Tal for months.

Opportunity came knocking, well knee-walking knocking anyway, in the form of three extremely intoxicated individuals—Barton and his gang of two miscreants. With his enhanced senses, Emet could smell the reek of alcohol—and vomit—from more than fifty feet away. Barton used a key to open the training room side door. Right before it swung shut, Emet took two leaps across the parking lot, covering the entire distance right before the door would have latched closed.

Emet held the heavy metal door pried open with his fingers for about a full minute, until he was sure Barton's group had moved on. He then crept inside, making sure the door closed securely behind him. He didn't need any security or partygoers sneaking up behind him while he was sneaking up behind Barton. The only light source in the weight room came from several fluorescent fixtures in the hallway. Which wasn't any problem for Emet. He quickly navigated his way through all of the piles of weights and arcane fitness devices laying about on the floor.

A quick look both ways up and down the hallway, a final check of his outfit and mask by looking in his reflection in the trophy cabinet glass, and he strode out into the hallway. Just another Nemeton High student who'd been to the bathroom and was now returning to the dance.

CHAPTER EIGHTY-SIX

So far, so good, Tal thought. That old saw about people seeing what they expect to see has proven true so far this evening. The Hunts School adults had led the way into the Nemeton gym. Principal Chiron, the HuntsMistress, Professor Elphinstone, Doctor Hardcastle, Professor SilverTongue, as well as several other administrative people Tal had seen but didn't know. The Archon and Queen Aine were also in attendance as "parent chaperones." The adults had been glamoured so they looked like regular run of the mill mortal adults. Mundane Munedans, you might say. The gaggle of Hunts students followed close behind and cruised past the front entrance check-in table without any problem. Tal stayed as far away as possible from that Angie Alison chick. She was kinda scary. Hot, but scary.

It had been a good call to go with the basic black Bauta mask. The Bauta covered most of his face. He'd guessed correctly that it was the no-effort dial-it-in default mask for several other Finalist guys, and at least half a dozen of the Nemeton students.

Borras was standing in front of Tal, head turning as his eyes continuously swept the gym, looking for possible trouble. Borras hadn't moved more than two feet away from Tal since they'd all left Fountain Flow. Tal knew Notos had been assigned to watch his six, and felt confident without even looking backward that Notos was obeying his Prime's order.

Borras had assigned Dysi and Anatolia the close quarters defense. The girls were both beyond lovely this evening. Dysi's hoop diamond earrings provided a nice frame for her short auburn hair. Her orange gown was off one shoulder, exposing some of the freckles on her left shoulder. She had chosen an ivory colored pantalone mask. The pantalone shape came to just under her nose but rose conically about eight inches above the crown of her head. The curved upper portion of the mask was hand-painted with a series of frolicking Renaissance cherubs. The height of the mask made her appear almost as tall as Tal and Anatolia.

Anatolia was dressed like she was, in a word, Anatolia. Always the fashion plate of the group, she was invariably perfectly coiffed and made-up, even for Combat class. Her dress was a full-length white ball gown, her straight shimmering blue-black hair had been apprehended and knotted up into some high falutin' upstyle do. Tal didn't know what the style was called, but it was upscale classy and suited Anatolia perfectly. Her signature fire opal necklace accented her long, elegant neck. Tonight she also had a pair of long, dangling matching earrings. White gold with uncut fire opals which caught and refracted the light as they swung in cadence with her head movements. Ana was wearing a plague doctor's mask, its face and long curved beak decorated in an Impressionist style with designs utilizing the same colors as those flashing from her necklace and earrings.

This didn't suck, Tal thought. It really didn't. Having two ethereal hotties, one on each arm, was pretty much the Winter Formal wet dream of every eighteen-year old dude. Granted, they were only there in case someone tried to commit murder most foul but the Nemeton High students didn't know that. Every Earth plane student must think he looked like the king boss daddy.

Borras's strategy was uncomplicated. Any thought of enjoying the field trip was out the window. The golden ticket to the Big Show was printed on Tal's ass. Job One—Priority One—

444

Only Thing That Mattered Tonight One—was safeguarding Tal during the dance and the return trip to Hunts School.

While his teammates continually updated their threat assessments, Tal was also scanning the crowd. Difference was he wasn't looking for danger, he was looking for two specific people. Emet…and her.

CHAPTER EIGHTY-SEVEN

Elle assessed the damage as she walked up the three metal steps to the stage. Son of a bitch. Not good. Not good at all. On the plus side, it looked like the instruments were intact. The guitars were scattered and the right keyboard leg was kind of doing that leaning Tower of Pisa thing, but they all looked intact and usable. The band members were a different matter. There was blood streaming out of both of Plato's nostrils and the lower half of his nose was at a seriously discordant angle to the upper portion. He was dabbing at it, trying to staunch the blood when she walked up.

"Are you okay?" Elle asked, knowing it was a lame intro but she wasn't really sure where to start.

"Do I fucking look like I'm okay?" he growled in response. She noticed blood was also coming out of his mouth from at least one broken tooth and a split lower lip.

"We're really terribly sorry. How about we take a thirty-minute break and I help you get everything back together and we just start over. Like nothing happened."

"Are you crazy? We're not playing anything else you stupid bitch! How do you think Socrates is going to play with a broken arm?"

Elle looked over at the other three members of the band.

Both of the guitarists were trying to help the drummer bind his right arm in a sling.

Plato was high-pissed. "We're going to the emergency room and I'm calling our lawyer on the way so he can get started on the papers to sue your asses off. Our tech crew will pack everything up tonight and we'll send someone to pick our stuff up in the morning." Plato got to his feet. Actually, he wobbled to his feet. There was nothing Elle could do but watch as he nodded to his Apologists and they all slowly walked down the stage steps, through the main Forest path, and out the front door.

Elle watched as the sound and light roadies started in her direction. She looked over toward the refreshment area where all of the Nemeton staff and the Little Rock congregation were hanging out. Then back toward the bathrooms. No sign of Angie. This may have permanently broken her, Elle decided. Well, somebody has to inform Principal Davis the band ain't coming back and that she should expect a process server sometime next week. As she slowly walked down the steps and toward the adults her thoughts turned back to her drunk ass brother. Mom and Dad were not going to be happy with Barton. They could fix the criminal charges, but Dad was going to have to pay some serious money to buy off the inevitable civil lawsuit.

Principal Davis stepped away from everyone to meet Elle. "What's the report?"

"It's not good, ma'am. The band has gone to the ER. They're not coming back and they're planning on filing a lawsuit."

"Well, that's just great," the Principal replied. "Your brother and his two idiot sycophants have gone too far this time. I'll deal with them later. What's your backup plan?"

Elle's response was a shoulder shrug. Pretty much said it all.

"That won't do," Principal Davis replied, her voice raising before she caught herself and lowered it. "We are supposed to have over five hundred students here tonight, not counting the more than sixty guests from Little Rock. Putting the unbelievable

448

embarrassment aside for the moment, your Committee sold tickets for a dance. How are you going to give everyone their money back?"

"I have absolutely no idea," Elle replied dejectedly.

"Then I guess you're going to have to fix this right now." Someone else had walked up to them by this time. Elle didn't know the man.

"Can I be of some assistance," the man inquired politely.

"I was just assessing the damage, Principal Chiron."

Chiron, Elle thought. Such an odd name. Greek mythology. Smartest centaur ever. Taught many of the heroes like Hercules and Jason. Grandson was Peleus, great-grandson was Achilles.

"And?"

"It's not good," Principal Davis replied, motioning toward the empty stage. "I'm afraid we're going to have to call off the rest of the evening. I know you've come all the way from Little Rock. I'm sure we can pay for the gas money for your bus, and maybe everyone would like to have some milkshakes at the diner before you head back."

Principal Chiron nodded his head and walked over to the stage area. He spoke briefly to the roadies who stopped what they were doing and headed back toward where their control boards were set up. When he got back to Elle and Principal Davis, he said, "Stay here a minute and let me talk to my staff. I might have a solution for us."

Didn't see that coming, Elle thought, as she and Principal Davis did as requested.

CHAPTER EIGHTY-EIGHT

Two matters were urgently competing for Tal's attention. The first was Principal Chiron's huddled conversation with the HuntsMistress and the Archon. The second was a tall well-built dude with a crisply pressed black tux and an attention grabbing golden Bauta mask. More specifically, what drew his attention was that this GQ-cover hunk walked up to the lissome redhead talking to Principal Davis and draped his arm over her shoulder in a pretty damn intimate manner.

Elle. She has a boyfriend, dammit, Tal thought, as he felt himself physically sag in response. Not just a boyfriend. Some top-notch grade "A" choice beef. Why not, dumbass? You've dropped the ball in every imaginable way with her so far. Plus you're into Väst. Remember?

Väst! Quit staring at Elle, Tal, you don't want anyone on an opposing team to realize you even know her. He flicked his eyes back to the adult confab. But not before he saw Nord looking at him and smiling malevolently.

CHAPTER EIGHTY-NINE

Borras took a step backwards to allow room for Principal Chiron, Ms. Empousa, and Alberich to form the center of a horseshoe configuration with Omada on the wings. The HuntsMistress raised a hand to shoo all of the other teams away from their immediate vicinity. Borras jerked his head backwards again and Tal saw Notos remain in place but turn his back to their group. Borras isn't taking any chances that this whole thing isn't an elaborate diversion, Tal thought.

Ms. Empousa spoke first. "Principal Chiron has spoken with his counterpart and the band has left for the evening. No band, no dance."

This is the best news possible for me and for Omada, Tal thought, barely able to keep his face from expressing his glee. Keeps me from getting busted as being on-site and gets me back to a secure dorm room until tomorrow morning. And I don't have to watch that asshat grope Elle all night.

Principal Chiron looked around their entire group before adding, "As it stands now the dance is effectively over, and we will be returning to Hunts School in the next few minutes." Principal Chiron turned a few degrees to look at Tal. "I understand you have a 'group' that you play Earth music with, is that correct?"

Dammit, Tal thought. He could feel the heat rising off of Notos's back and he was even two teammates over. What happens if I lie to the Principal? I'm sure there's some stupid lying to the Principal about Earth music rule in that stupid Hunts Rules rulebook. I simply have got to get a copy of that thing. "Um, yes, sir."

"The students you play with Omada Fifth, they know Earth Realm songs and they could play those instruments over there?" the Principal asked, motioning over his shoulder to the stage.

"They know Earth Realm songs and they know how to play non-electric versions of those instruments," Tal replied, trying his best to evade what was about to happen.

"Surely it would only take a few minutes to show them how to work the electrical versions?" Even though the Principal phrased his words as a question it was obvious he wasn't asking.

"That is correct, sir."

"They are, of course, not presently in the competition?"

"No, sir."

The Principal turned the other way to look at Alberich who left his place and walked over in front of Borras. "Omada Prime?"

"Yes, Archon," Borras responded, his body rigidly at attention.

"The field trip is an integral part of the Hunts School curriculum. All of the contestants, not just the winners, take the information they've learned back to their home Realms to teach their Folk about humans."

"I understand and I understand what you are about to ask of one of my team members," Borras replied. "Permission to speak freely, sir?"

"Certainly."

"Quint, the Omada Fifth, wears our talysman on his body, so we were unable to secure it in our team room or some other safe location. We have formulated a defensive scheme to keep him safe for the time we are here and until we can get him safely home. If he plays all night with his Hunts School group there is no way we can provide adequate protection."

Tal could tell from the Archon's upraised eyebrows he hadn't known about the Omada talysman and had some questions. "If I could insure that your Fifth is not subject to attack by any of the other Hunts students here or on the way back to Hunts School, wouldn't that actually leave you in a better position than if you declined to let him participate? Plus, his bandmates who weren't eligible to come would also get a once in a lifetime opportunity to spend time on Earth Realm, wouldn't they?"

Borras got a huge grin on his face. "Yes, your Highness. Absolutely, they would."

It wasn't until then that Tal realized just how tense Borras had been. Worry lines literally disappeared. If the Archon could swing it, not only would Tal be safe, but the rest of the Omada could enjoy the dance. Of course, the issue of him being recognized by the Nemeton side of the equation remained in play. On the flip side it did give him more time for Emet to show so they could hook up. Tal raised his hand. "I hate to interrupt but in all fairness the equipment doesn't belong to us, and none of the Hunts School students are going to know how to run either the audio mixing board or the lighting board."

"That's not a problem," Principal Chiron responded. "I have advised those gentlemen," he motioned toward the band techs, "that our school will pay them ten times their normal wages if they will stay and take care of the technical aspects. I sweetened the pot by telling them we will also buy an entirely new set of instruments for the band, and the band can keep both sets. All of that without any limitation on their right to sue the miscreants for the injuries caused this evening. They were most pleased with the proposed arrangement."

The Archon looked at Borras, who nodded. Then at Tal, who also nodded. Alberich next motioned to Aine, who quickly

455

walked over to them. "How may I be of assistance, my lord?"

"Omada Fifth, what are the names of your bandmates?"

Tal rattled them off. "Jimi, Jethro, Elton, Ella and Janis."

Alberich looked at him, clearly confused.

"I'm sorry, sir, that's their nicknames." He took a moment and mentally rolodexed their student numbers and gave them to the Archon.

Alberich leaned over and whispered in Aine's ear. She nodded in response. He clapped his hands over his head and she was gone, replaced by sparkling emerald motes hanging midair.

The Archon then snapped his fingers at the other four Hunts teams, summoning them over. "The human band will not be playing this evening. Rather than ending the evening early, I have asked the Omada Fifth if he and his Folk group will provide the entertainment."

There was a low murmuring from almost everyone. No one wanted to go home early. This was literally a once in a lyfetime opportunity.

Alberich continued. "As you know, all of the Folk, myself included, are forbidden to interfere with the Hunts. Directly or indirectly—whether to help or hinder—it does not matter. Such actions are *malum in se*. Which means although I have the power to place compulsions on all of you, I may not exercise such power for a Hunts related activity such as this field trip. Here's what we're going to do. I propose the following voluntary binding. If the Prime of each team will consent that no one on their team will attempt, directly or indirectly, to harm any member of the Omada until after our return to Hunts School, then that team shall be allowed to remain and enjoy the dance. If a Prime does not wish to consent, that is fine. I will use my teleportmagyk to send them back to Hunts School immediately. HuntsMistress would you call the roll of your Finalists, please?"

"Thank you, Archon. Shuzoku?"

"Shuzoku consent, HuntsMistress," Chuushin promptly answered.

"Pleme?"

Without a moment's hesitation, Sredina said, "Pleme consent."

Ulh-Ne-Ih didn't wait to be asked. "Hak"éí consent."

"Kabila consent," Kati added.

The HuntsMistress turned her gaze to Nord. "Släkt?" Nord did not respond. He just stood there chewing his lower lip. "Släkt?" Still no response from Nord as his team fidgeted around him.

The Archon stepped forward, preparing to send the Släkt home.

Nord spat the words out. "Släkt consent."

Alberich stepped back, cocked his head to one side and listened before snapping his fingers twice. Queen Aine and Tal's bandmates materialized at his side. They were all masked up and dressed to rock and roll. All five were staring quizzically at Tal.

"You didn't get the details?" he asked them.

All five heads shook no.

"I'll explain while we're tuning up," Tal told them. As he began walking toward the stage he saw the bathroom hallway door open and someone dressed in a white button down and navy dress slacks walk in to the gym. That someone was wearing a black Bauta mask and walked with a familiar gait. "Emet," Tal whispered to himself. "Thank goodness."

CHAPTER NINETY

Emet used his eidetic memory to snapshot a catalog of flash vignettes. Tal was easy to spot as they had ended up being identically dressed and masked. Something was definitely wrong though. He was walking with five unknown Hunts School students up the steps and on to the stage. The real band wasn't physically present and the instruments on the stage were scattered in an illogical pattern.

Not good, Emet thought. Not what we need to happen, Tal. We should be trying to keep this event on the trés shady side. His brain started rolling the possibilities. Obviously I am missing material information.

It wasn't hard to identify the rest of the Hunts School students and adults. Principal Chiron and the HuntsMistress looked exactly as Tal had described them. The four other Omada members were following Tal. Damn, Borras really is humongous.

Emet had a little more difficulty identifying the rest of the players, except for Nord and Väst of Släkt. Nord looked every bit as sadistic and foul as Tal had described him. Väst was the only one who looked different than Tal's descriptions. She was pretty enough, he guessed, but didn't seem like any big shakes.

Certainly no comparison to Elle, who was easy to spot wearing green, with her hair swept up in a some fancy up-do.

C'mon, Emet, you can do better than that. The word is, the word is…chignon. Emet marked Elle and her date's placement. Based upon height and estimated mass her date appears to be Holiman Richards. Tal isn't going to like that one bit, Emet told himself. Wait, how do I know that?

Speaking of Elle, he thought, as he sidled behind a small grouping of attendees, I need to stay as far away from her as possible while I try to get to Tal.

CHAPTER NINETY-ONE

Once they were all on the stage Tal called a quick huddle with his bandmates. They had all been involved in completely different Saturday evening activities when Aine materialized before them. Janis had even been in the shower. In a blink they had been magyked to Fountain Flow. Fully clothed, Janis was quick to add. They were also wearing masks. Queen Aine told them the Archon had need of their talents and asked if they each consented to use their musical gyfts for the benefit of Hunts School. They all jumped at the opportunity, bound the contract, and in a second blink they were magyked here. Tal finished bringing them up to speed on the events precipitating their presence, then broke the huddle.

Jimi walked over and picked up one of the electric guitars. "Wow," he drawled. "You mean we're going to use real electrified guitars."

"We've been over this, Jimi," Tal replied. "The answer is yes, but they're called electric guitars. I'm going to need you to take my place playing lead this evening." He saw all five of them staring at him. Quick, Tal, be quick, he told himself. Something that won't engender any further delay, but you can't be prominently exhibited up here tonight. Too much is at stake for you to be hauled off by the police. "The subject hasn't ever come up but there are a couple of girls here on Earth Realm who are more than a little mad at me, and it would be best if they didn't know I was here this evening. They both have extremely large boyfriends."

"I'm a little disappointed in you, Quint," Ella added. "I didn't peg you for a man whore. But we got your back anyway." She gave him a look evidencing a small amount of disapproval before heading over and taking her place behind the drum kit.

"So, Jimi, you take lead on most of the songs. Jethro, you've got rhythm, and I'm going to need you to sing the vocals instead of me on the rest of the guy tunes. Ella and Janis will do their usual split on the female vocals. Elton, there's a pretty sweet looking electric keyboard awaiting your loving ministrations." Elton flashed him a huge smile.

"I guess if you're going to play bass all night you're serious about fading into the woodwork?" Jethro asked.

"Deadly serious," Tal replied picking up his guitar. "Five minutes to sound check with the crew, and then we need to burn this mother down."

CHAPTER NINETY-TWO

Cautiously optimistic, Elle watched as the six Little Rock students tuned their instruments. What are the odds that our guests would have students who had their own band, she wondered. That thought was followed closely by—exactly how many degrees of terrible are they going to be?

While she was focused on the replacement group, Angie had walked up behind her. "What the hell is going on?"

"The Little Rock students have a band." Angie assumed the universally recognized outraged position of hands on hips. Before she could even utter a word, Elle continued. "Look Angie, the evening is a total disaster. If they're even half-ass okay, you come out looking like a competent disaster response manager. If we get lucky and they're good, you're going to get all the credit for saving the day."

Angie chewed her lip for a moment, apparently deciding whether she was being played. When she nodded her head, Elle realized Angie must have decided the risk-reward equation was in her favor. "I'm going to see if MY replacement band needs anything." Angie flipped her hair over her shoulder and marched toward the stage barking orders to any unfortunate committee member within earshot.

Elle turned her attention back to the stage. That guy playing bass, he's the same height as Tal. Wonder if he looks like him too? Can't really tell since he's wearing the same mask that at least a dozen other guys have on. First of all Elle, that guy is from Little Rock, not Nemeton. Just a short minute ago you saw some guy coming in from the bathroom hallway that you thought was Tal as well. He can't be two places at one time. And there's no way in hell he'd be stupid enough to put everything he ever wanted in jeopardy to come here tonight.

CHAPTER NINETY-THREE

Väst didn't dare talk to any of her other teammates about it but it was clear Nord was out of control. As if contingently selling his teammates to the wytch wasn't sufficient proof, he almost refused to bind the contract with the Archon so that we could stay this evening. If everything stays the same, it looks like we will be in second place after the Imbolc Feast tomorrow. Which means Släkt remains in the competition. If we don't end up winning the Tyrning, this will have been our only opportunity to experience the Earth Realm—the center of the known universe. If we do win, we need to learn as much as we possibly can about this plane so that we may guide the Folk to the best of our ability. And its not like Omada is being awarded any additional points for Quint's participation.

Nord's hatred of Quint has made him irrational. There are no provisions in the Hunts Rules for deposing a Prime Direction. Which is kind of interesting now that I think about it. The only way a Prime becomes not the Prime is death, or disability rendering him or her unable to continue participating.

Quit worrying about it now, Väst told herself. We're here. It's a singular experience. Enjoy it. Go mingle with the mortals while you listen to Quint's band. I don't get it though. He's standing all the way in the back, going to play the bass guitar.

Every time I've ever seen him and his group practice, he was front and center as lead vocalist. Surely before the evening is over he'll take his turn. Yeah, that definitely needs to happen, she decided.

CHAPTER NINETY-FOUR

"That was close," he mumbled, before catching himself. Don't blow it. Keep your hands away from your face, you can trace your scars later. After you've accomplished tonight's mission. Her magyk cloaking has held up even though we're on Earth plane proper. Even with the high and mighty Lord Alberich himself present.

It's a classic case of irony though. If it wasn't for the boy wonder Dust Child and his idiotic bunch of music groupies, the evening would have ended early and Her plan would have come to naught.

How much longer am I going to have to put up with all of this caterwauling? I'm ready to move forward. Then he heard Her. The softest whisper in the furthest shadows of his mind. *'You are my Creature and you will do as I say. One mortal, one nondescript meaningless mortal must die when darkness rules.'*

CHAPTER NINETY-FIVE

"Ready?" Tal asked his bandmates. As he looked, they each nodded in turn. "Don't let the electricity throw you, you know how to rock these bad boys. Let's start with set list number three. Okay, Jimi, take it away."

Jimi stepped up to the front of the stage. The roadies were obviously seasoned vets, used to taking things on the fly because as soon as Jimi stepped center stage, all lights were instantly extinguished, replaced with a single bright spot. Perfectly illuminating Jimi. "Good evening, ladies and gentlemen. We're pleased to get this opportunity to entertain you. We are 'Old School,' and as you've apparently already noticed tonight, you've got to fight for your right to party."

Jethro hit a long wailing intro chord and blue and white lasers leapt to life and began sweeping all over the stage as Old School lit into the Beastie Boys classic with every bit of their considerable talent.

They didn't even give the assembled students a chance to catch their breath before they moved on to Three Dog Night's "Mama Told Me Not To Come" and then "Any Way You Want It" by Journey. Next they cranked up The Trammps' "Disco Inferno." Tal smiled to himself. His peeps were killing it, they really were burning this mother down.

Tal took a breath after their initial four-song up-tempo onslaught. The crowd had grown, and there were now over a hundred masks of every kind bobbing and weaving out on the dance floor, anxiously awaiting the next tune. Quite a few of them were Hunts School competitors, including all of the Omada.

Mission partially accomplished, he thought. They've all forgotten the earlier bad mojo and they're ready for an excuse to be crazy-ass teenagers. Now let's seal the deal. He looked at Janis and gave her the signal for slow and smooth. Jimi stepped backwards while she took his place down front, the chaotically flashing lights stilled, and this time the spotlight was a steady light-hued blue. A perfect match to the lights high in the trees of the Enchanted Forest.

A capella, Janis hummed a few bars, as she began sensuously swaying, her body an erotic metronome, setting the beat. Then came the words. Slowly, distinctly, each word a compelling invitation for the attendees to take the hand of their significant other, drape their heads on each other shoulders, and totally surrender to the intoxicating idealism of young love. They all knew where they were headed after the third word of the song. Everyone on the dance floor was totally caught up, swaying when Janis swayed, pausing expectantly when she paused—waiting for what they knew was coming next.

"I'm—so—tired—of—being—alone..."

The rest of the band joined in, softly harmonizing while Janis threw down what Tal believed was one of the finest covers of the Reverend Al Green's iconic classic he'd ever heard.

As the final chords were playing out, Tal slowly walked his way over to Elton, and whispered in his ear, "Let's not let them off the hook, yet. You're up. Bounce straight into 'I'll Make Love To You." Old School didn't even give their audience a chance to untwine themselves before Elton hit the piano chords for the Boyz 2 Men hit. Tal watched as the dance floor grew even more crowded, and the bodies shifted from heads on shoulders to forehead softly tilted into forehead. This time the teenagers wanted to look into their dates' angst-filled eyes and say whatever it was their bodies felt needed saying.

CHAPTER NINETY-SIX

"They're wonderful," Elle thought, as she, Holiman, and everyone else on the dance floor clapped enthusiastically. She had been keeping an eyeball on the crowd's enthusiasm level, which just shot up another couple of notches as the band announced they were closing their first set with another Bon Jovi tune, "(You Want To) Make A Memory."

I've seen legit big time rock bands that have one or two folks who can sing but never a group where every member could front their own band. Well, except maybe the Tal look-alike bass player, who's been skulking in the shadows at the back of the stage. If it was Tal, it would be impossible for him to not sing. Unless he was trying to be incognito. Get a grip Elle, you saw that guy walk in with the Little Rock group. Speaking of getting a grip, she thought, as she swatted Holiman's hand off her ass, I'm going to have to tell this boy I've decided he's been relegated to arm candy status for the evening.

CHAPTER NINETY-SEVEN

After they finished their first set, Old School took a fifteen-minute break. There was a passel of students who met them as they came down from the stage. They began patting them on the back, high-fiving them, drunkenly trying to make out with a couple of members of the group. Tal's bandmates were having the time of their lives. It really was a once in a lifetime experience for people who before tonight had only met one human and didn't know squat about electricity. He even had to show Jimi and Jethro where the light switch was in the bathroom so they could see the urinals. They flipped it on and off about twenty times, erupting into laughter every time. They bailed about the time Principal Chiron came in and headed toward a stall.

Just a quick break though, Tal told himself, after he accepted congratulations from Borras and the rest of the Omada. Even Notos mumbled something that sounded vaguely complimentary. Well, at least it didn't sound like negative mumbling. Safest place for me now is on the stage, way in the background. He'd seen Emet signaling him a couple of times. With the crush of attention on Old School there simply wasn't going to be an opportunity to get with him until after they'd finished playing. Tal was hoping there would be a few minutes before they loaded up to go back to Hunts School when he could sneak away and get caught up with Emet. Find out where he was living. What he planned to do. Whether he had any updates on Mom and Pell and the twins. He wanted to tell Emet what he'd decided about the two of them moving forward. Most importantly, however, they needed to reestablish a reliable communication methodology.

Back on the stage they launched into their second set. Ella got to show her beautiful soprano and percussion chops on a version of Paramore's "Still Into You." Jethro took his turn covering Rascal Flatt's "Nothing Like This." The entire gym was seriously all up in their feels when Jimi sang, "Love's Divine," backed only by Elton on keyboards and Ella providing the background percussion thunder and softly holding the beat for them with her snares.

Everywhere Tal looked there was laughter and enjoyment. Even the Hunts School adults were foot-tapping. The Archon and Queen Aine stunned the crowd with the most gorgeous waltz to Pixie Lott's "Cry Me Out." Everyone else cleared the dance floor to watch two people, clearly crazy about each other, glide across the room. Together they moved as one. Tal took that opportunity to surreptitiously catch Väst's eye and was rewarded with a large smile from underneath her mask. Elle frequently drifted through his range of vision. Gobsmacking beautiful, almost six feet of grace in motion, whether she was dancing or performing some official committee duty. With that dipshit Holiman Richards constantly nipping at her heel. Be happy for her, Tal, he told himself numerous times. He had to do it numerous times because his altruistic response only lasted a few seconds.

CHAPTER NINETY-EIGHT

Tal decided it was a good thing he and the rest of Old School had put in so much practice time. Almost three hours of playing tunes, with only limited breaks, is a shitton of songs. They'd made it though. The last echoes were fading from their U2-inspired version of "Everlasting Love," when he looked up at the wall clock. Ten minutes until the midnight unmasking. Time for us to clear off the stage so I'll be on the bus by the time the Nemeton students start ditching their masks. No way in hell I need to be taking my mask off in this gym.

The whole episode kind of smacks of Cinderella and the clock striking twelve. Well, sort of. Call it what you want, this was an acceptable fairy tale ending to what could have been a horror story evening. "Ask not for whom the bell tolls," Tal paraphrased, as he lifted the guitar strap up and over his neck, and began walking to place it in its stand next to the stage right prop table.

"It tolls not for me," he finished. Not tonight anyway. Thank Amarantos. Now I have to figure out how to meet with Emet for a few minutes without being missed. Bathroom while everyone is still masked seems to be the best option. He looked up to try to locate the golem. Emet had wisely been ghosting through the Enchanted Forest most of the night, maintaining a safe distance from Elle. As Tal looked up, Emet was actually the first person to catch his attention. He was standing half hidden by a tree bough and wildly gesticulating, both arms windmilling. With Emet's mask blocking his face, Tal really couldn't get a feel for what was up. Emet must have realized that because he changed his arm motion, and began making a stabbing movement with his left index finger back over Tal's right shoulder.

As Tal was turning to look, he heard it. A single guitar chord. The crowd noise dropped to a hush as its reverberations caromed around the gym. The U2 song was our encore for that set. That's what we've always rehearsed as the clincher. And the time is ticking until the unmasking. I've got to get out of here.

Tal felt an ice-water cold shiver clutch his spine as the ripples of the first chord faded and a second chord sounded. This time the ice seemed to freeze solid as it forced its way up his spine and into his brain. Tal looked at the students standing right up front. Hell, half of them looked like they were holding their breath. Anticipating, anticipating…Tal's breath caught in his throat, waiting…praying…waiting.

The frozen mass exploded through his brain as he heard Jimi strum the third chord. When he looked across the stage, Jimi was smiling and beckoning him to step over and pick his guitar back up to join in on reprising the intro. NO, NO, NO, Tal was screaming to himself. The pumpkin is only a carriage until the last stroke of midnight. That's always the deal, those are mandatory fairy tale rules. I have six minutes to meet with Emet and successfully make my get away.

It was then that Tal saw her. Partially blocked by Jimi until she had taken a couple of steps backwards. Smiling underneath her mask, Tal saw the ridiculously gorgeous vision that was Väst. She'd obviously requested the song. Everyone else in his band kind of knew the notes, Tal had shown them the chords a few times.

Väst knew Tal would have to sing this song because she'd made him promise to never sing it to anyone else but her. Which is what she wanted him to do tonight, to sing it to her with all of the other people as witnesses.

The song was Howie Day's "Collide." It was their song. She'd asked him to sing it to her, and with her, often. What Väst didn't know was that it was also he and Elle's song and that he and Elle had also sung it together. Many, many times.

Holy crap! I was home free and now being a playa is about to get my ass killed, Tal thought, as he walked over and took hold of the guitar strap on the extra six-string on his side of the stage.

CHAPTER NINETY-NINE

Thank goodness Emet was there to help him. Realizing this was their final tune, the techs had pulled out all of the stops, which meant there was a spotlight trained on each member of Old School. Net result for Tal was that he could only see about a foot in front of the edge of the stage. Keeping one eye on Väst's location he looked at an angle, away from the lights, until he saw Emet. Emet knew what Tal needed to know—where the hell Elle was. Emet gestured off to his left. Tal saw her, head and shoulders taller than most of the ladies. She had been standing in the back of the gym over on Jimi's side of the stage. She was now walking purposely toward the stage. Which meant toward Väst.

Jimi wagged his guitar neck up and down, beckoning to Tal to hit the next note. Ella began tapping her drumsticks together over her head, pounding out a rhythm for the audience to pick up with their clapping. Which they did, a syncopated demand that Tal perform the song.

We'll knock out one quick rendition, Tal told himself. I'll just do this and get out of here still relatively unscathed. No one from Earth Realm knows it's me. No one on Earth Realm but Elle has ever heard me sing it so they won't know it's me. No one will ever know I was here. While the audience is wondering whether we'll do yet another encore I'll sneak off the back of the stage and meet Emet. He motioned for Emet to come around to the back and got a thumbs up in response.

Tal took a deep breath, slung the guitar over his shoulder, and walked up to the microphone center stage. When he was in place, Jimi began again. This time, Tal joined in. The crowd had now gathered close around the stage, expectant. Elle was about fifteen feet from him, but she also happened to be standing directly behind Väst.

CHAPTER ONE HUNDRED

Jimi motioned to Jethro to take up his part while he worked his way up front to Tal. "Sorry, mate," he shouted, over the crowd noise. "I know you said you didn't want to sing because of lady issues on Earth Realm but I thought, well, it was a specific request from a certain lady, that we all know that you…well, I felt pretty sure you would want to accommodate that individual for this one song…"

"It's not a problem," Tal replied, as he continued repeating chords in an elongated intro. The crowd was eating up the extra guitar play. Tal quickly glanced over to Elle and Väst, before repositioning himself on the stage where they were in a direct line visually, with Elle in the back. He saw his bandmates all relax into their usual roles as their leader bridged into the regular intro and began to sing.

CHAPTER ONE HUNDRED ONE

What is Tal doing, Emet wondered. He had it made, actually, we had it made. This evening was in the bank. Field trip completed. No one from Nemeton High any the wiser that Tal, or I, were here in violation of his suspension. Now he's let himself get roped into playing our song. Well, he and Elle's song. But she and I have done it a couple of dozen times together with me playing guitar and Elle on vocals, and she and Tal have worked it *a capella* while they've been together. She's going to know it's him.

Who was it that requested the song, he asked himself. Oh hell, who else would it be but Väst? Damn, I forgot. It's their song, too. Where is she? Shit, she's directly in front of Elle. Oh hell, now she's stepping toward the stage.

CHAPTER ONE HUNDRED TWO

Oh, this is much, much better, he decided. My instructions were to kill a random Munedan. I see now there is someone present who completes my mission…and more. I'll do what she wants and get a head start on my revenge. I'm going to make that son of a bitch pay. He's going to suffer like I've suffered. His pain begins tonight and I'm going to make sure it gets worse and worse until She finally lets me kill him. It's still not enough, but it will be fun to watch him suffer. Yes, much, much better, he thought, as he caught himself and put his hand down to his side. In his excitement he had been repeatedly tracing the scar on his face. That wouldn't do at all if someone noticed. There were Folk present who might see through his glamour if given an inroad. Oh, this is going to be good. She is going to reward me handsomely for my improvement to her plan.

CHAPTER ONE HUNDRED THREE

Angie is definitely going to get the win for this evening, Elle decided. Even with all of the early stress, it's been a fun night, and everyone seemed to have had a good time. Including the big city guests from Little Rock. Not the fun it could have been if Tal had been my date. Of course, he never asked me. Which is just as well, since he ended up dumping me. Which actually worked out well, I guess, since he almost got expelled, with one of his probation conditions being that he was exiled from any extracurricular events for the rest of the school year. I guess if I collate all of the events, it would have sucked much worse if he had asked me, then not dumped me, and then not almost gotten expelled because he still wouldn't be here with me and I would be dateless. Not that I blame him for stepping in to help Scooter against my dickhead brother and his posse. Actually, it was kind of, sort of, heroic. Except for the part where he dumped me. That was the most jackasserous action ever. So screw him.

"Everlasting Love" was obviously the band's encore as it was only a few minutes to midnight. As it concluded, Elle turned her back on the stage and started searching the crowd for Holiman. He'd lost interest and wandered off when he realized he wasn't getting any this evening. Probably for the better, she decided, since I have major operational cleanup duties.

Elle located Holiman at the same moment she heard a guitar twang. A second encore? She'd been told by Principal Chiron that the Little Rock group would be leaving right before the unmasking at midnight. Like they were going to turn into pumpkins or something.

The initial guitar strum was followed by two more chords. I know that sequence, her realization stopping her midstep. Her head whipped around, rising to look up toward the stage, as she began turning back to watch and listen.

Elle watched as the guy who'd taken on the role of lead singer most of the night looked across the stage expectantly at the bass guitar player. He hasn't sung a song all evening, she thought. Why now? And what kind of freaky coincidence is it that their second encore song is "Collide?"

Once the now former bass had picked up another guitar, the group started over. Elle watched his hands move across the frets, thumbing the strings. Then he opened his mouth and began singing...

Heat. She couldn't breathe for the heat. It was as if the pent up emotions that solar-flared to life sucked all of the oxygen out of the air around her. She tried to catch her breath and failed, her knees started to get all wobbly on her.

It can't be. He would be expelled if he got caught here tonight. All of his years of hard work, his scholarship dreams, all of it gone in the snap of Principal Davis's well-manicured but still tacky looking fingers. He might even face the possibility of criminal charges. He couldn't be that stupid. He couldn't. He wouldn't be that stupid even if he could be. Would he?

Elle walked back toward the stage as the entire audience became quiet and began to listen to that magnificent voice. It was Tal. She knew how his hands caressed a guitar from their many sessions in the band room. She knew his voice from their *a capella* duets walking home from the movies, or on the phone.

Shit! He's looking right at me. Even with our masks on, somehow, he knows it's me. He's singing our song to me, in front of hundreds of people. An act that could potentially result in him being a high school dropout, as well as a convicted felon. Oh, now that is fucking hot.

CHAPTER ONE HUNDRED FOUR

Väst smiled as a frisson of excitement washed over her. I knew he wouldn't be able to resist playing our song. Wow, just wow, she thought. Always before it was just us, in our room. Quint's voice, when he sings, it's like one of the ancient bards of royal-strength songmagyk from many Tyrnings past. The archives contained stories about mythological Folk whose voices when raised in song were so powerful the sound could raise great mountains and so intimate they could still the smallest ripples of a wind-battered sea. Songmagyk so beautiful it could actually remove the boundaries between one mind and another. In all of the thousands of known planes, the Folk haven't seen magyk like that for many generations. Yet here we are, on Earth Realm where magyk is prohibited, and the singer is Quint, a magykless Child of the Dust.

Our song. Which I made him promise to sing only for me. Last term when I was snared tightly by the geas and he was bound by the compulsionmagyk. Neither of us with consent freely given, yet now, if I could choose...now, that I can choose...

Väst listened to a couple more lines, enthralled as were all of the women present, and even some of the guys. He's singing it differently tonight, she thought. It must be because there are others present that he's singing it tonight with more feeling than he ever did before. I guess the good news is this means the compulsion hasn't fully dissolved, she thought with a sigh.

Quint obviously knew where she was. Even with his mask on she could tell from the angle of his body, the smile on his face, even the tilt of his head that he was singing it directly to her, only for her, as if she were the only person in the room...

EXCEPT HE WASN'T SINGING TO HER! Väst's breath was sucked from her lungs and her knees got faintish on her. HE'S SINGING OUR SONG TO SOMEONE ELSE! Myriad thoughts began whirring, slicing through each other. Before one could be completed it was replaced by the next. And then the next. I'm furious. No, I'm wounded. I was wrong, she concluded, I must be almost completely healed of the geas. Why couldn't I have left well enough alone? Wait a minute, she thought, as her brain kept up its endless supply of new comments. That two-timing son of a bitch has a girlfriend at Nemeton High? How can that be? He doesn't even go to school here, he's at Hunts School every day. Who is she? Where is she? That's easy, look at his line of sight. It's got to be the tall drink of water now standing only a couple of feet behind me. It's the one who wears green even better than me, and I'm the...damn, even without heels she qualifies as statuesque. Beautiful? How would I know the answer to that? Everyone has these damn masks on. Of course she's beautiful. Prettier than me? Stupid masks, I can't even tell how pretty she is...

STOP, she screamed to herself. Just stop. Fine, Väst, you've screwed up and fallen in love with a mortal. Hate to tell you but your broken heart doesn't rank high on the concern list right now. Tears. Breakdown. All of those things, you're just going to have to stuff those down deep inside until later. You know there's someone from the evil one here watching. They have to be. If they realize Quint is practically making love to someone else from the stage, they'll realize something has gone wrong with their spell on me. Something has to be done. Immediately—as in right now, Väst.

494

GO! Väst stepped sideways around the closely entwined couple right in front of her, took four quick strides to the side of the stage, hiked her ball gown so she could lift her leg, grabbed a railing, and stepped up on the stage. Before anyone could think about reacting, she walked in front of an unoccupied stage left microphone, halfway across the stage from Quint. And began singing her part in their duet.

CHAPTER ONE HUNDRED FIVE

Elle was singing her part of "Collide" softly in tandem with Tal when some Little Rock girl a few feet in front of her hiked up her dress, jumped on stage, and began singing with him. My part, Elle realized. She's singing my part. Beautifully, too. I've put up with a lot of shit the last few months but oh, hell no, Elle told herself as she took off toward the stage. Some slut from Little Rock is not gonna walk in here and steal my almost-but-not-quite-well-he-actually-dumped-me boyfriend. And sing our special song with him. OH, HELL, NO!

CHAPTER ONE HUNDRED SIX

Emet starting mentally scrolling his options the moment he saw Väst get on stage. My fault, what's about to happen is all my fault. I picked the song and played it for Elle. I helped make it their special song. When he saw Elle also headed for the stage, he kicked his option review process into high gear. The same answer kept repeating—follow rule number one. He and Tal had had quite a few close calls over the last few months, but by remembering how important rule one was there hadn't been any unexplainable situation. Although it ran counter to what he wanted to do, Emet knew that he and Tal simply could not be seen in the same place at the same time. The masks are getting ready to come off, and I can't compound whatever is about to take place by violating rule one, he decided, as he moved quietly toward the back wall of the gym.

CHAPTER ONE HUNDRED SEVEN

There was simply too much information for Tal's brain to sequence it into a video narrative, so it simply relayed the images as discrete photos—Väst singing...Elle reacting and heading directly toward him...the rest of the Omada as they stopped dancing when they sensed something was wrong with their teammate...Emet doing the smart thing and sliding backward, away from the potential friction.

Elle was almost to the stage now. He couldn't let her get up here and unmask him, or even worse get into it with Väst, there was no telling what that psycho Nord might do to her. Tal finally gave up trying to think it through. Okay, Panic, I'm all yours, he thought, as he abruptly stopped singing, laid the guitar down on the stage, and leapt off the stage right toward Elle.

CHAPTER ONE HUNDRED EIGHT

During the brief time Tal was airborne, the lights flickered several times—as if there were a transformer issue—then they went out completely. Well, except for the emergency floods in the gym which thrummed to life, creating eerie fluorescent shadows over the blue and white paints of the Enchanted Forest. With the spot having been in Tal's face, the light's absence now was as if someone had dropped a bag over his head.

Landing awkwardly, Tal stumbled, with his momentum carrying him into what had to be Elle. He finally stopped himself and steadied her at the same time. Her dress felt wet. Had she been crying?

"Elle, Elle, it's me. T…" He was stopped midsentence. Damn Hunts School geas, I can't say my psuche name here. "Elle? Elle?" There was no response. What's up with the damn lights anyway, Tal wondered.

Suddenly there was a warm fetid breath blowing purposefully across the back of his neck. Tal instinctively jerked away, pulling Elle closer, as he heard a voice whisper, pitched so low there was no possibility anyone would hear but him. "Darkness rules! Now it's your turn, you meddling, pisspot Munedan. Welcome to a small taste of the shit-eating hell I've been drug through for centuries. All of it, every last thing because of you, you bastard!"

I know that voice, Tal thought. Not the distorted, crazed, maniacal version of it but I do know that voice. Distracted, he almost didn't realize Elle was collapsing to the floor. Tal quickly lowered himself to support her in a controlled fall.

Suddenly the lights blazed to nova. Tal's pupils shriveled, then quickly began adjusting. Elle was lying in his lap, her hair falling across his thighs. Her mask was still perfectly in place. As Tal's eyes finally adjusted, it looked almost as if Elle was a porcelain live-action Sleeping Beauty, asleep in his arms. Waiting on Prince Charming to awaken her with a kiss. Except her throat had been slashed its entire width and the wetness Tal felt was her arterial blood spurting all over both of them.

CHAPTER ONE HUNDRED NINE

"HELP HER! PLEASE SAVE HER!" As Tal ripped his mask off, he screamed louder than he'd ever screamed in his life. He didn't move for fear it would accelerate Elle's blood loss. He wanted to scream for his teammates, but the geas prevented him from calling them by their names. Got to be a smart way around it. Turn the cube, Tal, turn it. That's it. I can't say their individual names. But how about… "Omada! Omada, to me!"

His yelling drew all of the attention in the room to him. To him, without his mask on. "Murderer!" he heard someone yell. "That Smith kid killed Elle," from someone else. "Everyone knows there's bad blood between their families, but killing a girl?" another chimed in. Tal felt the entire crowd starting to close around him.

Suddenly he saw Anatolia flying through the air. Well, not exactly. Borras had swept her up and with her in his arms had bounded over at least ten people to get next to Tal. Ana immediately laid her hands on Elle. Multi-colored tongues of fire erupted from the largest fire opal in her necklace, bathing Elle's entire body in a constantly morphing pastel rainbow.

Dysi was confounding the people closest to him by rapidly appearing and disappearing. Kind of like deploying the flares and chaff used by aircraft anti-missile defenses. Dysi would appear, grab a coattail, slap someone's face, or push someone over backwards. It worked to distract some of the mob from Tal—at least for a few moments. Tal watched as Notos strode right in front of him, to a spot Dysi had cleared. A hazy charcoal nimbus emanated from Notos. Anyone who got within two feet of Tal crumpled in a heap, knocked out by whatever Notos's magyk was.

They're having to use their magyk, Tal thought. Damn it, now everyone is going to know they've got their juice on Earth plane. They did it to try to help me. To try to save Elle.

ELLE!

The teachers and chaperones from both schools were now converging on Tal and Elle. He saw one of the Nemeton High professors with his phone out, obviously calling 911. The HuntsMistress was the first of the Hunts School crew to reach them. "You," she said pointing at Tal. "What have you done?" Looking to the rest of the Omada, she added, "How in the Five-Hells do any of you students have magyk on Earth Realm?"

Principal Chiron came running from wherever he'd been. "Lilith, all of that can wait for later. Right now we need to assist the Archon in tying up the loose ends of this emergency."

Then there was a blinding flash. For a second, Tal thought the lights had gone out again but then realized the flash had been so bright they were all momentarily blinded. He squeezed his eyes closed and when he opened them Alberich was standing before him. No longer glamoured as a mortal he was resplendent in his robes of office, holding his Archon's scepter. He quickly scanned the room, before speaking an unknown word to his scepter, which promptly lengthened until it was a staff. He banged the scepter/staff once on the floor. The whole room thrummed as the Archon commanded, "For this place, until I command otherwise, all mortals, excepting only Quint of Omada, shall be subject to Oblivion Plane Time."

Tal felt a wave of invisible energy flow outward from Alberich. As he looked around the room every human, except him, stopped moving. It didn't even appear they were breathing. The blood flowing from Elle's torn throat stopped in its place. It didn't congeal, it simply stopped flowing from her body.

ELLE!

CHAPTER ONE HUNDRED TEN

Borras was talking to Anatolia but their voices seemed garbled to Tal, like they were speaking pig latin. Underwater. Like they were speaking pig latin underwater. In all probability you're experiencing a dissociative shock reaction so that your mind may retain some measure of functioning capacity during the present overwhelming emotional crisis, Tal told himself. Shut the fuck up, he then also told himself.

"Can you save her?" Borras asked Anatolia, for what must have been the third time.

Anatolia kept her hands pressed firmly against the sides of Elle's head, the large opal in her necklace continuing to erupt in wave after wave of different colored flames. Ana's mask had come off while Borras was carrying her. She looked up at Borras, mascara running down both her cheeks and shook her head. "It's not just the blood loss, there is blackmagyk involved. It is far beyond my power," she replied, as she turned back to continue her efforts.

"Maybe, the Archon can…" Borras inquired looking up at Alberich.

"He is prohibited," Principal Chiron said quickly. "We are on a sanctioned field trip and any action on his part might have an unforeseen effect on the Hunts standings."

"She is not part of the Hunts," Borras argued.

"But your Fifth is," Ms. Empousa snapped back at him.

"Desist!" the Archon commanded, and Principal Chiron and the HuntsMistress promptly obeyed. Alberich's scepter had returned to its normal size and he passed it slowly, first over Anatolia, and then over Elle. "You may stop now. The mortal has left this plane. She is with the UnFading Spirit now." Anatolia broke into tears. The Archon reached down and placed his hand on her shoulder. "It is not your failure, Omada Fourth. A great evil has visited this place tonight. Even if I had not been prohibited by the Rules, I would have been unable to save the Dust Child. Someone here tonight has wielded a weapon of power, one that has been thrice-blooded."

The only thing Tal understood from all of the talking was that Elle was dead. But that was completely unacceptable. "NO," Tal screamed, putting his blood soaked hands over his ears to deny their words. "No, no, no. Y'all are magyk. You people have magyk. You're the Archon of the whole flipping universe," Tal said, his words finally dissolving into tears. Anatolia moved away as Tal fell forward over Elle's inert form. "You're magyk," he said, crying and pleading to Alberich. "Magyk."

The Archon leaned over to speak ever so softly to Tal. "I am sorry Quint of Omada. Magyk cannot turn back death."

I know the owner of the foul voice that killed her, Tal thought randomly. That terrible voice that whispered vengeance in my ear, but right now I can't get the resources online to ferret out any other details. Still overwhelmed, his mind kept trying to snap his thoughts back into order, only to have grief throw them to the four winds. Again, and again.

Tal happened to glance toward the far corner of the room. Even though most everyone had unmasked by now, Emet had had the presence of mind to keep his on. Emet mimed as if he were going to take his mask off and took a step to come over to assist Tal. Why isn't Emet moving in slow-time, Tal wondered. C'mon smart guy, get your head out of your ass. He's a magykal being. Everyone now knows about Omada's magyk working on

Earth plane, but they don't know about Emet. Tal gave Emet an almost imperceptible shake of his head. Emet, his mask still on, froze in acknowledgment, returning to acting as if he were one of the immobilized humans.

Tal's tears were free-falling now, mixing with the darkening red of Elle's blood stained green gown. He looked up at Alberich. "What just happened? Did you, did you just stop time?"

Tal could tell from the Archon's face that in another place and at another time the answer to that question would have included a large smile. "No mortal, Time itself belongs to Amarantos. The power to stop or turn back Time is beyond even the power of Chronos. We know of a Realm named Oblivion, where time moves ten thousand times slower than Earth Plane Time. One second there is almost three hours on this plane. I have temporarily encased this gym in a bubble of Oblivion Plane Time. Even with all of the power given me as Archon, I cannot hold the bubble for more than a few minutes. With that, he looked to Principal Chiron. "Aine will help you police the area. Be thorough, but be quick." Chiron nodded and moved away. "HuntsMistress," Alberich said addressing Ms. Empousa. "Get all of the other teams in that corner. All magykal beings will be leaving as soon as I get the all clear from Chiron." When he saw her look toward the Omada in their defensive positions around Tal, he added, "Leave Omada to me. Now, go. Do as I say."

As Tal watched he saw Principal Chiron and the other administrative staff carefully orchestrate a policing of the entire gym area, making sure any and all purses, coats, shoes, masks and other pieces of personal belonging that belonged to Hunts School students were picked up and secured. As ordered, the other five Finalist teams were all gathered in a tight knot around the HuntsMistress.

Alberich now addressed Borras. "Omada Prime Direction, do I understand correctly that because the mortal is on your team that the Omada are not limited by my Bane on Earth Realm?"

Borras nodded in response. "Not while we accompany our Fifth, Archon."

The Archon pondered a moment. "If the Rules have allowed it, then there is clearly no violation of the Hunts Rules." He looked back down at Tal. "Quint?" Tal didn't respond, his head deeply buried against Elle's neck and chest. "Quint of the Omada. I am the Archon and I command that you heed me."

Tal looked up.

"There is much to be done. Complications you cannot imagine are arising every second we delay in this place. I am going to use my magyk to transport all magykal beings back to Hunts School. I will also remove from every mortal's mind any remembrance that anyone other than the mortals were here this evening. Their minds will fill in the gaps of what they don't remember, which means that you are going to have to pay the pryce on two planes for the evil events of this evening. Do you understand?"

Tal nodded that he understood, although he really didn't. And frankly, he didn't care that he didn't.

"There are things that need to be done and meetings that need to take place. I must summon the Areopagus immediately if there is any hope of averting the inevitable demand for a bloodpryce."

Even in his stunned state Tal could tell the Archon looked sad as he made the last statement.

Borras spoke up. "Archon, Omada request permission to remain and assist our Fifth Direction."

"Permission denied," the Archon replied curtly. "It would prevent full implementation of my magyk removing us from the mortal's memories. Omada is to join the rest of the party," he said, abruptly waving them off to join the rest of the Finalists. None of the other four wanted to leave Tal but they had no choice. After they walked away, the Archon bent down on one knee and gently cupped his hand under Tal's chin. "Listen to me, Dust Child. The humans will remain as they are for ten minutes after all magykal beings have departed. Say or do what you must on the Earth Plane, then make your way to Sol's gateway. Terrible events have been set in motion at Hunts School that even I as Archon may be powerless to prevent." Tal nodded blankly. "Quint! Quint, no matter how dark your path may seem, remember you must always choose to Seek the Center. Choose love. Always."

The Archon stood to his full height and inhaled deeply. His scepter went supernova once more. As Tal squeezed his eyes closed to give them time to adjust, he tried to get his rational thought process reengaged. Emet, he finally remembered. I'm not all alone anymore, he'll be able to tell me what I should do. Tal opened his eyes. When they finally adjusted, he looked over to Emet to call him over.

Emet was gone, too.

CHAPTER ONE HUNDRED ELEVEN

Damn it, Tal thought. Of course, Emet's gone. He's a magykal construct. They probably didn't know he'd be along for the ride, but he's been transported to Hunts School with everyone else. Borras will look after him.

Tal gently moved Elle off of his lap, carefully laying her on the floor. Gently placing her mask beside her, he leaned over and kissed her lightly on the lips. "I'm sorry, Elle. I am so, so very sorry to have caused this." He stopped there, not knowing what else to say, not able to articulate any more words at that moment.

He slowly stood and looked to the wall clock to see how much time had elapsed. It registered no time had elapsed, not even a second. Of course, stupid, it's within the gym so it's on Oblivion Plane Time. How much time do I have left? Probably no more than five minutes.

He looked down at Elle. I don't want to leave her, but if I stay I'll be arrested. With everyone's memory being wiped of the Folk visit, I'd say the odds are pretty good I'd end up convicted of murder. Regardless of the long term result, if they catch me they'll hold me without bond until my trial. Which means I won't be at the Imbolc Feast tomorrow morning. Which means the Omada will lose the competition tomorrow. Which means, he realized, as anger seized him, I would never get the chance to avenge Elle against whoever did this to her.

Mom and Pell! I've got to go see them, explain what happened here tonight, before I head back to the Gas Station. Think, Tal. That type of reflexive action is going to get you caught. You have four minutes, at the most, until cellphones and police radios will be in full "hunt down the dangerous fugitive named Tal" mode. A search may already be under way in real time outside of the gym. You're going to have a hard enough time making it out of town and back to the portal. You can't even make it to your house in four minutes and you know it won't take law enforcement but a short period of time to get a trace set up on their home phone and your cellphone.

Tal jumped at the sound of the gym doors splintering inward. He looked up and saw that a police issue metal battering ram had been used to get the doors open. There was a fully geared up S.W.A.T. team, complete with vests and semi-automatic weapons at the threshold.

As soon as the leader jumped through the doorway he became frozen in mid-air. Like he was caught in some type of time syrup. The remaining members of his unit were standing outside the door, still in real time, chattering to each other and communicating over their radios. As Tal looked he could see the confusion on their faces as they looked at their leader hanging suspended two feet above the gym floor. The consensus must have been for the entire group to go ahead and charge the gym. Which they did. The end result being the prompt formation of the most realistic first responder sculpture ever created.

That settles that, Tal thought. My first goal has to be to get off of Earth plane proper. My cellphone is hidden outside of the Ladies' Room. I'll call Mom and Pell from there. Even if they trace it, they won't be able to follow me through the portal.

That's as good a plan as I can make. Emet is already at Hunts School, he can help me decide what to do next when I finally make it back there. Tal heard more sirens screaming only several blocks away. He took one last look down at Elle, wiped the last of the tears from his face with the back of his hand, and headed toward the back door.

CHAPTER CENTUM DUODECIM

Emet found himself standing in the dark, about halfway across Grass Grow. He was facing the side of Fountain Flow where he could see Mokosh's face. The fountain and the front of the Hunts School main building were brightly illuminated with their nighttime lighting. The school and fountain structures were every bit as magnificent as Tal had described them. Mokosh was perhaps even more regal looking than he'd imagined.

The Hunts School staff and students were arranged in a complete circle around the base of the fountain. The Finalists and their dates were standing grouped by teams, and the members of Old School were clumped together. Principal Chiron and the HuntsMistress were walking around the fountain perimeter making sure everyone was accounted for.

They're all clustered together now because the Archon had them stand together at Nemeton High, Emet realized. I'm about as far away from them now as I was at the gymnasium. Magyk must follow some electrical energy based physical laws. The Omada happened to be facing him. He waved broadly at Borras to get his attention. The moment Borras saw him he looked puzzled. He thinks I'm Tal, Emet realized. Emet placed his hand in front of his mouth. Borras expressed his understanding with a small nod, then stuck his hand in front of himself, palm downward and slowly, so as to not attract attention, lowered his hand a few inches to the ground.

Emet got the message and dropped himself flat on the grass. Even though the grass was short-cropped he was far enough from the lit areas that you might not see him even if you were looking for him.

Come on, Emet, you should have been ahead of the curve on that. To the best of our knowledge, no one at Hunts School except Omada knows I exist, and we need to keep that in our pocket for as long as possible. He waited and watched. The front doors were already closed for the evening so the entire group headed around the right side of the main building. The students were headed toward the dormitories, the staff to their apartments.

He watched as Borras slow-walked the Omada until they were about fifteen feet behind everyone else. He saw Borras stick his right hand behind his back, giving him the "come on" signal. Emet ran, staying in a crouch, and timed his arrival so that everyone else had rounded the building corner before he caught up with the Omada.

"Emet, I presume," the giant Prime whispered.

Emet nodded his head.

"It's nice to make your acquaintance. Unexpected but nice. Stay behind me, I should be able to block you from the view of the other teams. When we get to the boy's dormitory hang to the side until Notos and I can get you a clear path to my room. You'll be safe once we're there and we can debrief you then."

Emet nodded once more and tucked in close behind Borras.

CHAPTER ONE HUNDRED THIRTEEN

Tal's best guesstimate was that it must have been around four in the morning when he finally reached the Gas Station. He wasn't even sure what was keeping him on his feet at this point. It had been eight or ten hours since he'd had anything to eat or drink. Coming from Hunts School he'd had no wallet or money, although it wasn't like he could have stopped anywhere and bought anything. He'd seen plenty of signs on the highway that there was a full-scale manhunt in progress. It had taken him the extra couple of hours because he hadn't even been able to walk on the cleared highway right of way. After several police cars had driven by, Tal had decided he needed to climb through the brush and ditches by the side of the road.

He was filthy, scratched all to hell, cold, and wet. The worst migraine in the history of mankind was currently in residence in his skull and it felt like the Nyx brand was stabbing him in the ass every time his heart beat. Elle is dead and I'm bitching about a lousy headache and a sore ass. Get your head in the game, Smith.

During the entire trek to the station he'd reviewed his tenure at Hunts School, most specifically as it related to the use of Aurora's ring. Aurora told me I would need it four times but I only had three wishes and to choose well because it would cost me someone dear. I didn't listen, and it did. I could have killed Baba Yaga with Fragarach. I mean she asked me to. If I had, I would still have had one wish left. I could have saved Elle. But no, I had to act like I was some kind of fucking hero and try to save the wytch's soul too. Idiot. You're not a hero, Taliesin Smith. You're a run of the mill idiot.

Okay, you're here now. Get your thoughts in order. Priority one—check in with Mom and Pell. Tal retrieved his backpack from under the azalea bush and rummaged around in it until he found the phone. He turned it on and found that it had plenty of juice because it was hooked up to the extra battery. Emet. Bless that emotionless simulacrum golem of mine. Tal, remind yourself to give that boy an extra big hug when you see him. He checked the oldest messages first. They were from Emet. Every bit of the information on the texts was old news now.

Next he turned to the part he was dreading—the voice mails and texts from his Mom. He made himself listen to every one of the messages, to read every one of the texts. It was the least he could do. Damn, I thought I was beat down before. His poor mother was absolutely beside herself. Her messages alternated between crying hysterically, to trying to be angry with him, to Pell finally having to take the phone away from her. He would then ask Tal to please check in with them, and then he would tell him that they loved him. Add another huge bullet point to his list of sins. He was killing both of them. He thought about crying some more and realized he was too dried out, physically and emotionally, from Elle's death.

He did the two most rational things he could think of doing. First, he texted his Mom. He told her he was okay, in a safe place, and that he had not killed Elle. He'd first typed that he was innocent but he wasn't really sure that was a true statement. Not anymore. He told them that he was working on gathering proof of his innocence, and that he would contact them soon. Both lies, Tal. They're both lies. There's no way to prove you're innocent. And regardless of whether the Omada makes the third term cut, you're not going to be able to go home for a long, long time. Second, he opened up his phone and removed the battery. He wasn't sure if he was ever going to come back through the Gas Station Crossing again but if he did he didn't want there to be a dragnet waiting on him. He placed everything back in his backpack, shoved it as far as possible under the branches of the azalea bush, and covered it with leaves.

Okay, that's done. Now, through the bathroom and then it's a short walk across Grass Grow to my own room. Where food, water, a long, hot shower, and my bed await me. He opened the bathroom door, flipped the light switch on, and stepped through the threshold.

CHAPTER CENTUM QUATTUORDECIM

Notos had served as lookout to help Emet transition unnoticed from outside the dormitory to Borras's rooms. Once that was accomplished, Borras asked his Second Prime to go let Anatolia and Dysi know the golem was safe, that no one needed to mention the subject in public, and that they would meet at the secure team room at eight in the morning. That would give them plenty of time to share information before the feast. Hopefully, Tal would have evaded capture and made his way back to Hunts School by then. The feast didn't begin until noon, so that left them plenty of leeway timewise to address any unexpected twists.

After that Borras fixed a meat and cheese board for he and Emet. Emet inhaled more than his fair share of the food along with about half a gallon of water. It took Borras a few minutes trying to communicate effectively with Emet before he realized he needed to do most of the talking and that any questions he asked of Emet should call for yes or no responses. He got Emet a pen and paper, which helped but Emet found himself severely limited without his electronic communication devices.

Borras gave Emet all of the details of the last Journey and Tal's interaction with Baba Yaga. He then filled Emet in on the events at the dance prior to Emet's arrival. Emet wrote questions

525

as Borras delivered his information, and Borras answered them for the golem. The process was a little more laborious when it came to Emet providing information that Borras needed to know. By the time they'd worked their way through Borras's questions, Emet had been able to inform him about Tal and Elle's relationship and all of the activities of her brother Barton and his two buddies.

They had just begun brainstorming ways as to how Emet could sleuth out information that might help Tal with any criminal charges on Earth plane proper, when there was a knock at Borras's entryway door.

"It's after three in the morning, this can't be good," Borras remarked. He then gave Emet the signal for quiet before mouthing the words, "Go to the bedroom closet and hang there until I see what's up." Emet nodded and did as he was told.

About five minutes he heard Borras say, "All clear." When Emet walked back into the sitting area he saw the giant Omada Prime sunk into a chair, his head in his hands.

"It's bad. It's really bad," he said, looking over at Emet. "That was an emissary from the Ruling Council. They have convened a special meeting of the Areopagus. It is to take place at nine o'clock this morning, before the Imbolc Feast. An anonymous complaint has been lodged against Quint for a bloodpryce violation of the Hunts Rules." When he saw Emet's questioning look, he continued. "If convicted of a bloodpryce violation there is only one punishment—immediate and eternal incarceration in Five-Hells Realm."

Emet mouthed his response. 'Oh, shit!'

"Exactly. I've been ordered to report immediately to Fountain Flow. Quint is to be apprehended as soon as he steps on the Hunts School campus. As Omada Prime they're going to give me ten minutes with Quint. After that he will be sequestered until his trial." Borras stood, wearily. "Under no circumstances are you to open the door for anyone. I'll be back in time to take you to our team meeting and we will figure it out from there. You might as well use my bed to grab some shuteye for a couple of hours."

Emet was so shaken, he couldn't do anything but pace around Borras's suite for about fifteen minutes after the Omada Prime left. Fretting isn't doing Tal any good, he finally told himself. Do something useful, even if it's only getting some sleep so that you'll be clearheaded for what's about to go down. He took his shoes off, walked into the bedroom, and found that he had to leap up in the air to get on top of the mattress.

First, he told himself, go over your notes on the information Borras gave you. Emet found that Borras's pillows were oversized as well so he only had to place one behind him to comfortably prop himself up for reading. Emet could feel his subconscious slowly but surely turning the Rubik's cube of information. There was some correlation between the timing of Tal's final moments with the wytch and Emet's same time events on Earth plane proper. But, what? He read through his notes a couple of times and nothing leapt to mind. Oh well, let your subconscious mind do it's thing while you focus on something else.

He looked over at Borras's nightstand. There were a couple of textbooks. As he picked one up he realized the larger tomes were laying on top of a much smaller book. He freed it from its subordinate position and took a look. Well, well, well. He was holding a dog-eared, much used, literally falling off the binding, illustrated version of the sixty-ninth edition of the *Official Rules of the Tyrning Hunts*. He carefully picked the book up and turned to the Introduction.

CHAPTER CENTUM QUINDECIM

Ooof!

Tal had stepped out of the Ladies' Room and straight into a half-naked wall of man-flesh. What the hell, he thought, as he picked himself up off the grass. What are the sentries doing all the way out here? They've never left the front doors before. Wait a minute, they look exactly the same but these aren't the same six humongosoids. All of the Folk from that plane look the same, remember? Hello? he responded to himself. Been kind of a busy night. A busy, terrible, shitty night. I just want to touch base with Emet, with my teammates, take a shower, and crawl into bed where I can cry some more.

The giants silently took up positions in a row of three on each side. The rear left one motioned for Tal to begin walking toward the main building. This isn't good, Tal realized. Not at all. They aren't an honor guard, I'm under arrest. What was it the Archon said to me?

The procession marched swiftly across the dew-wet grass of Grass Grow. As they approached Fountain Flow, Tal saw a familiar figure sitting on the fountain's edge. It's my giant, Tal realized. Thank Amarantos, Borras is going to take care of everything. He's the best Prime ever and I'm sure he'll get this all sorted out.

Tal noticed the rest of his party stopped about twenty feet from Borras, leaving he and Tal space to have a private discussion. "Borras, thank goodness, listen…"

"Quint,…"

A shrill alarm claxon began in Tal's mind—'danger Will Robinson, danger!' I don't think I've ever seen Borras look so serious. And we've been through some serious shit together.

"The Ruling Council only gave me ten minutes to speak to you. I only got that because I am Omada Prime. You are to be escorted to a holding cell for the remainder of the evening."

"But…"

"Not another word, I don't want to forget anything you need to know. Emet is safe. Concerned for you but safe. For the moment anyway. The rest of the team is safe. I am so very sorry about the Dust Child. Emet told me what she meant to you." Then his friend paused, the first friend Tal had made when he arrived at Hunts School. The most solid friend, both physically and socially, Tal had ever had. "I hate to lay any more on you right now, Quint, but you must be prepared for this morning's events. The Areopagus has been convened."

"Why?" Tal found his throat so parched he could barely croak the word out.

"An anonymous complaint has been filed alleging you cold-bloodedly murdered a mortal during a Tyrning activity. If proven, it is a bloodpryce violation."

Elle! Tal wanted to scream her name in anguish, but there wasn't time, and he didn't have the energy. "I'm innocent, Borras. I swear it."

"We know you are, Quint. All of us. Normally, it would require a Folk murdering a mortal, but in your case it doesn't matter that you too are mortal because you are a team member bound by the Hunts Rules. The Ruling Council will determine whether you must pay the bloodpryce."

"What's the worst case scenario?

"If you are found guilty, you will be sentenced to Five-Hells Realm. For eternity."

What the hell, Five-Hells is really a place? Tal tried to swallow, but his throat was so dry it couldn't even complete the necessary contraction. Tal felt the looming presence of the six guards as they began walking in formation toward he and Borras. Borras is having a tough time here, too, Tal reminded himself. Help him out. "Could be worse. I'm already a dead man walking, remember? I've got to deliver Aislinn to Helblad before the Tyrning coronation or I'm scheduled to be his dinner. No matter what they do to me, at least the Omada will still be in first place."

Borras shook his mammoth head slowly from side to side. "No, Tal. If Omada loses you, we are out of the competition. The trial is taking place before the Imbolc Feast and if you're found guilty, sentence will be imposed immediately."

The guard detail closed ranks around Tal. Clearly, Borras's ten minutes were up.

CHAPTER CENTUM SEDECIM

Despite his best efforts, exhaustion claimed Emet right after he'd reached the annotations concerning Chapter 20—the provisions addressing bloodpryces. Something interrupted his sleep cycle and roused him. He looked at Borras's alarm clock. Holy hell, it's 8:45 a.m. Borras was going to come get me for the 8:00 a.m. team meeting. His plan must have met with some unforeseen impediment.

Maybe that's what woke me, Emet thought. No, that wasn't it, he realized. It was my subconscious messaging my conscious to let it know it had solved its assignment from last evening. There were, in fact, two events that apparently occurred simultaneously. One event on Earth Realm and the other on Baba Yaga's plane. After extensively reviewing the matter, his subconscious had issued a declaration of "not a coincidence," then passed the issue up the ladder to his conscious brain for further review.

A week ago Friday, when I started feeling "off" right after lunch, the afternoon I felt compelled to take action against Barton and his goons, that was the precise date and time Tal used his final wish to end Baba Yaga, not by trying to kill her, but by trying to help her to regain the ability to love again.

Borras had related in great detail Tal's description of the Baba Yaga events. What were the exact words Tal chose in making his last wish? *"If it is of the Center to restore Baba Yaga's humanity, let me not just be named Taliesin, but allow me to become the Taliesin of this time and place. Grant me the magyk of that Taliesin."*

'Grant me the magyk of that Taliesin.' That's it! Emet leaped off the bed, energized by his newfound knowledge. Even though it cost him his final wish, Tal chose to "Seek the Center" in resolving Baba Yaga's request. I know Tal has never seen himself the way the rest of us do. Maybe that's a constant in the human equation. What Tal doesn't see is that at every opportunity he tries to help someone else. He's always down on himself when his efforts fail, or his actions provide the opportunity for some then unknowable downstream bad damage to happen. That's not on Tal though, that's on whoever it is making the self-centered choices.

It was Tal's choice to try and do the right thing that led him to initially activate my lyfeword. Is it even possible that with the final wish Aurora gave him that Tal not only saved Baba Yaga, but also caused what I think has happened to me? Is it possible that by "Seeking the Center," Tal has transformed my existence from that of a "world of make-believe possible" into a "world that belief made possible?"

Emet ran into the bathroom, washed his face and brushed his teeth. Sorry, Borras, there was only the one toothbrush. He darted back into the bedroom and picked up the Hunts Rules book. Next, he found a piece of paper, wrote one short sentence on it, then folded it and placed it in his shirt pocket.

I now see what I can do to help, Emet thought. What I need to do to help. It's my choice, Amarantos, made of my own free will. I consent. Please grant Tal the wisdom to accept it as well.

CHAPTER CENTUM SEPTENDECIM

At least they don't believe in starving prisoners, Tal thought, as he ripped off a large hunk of bread and made a sandwich with the meat on the tray they'd left in his cell. Wait a minute, he thought, as he took his first bite. That's ouberos snake. Borras told me on day one of my Hunts School education that it was a delicacy and only reserved for special occasions. Tal scoped out the rest of the comestibles on the silver platter. Sure enough, there was also a large cut-crystal serving bowl heaped high with ambrosia. This isn't your run of the mill regular old "daily bread" he thought, as he washed the sandwich down with a large gulp from the matching silver flagon. And that's not water, it's mead.

HOLY CRAP! This isn't breakfast, it's my last meal. Well it may be my last meal, but it is also technically breakfast in the truest sense, as I haven't eaten anything since dinner last night and normally I would have slept between now and last night's dinner, so this…focus, you idiot, you may be going to hell today.

ELLE!

That one-word thought wadded his entire being up and shoved him right up against the brink of the black hole he'd been teetering on since last night's events. The "fault, it's all my fault" litany began echoing in his head as murky tendrils reached up to drag him further down into the bleakness of his own personal Gehenna.

Stop it, Tal. There's too much at stake here. Way beyond you and your sorry little life. There's the little mater of the fate of the known universe for the next three hundred years. On a more personal note, if you go to Five-Hells, then Emet dies as well. Use the gifts you've been given, Tal. Start with the fact that you're innocent until proven guilty. How are they going to prove you killed Elle? All you have to do is to tell them the truth.

Right, that'll take care of the matter. I'll just tell them a disembodied voice crept up behind me in the dark and said it had been seeking revenge on me for centuries, when I'm only eighteen years old. Oh, that truth? How about the truth that witnesses say they saw you leap off the stage right at Elle immediately before the lights went out? Not helpful. Of course, there's also the fact that her twin brother has sworn to kill you. Again, not helpful.

Tal felt himself falling over the edge, and this time he couldn't stop the blackness from enveloping him.

CHAPTER CENTUM DUODEVIGINTI

Borras didn't come get him until five minutes before the Areopagus was due to convene. When he finally arrived, he was sorely out of breath. "Sorry, I'm late. Lots to discuss. I'll talk while we walk. No time to stop for questions. The others will meet us outside the ziggurat. As I recall, Tal said you could really move when you put your mind to it. It's time to put your mind to it. Let's hit it." Before Emet could even grab him by his sleeve to try to get his attention, the titan was out of the suite, down the steps to the first floor, and out the door. Emet did have to "hit it" to keep up with him.

"It's bad, Emet. Really bad. Didn't have time to gather everyone together in the team room, so I got with Notos and he is supposed to fill the others in while they wait. Someone powerful is out to get Tal, and I don't think there's anything we can do about it. I don't really have time to explain about bloodpryces…" Emet ran a couple of steps to get within Borras's peripheral vision and held the Hunts Rules book up. Borras glanced sideways without slowing down. "Good. Way to be on top of it. We're going to have to pray to Amarantos for a miracle. But it's looking really bad for Quint right now."

Their hurried pace had brought them to the steps of the rectangular pyramid. The other three members of Omada were waiting at the top of the stairs, motioning for Borras and Emet to hurry. "Try to stay in the background behind me. Everyone is going to wonder how Quint can be in two places at the same time. Until they absolutely need to know you're a golem, they don't need to know it. Got it?" Without even waiting for Emet to give a confirmatory nod he was climbing the stairs, four at a time.

CHAPTER CENTUM UNDEVIGINTI

The Great Hall of the Ziggurat looked much the same as the last time Tal had been hauled in for an interrogation. Although it might even be fuller today. The noises and smells emanating from thousands of different types of Folk were a sensory overload. When you added the visual stimulus, it was truly overwhelming. Wings, claws, claws with talons, feathers, feathers with talons, scales, translucent hides thinner than parchment paper, pebbled hides thicker than tanned leather, heads with one eye or maybe eight eyes, necks as thin as celery stalks, neckless with heavily wattled shoulders. There were Folk with no discernible head, some with three-heads, even some with their heads literally up their asses. Pretty much every component from the super special extra deluxe build-a-monster boxed set was present and accounted for. They were talking, honking, snorting, beeping, purring, and roaring. Some were even vibrating their sounds in the absence of an orifice from which to do any true vocalizations. Anything and everything the most creative imaginist could possibly conjure for a menagerie of grotesqueries was present for today's Areopagus.

All five members of the Ruling Council were ensconced on their platform at the far end of the hall. Queen Aine, also in her usual place, occupied a seat at a table the next row down and over to Alberich's right.

Tal's guards escorted him to an open area away from the crowd and about forty yards from the faculty, the Finalists and the rest of the student body. The Omada had been placed closer to the Council's dais, maybe twenty yards away from the other Finalists. He caught each of his teammate's eyes in turn and gave them a little half-smile. Even Notos. Concerned stares were all he got in return. Even from Notos.

Thank goodness, Emet is here and safe, Tal thought. He hadn't realized he'd been holding his breath, waiting to see him, until he felt his long exhale. He was nestled in behind Borras. Tal looked quickly over to the Släkt. The first thing he saw was Nord, his head swiveling back and forth between Tal and Emet. The asshole's about to stroke out trying to figure out how I have a twin and why he's never been here before but he's here now. The next thing he saw was Väst. Her eyebrows indicated she too was perplexed by the double helping of Quint. Her eyes however were wide with fear.

Marid, Seneschal of the Ruling Council and the Suleman of all of the Djinn, didn't have to quiet the crowd this time as Tal was escorted in. The hall became a tomb in a split-second, the only sound being the perfectly executed cadence of the now two full platoons of guards serving as Tal's escorts. Whispering began, though as first the Ruling Council itself, then the entirety of the audience, began looking like the crowd at a professional tennis match. All kinds of heads and head substitutes—and yes, a few asses with heads up in them—were whipping back and forth trying to figure out how Tal was under arrest for something and how Tal was standing unfettered with his teammates.

Marid was the first to break the silence. Wisps of smoke were drifting lazily ceilingward off of his entire body. He pounded his great staff thrice on the floor, clearly in a ritual manner, as he intoned, "The Areopagus is convened to witness the trial of Quint, Fifth Prime of the Omada, Second Hunt Finalist in this year's Tyrning. He is charged with the cold-blooded murder of a mortal during a Hunt sanctioned activity. Parliamentarian?"

Raja Jin Peri, King of the Faeries of the Malay Realm, rose to his feet. His voice echoed through the enormous great hall bouncing off of sentient being and uncaring stone alike. "The charge is one of the most egregious under the Hunts Rules. If proven, there is only one possible punishment—immediate banishment to Five-Hells." Hundreds of whispers walked their way up and down the room as the Parliamentarian took his seat.

Marid pointed at the only woman on the Ruling Council, Márku, Empress of the HuldreFolk, and beckoned her to rise. As she did Marid announced that the Márku would be serving as Prosecutrix.

Why wouldn't anybody believe everything she says, Tal wondered. She looks so regal and prosecutorial. The entire hall waited as the Márku reviewed some notes in front of her, her cow-like tail swishing methodically behind her.

Finally, the Márku looked up and addressed the crowd. "All persons appearing to testify will be subject to a truth geas. Consent is not required because there is no contract being bound. The geas will be automatically imposed upon each and every witness. We will have the truth of this matter, and nothing but the truth, to make our decision. The first witness will be Borras, Omada Prime Direction."

Borras took two steps forward, bowed low to the Márku before saying, "I respectfully decline to testify."

"I think you misunderstand these proceedings, Omada Prime. I call the witnesses and they are compelled to answer my questions truthfully. Period. Now, is it true that the deceased mortal female..."

ELLE, damn it, Tal screamed in his head. Her name was Elle.

"...and the Omada Fifth had some type of romantic involvement on the Earth plane?"

Tal could see Borras fighting the geas, he could almost hear his supersized molars grinding on each other as he tried to keep his mouth closed. "Yesssss…" he finally and grudgingly replied.

"It will go easier for you, Omada Prime, if you voluntarily answer my questions. Is it also true the deceased mortal female had a twin brother?"

"Yes."

Oh hell, I can see where this is going, Tal suddenly realized. Borras was way ahead of me when he initially refused to participate.

"Would you categorize the Omada Fifth and the deceased mortal's twin brother as blood enemies?"

"That is the way the twin brother apparently views their relationship."

"Very good. One last question, Omada Prime. Isn't it true that the last thing you saw before the lights went out was your Omada Fifth throwing his musical instrument to the ground and leaping off the stage right at the deceased mortal female?"

Tal watched as Borras tried to fight the compulsion. It really looked to Tal like Borras's jaws, caught between the compulsion and his determination to not answer, were literally going to crack in half. He was pretty sure he could even hear them starting to splinter.

"Yes," Borras finally spat out.

"Thank you, Omada Prime, you may return to your team now. HuntsMistress." Ms. Empousa stepped forward. "HuntsMistress, what did you see?"

"Exactly what the Omada Prime Direction told you. The mortal female was alive and well. The Omada Fifth leaped off the stage, apparently to attack her, and when the lights came up, he was caught red-handed trying to get away from the scene of the crime."

She's been waiting all year for a chance to serve me up for death—or worse, Tal thought. What an evil bitch. Her testimony doesn't matter, Alberich knows she hates me and has it out for me. He won't believe her.

"Last witness," the Márku barked. "Principal Chiron."

Thank goodness, Tal thought. He's always been straight up with me and never looked down on me because I'm a Dust Child.

"Yes, Madame Prosecutrix," the Principal said, as he stepped forward.

"Prior to the field trip this evening, were you aware that the Omada had full magyk on the Earth plane because one of their team is a Dust Child?"

Tal could tell from all the exclamations and partial exclamations and ass-buzzings that the question rocked the house. It had been more than a thousand years since Folk could use their personal magyk on the Earth Realm.

"No, madam," Principal Chiron replied. "If I had known I would have restricted him to the Hunts School campus for the entirety of the school year and would have banned him attending the dance yesterday evening."

Tal nervously shifted his weight from his left foot to his right. That wasn't particularly helpful, but not damning by any means.

Proteus, Regent of the Olympians, interrupted at this point. "The boy is a Munedan. He has no magyk of his own. I understood that magyk was involved in the murder of the mortal female."

Principal Chiron raised his hand and the Márku nodded her assent for him to speak. "I was returning from the bathroom at the time of the unfortunate incident, and right before the lights went out I'm pretty sure I saw a flash of steel in the Omada Fifth's hand. Because of the Combat Challenge we know the Omada secured Fragarach, one of the greatest of the magykal swords, as one of their scavengyr artifacts."

The crowd went from quiet so as to not miss a word to full throat lynch mob in about a nanosecond. Why? Tal thought. Why would Principal Chiron say that. He knows he only saw the metal on the neck of the guitar I was throwing down.

"Does the prisoner have anything to say in his defense."

Tal stepped forward. "I'm innocent. I didn't do it. When the lights went out there was somebody behind me, somebody with magyk. He threatened me. I…the girl that was killed…I…," Tal reached that point and found that it was the end of his endurance. He simply couldn't go any further. Not with everything that had happened in the last twenty-four hours.

"Principal Chiron," the Márku demanded, motioning for him to step forward again."

"Yes?"

"Did you take a census before the bus was boarded?"

"Yes, Madame, I conducted it myself."

"And as part of that census did you account for all staff members and students?"

"Absolutely. The Archon and Queen Aine even rode with us."

"So there is no way some other member of the Folk could have traveled from Hunts School to Earth plane proper?"

"Absolutely none. The Archon relaxed the Sol Crossing wards only for our party."

"Thank you, that is all," she said, waving her hand for him to rejoin the other faculty members. She then turned and the five members of the Ruling Council conferred. Tal could tell from the arm waving and the posture of their bodies that the discussion was a tense one.

When they were done, the other four faded into the background and their seats as Alberich stepped forward. The five of them won the Tyrning as a team three hundred years ago but this was no "first among equals" situation. Alberich had worn the mantle of responsibility for the well-being of all the known Folk Realms for the last three hundred years. This morning, at this moment, this is the first time I've seen Alberich looking like a ruler with responsibilities almost too heavy for even his noble shoulders to bear. He doesn't want to do what he's getting ready to do, Tal thought. But he will, because above everyone else he has to follow the Law and to "Seek the Center."

The Archon spoke clearly, distinctly, and sadly. "Quint, Fifth Prime Direction of the Omada, it is the vote of the majority of the Ruling Council that you are found guilty as charged. It is a bloodpryce violation. Under the Hunts Rules there is only one permitted sentence, and it is required that it be imposed immediately." Alberich nodded at Marid.

Marid banged his staff sharply one time on the marble floor of the dais. "Veles, King of the Five-Hells Realm, thee art summonsed by Alberich, Archon of the all the Moiety, to perform thy duty under the Lex Immortalis."

CHAPTER CENTUM VIGINTI

Every eye in the Great Hall turned toward the wall farthest from the end occupied by the Ruling Council's dais. Tal followed suit. He saw the outline of a door appear. Well, it was about thirty feet high and fifteen feet wide but it was clearly a doorway. The outline continued to solidify until it was an actual wooden door. The door was made of great vertical planks of scorched and blackened oak, each plank five feet in width. There were three wide bands of black iron that ran horizontally, holding the door together. Three massive black iron hinges appeared on its right side.

As the door finished materializing, it slowly began to swing open. The second the door opened away from the wall, grayish smoke billowed forth and the hall was completely filled with a horrendous high-pitched keening. Tal tried to analogize the sound. The closest he could get was if what happened to him last night with Elle happened simultaneously to about a thousand Tals, that's how terrible the wailing and crying was. As soon as the door had swung fully open and was pressed flat against the marble wall of the pyramid, an even thicker version of the gray smoke erupted from the door. Out of that miasma stepped Veles, Lord of the Five-Hells.

Veles looked like nothing, or anything, Tal had ever seen. That was saying a mite, considering the present company. Veles looked to be as tall as Borras, maybe even a little taller. He was cut like a Greek god, well perhaps more appropriately, he was cut like a Slavic god. It was easy to tell how muscular he was, as he had no dermal layers covering his musculoskeleton. None. His muscles and sinews were interwoven strands of red ice and black fire. As his muscles moved, Tal could see they provided sheathing for bones of sparkling gray crystal. I mean really, the guy is made out of ice, fire and crystal.

There were only dead sockets where Veles's eyes should have been, his face only partially visible as it was surrounded by drifting dreadlocks of oily black smoke, which crawled slowly across his face before curling down his back. Veles was completely surrounded by a nimbus composed of equal parts steam and icy mist.

As he stepped completely through the threshold, Veles waved his hand over his head and the backing soundtrack of the damned ceased immediately. His head began turning in a clockwise direction, the empty orbits surveying the crowd. He's searching for something, or someone, Tal thought. Veles paused as his gaze took him to the Omada. Tal saw Notos take a step closer to Emet, so that he was also using Borras as a shield. Good to know there's something that scares the shit out of Notos too, Tal thought. Veles nodded slightly, as if to himself, before advancing to the portion of the floor fronting the dais of the Ruling Council.

"I have come in response to your summons, Archon," Veles stated, giving only the slightest hint of a bow to the head of the known universe.

In the absence of any lips or skin, Tal could see Veles's epiglottis open and close as well as the interaction of Veles's muscles and tendons moving in order to form the words. It would have been fascinating if it wasn't gross-scary as hell. What was it about this guy that made Mokosh want to take him as her lover?

"The Areopagus extends its gratitude and appreciation to the Lord of Five-Hells," Alberich replied. "I know it is painful for you to be physically present on this plane."

"All duty requires some level of sacrifice," Veles replied. "It has been many Tyrnings since I have been called upon to perform this obligation imposed upon me by the Lex Immortalis. I shall remain only so long as is required to collect the bloodpryce."

Tal gulped. This is where the rubber meets the road. I'm what he's come to collect. He quickly looked across the room to Emet, who remained partially hidden behind Borras.

"Offender, step forward," Alberich commanded as he pointed at Tal. He took a deep breath and stepped forward as commanded.

Veles snapped his fingers and immediately Tal's hands were cuffed in front of him. The cuffs looked to be made of the same materials as Veles himself. Thin, tightly wound cords of crimson ice and ebon fire. They hurt, too. Real bad. Tal whimpered. Several times. He knew it made him look cowardly but he couldn't help it. Everywhere the shackles touched his skin the point of contact either felt like it was on fire or being frozen. The nature of the pain constantly changed and repeated as the cuffs flowed around his wrists.

At the edge of his peripheral vision Tal saw Borras tense as if he were going to begin some type of rescue action. Tal quickly shook his head no and started to yell to tell Borras to let it go. As he opened his mouth to speak, Veles snapped his fingers a second time, and Tal discovered he was mute. He could open his mouth, he could try to talk, scream, grunt, whatever, but no noise emerged. Veles then crooked his left pointer finger at him and Tal's body started walking toward the King of the Five-Hells. Tal tried to stop but he couldn't. His legs were under the control of Veles, and they kept moving him away from the center of the great hall and toward the portal, until he was only a couple of feet away from Veles.

Veles snapped his fingers a third time, and Tal felt his body rotate until he was facing the assembly. He's a really versatile snapper, Tal thought. I wonder if he learned that online or if it comes with being the Grand Poobah of the damned. Tal's next thought was you're about to go to hell you idiot and you're interested in someone's skill set in finger-snapping? Tal heard another snap and felt the air move behind him as the great bound oaken door began to laboriously swing closed.

From across the floor, Tal could see Emet frantically tugging on Borras's shirtsleeve until he finally got Borras's attention. When Borras looked down, Emet gave him a small book he was holding in his right hand and with his left, reached into his front shirt pocket and took out what looked like a folded piece of notebook paper.

Borras quickly scanned the paper, resignedly shaking his head no, and tried to hand the paper back to Emet. Emet clearly wasn't through with the discussion because he reached up, grabbed Borras's left forearm as high as he could, and tugged on his sleeve until Borras finally acquiesced, lowering his great head down to Emet's eye level. It looked to Tal from his vantage several dozen yards away like Emet was talking to Borras. Which was of course, impossible. Emet had gotten pretty good at pantomiming words, Borras must be lip-reading.

This time when Emet got done, Borras had an entirely different look on his face. He got down on one knee in front of the golem, opened the book Emet had given him, and held out his hand out for the piece of notebook paper. Emet gave it back to him. Borras remained where he was as he reread it before looking back to Emet. He's asking him something, Tal realized. Emet is nodding his head, yes. Looks like he's repeating the question, Tal thought, as Emet again left no doubt from his head motion that he was saying "yes" to the question.

Borras smiled grimly at Emet as he stood to his full height once more before turning toward the Ruling Council's seats. He looked at the paper once again before speaking. "Master

Parliamentarian. Omada requests leave to speak. It is a critical matter involving the bloodpryce."

Raja Jinn Peri first looked to Alberich before responding. "Permission is granted, Omada Acting Prime," the Raja intoned ritualistically.

"Thank you. Pursuant to Rule 20.4, the Omada request permission to provide an Equivalynt to pay the bloodpryce."

Tal heard another finger-snap behind him, and felt the Five-Hells door begin to open wide again. At the same time Ms. Empousa leapt forward from her place in the faculty corner. "I am the HuntsMistress this Tyrning, and I am the one who will decide matters affecting the teams and the Hunts."

The Raja held up his hand to quiet her, before he turned and conferred quietly with all of the members of the Ruling Council. When they were done, it was again the Parliamentarian who spoke.

The Raja turned to face Ms. Empousa. "HuntsMistress, because the decision involves someone who is not a Hunts Finalist, the decision concerning the suitability of the proposed Equivalynt belongs to the Archon, with the advice and consent of the Ruling Council."

Even from half a cavernous great hall away Tal could see that Lilith Empousa was about to explode. Or maybe the actual event would be an implosion, Tal decided. Either way, he was pretty sure there would be some type of mushroom cloud and radioactive fallout. She didn't challenge the issue any further though, taking a step back into the group with Principal Chiron and the other faculty members.

Turning back to address the entire Areopagus, the Raja continued. "Pursuant to Rule 20.4, an Equivalynt may be substituted, if an Equivalyncy contract is bound. There is, however, a procedural impediment in the matter presently before the Council. Omada's Fifth Prime is a Dust Child. He is the only mortal to ever attend Hunts School. There is no other person present who would qualify as an Equivalynt."

Borras stood his ground. "Respect fully given, Master Parliamentarian, but your statement is incorrect."

The assembly's low-level babbling kicked up a few notches. At least until the Archon stood. Maybe he has the ability to strike them with lightning, Tal thought. Or maybe everyone knows a good show when they see one and they don't want to miss a word of this one. "Acting Prime, name the proposed Equivalynt."

What's Rule 20.4, Tal wondered. What the hell is an Equivalyncy? I knew I should have gotten a copy of that damn rulebook, he thought. Wait a minute, that's what Emet handed Borras, he handed him a copy of the Hunts Rules. Tal watched Borras straighten his shoulders before quickly looking down to his left. Where Emet was standing. Oh, no, Tal thought, finally realizing what was going on as Borras motioned to Emet, who stepped forward.

Tal tried to break his bonds, then he tried to move in any fashion, but he was held immobile. He tried to scream the words in his mouth but was allowed no sound. He tried to telepathically send the words to deafen anyone and everyone in the ziggurat who could hear that sort of thing. Of course, there was nothing.

Bereft of any other form of expression he scream-cried the words in his own head—No, Emet...No...NO!

CHAPTER CENTUM VIGINTI UNUS

"Fraud," a voice rang out. It was Nord, who apparently couldn't help himself. He got a look from the HuntsMistress that would shrivel a hundred foot hickory down to a twig. A runt of a twig, at that. It didn't stop Nord, though. Not this time. "It is impossible for another Dust Child to be on Hunts School campus. That thing is not Munedan. It is some trickery by Omada. A Creature of some sort."

The Archon addressed Borras. "Acting Prime, has Omada submitted a Creature as its proposed Equivalynt?"

"All respect, Archon," Borras responded politely. "That would not be of the Center. I suggest the Council question our candidate so that an informed choice may be made as to his suitability."

Tal relaxed into his bonds. Borras and Emet had tried a "hail Mary" pass to save his life. Thanks to Amarantos and the Lex limitation on golems it was going to fall incomplete in the end zone. Emet was safe.

Alberich's gaze first bore deep into Borras, and then he pulled focus to Emet. He maintained his unblinking stare for what seemed like an entire minute. He's thinking, Tal realized. But about what?

"Candidate, are you of the Earth Realm?"

Emet nodded, in response.

"Candidate, do you voluntarily choose to stand as the bloodpryce Equivalynt for Quint of Omada?"

Emet nodded again. A murmur went through the crowd.

"Candidate, do you understand if you are accepted that you will be banished immediately to the Five-Hells Realm, where you will remain indentured until the end of Time?"

Emet nodded firmly. Alberich somehow knows Emet's a golem, Tal realized. That's what's up with the questions that require no verbal response, but what can he ultimately hope to accomplish?

The Archon continued. "Candidate, were you made golem?" Tal could hear the word "golem" repeated and vibrated from dozens of mouths, and orifices that served the purpose of mouths. The response from the crowd was getting more vocal and hostile. Tal saw Nord actually licking his lips.

Emet nodded for the fourth time.

"The piece of paper you're holding, the one you've written something on, is that a note for me?"

Emet nodded.

"Hold it up, candidate."

Emet did as directed. Alberich waved his scepter at the notebook paper. The paper floated up out of Emet's hand. When it was about twenty feet in the air, Alberich waved his scepter again. The paper began expanding, and as it did it became three-dimensional. Tal tried to quickly count the object's sides—it's at least a hexadecagon, he decided. It may even have more than sixteen sides.

Alberich motioned with his scepter a third time, and one sentence appeared in huge fiery letters on every side of the object. The words were simultaneously visible to every person and thing in the entire Great Hall.

'ASK ME MY NAME!'

CHAPTER CENTUM VIGINTI DUO

Alberich paused to look to Marid, the Seneschal, who slowly pounded his staff on the floor. Once, twice, three times, four, and as the echoes of the fifth blow reverberated throughout the hall, Alberich spoke again. "Candidate, what is your name?"

It was as if someone had sucked all of the sound out of the entire pyramid. There was no clinking, no scratching, no tooting, no woofing. Absolutely nothing.

"My...name...is...Emet, your Lordship," Emet replied haltingly, but every word was crisply enunciated.

If the total silence that existed seconds before Emet spoke could be squared, then cubed, then multiplied by itself, that's what the magnitude of the silence in the room was now.

Emet wasn't through, though. "My name is Emet. I am of Earth Realm and I choose...to stand as bloodpryce Equivalynt...for the Omada Fifth Prime Direction."

Bedlam. Broke. Loose.

CHAPTER CENTUM VIGINTI TRES

Alberich stood there silently, allowing anarchy full reign for every bit of five minutes. It seemed an eternity to Tal. The moment the furor passed its zenith, the Archon raised his right hand. The room stilled immediately. He waited on purpose, Tal realized. Alberich allowed the Areopagus to vent their anger, using the release as a pressure valve. This way even though they aren't individually going to have a say so in the decision, they still feel like they've been heard.

The Archon now proceeded without equivocation. The perfect example of a leader, Tal thought, one who has been required on innumerable occasions to make the tough decisions, and who has always stepped up to meet the challenge. This might be his biggest decision ever, Tal decided. Even bigger than deciding to impose Alberich's Bane, which continued the moratorium on the use of magyk on the Earth plane.

"Hear me, all ye representatives of the Moiety. These are the facts. It is undisputed the candidate is not Principe, nor is he Folk." The gathering made various noises indicating general agreement. "It is also undisputed the candidate originated on the Earth plane." As before, the group seemed to be in agreement.

Clever, Tal thought. He deliberately didn't say, "created."

"Archon," Proteus exclaimed, leaping to his feet as he

interrupted Alberich. "Apologies, but whatever this abomination is, surely you cannot hope to construct a logical argument that it is human. It is not a legally acceptable Equivalynt." Proteus's opinion found support from a substantial portion of the crowd. Tal saw Marid nodding in agreement with Proteus.

"Regent," the Archon said, as he began his response to his longtime teammate. Tal noted Alberich made sure to address Proteus by his title, to show respect. The dude is uber smooth, I'll give him credit for that.

"Let us reason together," Alberich said as he continued. "What is the nature of the origin of the substitute?"

Proteus smiled, because the answer supported his position. "He himself has admitted he is a Creature."

Alberich replied, as he cut his eyes toward the Omada. "What kind of Creature is the candidate?"

Proteus's smile became more than a little smirky at this point. "Again, by his own admission, he is a golem."

"Specifically what kind of golem, Proteus?"

"Clearly he is a simulacrum golem," came the quick response.

"Fine, fine," Alberich said, tugging lightly on his carefully manicured beard. He's giving every physical indicator that he's pondering the matter, Tal thought, but he's known where this was going since he started this Socratic dialogue with Proteus. "Tell me, Regent, who established the Lex Immortalis?"

That was kindergarten knowledge for the Folk in all the known Realms. "The UnFading One, of course."

"You speak with great wisdom, Proteus," Alberich replied, nodding his head to accentuate his sincerity. Opening his arms wide to include the entire congregation, he asked his next question. "Do any of the Folk, singly or in the aggregate, have the magyk to change the Lex Immortalis?"

"Of course not, Archon," Proteus replied. He seems a little irritated that the questions are so elementary, Tal thought.

"One last question then. What is the restriction on golems that Amarantos herself placed in the Lex Immortalis?"

Holy hell, Tal thought, that's what he's been doing. Alberich went all major maieutic on the entire Ruling Council, as well as the Areopagus. He deliberately engineered a challenge from one of his own teammates so he could engage in this dialog in front of the entire Areopagus. Alberich made his point and made it indisputably using Proteus as his foil.

Proteus realized about then that Alberich had been using him as a living chalkboard. "Speech is the restriction," he growled through clenched teeth. "Golem are forbidden speech."

"Thank you, Regent. You may be seated." The Archon allowed Proteus ample time to regain his dignity and be seated before continuing. Makes sense, Tal thought. They're having a disagreement about this issue but they've been teammates for three hundred years now. I guess every team has to have its version of a Notos.

"Let me recapitulate. The candidate is neither Principe, Folk, nor Child of the Dust. It has been conclusively proven that under the Lex Immortalis, he is no longer Creature, having somehow transcended that origin. Emet is in fact a singularity in our entire known universe. One of a kind, there is no one and no thing like him."

Alberich next addressed Raja Jinn Peri. "As Parliamentarian, can you tell us if there is a provision in the Hunts Rules prohibiting a singular entity from standing as Equivalynt for either human or Folk?

The Raja quickly responded from his seat. "As such possibility could never have been anticipated, there is no such provision, Archon."

"Thank you." Alberich turned facing Emet once more. "That said, candidate, the bloodpryce punishment under the Hunts Rules is an eternal sentence to the Five-Hells Realm. This sentence can only be served by those with souls. We can only allow you to serve as an Equivalynt if you can prove to our satisfaction that you have also become ensouled. It is, of course, physically impossible to prove such metaphysical attribute."

Tal saw both Emet and Borras's shoulders sag. Thank

goodness, Tal thought. All of this Equivalynt bullshit just came to a screeching halt. How can anyone prove they have a soul? It's a Gordian knot on steroids.

Still immobilized, Tal stared at Emet, willing him to look at him. To let him know he appreciated the effort but to shut it down. Emet was deliberately avoiding looking at him. Tal knew that's what he was doing because that's what Tal would have done in the same situation. Instead, Emet was staring at a fixed point on the far interior wall of the pyramid.

Oh, hell no, Tal thought. He is doing what I would be doing right now. He's turning the Rubik's cube. He's using his brain—our brain—to solve the puzzle. Stop! Tal sent his thoughts as hard as he could to the golem. Stop it, right now!

When Emet finally ceased his computational activity he looked over to Tal, and smiled. It was a little on the anemic side but it was enough of an "I did it" upward turn of the lips to let Tal know that his brain—their brain—had been sufficient to the task.

"Lord Alberich," Emet began. Alberich looked a little surprised that Emet had anything else to say but nodded his head and waved his hand for Emet to proceed.

"I have determined that in my unique case, objective physical proof can be presented to satisfy your requirement."

"Physical proof to prove the existence of the metaphysical? What is the nature of your proof?" Alberich asked.

"I will bind a contract with the Omada Fifth to unbind my lyfeword. If I die, then I was still a soulless Creature. If I survive, if I continue to exist independently of any external magyk, then as an ensouled unique entity I am clearly sufficient for you to declare me an acceptable Equivalynt."

Damn it, Emet! Damn you and that beautiful brain of ours, Tal thought. You went all Star Trek "Kobayashi Maru" scenario on us. Presented with an impossible "no-win" problem you "cheated" to solve the problem.

Tal tried again to move toward Emet, to stop this train wreck before it could get any worse. No luck. Veles stood right behind him and unless he snapped his fingers, Tal wasn't going anywhere.

Alberich nodded his head in acquiescence to Emet's proposal. "So shall it be done."

Marid proceeded to again pound his staff on the floor. Once. As the sound reverberated and the members of the Areopagus watched intently, Emet started slowly walking toward Tal. Twice. Three times. Four times. Emet was within an arms length of Tal when Marid struck the floor the fifth time.

CHAPTER CENTUM VIGINTI QUATTUOR

Veles snapped his fingers, and Tal discovered that although he was still shackled, movement and speech were restored to him. "No," he said preemptively. "Turn around and go back, Emet. I'm not playing this game."

Emet took another step toward Tal before leaning forward and whispering in his ear, "I consent. Do you?"

"Listen to me dammit. I said no," Tal replied angrily, as the advance guard of a battalion of tears began a tortured march down his cheeks and onto the floor. "I am not going to let you die in my place. You are not less than me. We are equals, we are the same."

Emet grabbed Tal by the shoulders and pulled him so close their lips were almost touching. In the softest of whispers he said, "Tal, listen to me. I am only golem, a Creature."

"No, you're not. You've changed. You were golem, but it's not who you are now," Tal replied, as his body began to spasm. From sadness, and fear. From loss. First Elle and now Emet?

"What is my name?"

"Emet," Tal replied, the tears now freely flowing.

"And what is it's etymology?"

Tal realized Emet was doing one of their drills, going

back over something they'd previously discussed. He's attempting to settle me with logic. "In the Earth plane Hebrew language, Emet means 'Truth.' "

"Exactly. That is what I am speaking to you now. I would not survive your death." Emet leaned back erect, before stepping backward one small step.

"You're as human as I am now," Tal responded.

"We don't know what I am now."

"Yes, we do, Emet," Tal said, tears still streaming. "I do anyway. I know who you are—you're my brother."

Emet paused a moment before answering. Tal saw the moisture now brimming in Emet's eyes as well. "And you are mine, but if you die we don't know if I will still die as well."

"Then we will go together," Tal replied. "Elle is dead because of my choices. Now I'm supposed to be responsible for your death as well? No. I can't. I won't. I do not consent," Tal stuttered, as he started losing the small amount of his remaining emotional control.

"Pell and your Mom and the twins. They need you."

"I can't do it, Emet. I can't." Tal realized if Veles didn't still have some partial control over his body, he would probably already have collapsed to the floor.

Emet grabbed Tal by the shoulders, shaking him. "Stop being selfish, Tal. Gas Pump Number Unus told you the future of worlds depends on your choices. Not my choices. Yours. Arthrys, Excalibur, Perun, Myrddin. Helblad. Baba Yaga. Every one you've met and everything you've done thus far verifies that statement." Emet stopped, his voice dropping to a whisper again so that no one else could hear. "Taliesin, Baba Yaga intentionally placed the talysman on your skin. She could have given you any of her belongings as a sufficient talysman. She branded you. On purpose. For some unknown, important reason."

"Like what, Emet," Tal yelled. "What could be more important than your life?"

Emet remained calm. "You know the answer. It is much more important that the only team truly Seeking the Center win this Tyrning. Tal, someone or something very powerful has set this whole thing up. The Wytch Hunt does not end until the Imbolc Feast immediately after this meeting is over. The talysmen will be presented there and the three remaining Finalist teams will be determined. If you walk through that doorway with Veles, the talysman goes with you and Omada is out of the competition. You know it and I know it."

Tal stood there silently a minute longer before Emet again stepped close, this time wrapping his exactly-the-same-size-as-Tal's arms around Tal. "It's okay, Tal, it really is. I am alive today because of your choice to Seek the Center. It is because you used your last wish trying to help Baba Yaga regain her humanity that I have become more than Creature. Tal, it is because you first loved me that I learned how to love in return. Thank you for my life and for giving me my own opportunity to Seek the Center. Amarantos has a plan for all of her children. Which includes me. Now quit acting like a baby and do what we both know you must do."

With that, Emet took two steps backwards. He quickly unbuttoned his shirt, before stripping it off. Bare-chested, he next slipped off his loafers. After that he dropped his jeans. Staring Tal straight in his eyes, Emet put his thumbs in his boxers and pulled them down. Emet was now as naked as he'd been when Tal had first chosen to bring him to life. He turned his right leg outward so the lyfeword on the inside of his thigh was clearly visible to the entire assembly. "I consent. Do you?"

Tal replied, his voice wavering, but clearly pitched loud enough for all to hear. "I consent."

As the thousands watched in silence, Emet's name faded from his leg, leaving only unblemished white skin. The collective silence changed into a collective gasp followed immediately by a collective clamor. Tal saw Alberich's hand go up, quieting the Areopagus. As soon as he had everyone's attention, he nodded his head to Raja Jinn Peri.

It was apparently the Parliamentarian's obligation to make the official pronouncement. "The bloodpryce Equivalynt is accepted."

Tal heard Veles snap his fingers. The restraints disappeared from Tal's wrists, and promptly reappeared on Emet's, binding his arms tightly in front of him. As Tal half-turned toward Veles, he saw wave his arm over his head, and the mammoth door begin to swing closed once again. As it did, flames and ice erupted outward, followed immediately by the terrible, worse than fingernails on a chalkboard screaming.

Expressionless and mute, Veles motioned for Emet to step in front of him and toward the portal. Emet did as directed. Emet then stepped through the threshold and disappeared, followed closely by Veles. As the King of Five-Hells reentered his domain the oversized door clanged shut behind him, became an outline on the marble wall, and then was gone.

Complete—almost suffocating—silence ruled.

The Seneschal banged his staff once on the floor. "This Areopagus is concluded. All students and faculty are to report immediately to the cafeteria for the Imbolc Feast followed immediately by the presentation of the wytches' talysmen." At the conclusion of his announcement, the non-school members of the Areopagus began streaming toward an exit to get in line to use the Prime Omphalos.

Tal was seeing everything as if it was an enormous multi-scene diorama in a museum. His logic center was trying to whisper the word "shock" to him. He acknowledged the voice but it made no difference, not after everything that had happened.

He saw Nord and the rest of the Släkt, hopping and yelling. Like somebody had kicked over an anthill of exceptionally petty ants. A really small anthill of exceptionally petty ants. Well, all of them were yelling—except for Väst. She was staring at Tal, unblinking. Her eyes were abnormally large and bright with the sheen of nascent tears. The HuntsMistress's violent arm movements and contorted features in her "conversation" with Principal Chiron evidenced she was beyond high-pissed and pretty far up the livid depth chart. Tal saw Aine, from her place of honor, looking at him with—well, with either pity or compassion. He couldn't decide which. At this moment he was incapable of caring.

As the Ruling Council filed out, he saw Alberich trailing the group, his eyes inscrutably focused on Tal. And then there were his Omada teammates, all of them, slowly walking over to him. To comfort him, to tell him he did what had to be done.

The part of his brain governing emotions seized control, pummeling his logic functions into submission. I can't do this any more, Tal decided. Not after everything that's happened. He turned away from the Omada, and walked toward the farthest exit.

As soon as Tal got outside the ziggurat, he did the only thing that seemed right—he began running. Toward the Gas Station Crossing.

Crying. Running. Trying to run so fast his thoughts couldn't keep up with him. But they somehow managed to keep pace.

I'm out. *You can't be out, you have the talysman.*

I can't be responsible for any more deaths. *You've saved countless lives by finding Excalibur and helping Arthrys become Archon.*

It's my fault Elle is dead. *You're the reason Väst lives.*

Emet is dead because of me. *Emet lived and became something unique because of you, because you loved him.*

Shut up, Brain! Shut up! SHUT UP!

Don't you get it, Brain? Life is too hard. People I love are dying, because of my choices. Who's next? Mom? Pell? The twins? The rest of the Omada? What does a stupid, broken down gas pump know anyway? Worlds depend on me? That's gotta be some sick joke. One person can't possibly make that kind of difference to the universe.

Finally, breathlessly, Tal was to the threshold of the Gas Station Crossing. His next step would take him across.

Tal, is this what you really want to do? Yes. Fuck Seeking the Center.

I'M DONE.